ESCORTING A WITCH
EMERALD WITCHES BOOK 2

HEATHER McCORKLE

FOR THOSE STARTING ANEW.

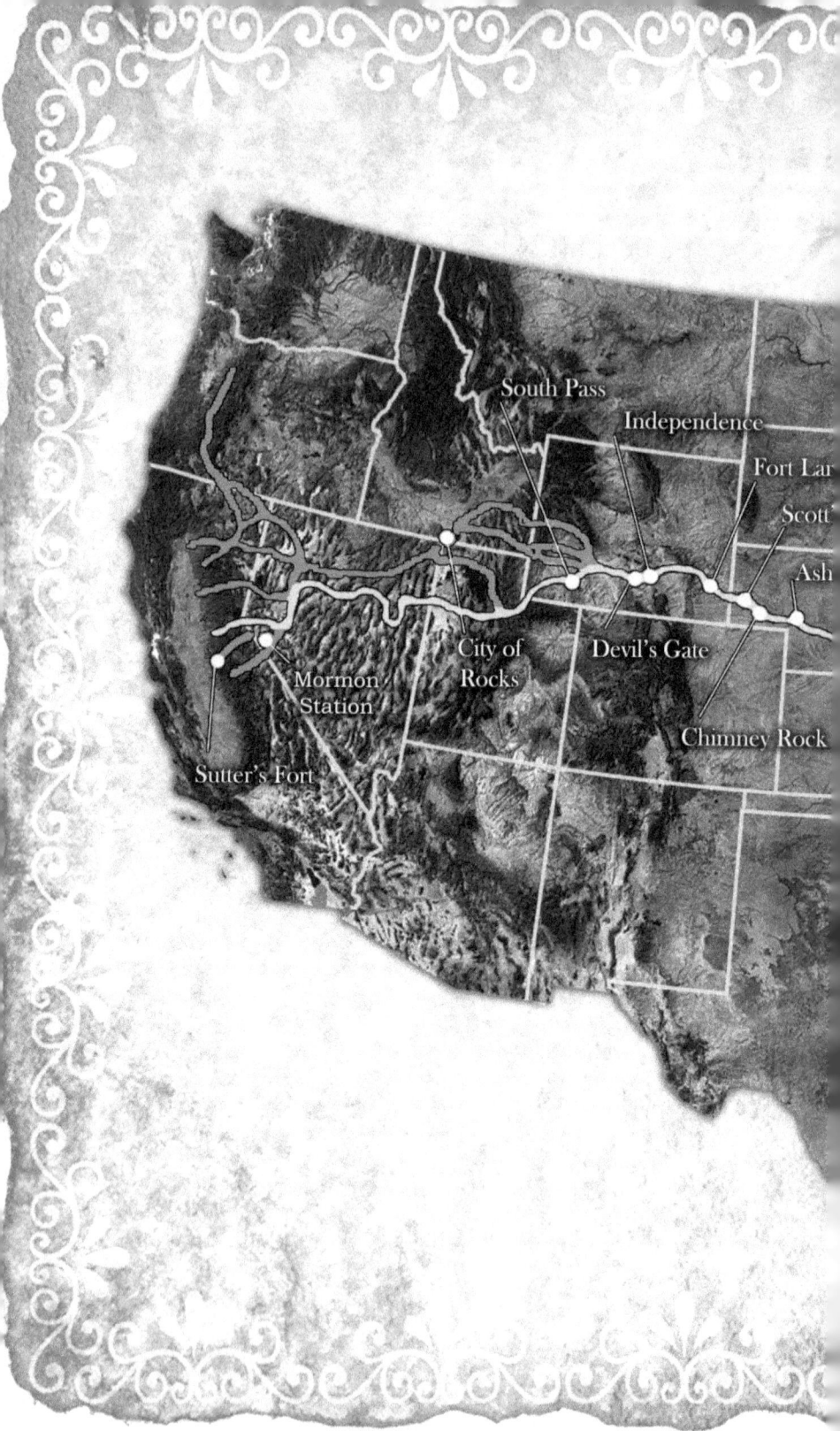

ESCORTING
A WITCH

Escorting a Witch
An Emerald Witches Novel

Copyright 2023 Heather McCorkle

Ebook ISBN: 978-1-939469-26-7
Paperback ISBN: 978-1-939469-27-4
Hardback ISBN: 978-1-939469-28-1

Cover images from Deposit Photos. Cover design by McCorkle Creations.

Compass Press release date: July 2023

OTHER BOOKS BY HEATHER MCCORKLE:

Emerald Witches Series:
Honoring a Witch's Heart
Escorting a Witch
Desiring a Witch (November 2023)

Children of Fenrir Series:
Clawed & Cornered (novella)
Bitten & Beholden
Tempered & Turned
Bared & Betrayed

Shifter Seeker Series:
Holiday Hunting (novella)
Raven Rousting (novella)
Coyote Calling
Tiger Tracking
Bear Baiting (Coming Soon)

Channeler Series:
Born of Fire (Short Story)
Fire With Fire (Novella)
The Secret of Spruce Knoll
Channeler's Choice
Rise of a Rector

Channeler Novel Stand Alone:
To Ride a Púca

AUTHOR'S NOTE:

This novel began its life as another novel in another genre as Courting a Corporal, a historical romance. My intention was for it to be a historical fantasy about fae descended Irish women making their way in America during and after the Civil War. It was intended to be a story not just of tragedy and hardship, but also filled with the magic and wonder of Irish folklore. However, when I got the idea for it, I talked to my agent about it. They convinced me there wasn't much of a market for historical fantasy. It was too much of a mashup of genres, they said, and they wouldn't be able to sell it to a publisher.

They convinced me I should write it as a historical with no fantasy elements. After extensive, exhaustive research on all things American Civil War related, I did so, and they helped me sign it with a publisher. I hold no ill will whatsoever to that agent. They had good intentions and advised me as they thought best based on the selling genres of the time. But, it did crush something in me to compromise on what I wanted for the story.

After several years of mediocre sales, I got my rights back, and now I've rewritten not just this book, but the entire series as it was originally intended to be. Here's hoping the industry was wrong, or at least has changed enough, and you love this book of my heart just as much as I do.

CONTENT WARNINGS:

These content warnings contain mild spoilers, but my hopes are that they won't detract from the enjoyment of the novel for those who would like to check the trigger warnings before proceeding.

This novel is about a widow whose husband was verbally, mentally, and physically abusive, but it does not graphically cover any of those incidents. It focuses instead on her growing and recovering after her husband's death in the American Civil War. She is attacked by a man attempting sexual assault but it is not covered in detail, and she fights him off. There is a separate choking incident by someone she trusts (not sexual). There is mention of a miscarriage due to abuse, but only briefly and not in detail.

This novel also deals with the oppression of women, African Americans, and Native Americans as is historically accurate during that time. These incidents do not glorify those committing the acts.

Triggers are a very personal thing and are not the same for everyone. As such, there is a chance I may have inadvertently missed calling attention to something that may trigger some readers. I hope this isn't the case, as it is not my intention to overlook any potentially triggering things.

GLOSSARY:

Please keep in mind, each of these terms is in relation to the fictional beliefs and systems in the Emerald Witches world, and may not match Irish mythology exactly.

Failinis: a legendary warrior dog of the fae

Tír Na nÓg: the fae land of eternal youth and abundance, where the Tuatha Dé Danann and other fae are said to have fled after being defeated in this world by the Fomorians.

Dullahan: the darkest of fairykind, sometimes seen as a headless horseman.

Dubnos: the fae underworld, realm of the dead, thought to be hell-like by some.

1

Catriona

New York

The whispers frayed at her last raw nerve. With careful precision, Catriona set the delicate crystal wineglass down on the marble table. The dark red liquid didn't so much as ripple. Such quality wine was hard to come by, she didn't want to waste it in anger. Her fingers closed into a fist, her nails biting into her palm. But it was a good pain, the kind that helped bring focus and calm so she didn't do something foolish. As the founding board member of the organization, she couldn't very well fly off the handle every time someone spoke ill of her beneath their breath.

Gathered like a brood with their coiffed hairdos leaned together, half the board members cackled all manner of derogatory things about her. Their too-loud whispers from behind their fans were clearly meant to be heard.

"New money and she thinks she deserves a place among us."

"And I hear she is a witch who communes with animals."

"Already out of mourning clothes, it is disgraceful."

Over half the eyes in the packed tearoom rested on her. Her skin crawled and her cheeks heated. The old Cat would have torn into them like a wild thing, but sadly, she hadn't been that woman for a long time now, not since she'd gotten married.

Beyond the women, muted sunlight filtering through the grapevine-framed window beckoned her. She wanted nothing more than for this meeting to be over so she could return to the stables where she could find a bit of serenity. On the edge of the windowsill sat a lovely black and white bird—a warbler—tiny eyes staring at her as it rotated its head. The tranquility of its mind soothed her much like the trickle of a stream. Not to say it didn't have thoughts, for it certainly did. And she could hear them as clearly as she could hear the horrible women in the room behind her. The warbler eyed the colorful sweet cakes on the table near the window. It was hoping she had some of the lemon variety it liked so much.

She touched the little bird's mind and sent it a promise to set some out later. To do so now would attract the attention of the ladies in the room and only heighten the chatter about her. While she was no witch, not exactly, they wouldn't understand or care about the difference. That the fools even thought a witch was a bad thing spoke volumes about their ignorance.

A delicate hand came to rest on her shoulder just as a full skirt brushed against her own. Gentle though the touch was, it was all she could do not to flinch. The white lace glove could have belonged to anyone, but the almost hesitant hand within it could belong to only one person.

"You pay them awful women no mind now, Catriona. They are jealous is all," came a carefully measured feminine voice with just the barest hint of what had been an African accent a few generations back.

Brown eyes as gentle as her voice gazed out of a lovely face nearly the color of obsidian to bathe Catriona in sympathy. She managed to force a tight-lipped smile.

"Aye, but they are jealous for the wrong reasons," she all but whispered. "But thank you for your kindness, Sadie. You are a treasure." She patted the lady's hand where it rested on her arm.

Many of the ladies in the finely furnished sitting room shot frowns their way. Some likely because such familiarity with one's servants was looked down upon. But then, even allowing Sadie to attend was frowned upon by most in the room. While the north had been the first to free their slaves, they still believed in separatism. Not Catriona, though, and on that she stood up to these hens. Sadie was a widow of a soldier of the 69th infantry, which gave her every right to attend these meetings. Besides, she was more than just Catriona's housekeeper, she was her friend, and for her Catriona would withstand all the evil glares those hens could dish out.

Lovely dark brows drawing together, Sadie waved a dismissive hand at the group of women. "The hens wouldn't believe the truth if it slapped them upside their pampered backsides," she said.

At that image, a genuine smile turned up the corners of Catriona's lips. If only they were hens. Those she could understand, those she could talk to.

The sight of a black-haired woman with skin the color of

porcelain descending on the group of board members like a storm wiped the smile away. Trouble flowed around the immaculately dressed young woman like a cloak of dark foreboding. Along with it came a press of power that heated the air in the room. Thankfully these hens wouldn't know it for what it was, for what it meant *she* was.

"Oh no," Catriona murmured.

Sadie laughed quietly. "Don't you worry. Our Miss Deirdre there is going to give those ladies a taste of what they've got coming," she said.

Catriona groaned. "That is precisely what I am worried about."

All those coiffed heads raised at once, sharp eyes darting to Deirdre as if they could pin her back with their glares alone. But Catriona knew it would take far more than icy looks to stop Deirdre. Chances were not even a battalion of southern troops could do so.

The pointed chin of her lovely, heart-shaped face lifted, and her long lashes swept down over dark blue eyes that looked as black as her hair without the light hitting them. She focused the weight of her gaze upon the brood's ringleader: a tall woman with a prominent nose. "To speak ill of your founder is to speak ill of the very manner in which you spend your free time." Deirdre thrust that delicate-looking chin of hers in the direction of the double doors leading from the room. "The wind would most certainly be at your back should you choose to walk out that door."

All five women in the brood stiffened, eyes filling with disbelief as they widened. The worst of the lot stood her ground, angling her chin up so she could look down that prominent nose at Deirdre. "Our founder merely shocks us all by coming out of mourning so soon. Had any of us landed the catch of the century for a husband, we would have extended our mourning period," she huffed.

One of Deirdre's hands went to her hip. Catriona couldn't help but notice it had curled into a fist. The heart-shaped leaves of the vine-like pothos plant that wove along the bookcase behind her fluttered as if in a breeze. But Catriona knew better. The plant was reaching for her, reacting to her power. She held her breath, hoping the other women wouldn't notice.

Deirdre sneered at the women. "Would that you had, then it could have been you who felt the snap of 'the catch of the century's' jaws instead of my dear friend."

Gasps traveled through the brood. Gloved hands flung up to cover gaping mouths.

"What exactly are you implying?" their ringleader demanded.

Deirdre took a step forward. "That Michael O'Brian was a—"

"Enough, Deirdre!" Catriona finally found her nerve and her voice.

As much as she appreciated her friend defending her, the last thing she wanted was for these horrible women to know any of their darkest secrets. Deirdre's mouth snapped shut and she spun away from the women on what Catriona knew to be a scandalously high heel—though it was well hidden beneath the hoop of her burgundy gown. Once again the leaves of the plant reached for her. Thankfully, this time it only looked as though they danced in the draft creating by her skirts. Head held high, she pranced like a prized, gaited mare to Catriona's side, spun back toward the women, and looped an arm through Catriona's. With her friends to either side of her, they stood as a unified front. All eyes in the room turned to watch the drama unfold.

Catriona took a deep, steadying breath before speaking. "After today's testimonies we are all a bit emotional. We need to keep focused on what we are here for, to support one another." A bit of her old strength and confidence helped her voice carry throughout her five-hundred-square-foot tearoom.

Fingers gripped her arm tight, pulling her attention to a wide-eyed Sadie. But she wasn't looking at Deirdre, she was looking at the door leading out of the room. She leaned in and whispered in Catriona's ear. "I'm sorry I didn't see it earlier, but you've a visitor coming, a surprising one at that."

Puzzled and more than a touch alarmed, Catriona could only stare at her. She wasn't expecting anyone other than those attending today's meeting. Though Sadie wasn't the same as Catriona and Deirdre, she had a magic all her own, one that allowed her glimpses into the near future.

"No need to apologize. 'Tisn't your fault the ability is sporadic," Catriona whispered back.

The head hen facing down Deirdre opened her mouth to respond, but a door banged open, halting her words. Her friends' arms withdrew from hers, allowing Catriona to turn. Dread made her movements slow. Little on this green earth could cause her help to throw a door open with such carelessness. The last time it had happened, news of her husband's death had followed. What sort of visitor might be darkening her doorstep?

A young Irishwoman, her pale face flushed red, stood in the doorway, a hand clutched against her heart, her wide eyes seeking Catriona.

"Mrs. O'Brian, please pardon the intrusion, but your sister-in-law, Mrs. MacBranain, is here," she gasped.

Stomach churning with a mixture of joy and dread, Catriona dipped her head to the servant girl. "Thank you, Emily. Please make her comfortable in the sitting room. I shall be along shortly." With that, she swallowed her emotions, ensured her expression was one of regret, and turned to face the waiting group of women.

"Ladies, I fear I must adjourn this meeting of the Widows of the 69th as I have pressing business to attend to. Thank you all for coming. My servants will bring your wraps and cloaks along post-haste," she announced.

Murmurs spread throughout the women with the speed and relentlessness of the pox. Many, like the hen and her brood, didn't even try to whisper their comments.

"Isn't that Michael's sister?" one woman asked.

"Yes, it is! I am sure of it. And she was so close to Michael. Whatever will she have to say about Catriona being out of mourning already?"

Grinding her teeth against scathing replies, Catriona ushered the women out of the room and into the hallway where her servants were already bringing their belongings. Warm as it was outside this June afternoon, most of them hadn't worn cloaks or shawls, but almost all had brought either a bag or a parasol along. Though she was near to exploding with anticipation, she played the good hostess and bid farewell to each woman as she departed, even the horrible brood. When the worst of them shot her a cold look, she had to remind herself that they had all lost husbands, and many bad feelings were merely born from that. Still, women like her made Catriona wish she hadn't opened the organization to all widows of soldiers of the 69th without thinking what that meant.

A very unladylike snort came from Deirdre, who stepped forward when the head hen—the last to leave, by no accident for sure—made a snappy remark. Flinging her long, black hair over her shoulder, Deirdre looked down her nose at the woman.

"Hasten your step through the doorway now, Mrs. MacNeil, else your bustle may get closed in it," Deirdre said in a wickedly sweet tone.

Powdered brows rising into her carefully arranged brown bangs, Mrs. MacNeil gasped almost comically loud and stormed out of the parlor. Sadie giggled behind her gloved hand and Catriona groaned as she covered her face.

"She'll be impossible now," Catriona said.

Another snort sounded from Deirdre. "Oh aye, she was completely congenial before."

Catriona slapped playfully at her friend's arm. "You know what I mean."

Looping an arm through hers, Deirdre walked with her and Sadie to the front door. "I do indeed. You take too much from those hens," Deirdre said. "You should talk their horses into running their carriage off the east bridge."

"Deirdre!" Catriona whispered harshly.

"A jest, merely a jest! Perhaps off the canal bridge where they would only suffer the indignity of a good dousing. We wouldn't want the horses to get harmed."

Laughing, Catriona hugged her friends in turn as they waited for her servant to bring Sadie and Deirdre's parasols.

With a shake of her head, Catriona leaned close to

whisper lest the help hear. "By the Tuatha, Deirdre, you must be careful. I thought that pothos was going to start shooting sprouts out and wrap around the women!"

Full lips quirking to the side in consideration, Sadie cocked her head. "Wouldn't that have been a sight! Ha! And now that I think upon it, they could do with a bath, wash that interminable powder out of their hair." She winked. "I shall escort Deirdre home, then return post-haste, unless you would like us to stay for moral support?" Sadie asked.

Catriona smiled as she grasped her friend's hand. "Thank you, but no. Ashlinn and I were friends, of a sort. I will be all right."

With a nod, Sadie stepped out onto the wide porch into the brilliant sunshine and opened her parasol. She stepped onto the public walk without even looking, her gift of foresight protecting her from any collision that another might suffer by such boldness on a bustling day. The clop of many hooves on cobblestones echoed into the house, accompanied by the din of voices that seemed constant in the heart of New York. What Catriona wouldn't give for the quiet of the country home she had grown up in. Days like these made her long for seclusion, well, seclusion from everyone save her friends.

Deirdre joined Sadie outside but turned back to give Catriona a stern look. "You send for me as soon as they are gone. I do not want you to be alone after such a visit."

She gave her a mirthless smile and nodded. "I shall. Now, off with you so I can get this over with."

Waving, they descended the wide stairs leading up to Catriona's grand home and started north down the sidewalk. A deep breath steeled her enough that she was able to turn away from the sight of her retreating friends and nod to her servant girl to close the door. The click of the mechanism securing it behind her stirred a burning anxiety within her chest. Her hands fumbled with her green skirt. Of all the things she could have worn today, this was perhaps her most cheerful dress. Never had she regretted being out of mourning clothes so much as she did in that moment. Hiding it as best she could, she strode to the parlor doors and pulled them open without hesitation.

Sky-blue dress arranged about her, Ashlinn sat on the edge of a plush couch, looking as though she may burst from anticipation. Blue. She wore blue, not black. Relief rushed through Catriona, passing her lips in a long breath. And her powerful energy radiated joy and contentment. A man clothed in a respectable gray suit stood beside Ashlinn, one hand resting on her shoulder. Short brown hair framed a handsome face with dimples that suggested a grin often graced his face. The smile soothed her fears enough to loosen her tongue.

"So this is the man who won my sister-in-law's heart," Catriona said as she stepped into the room.

The smile that spread across Ashlinn's lovely face as she laid eyes on Catriona eased a bit more of her anxiety. Golden hair floating about her like the cloak of a fae queen, Ashlinn flew to her feet and crossed the distance between them to embrace her. She stiffened at first.

In many ways, her sister-in-law felt like a real fae queen; the way she commanded the attention in a room, had always kept her brothers in line with ease, and held the interest of everyone in high society as if they were her court. It came as no surprise her family could trace their lineage back to royal members of the Seelie Court. All that aside, she'd always been kind to everyone, especially Catriona.

The gentleness of her embrace soon made Catriona relax. The woman's joy slowly began to dissolve her trepidation. Ashlinn drew back, took her by the hand, and led her to the couches.

"My deepest apologies that it took us so long to come visit. I wanted to come to you right away, but we got caught up in Chicago while Sean was recruiting new troops, and then the riots made it impossible to travel to this side of the state from where we were. Still, 'tis a poor excuse for keeping me from my sister-in-law," she said.

For a moment Catriona found herself speechless. Never had she heard Ashlinn allow her Irish brogue to slip through like it did now. She looked harder at her sister-in-law, surprised to see a woman filled with light and happiness, a woman very unlike the one who had followed her brothers into war.

"'Tis a fine reason, for which you have no cause to apologize," Catriona finally managed.

Ashlinn stopped beside the man whom Catriona presumed was Sean.

"Mrs. Catriona O'Brian, 'tis my pleasure to introduce you to my husband, Sean MacBranain. My only regret is that you were unable to attend our wedding. I would so have loved for you to have been there," Ashlinn said as she clutched her right hand.

The sincerity in her clear blue eyes touched Catriona, but the hint of shame in them confused her. Surely such emotion wasn't just from not being able to visit sooner.

Sean bent at the waist, bowing deeply to her. "'Tis a pleasure indeed to meet you, Mrs. O'Brian. I apologize that we were unable to bring you news of Michael's death in person, or to return his body to you."

For a moment she was struck silent. The man was human, unlike like her and Ashlinn. To marry a human wasn't exactly forbidden any longer, but it was frowned upon. Not that she cared. Such prejudice was unthinkable to her. As long as he treated Ashlinn right, he could be an orc for all Catriona cared. Not that there were any orcs on this world. Marriage itself was what she feared now. She shook her head. "Please, there is no need to apologize for something outside of your control."

Out of habit, Catriona cast her gaze to the floor and nodded, effectively hiding the lack of an emotional reaction to the mention of her husband's death. She didn't want to give Ashlinn and her nice husband the wrong idea about her feelings, or worse, the right idea. Ashlinn took one of her hands in both of hers and pulled her down onto one of the couches beside her.

"I know what you're thinking, I can see the burn of your cheeks. But you have nothing to worry about, we may speak freely. Sean knows what I am, what we are," Ashlinn said.

Gasping louder than was proper, Catriona's head snapped up and her gaze locked upon Sean. "You know that we're..."

"Fae, aye. And you have nothing to fear from me," he said, his tone as kind and genuine as his face.

The loving smile Ashlinn basked him in left Catriona as speechless as the man's profession. "We've much to discuss," Ashlinn said in a guarded tone that made the hair on the back of her neck stir.

It was what she had come to think of as the woman's "physician tone," the one she used when she removed herself emotionally from a situation. Catriona had witnessed her do so several times while working with patients in the family practice down the street. What could cause such detachment now, though, she had no idea. Behind her eyes, regret stirred.

"I could tell you that Michael died honorably, fighting to unify our country and end slavery. I *should* tell you that. But I won't lie to you," Ashlinn began.

Prickles of concern danced their way across Catriona's skin. While Ashlinn had always protected and doted on Michael, she had seemed ignorant of his true nature. No ignorance shone in the depths of her eyes now. Catriona wanted to ask her not to go on, but she couldn't find her voice.

"I am deeply sorry, Catriona, but Michael was a deserter who nearly got both myself and Sean killed with his foolishness. I do not tell you this to hurt you, or cause you shame, but because you deserve to know the truth," Ashlinn said softly.

Heart sinking, Catriona's mind began to race. This made her the disgraced widow of a deserter. If she left soon enough, before word spread, perhaps she wouldn't be stoned to death on her way out of town. A shiver went through her as she recalled the stories of such things happening—particularly to women like her who were viewed as…different. She had no family to go back to, the pox had seen to that after she'd been sent off to marry Michael. And there was no way she would even attempt to impose upon her friends. Awful as this news was, it didn't surprise her. Nothing horrible that came her way through her deceased husband surprised her anymore. A deep breath helped her straighten her back and swallow her emotions.

"I understand. I will gather my things and be gone by

morning," she said.

She fought back the instinct to beg for time to leave before Ashlinn made the announcement. The words hung heavy on the back of her tongue, but she bit them back. If Mrs. MacNeil from the Widows organization found out, she'd lead the stone throwing herself. It wouldn't even surprise her if she cried witch and blamed her for causing Michael's cowardice. The thought of giving that woman any reason to hate her more turned Catriona's stomach.

Ashlinn's eyes flew open, moisture gleaming in them. Her grip on Catriona's hand tightened. "No! You misunderstand. No one but you, Sean, and I will ever know about Michael's disgrace. I do not seek to disinherit you, or have your position in society threatened in any way. You are my sister as surely as if we had been born of the same mother, and not because we are both fae descended. I will never allow harm to come to you, especially because of something my foolish brother did," Ashlinn swore.

Catriona's mouth moved, but she was unable to give voice to any words. Leaning toward her, shadows in her eyes, it was Ashlinn who filled the silence.

"I saw something in my brother that day, something dark and terrible. It was as though he were in the grip of a dullahan. And while it would do my heart well to blame his actions on a dark fae, I know 'tis not the truth. The darkness within him was his own. It is a darkness I fear perhaps you were a victim of in more ways than one."

Tears scorched lines down Catriona's face. Though she dropped her head, her hair was bound back with pins and clips, offering no way to hide her shame. Not so much as a single scarlet strand hung free. A strangled curse thick with emotion came from Ashlinn.

"Oh by the Tuatha, you did. I am so sorry, Catriona." Ashlinn drew her into an embrace.

Silent sobs shook Catriona to her core. Tears streamed from her eyes to fall upon her sister-in-law's fine silk shawl. They sat like that for some time, with Ashlinn patting her back and murmuring comforting words into her ear. When her tears finally dried up, Ashlinn drew back and offered her a handkerchief. As she saw to pulling herself back together, Ashlinn drew a large envelope out of her bag.

"My brother purchased a plot of land in California. Michael gave me the deed before he died. I want you to have it. You deserve it after all that you have been through." She handed the envelope to her.

Both excitement and trepidation shook her hands as she accepted it. California, the land of sunshine and gold. More intriguingly, a place with at least a nine-month growing season. Waves of amber grain where huge brown animals called buffalo roamed were said to stretch as far as the eye could see. She had only ever heard stories of it, wondrous stories. It could be much worse. Ashlinn could be banishing her to Nebraska, or simply disinheriting her altogether.

Ashlinn touched her arm. "Do not misunderstand me, Catriona. You don't have to go if you don't want to. You may stay here in New York, in this very house, for the rest of your life if you so wish. Or you may sell and use the money to build a new home in California. I merely want you to have this land, this choice, because it is rightfully yours."

The tenderness in Ashlinn's eyes revealed the truth of her

words. She had always been kind enough to Catriona, but this was completely unexpected. Even among their dwindling kind such generosity and support was not expected.

Catriona shook her head. "No. Rightfully this belongs to your family, as does this fine house. You are too kind to me."

"You are part of this family. Even if you decide to remarry in time, you will still be my sister. If you choose to go to California, this home, Michael's inheritance, all are still yours and always will be."

Had she any tears left, she would have wept again, but, thankfully, they were gone. A huge part of her, a part she had buried four years ago, wanted out of this city in a desperate way. She loved rolling fields filled with horses and cattle, gardens filled with fairies, gnomes, and even mischievous brownies. Those things soothed her soul in a way society never could. But she had ties here now, friends, and from the look of devotion on Ashlinn's face, even family. Did she dare? Her fingers fumbled with the envelope until she finally managed to extract its contents. Smiling, Ashlinn helped her.

"To be honest with you, I was tempted myself when Michael gave me the deed. But something told me it was meant for you," she said in a wistful tone.

As Catriona pored over the documents, her sister-in-law went on. "It is a total of four hundred and eighty acres, a lot, I know, but three plots really. My brothers wrote to a friend of theirs in California, paying him to put in for a plot under the Homestead Act while they were in the war. Unfortunately, that means it has already been two years, leaving you only three to make the required improvements on the land to keep it."

She heard every word, but it was background noise to the

words on the pages before her. Sonoma Valley California, near San Francisco. Almost five hundred acres was hers if she built dwellings on the three plots and improved the land by 1867. *Hers*, by her own hand and hard work. She hadn't had anything like that in a long time.

"Three dwellings," she murmured.

The very idea of such a cost made it hard to swallow. Ashlinn leaned forward, pointing to a line lower on the page. "'Tisn't as bad as it sounds. They only have to be twelve by fourteen feet, a shack really. You could build a manor house on the prime plot and two small guest houses on the other two, and still have coin from Michael's inheritance left for cattle, horses, or whatever you choose to do with the land," she said.

Not an ounce of push tempered her tone, it was merely matter-of-fact. "If you don't want it, don't worry, I can send along a cousin of ours to settle it. Take a few days to think it over. We can discuss it more over the week if you like."

Grinning, Catriona set the papers aside. "You will be staying awhile?" She tried not to sound too eager, but feared she failed terribly.

The few times she and Ashlinn had been able to visit with one another before the war had always been filled with interesting conversation and fun. Michael had been happier when she was around, as if his sister brought out the best in him. It had made her visits the highlight of Catriona's married life. Now, with Michael gone, she longed to have her sister-in-law all to herself. Guilt stirred within her over feeling that way, but she pushed it down. Aside from herself, Ashlinn and Deirdre were the only three fae she knew of in New York, the only people in the entire city she could be herself around.

"Yes, we are staying in the hotel down on main street, and visiting whenever 'tis convenient for you," Ashlinn said.

Catriona shook her head. "A hotel, no. You must stay here. There are dozens of empty rooms in this house, and you and Sean are more than welcome."

Eager gaze going to Sean, Ashlinn inclined her head. He grinned and nodded.

"Only if you are sure we are not imposing. We did arrive unannounced, after all," Ashlinn said.

They clasped hands and grinned at one another like schoolgirls. "O' course not, you're family!" Catriona insisted, her voice shaking slightly with the threat of tears.

After a bit of giggling and more hugging, Catriona called for her servants to ready the rooms and heat water for baths for both Ashlinn and Sean. She would see to it that her sister and new brother-in-law had every comfort she could provide. As they headed up to their rooms to retire for the evening, Catriona called for one of her servants. The head of the household help sent along a skinny young man who either hadn't filled his clothes out yet, or had just gone up a size due to a growth spurt. A shock of hair almost as red as her own peaked out from beneath his cap. Catriona handed him a letter.

"Please deliver this to Mrs. Deirdre Quinn, and ask the stable hand to ready my horse," she told him.

Accepting the letter, he bowed deeply then hastened out the door, closing it carefully behind him. Her heart began to beat a steadily increasing rhythm. A ride out of the city was in order. The fresh air and time with her horse would clear her head. Once that was done, she needed desperately to speak to her friends.

18

2

Catriona

The setting sun cast a lovely orange glow on the open marketplace by the time Catriona finished explaining. Open mouthed, both Sadie and Deirdre stared at her. The silence from her friends stretched her nerves until they were taut as a fiddle's strings. No disappointment or suspicion played upon their faces, only shock. She had told them every word and every nuance of character that had come to pass in her parlor, leaving no question as to her sister-in-law's meaning or intentions.

Purple light—and something else began to fill Deirdre's dark blue eyes as she leaned forward. "What an adventure! Are you going to do it?" she asked.

Joy at the very idea brought a smile to her face at the same time anxiety flipped her stomach upside down. "I couldn't possibly," she murmured.

While her gaze was cast out over the fruit stands and merchant carts, she saw neither the people who walked the cobbled city center, nor the wares they searched for. Instead, she saw rolling fields of green dotted with horses, maybe a few sheep or cattle, all bathed in brilliant sunlight.

"But you have always wanted a farm filled with animals! Can you imagine it, the land of sunshine, the Wild West!" Deirdre exclaimed, her hands moving with each word as if they spoke for her as much as her voice did.

She turned a circle, twirling her burgundy skirt out, pausing halfway around to fetch an orange off a merchant stand. Eyebrows rising, she held the fruit beneath Catriona's nose. "A place where things like this grow wild, they say!"

Though she shared her friend's enthusiasm, fear held her back from expressing it. Plaintive calls for her to handle the expensive fruit carefully came from the vendor behind her, but Deirdre seemed not to hear.

Sadie nodded. "You would thrive on a farm filled with animals."

The vendor behind them began to beseech their better nature. His desperate pleas finally made Catriona dig a few coins from her purse and press them into his hand as they walked by.

"You want to. I can see it in your eyes. Why stay here where the hens of high society sneer down their noses at you?" Deirdre leaned close and whispered, "If they ever found out what we are, you can be certain they would use it against us."

Catriona's gaze moved from Deirdre's flushed face to Sadie's guarded one. "I couldn't leave you two. Sadie here would be out of a job, and who knows what trouble you would get up to with me gone. You'd likely have the foliage and fauna tormenting the ladies of high society at every turn," she said, one eye narrowing at Deirdre as her gaze returned to her.

Laughing, Deirdre threw an arm around her as they walked. "That is certainly true, on both counts. But what if we both went with you?" Not so much as an ounce of tease peppered her tone, excitement, but not teasing.

"You're serious?" Catriona asked.

She watched as Sadie's brows rose, her head tilted, and a smile started to lift the corners of her lips. Deirdre draped her other arm around Sadie and leaned down to whisper in her ear.

"Sunshine, trees that reach up to the sky, beaches, a warm ocean, all within a few days' travel," she tempted her.

The smile playing at Sadie's full lips spread. The joy on her face stripped away the aging her husband's death had wrought upon her, making her look her true twenty-five years once again. "It would be an adventure, would it not?" she asked.

Deirdre nodded. "The grandest adventure, indeed! Far away from the cackling hens of New York high society, in a place virtually untouched. Imagine it, the three of us forging a new path." Her arm tightened around Catriona. "Three plots, one for each of us. That means it is meant to be. I would be happy to pay the fees on one of the plots and build a home on it. And Sadie could settle the third." She held up a hand just as Sadie's mouth opened. "I know what you are going to say, it would not be charity. You are more than just our friend. You are an intelligent, competent woman who knows all about farming and could help us in whatever endeavor we undertake with the land."

The passion in her friend's voice moved Catriona, stirring an excitement in her that she hadn't realized had been sleeping there.

Casting her gaze down, Sadie shook her head. "I'm just a housekeeper now. It's been years since I worked the land."

A humming noise came from Deirdre. "You miss it, I can feel it in your energy!" she said as she brushed a tight black curl back behind her ear.

"But what venture would we undertake?" Sadie asked, her tone making it evident she was teetering on being convinced.

Catriona's thoughts went to her garden where she sat with all the birds and squirrels, the only part of the house that felt like hers. The idea sprung immediately into her mind, as if it had merely been waiting for the right prompting. "A winery, and horses, o' course." She looked to Deirdre. "With your talents, I have no doubt the grapes would thrive."

Springing up, Deirdre skipped ahead of them, spun around to face them, and clapped her hands together. The woman's girlish enthusiasm melted away the last of Catriona's resistance. "That would be perfect! With our connections here in New York, we could even sell to buyers here!"

Eyes alight, Sadie grabbed one of Deirdre's hands. "Your mother's grapes! You can take the vines. That is perfect," she said.

Those vines were the one possession Deirdre's mum had brought all the way from Ireland, nursing them in American soil before she had even been born.

Shaking her head, Catriona stopped on the sidewalk before one of her favorite stores. Bailey's Spirits. The mercantile sign hanging over the solid oak door announced that they sold wine, tobacco, and spirits. That they had ended up before this very shop struck a chord deep within her. But then, she had a feeling Deirdre's tugging and prompting had a bit to do with that.

"Could we really do it? *Should* we really do it?" Catriona whispered.

"Yes!" Deirdre and Sadie said in unison.

The bubbling excitement building within her threatened to boil away her reservations. Her friends' eager faces fed the latter rather than the prior. Chin tucked, Deirdre peered at her from beneath her dark eyebrows.

"We try it, if it doesn't work out, we come back. You said yourself that Ashlinn is leaving you the house here in New York, along with Michael's inheritance. You have nothing to lose save for the experience of a lifetime," she said.

Those words fell like a finger on the wrong key of a piano during a beautiful song. Ashlinn was being amazing to her, treating her like family despite the fact she no longer had to. Letting out a long breath that eased the pressure from her corset, she nodded. "All right. We'll try it. But after her generosity, we must invite Ashlinn along as well."

Squeals of delight pierced her ears as her friends hopped about like young lasses and took turns embracing her.

"O' course! It would be only right. We can split my property." Deirdre said.

"Or mine," Sadie chimed in.

Deirdre clapped her hands together and rubbed them. "We must celebrate!"

"Yes, we must!" Sadie agreed.

Eyes going to the shop door to their left, Catriona smiled. "I'll buy the wine. 'Tis only appropriate that we do so with a special bottle."

Sadie looped an arm through Deirdre's. "We'll pick up the cheese. There's a shop just down the block that has the finest in all of New York," she said.

Deirdre nodded to her. "Excellent plan. We'll meet you back here in a few moments," she told Catriona.

With a nod and a wave, Catriona began to ascend the stairs to the shop. Deirdre's voice rang out, making her turn her head back in their direction. "Red or white?"

"Red," she called back as she kept climbing.

Foot halfway up the next step, she turned her head back around, and smacked into an unyielding body. The momentum of the person descending the stairs redirected her own, and she began to topple backward. A pair of striking green eyes widened within a face boasting fine cheekbones and a strong jaw that hadn't seen a razor in at least a week. She had just enough time to fret over a handsome man—rugged though he was—seeing her tumbled to her arse, before his hand dashed out and grabbed hers. One moment she was falling, the next she spun around and landed in strong arms.

Pressed up against a firm chest as she was, she could scarcely draw enough breath to cry out. Arms that bulged with muscles barely contained within a simple cotton shirt engulfed her. The scents of lavender soap mingled pleasantly with the subtle musk of man. Something about him felt comfortable, soothing, things she felt only around animals and those of fae blood. It snatched away the words she'd been about to say.

"Easy there, ma'am. The path ahead is more important than the one behind," a deep voice thick with a brogue that didn't quite seem all Irish resonated from the chest against hers.

Finding her balance, she pushed away from the hard planes of muscle, freeing herself from arms that tugged with a slight reluctance to release her. She had to crane her neck back to take in all of the man who towered over her, and not because he was a few steps up from her like she had thought. He stood on the same step she did, he was just that tall. Breeches filled out quite nicely—she hated to admit—went along with the simple shirt and an ankle length leather duster. The outfit created the picture of a rugged man who looked like he belonged out West rather than in downtown New York.

Her cheeks heated as she realized he had said something, and she couldn't recall for the life of her what it had been.

One of his brows rose into dark brown hair that hadn't seen a barber's scissors for at least a year, maybe longer. The motion made his green eyes all the more alluring, as if it increased their magnetism.

"Cat got your tongue?" he asked.

He didn't even attempt to hide his brogue. Either he wasn't from New York, or he had not undergone years of lessons to strip the Irish from his voice. Either way, his lack of concern over the matter both incensed and intrigued her—though she would never admit the latter to anyone save herself. And to speak to her with such familiarity, well it simply wasn't done. Nor did it help that he used her old nickname. Hearing it reminded her of all the things she no longer was. And those reminders hurt.

Deep laughter rumbled from him when she didn't answer. Straightening her shawl, she took a step back, skirt swishing against the steps as she did so. The material caught beneath her heel and she began to slip. His hand shot out and gripped her elbow, steadying her. The warmth of his hand on her arm felt wonderful. Sensations she hadn't experienced in years began to stir deep in her bosom. They were things she hadn't ever wanted to feel again. Her judgment of men's character, her attraction to them, couldn't be trusted. Eyes narrowing, she tugged free.

"That is twice you have put your hands on me, sir. Such a thing is quite improper, and I will thank you not to do it again," she huffed.

A corner of his mouth lifted into a crooked grin that caused things low in her body to betray her by tightening. "But if I have to do it to save you from falling, again, your thanks will then be for naught," he teased.

Her brow furrowed so deeply she could see the carefully shaped hairs of it. Such a look would cause wrinkles, her mum would say, yet at the moment she didn't care. "I shall forgive you since you are not from around here, and clearly do not know the rules of proper society."

The man tucked the package he was carrying under his arm and fixed her with an amused look. "You should instead thank me for not letting you fall on your arse, twice."

Mouth dropping open, she could only watch mutely as he gave her an exaggerated bow, turned, and strode down the steps. Her gaze remained riveted upon him. The duster billowed out around him, sending his leather and lavender soap scent to her on the breeze. An arse of a man simply should not smell so good, or have the ability to make such a simple outfit look so appealing. Shaking off such thoughts, she lifted her head and strode up the stairs, determined not to allow the frustrating encounter to ruin her good mood. She had a bottle of wine to buy and a change of destiny to celebrate.

3

Rick

Two days later, the spunky redhead Rick had collided with on the stairs before Bailey's Spirits still filled his thoughts. The way her cheeks had flushed as red as her hair, the look of indignation that had filled her ultra-green eyes, and those curves… *Oh those curves…* It should have been enough that she was clothed in all the finery that marked her as a lady of high society to banish her from his mind. But the fine silk and lace had framed her generous bosom oh so nicely. And then there was the problem of her lineage which had been as unmistakable in her scent as her gorgeous red hair was upon her head. Fae did not mix with his kind, or really any kind for that matter.

It was a good thing he always wore the obsidian necklace his Navajo shaman friend had given him. It shielded his power from other supernatural races, allowing him to avoid detection. If she had realized what he was, the scene would have been much worse. Though he hated himself a bit for it, he couldn't help but hope he'd run into her on the streets of New York again. Much to his dismay—and relief—he didn't.

Even now though her fresh hay and lilac soap smell clung in his nose. He imagined it was more likely that he simply couldn't get it out of his head.

One more thing to attend to and his business in New York was finished for the year. Bottle of wine in hand, he stopped at the door to his friends' place and rapped soundly upon it. Rain began to beat down on him, stripping some of the heat from the early June evening. The door opened to a lovely young woman in a yellow dress that beautifully set off skin the hue of mahogany oiled to a dark finish. He inclined his head in a slight bow and smiled.

"Hello, miss. I am Corporal Fergusson. Mr. and Mrs. MacBranain are expecting me," he said.

The woman smiled and stepped aside. "They are indeed. Please, do come in, Mr. Fergusson." She stepped aside and swept an arm out wide. "My apologies for the informality but our doorman has the evening off."

Just a hint of an accent touched her words, marking her as one who had been born in the north rather than fled here for freedom before the war. While it wasn't completely uncommon for a woman of color to be a maid, most houses in New York high society that he knew used Irish servants. Perhaps she was a nurse friend of Ashlinn's. But then, she didn't have that haunted look those who had seen battle carried with them.

"No apology necessary. Thank you, miss."

His wet boots clunked against the marble floor as he stepped inside the foyer, leaving tracks of mud and droplets of water behind.

"I apologize for the mess, miss. 'Tis raining with a vengeance out there," he said.

The woman smiled. "No need to worry about that, sir. It cleans up easily enough."

The scent of roses wafted to him from where they sat within a delicate vase on a table near the arched wall that separated the space from the rest of the house. Beneath it he smelled the earthy, sweet scent of a fae—Ashlinn's scent. Yet it reminded him of the lovely redhead on the steps of the wine shop. Would he ever get her out of his head?

Beyond the arched opening, a wide staircase yawned that forked both to the left and right after a short flight. The oak banister was garishly decorated with cherubs and vines. Such over the top trappings were a surprise, but then, Sean had said this was Ashlinn's sister-in-law's house, not hers.

"Oh, Sadie, is that the postman? I have a few letters to go out," a very familiar female voice called.

"No, Miss Catriona. It's the visitor the MacBranains have been expecting," the woman called back.

That voice… Surely not.

His eyebrows rose at the unusual familiarity with which the maid addressed her mistress. Such a thing wasn't normally done in high society homes, not even up here in the north. He liked it. It reflected well on the mistress of the house.

"Ah, excellent! I am eager to meet him," the woman called above the echo of narrow heels clicking on marble.

It couldn't be. Surely, his mind—and his nose—was merely playing tricks on him. She rounded the corner and his eyes confirmed what his senses already knew. Long red hair swung unfettered about shoulders that were far more slender than they had looked beneath her shawl a few days ago. Green satin and black lace hugged curves that bordered on being skinny, likely thanks to the abhorrent societal trend, all save for a bosom with deliciously deep cleavage. Green eyes widened, her gaze skittering across his frame, catching on the wine bottle in his arm, going to his muddy boots, and back to his face.

Pasting on a badly faked smile, she touched the maid's arm in a casual way that suggested they might be friends, which made her even more interesting. "I am afraid you are mistaken, Sadie."

The smile dropped and her top lip pulled back from her teeth as she turned to him. "It seems quite counterproductive to track mud all over one's floor while coming to apologize."

"'Tis you who are mistaken, ma'am. I am not here to apologize for some imagined slight, but am instead here to see the MacBranains."

Triumph shot through him when a blush stained her cheeks. "*You* are Corporal Fergusson?" she demanded.

He nodded. "None other."

"No," she insisted with enough vehemence to make his brows rise.

Hands out, palms up, he looked down at himself. "Yes."

Her eyes widened. "No!"

Emitting a wordless cry, she spun and stormed out of the room, heels clicking out a battle rhythm as if launching an assault on the marble floor.

"Truly, I am," he called after her, which elicited another wordless cry of frustration.

He turned to the maid only to find her regarding him from

beneath raised brows, head cocked. "You as puzzled as I am by that, Miss Sadie?"

Her full lips began to twitch with a coming grin. "Perhaps not as much." She nodded toward the bottle of wine tucked into the crook of his arm. "Is that from Bailey's Spirits?"

Not sure why it was relevant, but not seeing any reason to withhold the information, he nodded.

"Well, Mr. Fergusson, I fear Miss Catriona's reaction will not be your only surprise of the day," she said.

Even as he contemplated the strange words, his eyes followed the redhead as she disappeared around a corner. A fiery name to match a fiery personality. He liked both far more than he wanted to. Words raised in a heated discussion centered around him drifted back into the foyer. Among them were both Catriona's voice and the gentle, soothing voice of a friend he remembered oh so well. Not wanting to track mud all across the foyer, he leaned to the left as far as he could, trying to see around the corner.

The back side of a man clothed in a fine suit appeared in the opening, pulling double doors closed behind him. The feminine voices cut off to all but his sensitive ears. Spinning on a heel, the man turned toward him. Though his hair was shorter and a scar marred his forehead, the confidence and self-awareness made him instantly recognizable. Cheeks aching from a grin so huge it had to look maniacal, Fergusson took a step toward the man.

"Sergeant!" he said as he advanced, forgetting his muddy boots.

The man grinned just as wide in response. They met in the middle of the floor, embraced heartily, and pulled back apart.

"'Tis just Sean now, me friend," he insisted.

Fergusson grunted. "It will always be Sergeant."

Waving the comment off, Sean grinned and slapped him on the shoulder. "Come now, Rick, let's dispense of such things. Tell me, how on Earth did you manage to make such an impression on Catriona already?"

"I have a talent, I suppose." He held the bottle of wine out to Sean, who accepted it with an impressed look. "A late congratulations on your wedding. Sorry I couldn't be there, but, you know, war to finish and all that."

Sean tapped the scar on the side of his head. "Sorry I couldn't be there to finish it with you. Head wound and all that."

Fergusson clapped him on the shoulder a bit more vigorously than he intended, making his friend stumble a step. Laughing, Sean shook his head and motioned to the door.

"Walk with me a bit. I have something for you in the carriage house. It will give the ladies time to talk things through," Sean said.

Before they reached the door, Sadie pulled it open. The clip clop of horses and grind of wagon wheels against cobblestone drifted in from the busy street not far beyond the front garden of the house. Pattering beneath it all like the erratic rhythm of an untalented drummer boy was the constant deluge of rain. Nose wrinkling from the stench of wet horse manure, oil lamps, and far too many people, Fergusson tipped his head to Sadie in thanks, then stepped out before Sean. He flipped his collar up and ducked his head low so his almost shoulder-length brown hair kept the rain from running down the back of his coat.

On the way out the door Sean paused and handed Sadie the bottle of wine. "Would you please have the cook put this on ice for when we get back?"

"Of course, Mr. MacBranain."

Sean waved a hand. "Please, call me Sean."

The words convinced Rick the woman was indeed no mere maid, but a friend of the lady of the house. *Intriguing.*

She grinned and nodded, her expression making it clear she would do no such thing.

Following a stone pathway that cut through the garden and around the side of the expansive brick house, Rick spared a glance back at Sean. "Ice, in June? Damn, Sarge, you really did marry into money."

From behind him, Sean called up. "I did, but as you might guess, Ashlinn is the true treasure."

Does he know she's fae? A sparkle in his eyes suggested maybe he did. But Sean was human. One of the cardinal rules of faekind was not to reveal their race to those outside of the supernatural—a creed all supernaturals held in some form or another. He and Sean had fought together in the war, bled for one another, and he still hadn't revealed his true nature to the man. "True enough, she is at that. So I trust the marriage has gotten off to a good start?"

Catching up and passing him, Sean opened the wrought iron gate that led around to the side of the house. "Aye, you could say that."

Though he couldn't see his face, Rick could hear the smile upon it.

"No little ones in the oven yet, though?"

34

"Not yet, but it has only been a bit over a year. All in due time."

A slight overhang kept the rain from them as they made their way along the path to the huge carriage house. Sean opened a man door beside the double doors and motioned for Rick to go first. The scents of hay and horses enveloped him in a rush of warm air as he stepped inside. So did Catriona's unique scent. In fact, he smelled it more strongly here than in the house, as if she spent more time in the stables. Six stalls lined a wide, cobbled walkway. The horses within snorted and pawed, smelling him.

"Easy, you've nothing to fear from me," he soothed.

One by one, they settled under the calming energy he sent out. When his energy touched something else, something deeper in the building, he gasped. It felt wild, untamed, but full of innocence and curiosity. It smelled like fresh rain falling over the hills of Ireland.

Behind Sean the door clicked shut, muting the sound of the falling rain. An inquisitive, young-sounding bark punctuated the noises of horses eating and rustling about in their stalls. It came from the source of that other energy and brought to mind the massive Irish wolfhound that had followed Ashlinn and Sean everywhere during the war. He had nearly forgotten that the hound was pregnant the last time he had seen her, and that he had asked for one of the pups. But knowing the true nature of the hound, he hadn't expected Ashlinn would willingly give up any of her offspring.

A childlike joy he hadn't felt since long before the war swelled within his chest at the sound of clawed feet pattering against cobblestone. But it had been a little more than two years since then. There was no way the youthful bark he had just heard could be from a two-year-old dog. He shot Sean a questioning look, but his friend only grinned. Another soft bark of greeting sounded.

Rounding the corner that led down to the horses' stalls came a canine that already stood at least two and a half feet at the shoulder but still had that young pup look to him. Paws the size of a lady's hand proved he would grow much bigger. While he certainly had the look of an Irish wolfhound, something otherworldly lingered about him as well. His body was broader, fuller, with a fluffy tail boasting long hair. Gray dominated his slightly long coat, but a ring of white framed his chest and head like a lion, along with white areas around some of his feet, and down his back.

On instinct, Rick went down on a knee, grinning, yet holding his lips closed over his teeth. He dared not foul this up. Despite how he looked, this was no mere pup. For such a creature to accept him would be no small thing. If it did, it would be a companion for life, which was longer for Rick than most folk.

"Look at you," he mused.

"Ashlinn is very particular about who we give the pups too, but for you, she agreed. This fellah is from the second litter. Something told me to bring him to you," Sean said.

The pup trotted right up to him, bushy tail wagging, floppy ears perked. Unlike many other animals, not a hint of fear lay in his eyes. His pink tongue darted out to slather Rick's hands. Laughing with relief, he petted the pup's head and scratched behind his ears.

"He's fantastic. Are you sure you and Ashlinn don't

mind?" Rick asked.

Crouching beside the pup, Sean petted him as well. "O' course not. He was meant to be yours, I'm certain of it, and so is Ashlinn."

The words stirred something that slumbered deep within Rick. He scratched beneath the pup's chin with both hands, looking into its unique gold eyes as he did so. Tongue lolling out the side of its mouth, it seemed to smile at him. Within its eyes rested the gentleness customary to the Irish wolfhound breed, but something else sparkled there as well, his supernatural side, along with mischievousness, and a sense of adventure.

Watching the little fellow wriggle beneath his attentions, trying to lick him again, Rick grinned. "Your instincts were spot on. He's perfect."

Sean rose to his feet. "Fantastic! What will you call him?"

Caught up in the pup's gold eyes, Rick thought hard for a moment. "Lincoln, after our esteemed President, may he rest in peace."

"A fine name. Now that I have softened you up a bit, there is a favor I must ask of you, me friend," Sean said.

The serious tone his voice took at the last part made Rick rise and meet his gaze. "Anything." Whether or not Sean knew the value of the gift he had just given him didn't matter. Rick would do anything for him in turn regardless.

Sighing deeply, Sean ran a hand through his short hair. "Don't be so quick to agree, you haven't heard what it is yet."

Rick dismissed the words with a laugh and a wave. "It doesn't matter. You saved me life on more than one occasion.

We're blood brothers. You have but to ask and 'tis yours."

Sean made his way over to a bale of hay and sat down. His friend's disregard for his fine pants raised one of Rick's brows, and his concern.

"I trust you are still guiding people to other states?" Sean asked. Though the question was innocent enough, the hesitation in his voice led him to believe far more weighed on it.

He sat down on another bale next to him. "Aye."

The pup bounded up to him, sat on his feet, and thrust his head into his hands for more petting. He scratched absently behind its ears as he watched Sean's guarded face.

"Ashlinn's family is heading west to settle some property in California."

"Which part?"

Sean's smile stretched to a painful looking size. "Sonoma County, right in your backyard, quite literally, according to the county records, I believe."

Scratching his own bristly chin with one hand, Rick tried to catch his friend's gaze and failed. "Um hum, but I'm guessing that's not why you want me to do it."

"No, 'tis not."

They stared at each other for a long moment that swelled with unsaid words. That knowing look made his skin prickle as if brownies trod along it, digging in with their wickedly sharp claws. He began to fear he was going to have to literally pull it out of him. "How many people?"

"Three." The tension in Sean's voice was building, which Rick knew to mean they were getting closer to the meat of the issue.

"Three people, a wagon or two, doesn't sound so bad.

Why is it you fear I'm going to say no, then?"

A long sigh rattled out of Sean as he finally looked up and met Rick's gaze. "'Tis Catriona O'Brian and two of her friends."

Rick shrugged. "'Tis no bother, Sean. True, the woman doesn't like me much, but we can get along well enough for three to four months on the trail together."

Still, Sean looked doubtful.

"Out with it, man. What else is there to it?" Rick prompted. The pup gave a little bark and licked his hand.

Again, his friend sighed. If he kept it up Rick feared the man may swoon like a lass. "Her friends are women. I am asking you to guide three women to California."

Rick shot to his feet. "For the love of the Tuatha, man, what are you thinking?"

Hands held out, Sean rose to stand beside him. The pup let out a louder bark and danced between the two of them as if it were a game. "I know, I know. But you're the only person I trust for the task. This is Ashlinn's sister-in-law, after all. She assures me she's quite capable. We will pay for armed men, however many you need."

The desperation in his friend's eyes tugged at his heart like sutures. "People die on such a journey all the time. While armed men can help protect against hostile natives and predators, they can do nothing against illness and weather. The risks are high, Sean. I only want you to enter into this with your eyes wide open."

Sean clapped him on the shoulder. "I know, and I am. These women are not like the frail lasses of high society. They are strong, independent, and they know the risks, as do Ashlinn and myself."

Not like them indeed. Again he wondered if Sean knew just how unlike them Ashlinn and Catriona were. These friends of hers he didn't know, but he had a feeling since both Ashlinn and Catriona were fae, their friends likely were as well. That made them hardier, for sure, longer lived than humans, but still just as likely to succumb to bodily harm.

The deep breath that blew from Sean snapped Rick's attention back to him. "And I know you are…"

Eyes widening, Rick swallowed hard as he waited for the end of the sentence. Again they locked gazes and shared a long look.

"More capable than most," Sean finished at last, his tone making it clear he meant more than the words revealed.

He knew. Maybe he didn't know exactly *what* Rick was, but he knew he was…more.

Mouth gaping, Rick blinked several times, unable to find words. No judgement, fear, or suspicion lay in Sean's eyes. Neither did any pressure to explain or tell his story.

Nodding, despite everything good sense told him, Rick echoed one of Sean's many sighs. "All right, then. I hope they can prepare quickly, because we need to depart within the week to make it before the weather turns."

A whoop of relief echoed off the rafters, making a few of the horses around the corner jump in their stalls. "Thank you, me friend. I'll owe you greatly for this."

Rick shook his head. "Don't thank me until I get them all there safely."

Sean's answer was cut off by the pounding of a pair of feet running toward them. They both turned toward the corner to see a gangly young footman. He nearly slipped in the hay scattered across the floor but managed to right himself at the last moment. His wide eyes fixed on Sean.

"Mr. MacBranain, sir, please pardon the intrusion. A letter has arrived that has the ladies most disturbed. Mrs. MacBranain requests your presence straightaway," he huffed.

Motioning for Rick to follow, Sean started for the door. "Come along. Once I get them calmed down, we'll open that bottle of wine."

Reluctant though he was, he followed anyway, fighting the urge to roll his eyes. Ladies in a lather over a letter? What was he getting himself into?

4

Catriona

Slight heels clicked out a frantic rhythm as Catriona paced, their sharp sound serving to aggravate her further. At least half a dozen birds sat on the windowsill, screeching in response to her agitation. She hated that her distress bothered them. Yet her mind could not stop, so her feet couldn't either. While she paced, Ashlinn sat calmly on one of the plush couches of the parlor, bent over a coffee table, writing away. Considering her sister-in-law worked on a list of things Catriona would need on her journey, her actions were far more productive than Catriona's own. Not even that knowledge could halt her momentum.

At last, a knock sounded on the parlor doors and upon her word, they burst open, spilling forth a flushed Deirdre with Sadie on her heels. Shoving a long, black lock that had come free from a hastily-made-looking bun, Deirdre curtsied to

Ashlinn and murmured a quick greeting. In her rush, Catriona introduced them quite poorly, begging forgiveness from both women as she did so. Ashlinn waved off her apology and motioned for Deirdre to sit opposite her on a second couch.

"And here I thought I'd met all the fae in New York. 'Tis a pleasure to make your acquaintance," Ashlinn said.

"Now you *have* met them all," Deirdre said with a sweet smile. "And 'tis a pleasure to make your acquaintance as well. I have heard nothing but wonderful things about you." Pleasantries out of the way, her dark blue eyes turned up to Catriona. "Please, do read it to us."

With shaking hands, Catriona unfolded the letter. Two pairs of booted heels marching into the room stopped her before she could begin. Sean in all his polished glory, looking every bit the gentleman, clashed with the wild appearance of Corporal Fergusson with his week-old beard and ankle-length duster. The very sight of Fergusson only added to Catriona's frustration. She did not want the uncouth human rogue to know her business, but then, if Ashlinn was right and he was her only hope, she had no choice. Her sister-in-law had assured her the man knew nothing about her true nature, nor was he the type who would pry at curiosities in her mannerisms. Still…

She made hasty introductions and curtly invited Corporal Fergusson to sit. To the corporal's credit, he barely spared Deirdre a glance and a kind word where most men all but ogled her and fell all over themselves to impress her. Not that she wanted the man to be curt with her friend… *Oh, hells.* Her mind was simply all over in its state of unrest.

Taking a seat beside his wife, Sean nodded to Catriona. "Please, don't allow us to interrupt. You were about to read the letter."

Eyes shifting from Sean's concerned expression to Fergusson's wary gaze, she took a breath and began to read.

"Dear Mrs. O'Brian, Thank you kindly for the fine wine and chocolates that you sent all the way from New York, as well as your assurances that you will make a richly contributing patron to Sonoma County."

She paused and shot Ashlinn an inquiring look. Her sister-in-law gave her a half-smile and shrugged. When she had read it aloud to Catriona a few moments ago, she had left that part out. Ashlinn must have reached out on her behalf. She wanted to thank her, should thank her, but she couldn't focus enough to do so now. Attention returning to the letter, she went on.

"As you know, the gold rush has brought many settlers to California and the railroad is bringing even more. Demand for land is high and those who will utilize it to its full potential, a potential that best furthers the fine state of California, must be given preference. The man who originally petitioned for the grant on your land, a Mr. Ainsworth, has written to me to ask to reclaim the grant should the O'Brians fail to claim it. Seeing as you are a widow with no male children to help improve such land, I am giving you until the middle of this August to lay claim to the land, or it will revert to Mr. Ainsworth. I do so in the best interest of our fine state of California. I wish you the very best of luck."

Her voice choked on the man's name and title. Suddenly both Sadie and Deirdre were at her side, offering comforting words and touches.

Corporal Fergusson made a sound close to a growl.

"Ainsworth, the blaggard. It figures. I'm sorry your husband had the misfortune to purchase the claim from him." Indignation furrowed his brow.

"You know the man?" Sean asked.

"Aye. He's an Englishman who's been buying up as much of the valley as he can, selling off the bits of land he doesn't want or can't get to in time." The way he stared hard at the fireplace as he talked made Catriona think there might be more to the story. But right now the why of it didn't matter. What did was that someone wanted to take her dream from her before she even had a chance to fully realize it.

Face heating, Catriona blinked tears away, straightened her back, and gave her friends what she hoped was a determined look.

"I have to do this," she told them.

Until it was being snatched away, she hadn't realized just how badly she wanted this opportunity. To get out of this house and away from its bad memories, start a life with her friends from which the fruits would be born of her own hard labor, it was more than she had ever hoped for. And moving to the country where they could be close to the land and its creatures and plants would strengthen all of their power.

Wisps of tight black curls hair floated about as Sadie shook her head. "But it's impossible to make it that far that fast."

Catriona's look hardened as her determination grew. "For a few wagons and an entourage of armed men, yes." Gaze steady, she looked to Corporal Fergusson. His head was cocked and green eyes were wide with curiosity, as if she suddenly intrigued him. "But not for two people on horseback." Those green eyes snagged on hers and wouldn't look away. The weight of interest in them both bothered and thrilled her. Just for a moment, something about the man felt otherworldly. But before she could put her finger on it, it was gone.

"No!" Ashlinn cried as she flew to her feet in a flurry of yellow satin skirts.

Rather than grab hold of her as she expected her to, Ashlinn took hold of one of Sadie's arms and one of Deirdre's. "Please, turn her from this foolish idea. Such a thing is not done, a woman traveling alone with a man, with no escort. And, 'tis too dangerous." The last part was no more than a whisper.

To her friends' credit, they both shook their heads. A smile spread across Deirdre's face. "I want to go as well!"

Gaze snapping back to Fergusson, Catriona saw alarm flash in his widening eyes. Now it was she who shook her head. "No. Corporal Fergusson will have an easier time keeping only one person safe. Is that not right, sir?" she asked.

"True enough. Two people can make the trip almost unnoticed, and within the timeframe, more would complicate matters," he said, sounding impressed.

His green eyes held her a bit too intimately for her comfort. Her power thrummed with recognition, as if it saw and connected to the animal in him. *Odd. That has never happened with a human.* And yet, he certainly was human. Some people were more in tune with their animalistic nature, especially those used to fighting for survival like him. That must be it. Pulling her gaze from him, she smiled at her friends. "You can leave in a week as we planned. You'll just have to have a different escort, and will arrive a after I do. I'll be all right. Corporal Fergusson is a war hero trusted by my sister-in-law and her husband. I could not be in better hands." At the last, her attention shifted to the strong hands of which she spoke.

At over six feet tall and roped in muscle, the man was formidable indeed. Her friends could hardly contest that. And if Ashlinn trusted him, surely she was safe with him, despite the gleam of interest in his eyes. Most likely that had to do with her hiring him and nothing else, especially considering the nearly disrespectful manner in which he had spoken to her upon their first meeting.

Ashlinn strode to her husband's side, hooked an arm through his and Fergusson's, and inclined her head to Catriona. "If you will excuse us for a moment."

"O' course," Catriona said.

As the three of them left the room, Fergusson's gaze remained locked on her until the door closed behind them. Sadie and Deirdre began bombarding her with rushed questions and suggestions the moment the door clicked shut. She could scarcely keep up with them, especially with her mind going in so many directions. Half-hearted answers and reassurances passed her lips while her mind contemplated one thing, and one thing only. She would be alone with a man for a month. A wild, rugged—and admittedly quite handsome—man who seemed to have little care for propriety and boundaries. It was a bit harsh to judge him as such, she knew, but it was hard not to considering her distrust of strange men. Or all men in general, really.

"Alone on the trail with a man, it's not done, Miss Catriona. Surely, at least I should go with you," Sadie cautioned in a hushed voice.

Smiling, Catriona took up one of her hands. It had taken

quite a bit of time for Sadie to become comfortable enough with the two of them being friends, equals in Catriona's eyes. She wanted to be careful what she said so she didn't undo her fragile confidence.

"He is a trusted friend of the family, and an honorable soldier to boot. You need not fear for me, and the very act of the three of us ladies settling on our own in California steps outside the rules of propriety as 'tis, so I am not worried about that. Besides, if I feel threatened, I can always charm a rattlesnake or a bear to help me out," she told her, proud that the words sounded convincing when she herself wasn't so convinced.

Practically skipping over, Deirdre took hold of their grasped hands in both of hers. The sweet tang of her self-made lilac and vanilla perfume wrapped around Catriona. Eyes shining behind her dark locks, she grasped her bottom lip between her teeth as if trying to keep her smile from growing too large. She failed.

"Traveling alone across America with a handsome, rugged man, I envy you so! You must do it. It will be the adventure of a lifetime, one you can tell us all about in September when we arrive with the wagons," she said.

Sadie groaned. "An adventure, oh Deirdre."

Laughter bubbled from Deirdre. "Indeed! Now enough of this fretting, we must prepare."

Fighting Deirdre's enthusiasm was like fighting an outgoing tide, impossible and exhausting if one tried too hard. Catriona gave in and allowed her own smile to slip through. Part of her wanted to jump at the chance, *had* to, but the ever-cautious part of her that usually won out sort of hoped Corporal

Fergusson would say no.

The doors to the parlor opened and in walked Ashlinn, Sean, and Fergusson, as if her thoughts had summoned the man. Gazing intently at her from behind overly long brown bangs, the man all but commanded her attention.

Damn, but he is attractive. Burying the thought, Catriona cleared her throat. "Well, Corporal Fergusson, will you take on the task?"

"Aye, I'll do it."

And upon those four little words, her life was about to change.

5

Rick

Three days later, as he strode into Mrs. O'Brian's carriage house and laid eyes upon her, he wanted to eat those words. The woman stood in the aisle cinching up an English saddle onto her tall thoroughbred. In a man's riding breeches that hugged her shapely hips and long legs, she was a sight to behold, one that had him fearing he may swallow his tongue. He had only ever seen one other woman in breeches and had enjoyed the wicked sight. This second look, at this particular woman dressed in such a manner, nearly undid his control. The morning light played across a dark red plait of thick hair that hung down between her shoulders, reaching almost to where her nicely curved behind disappeared beneath a mid-length wool coat.

More captivating was the aura of softly glowing green power surrounded her. It took his breath away. Speaking soothing words to her horse, she stroked her neck. The creature's eyes fluttered closed as he calmed beneath her attentions.

Something both within Rick, and without, stirred at the sight, so much so that he casually closed his coat to hide the effect she had on him. He had promised Sean he would be the epitome of a perfect gentleman, and here he was getting hard at the first sight of her. Reminding himself she was just another high society woman whom he would have to keep alive helped dampen his desire. And a fae to boot. In his experience, her kind looked down on his, which was why he kept his own power under tight lock and key so she wouldn't know what he was.

"Mrs. O'Brian, that'll most certainly not do," he said.

Startling at his voice, she spun toward him. For a moment he caught a glimpse of a glowing knotwork symbol on her forehead. It faded in an instant. The big brown thoroughbred darted away from him as far as the leads clipped to either side of its halter would allow. Steel clashed against cobblestone in a terrible racket as its shod hooves clattered about. The beast didn't get far, and thankfully didn't step on the lady's feet, but its wide eyes and high head proved it would not settle for a while.

"Case in point." Fergusson indicated the horse with a nod of his head.

To her credit, Catriona quickly subdued the animal with a few soothing words and a stroke of its neck. Her green aura pulsed when she did. Most fae had a way with animals, but hers was something to behold.

"What, my horse? She is a bit spirited, admittedly, but she is fast and reliable, the very best hunter in my stable. And I can ride quite well. You have no cause to worry over that."

Slowly, so as not to spook the beast again, he approached. Paws slapped on the cobblestones behind him, claws clicking in time to them. He spared a scathing look down at Lincoln's gray and white head, but the pup only seemed to grin up at him. Apparently the "sit, stay" commands still needed work. Considering the pup's true nature, he wasn't surprised or even the slightest bit disappointed in his willfulness. On the contrary, it delighted him.

"I've no doubt you can ride, but mustangs will steal a mare away the first chance they get, leaving you riding with me," he said.

Heat flushed his face. He hadn't meant for the words "with me" to come out sounding so husky, but he couldn't help it, not with her curves looking so tempting in those tight breeches. His traitorous mind dropped the word "with," giving him an all too intimate picture. For the second time already this morning he was glad for his long coat.

Catriona lifted her chin, her pert little nose cutting the air. "Nonsense. She may be a bit high-spirited, but I can control her quite well, I assure you."

Unable to resist her magnetism, he took a step closer. It worked both to bring her alluring lilac scent drifting to him, and to bring a glare to her lovely face as she had to crane her neck back to look up at him. He leaned so close their bodies were only inches apart.

"I don't doubt your powers of control over your animal. 'Tis the mustangs you can't control. When they see a mare they want, they take her, and there is nothing you can do about it." Since his voice dropped several octaves from repressed desire, the words came out sounding breathy and dirty. The flare of desire in her eyes ensured he didn't regret them, though.

He fingered the edge of her close-cut riding jacket. "This will not do, either. Such clothing will shred on the trail." Tuatha help him, but he was picturing just that.

Huffing in a deliciously cute way, Catriona tugged away from him and tried to pull the edges of the jacket down as if she could make it longer. "Ashlinn suggested the breeches. It seemed a good idea. What do you propose I do? Ride a stallion and dress in leather like a savage?" she called over her shoulder.

Damn if the crotch of his breeches didn't threaten to give way from the pressure of his erection at the image *those* words elicited. The sight of her breeches hugging her toned buttocks only made it worse. Turning away, he cleared his throat and wrangled his control. This woman was having far too powerful of an effect on him. He needed to get a hold of himself.

"The trek is one that takes a special kind of horse. I'll lend you one of mine. As for the clothing..." He had to pause and steady his voice. "You got the idea half-right with breeches, but I do recommend treated leather, both chaps and coat."

She spun toward him, eyes wide beneath a furrowed brow, mouth gaping in a most distracting manner. "Leather? In June? I shall melt in the heat."

He nodded. "Aye, it will feel like it at times. But you won't catch your death in the driving rain or hail in Nebraska territory, nor the blowing wind of Wyoming territory. When the heat of the Utah territory and the state of Nevada becomes too much you can roll your coat up and strap it on the back of your horse."

At the mention of each state and territory, her eyes grew wider, as if she hadn't considered just how much land they would be crossing in such a short time. He couldn't fault her. The reality of it was daunting.

"An entire continent... Is that why they call the California trail the Elephant? Because it's so long?" she asked in a hushed voice.

Having crossed it multiple times, he found it an odd comparison, but not an altogether inaccurate one. "Partly."

Letting out a long, dramatic sigh, Catriona stroked her mare's neck. "Well, you're right about one thing. I shouldn't expect such a creature to carry me across the wilds of America."

Not quite sure how to respond without sounding as though he were gloating, he watched in silence as she removed the horse's tack and placed it back into a room nearby. The view of her coming and going was well worth not getting in a jibe. When finished, she unclipped the horse from the leads and took it back into a large stall.

"Sorry, girl. You shall have to come along in a few months with my belongings," she quietly told the animal. It nuzzled into her hand and blew out a breath.

Head held high, she strode back out into the aisle and placed her hands on her nicely shaped hips, fixing him with a hard look. "We'll have to stop at a leather shop along the way. I do not own any such garments. Let's see this horse you would have me ride."

With a nod that made his chin-length brown hair sweep down and cover his face, he grinned. Taking the lead, he walked toward the back of the stables where he stalled his horses.

"Oh, well hello there. I didn't see you come in." Catriona's voice had taken on a gentle tone that struck an entirely different chord in him. "I'm sorry, I did not bring along any treats for you today."

Both her tone and words told him she had discovered Lincoln. Tension straightened his spine. Since she was a fae, there was no doubt in his mind she knew the pup's true nature. He couldn't help but wonder how she'd react when she realized he now belonged to Rick. The questions it could raise... One word she said in particular struck curiosity into him. He looked back to where she crouched beside his pup, scratching behind its floppy gray ears. "Today?" he asked.

Joy and affection softened her expression. It almost rankled him that such a look was cast on the pup and not him. But he knew better. Truly, it was an arrow best dodged, for the affections of such a woman led nowhere good.

When she finally turned her gaze to him, it was guarded, as was her tone. "I have brought Sean's pup treats since their arrival here. I shall miss this little fellow. My late husband never much cared for hounds, but I adore them." The last sentence faded almost to a whisper as she rose and they continued walking.

The pain in her voice stung him, especially knowing he had brought up the memory that put it there. He almost made a comment about the kind of men who didn't like dogs, but good sense stopped his tongue before it could wag.

"Good news, you won't have to say good-bye. Sean brought him as a gift to me. He'll be traveling with us,"

Fergusson said.

As if he knew exactly what Fergusson's words meant, Lincoln's fluffy tail curled up into a half moon and wagged furiously as he trotted to catch up.

A scowl greeted him as she rose. "Sean and Ashlinn gave this pup to you?" she asked, tone doubtful.

Playing innocent was in his best interest at the moment. "O' course. And why wouldn't they?"

She started, stopped, and sputtered, unable to gather her words. At last she did. "Well because, Cliste and Scáth's offspring are precious to them, family even."

Rick inclined his head. "As am I. Sarge and I bled for each other and saved one another's lives on more than one occasion. That makes us blood brothers."

The weight of all the words she wanted to say and clearly wouldn't held her mouth open. Never one to be speechless for long, she shook off the stupor. "That hardly seems wise. The journey surely cannot be safe for a pup."

Laughing, Fergusson turned the bend in the aisle. "Ma'am, the journey isn't safe for *us*." *No sense in sugarcoating it.* Besides, he knew full well that she was privy to this pup's true nature, and in being so, knew it had very little to fear on their trek.

She made a soft grunt that he could only interpret as defiance.

The big crème-colored nose of his buckskin gelding came over the stall door as he approached. The horse's eyes slid closed as he scratched beneath its long, black forelock.

"You expect me to ride that big fellow? It sounds to me as though he is more interested in sleeping than crossing

America," Catriona's amused voice came from behind him.

"Sounds?" he asked.

She twitched as if startled. "Looks. I meant looks, o' course," she said quickly. The slip up gave him a clue as to her fae power—which could be one or more of several different things related to either the elements or the planet and the creatures on it.

In an attempt to keep things light, he laughed. "Right. He sleeps when given the opportunity because he knows the amount of work that will be asked of him when he is awake. Unlike your thoroughbred there who would lose its wind in the morning and not be able to run from the wolves nipping at her heels in the afternoon."

Ignoring the gasp she let out, he moved to the next stall and clucked at the horse within to draw it to him. A gelding with a dark red head broken up by a long white blaze down its face poked its nose over the door. Unlike his own horse, this one's coat was a patchwork of white, black, and dark red.

"A painted mustang?" Catriona exclaimed. Her tone wasn't derisive as he had thought it would be. Instead, it sounded almost fearful. Peering from the horse to him through narrowed eyes, she placed her hands on her hips. "You expect me to ride a native pony? But aren't they wild like the west they hail from?" Interest hid behind the words; he could see it in her eyes.

Eyebrows rising at her, he absently stroked the horse's forehead. "It seems you have much to learn about both."

He opened the stall door and stepped inside.

"Pardon me?" she demanded.

He almost bowled her over as he led the horse out into the

aisle. "Not until such pardon has been earned, ma'am."

Huffing, she stepped aside, shying back from the horse who noted her presence only with a lazy sideways glance.

"Mustangs are the most sure-footed horses I've ever come across, and they have the good sense most of your 'acceptable' breeds lack."

Delicate red brows drew low over her eyes as she crossed her arms beneath her breasts and watched him walk to the tack room. The way she stared at his horse with her head cocked as if listening, made him curious. That she was a capable horsewoman was clear. But he had a feeling it might be more than that.

The scents of leather and oil overwhelmed him for a moment, nearly making him sneeze. He lit the lamp sitting on a table beside the door. Rows of English style saddles stood on racks, a dozen easily, and twice that many bridles of varying types hung on the walls. It was an impressive selection for such a small stable. A few moments later Cat's soft footsteps sounded on the wooden floor behind him.

After perusing all the bridles, he handed her one that looked like it would fit the horse. Drawing back, she lifted her chin and cast him a sardonic smile. "A snaffle bit for a mustang? You must have quite the confidence in my ability to ride."

He lifted a brow. "That remains to be seen. But 'tis all he needs. And you still need to have soft hands with him."

The look of indignation faded and behind it he saw what he thought might be pain. "My hands are always soft on the bit. I'm gentle with all animals," she said quietly.

Something about the way she said the words made him

look harder at her. Yes, it was definitely pain peeking through her guarded eyes. The mortar in the walls around his heart lost some of its solidity, and he hated it. "I didn't mean to imply that you aren't. Me apologies." He turned back to the tack and steeled himself. "I recommend taking a saddle you don't mind parting with. We'll have to trade it at the leather shop in Omaha for a suitable Spanish saddle."

She groaned. "Must I really ride in one of those ungainly looking things?"

"English saddles are designed to carry only you. The ones used out West are designed to carry much more."

To his surprise, she put the snaffle bit bridle back and picked up one that resembled a halter more than a proper bridle. It had no bit, though it had reins attached to it. Her gaze flitted to the right, landing on one of her saddles. She moved to pick it up, but he grabbed it before she could and started out the door, leaving her to get the saddle pad. On one hip he balanced the saddle while patting a large red patch on the mustang's neck. As she positioned the saddle pad, he did his best not to watch how her coat pulled up, revealing the snug breeches hugging her rear. He failed utterly. Why she captured him so completely and demanded his attention whenever she was near, he had no idea. It both aggravated and thrilled him.

"A Spanish saddle is also bigger, distributing weight better across the horse's back for long rides. 'Tis more comfortable for both you and him, trust me," he said.

The moment she stepped back, he swung her old English saddle onto the horse's back, adjusted the pad, and began cinching it up. Much to his surprise, she grinned. "You're the expert." Not a bit of sarcasm touched her voice. It made him suspicious. The excitement in her eyes explained it, though.

"What are their names?" she asked.

He scratched the nose of the crème-colored gelding as it poked its head out the stall again. "This here is Ayegi."

"A unique name to be sure. Not Irish or English. 'Tis native perhaps?" she prodded.

"Indeed, Cherokee to be exact," he admitted.

Her eyes widened with interest. "Truly? What does it mean?"

The memory made him smile. "Awake."

She all but beamed in return, the look transforming her face into a thing of such beauty her fae lineage shone through. The way she had of turning his mind to something pleasant disturbed him. It made it hard to keep the walls up that kept her out.

"An interesting name, to be sure. Why in the world would he be named that?" she asked.

With a lift of his chin, he indicated her mount. "Because *his* name is Galiha. It means asleep in Cherokee."

Her brows scrunched together and one rose. While a bit odd, the look transformed her from otherworldly to adorable. "Odder still," she said.

He laughed at her expression as much as at the memory. "Aye, but truly, 'tis me fault. That was the way the Cherokee man described them to me when I traded for them."

Those alluring green eyes widened, drawing him in like a moth doomed to get scorched. "You traded with the natives. Aren't they dangerous?"

Instinct screamed at him to shut the conversation down. But he couldn't bring himself to, not when it clearly delighted her so much.

"During the war I learned how hardy and reliable their horses were. I knew they'd be perfect for escorting people across the territories. As for dangerous..." He shrugged. "All people are dangerous when their home is threatened. These particular natives were a lot less so than others."

A terrible darkness flashed in her eyes. The look made him want to take the words back more than anything in the world. Not only did the Irish know all about being pushed out of their land, but the fae in particular were painfully familiar with it. He scrambled for something, anything to rectify the mistake. "These Cherokee were on a reservation. They were peaceful. They were a sight to see, for certain." A sad sight considering all they had lost, but he left that part out.

He didn't dare describe things too gently though. No matter what hardships she'd been through in her soft high society life, it wouldn't compare to what she was about to undertake.

As he took the bridle from her and adjusted it to fit the horse, he shook his head. "This'll not be a pleasant outing. I hope you understand the hardships that lay ahead," he said.

Excitement still shining in her eyes, she met his gaze. "They're much better than those that lay behind, I assure you."

With a shake of his head, he steeled himself for what had to be said. He would not spare her his customary lecture because she was Ashlinn's sister-in-law. If anything, he owed it to her that much more. Embarking on such a journey unprepared either mentally or physically was what got so many killed.

"I mean no disrespect for the loss of your husband,

ma'am. I'm sure that was terrible beyond measure. The hardships I speak of are ones that could cost you your life. Starvation, dysentery, hostile natives, predators...hell, even a simple fall from your horse."

His lecture didn't even chink the armor of her hardened gaze. "As I said, they're better than those that lay behind me."

Unable to comprehend such stubbornness, he shook his head and started back toward his horse. With the ones like her he knew there was nothing he could say. Experience would teach her soon enough. Lincoln trotted along ahead of them as they led their horses out into the courtyard where a small crowd waited in the carefully groomed pea gravel. Among the people stood Ashlinn and Sean, the feisty black-haired woman, and the woman who seemed more a friend than a maid of Catriona's, as well as a slew of servants clothed in black and white finery.

Sunlight warmed his shoulders as he moved out from beneath the overhang of the carriage house. Above him stretched a clear blue sky, a good omen for the first day of travel. The clack of hooves and grind of wagon wheels drifted to him from beyond the green space beside the O'Brian estate where too many roads choked through too many buildings. The itch to leave the city behind began to grow into a full-blown burning sensation that made his muscles ache.

He gravitated toward Sean and Ashlinn as Catriona spoke with her people in quiet tones, touching arms or shoulders, and hugging a few. Even here in the north he had never seen a high society lady be so familiar with her help. It was refreshing. He shook the notion off, refusing to allow anything about this woman to be "refreshing."

Sean clapped him on the shoulder. "You're having

doubts, me friend. I see it in your eyes."

Scratching his two-week-old beard, he nodded. "O' course I am. She means a lot to you both, and that means a lot to me. This trip is hardest on those of high society."

Ashlinn hugged him tightly, saying softly to him, "She is more than she seems. Your concern is part of why you are the only one we trust to escort her."

At a loss for a reply, he merely nodded. The words intrigued him, but he didn't want to ask with Catriona within earshot. For one, it was improper, for another, he didn't want her to think he was actually interested in anything about her. The two servants standing not far behind Sean holding the reins of two tall thoroughbreds gave him cause for distraction.

Thrusting his head in the direction of the horses, he asked, "You're coming with us to the train station?"

Ashlinn nodded. "I want to see her off properly." A bit of a sniffle followed the words.

Out of respect, Fergusson turned his gaze elsewhere. Like a needle pulled north, it landed on Catriona, where she stood hugging her friends. Though her eyes glistened, not a single tear made tracks down her cheeks and her steady jaw suggested they wouldn't any time soon. Thanks to his true nature, he couldn't help but overhear their words, or so he told himself. It sounded better than admitting to himself that he was eavesdropping.

Sadie drew back from hugging Catriona and handed her a package. "A brick of my homemade cheddar for your journey. You send a telegram to Miss Ashlinn at every outpost and city that has a device, let us know you're all right," she told her.

Catriona nodded with a solemn look. "I will, and you do

the same once you and Deirdre set out."

Warmth equal to that of the deepest friendships he had ever seen radiated between the two of them. It was evident in their smiles and the concerned looks they exchanged. Such a breach of propriety both impressed Rick and made him curious, neither of which he wanted to allow himself to feel about this woman. Watching her thank her friend and say her good-byes, he had to forcefully remind himself that she was a job, nothing more.

Not waiting for the two to stop embracing again, the black-haired woman with crème skin and rouge lips wrapped them both in her arms. Deirdre, he thought he recalled her name being.

"Three months! We have not been apart since my wedding. Whatever will Sadie and I do without you?" Deirdre asked.

A full-bodied laugh tittering with a touch of nerves sounded from Catriona. Tuatha help him but that was an appealing sound.

"Without me? Ha! Sadie has kept me in order as much as my home, and you challenge me each day to be better. The true question is, what shall I do without you two?"

Those rouged lips curled up into a half-smile as Deirdre handed Catriona a small, sheathed knife and a pistol. Catriona's eyes widened, and for a moment it looked as though she might drop the items.

"You will have the adventure of a lifetime. But I will not have you doing so without a way to protect yourself. Please keep these on you, I'll feel better knowing you have them." Deep blue eyes shifted to him from beneath a furrowed brow as

Deirdre wrapped Catriona's hands around the weapons. "For protection from *all* threats," she finished as if speaking directly to Fergusson.

Inclining his head in what he hoped came across as respectful acknowledgment, he hid a grin behind his hair. The woman had tenacious friends. Their dedication spoke well of her. To his surprise, Catriona nodded and tucked the weapons into her saddlebags. He wondered if she would ever take them back out.

The women all hugged again, and just when he thought he was going to have to tear them apart, Catriona gave Galiha a good scratch then swung up into the saddle. Seeing her straddling the horse like a man stirred something in him that was part desire and part respect. He was still stifling it down when her gaze caught on his.

"Certainly you did not expect me to ride side-saddle all the way to California? Especially considering the saddle I put on your horse," she said through a wicked smile.

Of course he hadn't, but knowing it and seeing it were two entirely different things. He used the excuse of swinging up onto his own mount to delay his response, giving him a chance to steady his voice. "Course not. You just didn't strike me as the type of lady who'd be willing to."

Challenge gleamed in her eyes. "And what type of lady do I strike you as, Mr. Fergusson?"

Leather creaked as he settled in the saddle. "A proper lady of high society, but o' course, Mrs. O'Brian," he said, deciding to play it safe.

She laughed and shook her head. Her mouth opened but her words halted as hooves clopped against cobblestones.

Sometime during their exchange, Ashlinn and Sean had mounted up and Catriona's servants and friends had retreated to the porch of the house. How had he allowed himself to become that distracted?

"Shall we?" Sean asked. Though his voice was level and clear of any humor, amusement shone in his eyes.

Sean's shortly trimmed mustache rose in the beginnings of a smile, and he nodded. *Damn it all.* He'd been caught. Turning back to the servants and the two women waiting on the porch, Rick dipped his head in respect. Both of Catriona's friends waved and grinned like young lasses watching their friend step onto the dance floor with a handsome man.

A word or two muttered in Gaelic passed his lips as he cast his gaze back to the three riders drawing away from him and urged his horse forward. They couldn't get to the train station soon enough. The ride to Omaha and the end of the tracks would give him time to gain perspective and distance. He was going to need a clear head for the long ride that came after.

The rounded perfection of Catriona's cheeks meeting the saddle drew him like an unrelenting magical force. Tuatha help him indeed.

6

Catriona

Omaha, Nebraska

The close-fitted breeches and brown leather chaps over the top of them made Catriona feel as though her legs were virtually bare. She'd had to resort to wearing only drawers beneath the breeches, as a chemise proved completely impractical to tuck in. Only her corset and corset cover lay beneath the long-sleeved tunic that covered her upper body, leaving her feeling terribly underdressed. Already the June morning was warm, but regardless, she donned a knee-length oilskin duster as she stepped from her hotel room onto the porch. It had a bit of an odd smell to it but right now all she cared about was that it covered her.

With her long red hair plaited back into a braid and a

bowler hat atop her head, she hoped no one would recognize that she was a woman dressed like a man, at least not at first glance. Never in her wildest imaginings had she ever thought of dressing as such. Disconcerting as it was, she had to admit the clothing was quite comfortable. The realization made her a bit envious of the simplicities of men's wear.

If only the ladies of the Widows of the 69th organization could see her now… But then, it wouldn't matter if they did because she would never see any of them again, save for Deirdre and Sadie, the only two who really mattered to her anyway. That realization made her smile.

The first bright yellow rays of the sun cut through a cloudless horizon, slicing their way through the dust of the street. Neither the rolling hills in the distance nor the short buildings lining the rough street rose high enough to challenge the light. Why in the world the corporal had them out here on the far western edge of town she could not fathom. Last night when their train had pulled into the Omaha station she had been ready to collapse at the nearest hotel, of which there had been plenty.

Claws clicked out a rapid rhythm against wood, drawing her gaze down the porch to the right. The large gray and white pup of Fergusson's trotted toward her, fluffy tail arched high over its back, bright pink tongue lolling out the side of its mouth. Lincoln, she had learned his name was on the train from New York to here. A fine name, despite her desire to disagree with everything the aggravating Fergusson said and did. The important thing was, the pup liked it. Though he was so young and still small—for his kind, at least—he made her feel safer and better about the trip overall. She held no doubts that her safety had played a large part in Ashlinn's decision to give the pup to Fergusson. For like her, Lincoln was far more than he appeared.

Pretty lady. Smells good, like ancestors' people-pack. Keep her safe, the pup thought.

The pup's thoughts and happy, carefree expression made her smile and eased some of the anxiety twisting her stomach. More than happiness glowed behind his eyes. The truth of his nature, of his species, lay there like a promise.

Thank you. I will do my best to keep you safe as well, she said in his mind. Not that his kind needed much protecting, but he was young and rare, and protect him she would.

She bent to pet his head, wincing as the Colt pistol Deirdre had given her bit into her side. Damnable thing. She would have left it in New York if Deirdre hadn't made her swear upon her mum's soul that she'd carry it. The fact that it only had a four-inch barrel and was a .31 caliber hardly made it ladylike in her eyes. She felt silly enough wearing men's clothing, but wearing a pistol as well just seemed daft. Lincoln would provide far more protection.

"Ouch," she murmured as she adjusted the gun belt.

"That's because you're wearing it wrong," came a deep voice from behind her, sliding over her like the finest silk sheets.

Ignoring how that voice tightened the skin of her breasts, she stepped swiftly away and spun around. Fear and surprise mingled unpleasantly in her chest. Not until she saw Fergusson's wide eyes fall on her waist did she realize her hand had gone to rest on the weapon.

"Good instincts, though," he said through a grin.

"Whatever do you mean?" she demanded. The breathless way her voice came out made her brow furrow all the deeper.

She didn't like that her gaze traveled the tall length of Fergusson's body, but she didn't stop it either. In leather chaps that bulged nicely at the groin, a beige linen tunic, and his leather duster, he struck an imposing figure. More than that, he struck a handsome one despite his two-day-old shadow of a beard, wide-brimmed vaquero-style hat, and gun belt. Or perhaps it was because of all that. The man also possessed an aura of confidence and power that pulsed behind carefully erected walls. It left her believing there was more to him than met the eye.

His confident stride as he approached her was absent the jingle of the Western spurs she had expected. When her gaze finally made it down his solid form to his leather boots, she found they bore no spurs whatsoever. She liked that, a little too much. A man who understood horses didn't need that kind of prompting was rare. During her blatant perusal of his person he moved ever closer until he stood only inches from her. His leather, soap, black powder, and some kind of pleasant musky spice scent enveloped her so intimately she may as well have been in his arms. Heat flushed through far more than just her cheeks at the thought. Only her heaving breast moved as he reached for her waist.

It should have scared her, being this close to a man she barely knew and didn't trust. But something about him felt safe. Despite challenging and rankling her at every opportunity, his energy—though subdued and guarded—felt comforting in a way unlike that of any man she'd ever met.

Those big, strong fingers of his undid her belt and she

found herself immobilized, like a fly in honey. Though the streets were empty this close to dawn, part of her worried over someone seeing them acting so familiar with one another. His linen shirt clung to the hard planes of his chest, drawing her eyes, which were only inches away. Thoughts of other people melted away. To her disappointment—which quickly transformed into relief—he only tightened it up and re-buckled her belt.

"It'll be much more comfortable this way," he said, voice deep like the rumbling of distant thunder.

It took several moments for her to focus on what exactly would be more comfortable with her belt cinched up. "The illustrations in the penny novels always show the cowboys wearing their belts low on their hips," she said, happy she didn't sound as breathless as she felt.

He made a sound halfway between a grunt and a laugh. "That's why they call them Penny Dreadfuls. Trust me, this will feel better. Try bending now."

The only way to bend was right into him or backward, which would press her breasts out toward him. Neither of which she was willing to do. She placed her hands on her hips and fixed him with a hard look. Inclining his head and sweeping his hand out in a dramatic gesture, he stepped back. Swallowing a tart answer she knew would only sound breathless, she did as instructed. It didn't pinch.

"Thank you," she said.

He nodded and walked past without so much as offering her his arm. The wonderfully masculine scents of him swirled about her, enticing her to follow. But she had been enticed by such things in the past and they had only brought her swiftly to heartache. And her mother always taught her that their own kind would treat her better. Considering her late husband had been fae, she couldn't bear the thought of someone treating her worse. And, this man had the manners of a street urchin and could barely stand the sight of her, which was evident in the way he marched so quickly toward the stables.

The pup reached up, licked her hand, then darted after Fergusson. That Lincoln approved of him meant little. Scáth, Lincoln's father, had been Michael's hound. While Scáth's loyalty to him had been begrudging and he had done everything he could to shield her from Michael, he had still been loyal to him. Though that was hardly the hound's fault. His kind bonded to a person when they were pups and almost always to warriors. It was part of why Scáth had stayed with Ashlinn and Sean after Michael had died. She was certainly no warrior.

Lifting her head, she called over her shoulder. "I shall settle our bill."

"No need," he called back, boot heels never slowing.

She spun back in his direction. Despite the sound of protest she made, he didn't even slow. The edges of his leather jacket flowed with each quick step, revealing a slit in the back that went to midthigh, giving the barest glimpse of his legs. Fearing he meant to skip out on their bill, she rushed to follow him. They rounded the side of the building before she caught up.

"Excuse me, Corporal Fergusson, whatever do you mean?" she demanded as she grabbed his arm.

The scathing look he gave her made her pull her hand back immediately. "Please, don't call me that." The pain in his voice leeched the heat out of his eyes, making her realize the words were not said in anger.

He began walking again, his long legs stretching out into an even faster pace. The pup dashed ahead, slipping into the open door of the barn.

"I did not know you held animosity toward your title. My apologies."

Gaze never wavering from the wooden sidewalk before them, he shook his head. "'Tis not the title I hold animosity toward, but all that was required of it."

She tried not to allow such words to harden her heart but failed. Many soldiers were bitter that the war focused on ending slavery more than it did preserving the Union. Not that they wanted to keep slaves. But the popular belief was that if the president had focused on the latter, the South would have acquiesced more readily, resulting in a lot of lives saved.

"You fought to preserve the Union then, as my husband did, not to end slavery." She tried to keep the bitterness from her voice, and only partially failed.

At that, Fergusson halted so quickly that she jumped a good foot away from him, arm raising to block a blow. The anger melted from his face and his eyes turned soft. Part of her hated that softness, but only because it made her like him a little.

"O' course not. The possibility of ending slavery was the only thing that kept me going through those long years."

She couldn't see his face as he stepped into the stables, but she had a feeling the pain lacing his voice would give away more than his stoic expression. Breathing deep of the comforting scent of horses and hay, she followed him inside.

"I misunderstood. My apologies."

He turned to her, taking a step closer. His tall figure hovered over her, the shadows of the barn obscuring his face from her. While his body seemed relaxed, she still couldn't help but be a bit fearful of his reaction. This time, however, she did not allow herself to flinch away.

"You apologize too much for things you needn't."

The scents of leather, soap, and spicy musk drifted over her again, twisting her tongue up and clouding her mind. "My apolo—fine. Mr. Fergusson, what do you mean by saying there is no need to settle our bill?"

She couldn't help but wonder how much of a rogue this man might be. *He wouldn't skip out on paying our bill, would he?* Surely Sean and Ashlinn wouldn't trust her in the company of a man like that. *But how could one such as he afford a fine establishment like the one we'd stayed in last night?* Well, *she* wasn't about to skip out without paying. To start her journey in such a manner was unthinkable.

"I already settled it," he said.

The surprise must have shown on her face because he rolled his eyes skyward and shook his head. His arm reached toward her and just as she was about to flinch back, his hand closed on a door handle directly to her right. She let out a breath. Wood ground against wood as he slid the door open, revealing a dark tack room. Leaving her gaping, he stepped inside.

"There was no need for that. I'm funding this journey," she said.

She was forced to step out of the way as he walked out of the room carrying a saddle in one hand and a bridle in the other. The morning light pouring in through the open door of the stables afforded her a glimpse of his blank face.

"I chose the hotel," he said as he walked past, eyes flicking out the door for a brief moment before he turned down the aisle toward the horses.

His long legs stretched out into a quick pace, as if he were in a hurry to get away from her. Did this topic bother him so much? She did not want him paying for this on the principles of being a gentleman, not when she clearly had more coin than he did. Besides, it indebted her to him, and she liked that far less. Trying not to stomp like a child, she stormed after him.

"Well if I had known you were going to pay for it, I would have insisted on a more frugal hotel."

He entered his horse's stall without even glancing back at her. "'Tis done, forget about it. Now if you'll please saddle your horse, we need to get moving."

Though she couldn't see his face, the impatience in his tone told her all she needed to know.

"Fine. But I am paying you back for the expense."

When he didn't answer after a moment, she gritted her teeth against a growl and stormed back to the tack room. Lincoln gave a playful little bark and bounded after her. She patted his head before fetching her saddle and returning to the horses. Aside from the pup's playful antics, they saddled their horses in silence. The big painted horse stood quietly for her, solidifying her concerns that he may fall asleep on the trail.

As she slowly worked at snugging up his cinch, she touched his mind. *I am so sorry. I know this is about as comfortable for you as a corset is for me.* Along with the words, she sent her emotions and images, knowing some animals understood those better than words spoken in their mind.

His lids fluttered open and his gaze fixed on her. Interest sparked within the brown depths. She sent another thought to his mind. *I'm part of your herd now. I will do everything in my power to keep you safe.*

Feelings of warmth and welcome returned to her. *Friend,* he thought.

Yes, friend, she assured him. *I promise to compensate you generously for carrying me to California.* Aloud, she said, "There are many more of these to come." From her pocket she drew out a special treat she had made for her own horses, a baked mixture of alfalfa and berries.

Nostrils flaring, eyes widening, Galiha nickered eagerly. Fingers flat, palm up, she offered it to him. He grabbed the treat with his lips and pulled it into his mouth and devoured it. Laughter bubbled from her as he pushed his nose into her hand, then into her armpit, searching for more.

Good friend, he thought with eager contentment.

Sneaking looks at Fergusson's mount as he worked on the packhorse, she tried to figure out the proper fitting for the rear cinch and breast collar. Both looked loose compared to how she had put hers on the painted horse.

"Too tight," came Fergusson's voice from directly over her shoulder.

Though she jumped inside, she managed to hide the reaction. He loosened both the breast collar and the rear cinch a little then handed her something that fit in the palm of her hand. She flipped the cool, metal object over. A compass. Brows rising, she gave him a hard look.

"Do you expect we'll get lost?" she asked.

"No. That's for if we get separated so you can find your way to the next station."

She clutched the compass tighter. "Why would we get separated?"

He retreated to his own horse, calling over his shoulder as he walked. "Weather, animals, natives. If it happens, you keep going, get to the next station, and I'll meet you there."

"Station?" she asked, feeling terribly clueless.

"The old Pony Express stations. We'll be traveling close to the trail they established, and there were stations every ten miles or so. It doesn't matter if they've been repurposed or not. Even if they're burnt to the ground, we can still meet there." His matter-of-a-fact tone grated her all kinds of wrong ways.

Without so much as another word, he swung up into the saddle of his buckskin gelding and turned him toward the back door to the stables. Considering he had not even offered to help her onto her horse, she surmised that his paying for the hotel had not been a gentlemanly act so much as one of pride. *It figures.* She tucked the compass into a pocket.

To her delight, Galiha stood still as she swung up into the odd saddle. Sleepy he may be, but at least he was kind and patient. The saddle held her securely, rising up both in front of and behind her. It was a bit snug for her liking, considering she had only ever ridden an English saddle, or bareback. The tails of both Fergusson's buckskin and his speckled packhorse drew quickly away. Lincoln trotted on ahead, darting out into the sunshine. By the time she took up the reins Fergusson was nearly to the open back door.

"Is there a reason we're going out the back?" she called to him.

"Aye."

She waited, but only the clop of his horse's hooves on the packed dirt outside broke the silence that fell. With a squeeze of her legs, she urged her horse to catch up. The gelding leaped into a trot, surprising her with his enthusiasm. She quickly caught up to ride alongside Fergusson. His gaze remained fixed on the road ahead. It was a back road that skirted along the edge of town the best she could tell. At some unseen command from him, his horse began to trot, the packhorse instantly picking up the gait as well. Though her horse's ears perked forward, he didn't pick up the trot until she squeezed with her legs. At this point, she wasn't sure if it was good training, or just laziness. A gentle brush of his mind confirmed he was just being kind and taking care with her until he knew her abilities.

You're sweet as rain on a newly planted field, she told him.

The happy nicker he gave in response warmed her heart and gave her a small measure of hope for the journey ahead.

The town began to fall behind them. Their little side street came around a grouping of cottonwood trees who's green, heart-shaped leaves blocked the sun for a brief moment. Once past the trees the road joined the wide main road leading out of town. Fergusson glanced back toward town, his shoulders relaxing before his gaze went back to the road ahead. They kept to the side, near the grass, avoiding the wagon wheel ruts. Since he didn't slow, she forced herself to sit in the saddle rather than post through the trot as she had been taught. It felt a bit unnatural, but if they were going to keep this pace up, she would quickly tire by posting.

"Are we in a hurry for some reason?" she asked.

"Aye."

Damn that man and his simple answers. She opened her mouth to unleash a tart reply when he spoke again.

"You said you ride well." It was more of a question than a statement.

"Yes, I do."

Green eyes sparkled with mischief as he shot her a grin. "Let's find out then."

Joy and excitement shot through the buckskin's mind a moment before his haunches dropped down and the horse dug in, then launched into a gallop. His spotted packhorse followed suit a pace later. She was suddenly glad she had left all her valuables for the wagon to bring, particularly the breakable ones. Galiha became a bundle of tense muscles and energy beneath her but waited for her command. Gritting her teeth and dropping her heels low to gain a deeper seat in the saddle, she sent him a thought. *Go*. He bolted after them, quickly catching up to run alongside Fergusson. Beside them, Lincoln ran with all the glee only a dog could, ears flopping and tongue lolling out the side of his mouth.

The pup began to lag behind, not out of exhaustion, but distraction. Thanks to the type of fae creature he was, if it came down to it, Lincoln could run all day, all night, and then some. So many scents and moving things awaited in the grasslands beside the road, all of it so new and wonderful to him that his mind was abuzz. *Hopping thing! Buzzing thing! Must chase them all!* Catriona laughed at his enthusiasm.

Fergusson reined his horse back into a slow lope and settled deep in the saddle as if for a long haul. Brows raised high, he gave her a nod that she took to mean he was impressed with her riding ability. However, the grin on his face looked a bit too stretched. Out of the corner of her eye, she saw him glance behind them again. Chills began to creep up her spine as she wondered what he was looking for.

7

Rick

Throughout the day, he pushed them as hard as he dared. He paused only to pick Lincoln up and set him on the nest he had made between the packhorse's saddlebags for just that purpose. He knew Lincoln could run all day and all night for who knew how long, but he was still a pup and was prone to mischief. The nest would help reduce that.

The training and practice he had done with him before leaving paid off, and he stayed put until they paused at the swampy edge of the Platte River to rest at midday. Catriona scarcely said a word, as she was too busy devouring her lunch and catching her breath. He gave her little time to do either, getting them back on the trail the moment the horses breathed easy and became picky with their grazing.

In an effort to cover more ground at a consistent pace, he alternated between a trot and a brisk walk. The gallop out of town had served its purpose and he had no intentions of picking that pace back up unless they had to. They'd make faster time at a trot since the horses could maintain it longer. By the time darkness began to spread across the land, they had covered over forty miles by his estimate. They had long ago left the trail for the rolling grasslands farther away from the river. He hadn't expected Catriona to tolerate riding for so long. But she did so with a wistful half-smile, her eyes always on the horizon. She patted, scratched, and talked to Galiha a lot, often starting in the middle of a thought. Much to his irritation, he found it adorable.

Damn if she isn't enjoying this. He couldn't help but wonder how she'd feel in a week.

He also found her interactions with Galiha intriguing. Could it be a clue to her fae abilities? Or was she just fond of horses? The desire to ask ate at him, but he didn't dare. The fact he could feel what she was would out him to her, and they were nowhere near that level of trust yet. Unfair since he knew what she was? *Perhaps. Definitely,* he corrected himself.

Nearly a mile off the main trail, he guided them to an offshoot of the river deep in the cover of birch and cottonwood. The sun hung low on the horizon, barely clinging to it.

After a long yawn, Lincoln leaped down and trotted straight to the edge of the stream to drink alongside the horses. Removing his hat and leaving it on the saddle horn, Rick dismounted and dropped his horse's reins, trusting the gelding not to stray far. A groan from Catriona drew a lazy smile from him, one that he didn't even try to hide as he went to stand beside her horse. When her feet touched the ground, her knees gave out. Ready for it, he caught her in his arms.

She righted herself and pulled away. With nowhere left to

go but into Galiha, she remained pressed against his chest. The soft mounds and curves of her body stirred more than just a longing in him. He drew swiftly away before she could feel his body's response to her, or worse, the surge in his power.

One hand going to the stirrup, she steadied herself against the horse, putting distance between them. Her eyes shot open wide. "Taking liberties again, Mr. Fergusson? I know we need to get there quickly, but do you not think you are pushing us a bit hard?"

Is that masked amusement in her eyes? He wasn't quite sure. "What, no 'thank you'?"

Her gaze narrowed. "For what, groping me?"

Shaking his head, he returned to his horse and began removing the saddle. "For not letting you fall on your arse," he called back.

He chose a spot beneath a large birch tree and began to pile his tack there. Fetching a brush from his saddlebags, he returned to his horse. Behind him, Catriona huffed as though she couldn't come up with the proper comeback. That or she was too ladylike to curse at him as she so clearly wanted to do. Grinning, he removed Ayegi's bridle, leaving the animal in only his rope trail halter, then began to remove the packhorse's gear as well. Catriona had the saddle and bridle off Galiha before he could get to it.

She finally found her voice. "Well, I still say there's no need to push so hard. Though it was an invigorating ride."

Face set in hard lines, Rick turned to her as he began to strip his long jacket off. Her eyes widened and swiftly traveled the length of his body before rising to his face. The lovely color of pink that brightened her cheeks almost cracked the hard mask that hid his mirth. He stared her down as he loosened his gun belt.

"This is the easy part of the trail, Duchess. 'Tis best to ride this part quickly to make up for time we'll lose in the Utah territory and Nevada."

Carefully, he lay his gun belt beside his other gear, then stripped off his tunic. That lovely gaze of hers traveled across the muscles of his chest and arms, and damn him but he loved it. Her bottom lip pulled in between her teeth before she looked swiftly away.

She huffed as she spun away from him. "Whatever are you doing? And why on Earth would you call me duchess?" The indignation in her voice failed to cover how breathy it sounded.

That sound caused a reaction in his body that made him glad her back was turned. Willing blood to flow to anywhere but his groin, he turned toward the river as he removed his chaps and breeches. Though the air was warm and muggy, it felt wonderful on the lower half of his legs that his thin, cotton underpants exposed.

"Because you're acting like one. Would you prefer princess? Hmm, yes, I think *I* rather prefer that. Well, Princess, I am preparing to take a bath, but never fear, for your modesty's sake, I shall leave me pants on."

"That is hardly a comfort."

Brush in one hand, horse's lead rope in the other, he shook his head as he walked into the water until it came to his waist. Ayegi's head dropped to drink, his eyes sliding closed in indulgence. Wetting the brush, Rick began to scrub away at the sweaty patches that the saddle had left on his horse. To his surprise, Catriona laughed and turned back around toward him. Her eyes widened but she didn't look away.

"You know nothing about me, Mr. Fergusson."

"In that case, Mrs. O'Brian, enlighten me."

Blood rushed to her face and tears shone in her eyes. Her jaw tightened and she gave him a look that could stop a raging bull in its tracks. "Don't call me that, please."

The pain in her voice drained the mirth right out of him. He hadn't meant to be insensitive, only to return her orneriness. "Me apologies. While I'm particular to princess, what would you prefer I call you?" He kept his tone gentle, the playful words an attempt at a truce.

Much to his surprise, she removed her coat and started to unbuckle her gun belt. Once that lay on the ground, she worked at the laces of her chaps. Eyes wide, tongue tying in his throat, he turned away to focus on washing his horse. The image of her waited behind his eyelids. *How much will she take off?*

"I trust you will be the gentleman you promised the MacBranains you'd be," she said, a teasing note in her tone.

He cleared his throat and turned farther away. "O' course."

Lincoln swam by, his gray head floating above the water as his huge paws paddled him about. Tongue hanging out the side of his mouth, he seemed the very picture of happy and relaxed. Fergusson envied the pup's carefree manner more than he cared to think about. More than that, he envied that Lincoln swam behind him, straight for Catriona.

"Since we're going to be on the trail together for over a month, we are certainly no longer strangers. You may call me Catriona. What's your given name?" came her sweet voice.

Doing his best not to picture her undressing behind him, he cleared his throat. "Rick."

A short laugh came from Catriona, making him glance over his shoulder. The woman stood there in only her drawers, a corset, and an undershirt. Back to him as she was, he saw her small, long-fingered hands working at the laces of her corset. He realized it might actually be possible to swallow one's tongue.

"As in Richard? An Irishman with an English name, truly?" she teased.

She began to wiggle out of her corset, making him very glad for the cool water that reached up to his navel. If only women didn't wear so many layers, even beneath a corset…

"Hells no," he couldn't help but snap.

Standing now in only a thin undershirt and her drawers, she turned her head toward him. He snapped his attention back to Ayegi and continued brushing him.

"What then?"

Though he hated telling people, he couldn't allow the challenge in her voice to go unanswered. "Patrick."

"'Tis a fine Irish name. Why do you sound ashamed to say it?"

Hearing the very same words his mum had always said both made his heart ache and his lips turn upward. "Partly because the name is so common, others use the term 'Patty' to describe all us Irish, and they do so as if the name is a curse, as if we're a curse." His voice dropped on the last, imparting far more emotion than he had intended to let slip out.

Cool water splashed across his back. Ayegi turned his head to look behind him. He almost did the same, but caught himself at the last moment. While he had no interest in acting the man of proper society, nor was he about to turn to see her nearly naked. What would Sean think? More so, much as he wanted to, he refused merely because she might be goading him to do so.

"They are fools, Rick Fergusson. It seems to me anyone named after the so-called saint who drove the 'snakes' out of Ireland should be a bit of a rogue and you seem to fit that bill quite well," she said.

He laughed. "You know nothing about me either. I *could* be a saint for all you know." He was feeling rather saintly, what with his restraint and all. Saints, sinners, and the like weren't in his wheelhouse of beliefs, but she didn't know that. And clearly she was holding out an olive branch.

Her laughter echoed after his. "Hardly. Of that I'm certain."

The sound of feet moving through water to his right told him to turn his head left. *Tuatha, is she coming around in front of me?* Water splashed nearby. "What do you think you're doing?" he asked, eyes clenching shut.

"The same thing you are. Keep your mind on a proper track, Mr. Fergusson. I'm only getting in deeper water to cool off. Simply because society deems a woman shouldn't do a thing, doesn't mean she cannot."

He shrugged. "I have to agree with you there."

She didn't swim around in front of him after all. Disappointment hung heavy on his shoulders. Perhaps he wanted her to tease and goad him so badly that was imagining it. He suddenly felt the fool.

"Really?" The surprise in her voice almost hurt.

"Really," he grumbled.

Part of him wanted to elaborate, to tell her that he was a forward-thinking man who believed a woman could—and should—do whatever she wanted to. But to do so would bare more of himself to her than he cared to. The less personal they allowed things to get between them, the easier this trip would be. For him at least. Knowing she was soaking wet in no more than her underclothes only feet behind him shot that theory full of holes.

Oh hell, there I go picturing her wet underclothes!

His horse pawed at the water, a sign that he was about to try to roll in it if Rick didn't hurry. A quick pat on the belly kept him upright. As fast as he could, he finished washing Ayegi and himself, then led the horse back up the sandy bank. Though of course Ayegi couldn't understand him, he sent the creature thankful thoughts for bringing his mind back to the important things at hand. He would feel the energy and that would be enough.

While Catriona bathed, he busied himself by setting up a picket line and tying the horses to it, then on to setting up their camp. He was determined to be the proper gentlemen. The fact that she teased him about not being one made him want to try all the harder. Since he wasn't building a fire or setting up a tent, he didn't take as long as she did.

"Will we not be sleeping in tents?" came her voice from behind him, her bare footsteps soft on the sand and grass.

For more than one reason, his body went so tense his spine straightened. "Sorry, Princess. We need to be able to pull up camp quickly. As I have already proven, your virtue is safe with me, no worries there."

Cloth rustled and the buckles on a saddlebag rattled. He tried not to picture her changing into dry drawers and failed so miserably he had to fight the urge to curse his imagination. He focused on the gold and orange patches of sky he could see through the trees. Several moments later, she walked around in front of him and eased herself down onto her as-yet-unfurled bedroll. So active was his imagination that for a moment he thought he glimpsed round breasts and pale skin. But it was only the beige tunic she had put on over her corset, which still managed to push her breasts up enough to reveal a touch of cleavage. Sunset shadows cloaked her, preventing more than a glimpse of golden light on skin or fabric here and there.

Pale green eyes pinned him like a bug. "You pushed us hard all day, and now you want to be able to break camp quickly. What are you not telling me?"

The shadow of his mustache tickled his nose as he scrunched his top lip up and shrugged. "We need to get to California fast is all."

That needle-like gaze refused to let go of him. "I am no lass who will swoon at the first sign of danger. Tell me the truth, Rick."

"All right. We're being followed."

Her eyes widened and her left hand moved a little closer to her pistol. Such instincts breathed to life a new respect for her. "Who would follow us?"

"Someone who doesn't want you to reach California. Someone hired by Ainsworth, no doubt."

She swallowed so hard he heard it from where he sat ten feet away. "He would do that?"

"Oh, aye, he certainly would."

"Why would he do such a thing?" she whispered.

One of the horses on the picket line behind them snorted and she jumped. Despite the slight tremble of her limbs, he wasn't about to pretty this up for her because if he did, then he would be responsible for any mishap based on her lack of knowledge. Or at least he would feel as though he was.

"That's the type of man he is. He unloaded land he didn't want for a minimal profit, went off to war like the rest of us, and now that the dust has settled, he wants it back."

The lengthening shadows of the coming night made it hard to tell, but he thought he saw her jaw set in a determined line. "I know his type all too well, and I shall not be intimidated by him. This only strengthens my resolve."

Part of him thrilled at her resilience. Part of him raged against it. He had become fond of her, despite his resistance. Besides, her kind were just as rare as his. He didn't want anything to happen to her. "All right then." He stood and spread his bedroll out on the grass.

"We're to sleep on the ground then?" Her voice was hesitant, edged with a touch of fear.

A grin worked at his lips as he rolled up his coat, set it at the top of his blankets, and lay down. Placing his arms behind his head, he gazed up at the darkening sky where the twinkle of stars began to show through. "Yes, Princess, on the ground." He took far too much pleasure rubbing that in, he knew, but he couldn't help it.

As she stood and picked up her bedroll, he thought he saw her hands shake. A very small spike of guilt worked its way into him.

"Will the moisture from the ground not soak up into the

blankets?" she asked in an admirably steady voice.

"No. The backside of the bedroll is canvas treated with wax, a little trick I picked up from the war. Put that side down and you'll be fine."

He kept his head pointed at the stars but watched her out of the corner of his eye. Mumbling to herself, she unrolled the blankets and fussed with their arrangement. A curse word or two in the Irish vein of Gaelic was punctuated by something about bugs. So there was an Irish lass under that proper high society lady after all. It was good to know. Laughter tried to work its way up his throat, but he choked it off. With the way she was going on, provoking her now would ensure neither of them slept for quite a while. As if sensing his thoughts, she mumbled something about not being able to sleep on the ground without even the semblance of a roof over her head. Despite her seemingly heartfelt words, her breathing evened out into that of deep sleep only moments after her head came to rest on her coat.

Though weariness crept up on him, he knew sleep wouldn't come for a long time. If it came at all. Concern over keeping the lovely, cantankerous woman across from him alive would not allow it. And if that didn't work, there were always the nightmares to keep him awake.

8

Catriona

Day Two

Something rough and wet brushed along the side of Catriona's face. Eyes snapping open, she pulled back from the sight of white canine teeth and a long pink tongue inches from her. Before Lincoln's happy puppy thoughts filled her mind, she had backed right out of her sleeping roll and smacked into a tree trunk. Nasty puppy breath clung to her like the most odious of perfumes. On instinct she brushed the canine saliva from her face with the back of her hand.

"Ick," she mumbled.

Gray ears with white peeking out from where they flopped over perked up as Lincoln bounded to her side. She stopped him before he could get close enough to lick her again. Keeping him and his tongue at bay, she petted him, wiping her hand off on his fur as she did so. Oblivious and happy, the pup nuzzled into her. She almost said something aloud to him, but caution born from years of needing to know her surrounding and situation before making a sound held her tongue. It was bad enough that she had mumbled before. No need to take further risks.

Good morning. I'm happy to see you too, she thought to him instead.

Fun to be had. Mice to chase. We go! he thought back.

Things certainly sounded safe enough if his mood could be trusted. But considering the nature of his kind, it certainly couldn't. A pride of lions surrounding them might delight him.

The dim light of the start of sunrise softened the trees and stream bank, giving them an almost dreamlike quality. Already it was warm enough that even in only her nightshirt and drawers she felt comfortable. *Oh dear Tuatha.* She wasn't wearing her corset. What would Rick think of her if he noticed? There was a time when she wouldn't have cared. Life had changed that, and so much more, about her. The man was all but a stranger to her. A strange, alluring man who looked incredible without a shirt on, but a strange man nonetheless. She wanted to go back to her bedroll, her pack where her clothes were stored, anywhere with something to cover herself. But practiced caution overrode the strong desire with ease. Instead she froze against the tree with the pup in her arms, listening, looking.

The soft, trilling chorus of frogs filled the air, but oddly no birdsong accompanied them. Her eyes darted to where Rick had been sleeping. His bedroll was not only empty, but gone. Slowly, she leaned out around the tree to check on the horses.

All three stood with their heads drooped in sleep, saddles and packs on their backs. The only gear missing on them was her personal bedroll and pack. Was he planning on leaving her? She tried to recall if she had said anything particularly abrasive the day before, but it was all a jumble of sore muscles and irritation. The possibility was strong that she had.

Soft yellow rays of light filtered through the tree trunks and leaves here and there, marking the sun's progress toward the horizon. The birds should be singing, yet they remained silent. Her gaze traveled up into the trees. High up in a birch, nearly hidden by the bright green heart-shaped leaves, perched Rick. Held to his right eye was a sailor's spyglass. After several moments, he tensed, pocketed the spyglass, and began to climb down. Catriona scurried over to her bedroll, grabbed her pack, and fled into the bushes with it.

Quick as she could, which wasn't very quick considering how difficult it was to get into a corset by oneself, she dressed, brushed her long red hair out, and started back to camp. The thin trees provided such little cover she could only hope he hadn't seen her. Rick was tying her bedroll onto the back of her horse as she approached. Brow pinched with tension, he regarded her for a moment without saying a word. At first she thought him angry, but then she noticed how his eyes flickered across her body and hair with admiration.

"We need to get moving," he finally said as he handed her Galiha's reins.

As he passed her, he scooped Lincoln up from where he sat at her feet and placed him in the nest on the packhorse. The urgency in his voice had her swinging up onto her horse without question. Her groin muscles and the tender flesh of her buttocks and womanly parts protested with stinging pain, but she ignored it. Sitting the trot was not all it was cracked up to be. She began to wonder if it wouldn't be better to post like a civilized rider and have the pain in her legs instead of her nether regions.

Rick's eyes shot to her as he swung onto his buckskin horse. "I know what you're thinking, and don't. If you try to post today you won't be able to walk tonight."

Brow furrowing so deep she could barely make out his jade-green eyes, she squeezed her horse forward. "Don't do that, 'tis quite disconcerting."

Eyes wide in feigned innocence, he placed his hat on his head and squeezed his horse into motion. "Whatever do you mean?"

His horse launched into a fast trot and he made no move to slow it down. On the packhorse behind him, Lincoln hardly noticed the bouncing in the soft hammock created between the two sides of the packs. Teeth clenched against a tart reply, she urged her own horse into a trot that stung with every beat and found herself envious of the pup. Instead of leading them south, back to the trail they had abandoned yesterday, Rick kept them pointed north, deeper into the plains.

She urged her horse up alongside his. "Will we not lose time by going so far north of the main trail? We'll miss the township of Lancaster."

"Not enough to matter, and we've no time or need to stop there. We're only going another mile or so deeper into the hills, out of sight of the main trail," he answered.

"And in a hurry. Would you like to tell me why?"

His gaze remained fixed on the fields of green grass

ahead. "Nope."

"Well, will you?"

A long sigh blew from his stubble-lined lips. "Ainsworth's man is behind us."

Alarm shot through her, and though she wasn't sure she'd use it, she was suddenly glad for the weight of the pistol at her side. "Are you certain?"

"Aye."

As Galiha felt her desire to go faster by the clenching of her legs and change in her seat position, he sped into a trot that jarred her with each long stride. Posting would have made it smoother initially, but Rick was right. She couldn't post all day. She'd have to sit through the trot and find its rhythm. "Should we not go a bit faster then?" she asked.

Calm as a man waiting for a fish to bite, he shook his head. "Nope. Trotting disturbs less ground and the horses can keep the pace up longer, thereby going farther."

A frustrated grunt escaped between her clenched teeth. The one corner of his mouth that she could see rose into a grin. For a fleeting moment she hoped his horse stumbled, tossing him to the ground so that smug look would get ground into the grass and dirt. Though she was careful not to send that thought to Ayegi. Not that his loyal horse would listen, but he might think her terribly rude for thinking it. The more pressing matter of the pain in her posterior each beat of her horse's hooves caused quickly distracted her from such thoughts. That, and the idea of someone following them. No, not following them. Tracking them down so they could ensure she didn't make it to California. She clung to the hope that they only meant to scare her off rather than something far more nefarious.

Stolen glances over her shoulder revealed no more than shadows and bushes amidst the tree trunks. The hoof beats of Galiha and Ayegi drowned out all other noise. Sunlight poured over them as they emerged from the trees and started out across the sweeping grasslands. While the bright light made her squint, the warmth it brought helped her relax enough that the bouncing motion of the trot eased a bit. The big horse actually had quite a smooth gait, but after having ridden for eight hours straight the day prior, even a smooth gait was painful. Soon they crested those hills Rick spoke of and dropped over the other side, preventing her from looking back through the copse of trees they had camped in.

The anxiety that had been building in her chest like a teapot under pressure released as those trees disappeared. A long breath eased from her, tension going with it, allowing her to relax in the saddle. Knowing Rick wouldn't stop for hours, she dug into her coat pocket where she had some hard tack stashed. It wasn't exactly the breakfast she'd been hoping for, but it would have to do.

As Rick promised, they didn't ride north for long. In what felt like less than half an hour, they put their backs to the sun and maintained a brisk trot through the slight hills. Irritated as she was at having been shocked from sleep and hurried onto horseback, she found herself watching Rick ride with something akin to enjoyment. He rode well, that was all. Like a man who had been born riding a fox hunter. Or so she told herself. Yet it was not his straight back or low heels that she admired, but rather the way his biceps and chest stretched his shirt seemingly to its limit. Despite the early hour, the man's coat was rolled and tied atop his bedroll.

His blood must run hot. That thought did all kinds of wonderfully sinful things to her body.

She shook her head. It had been a long time since she had looked upon, or thought of, a man in that way. Years. The excitement of the journey must be affecting her, because this mannerless rogue certainly wasn't.

"What? Upset at having your beauty sleep interrupted?" Rick asked.

She started, causing Galiha to speed up as he felt her tense. Had Rick noticed her watching him, or was it just the shake of her head that had drawn his attention? She was suddenly glad she hadn't had time to braid her hair back, for it helped hide her embarrassment. How dare he speak to her as if she were a pampered, spoiled, rich woman. *If he only knew...* But if he did, he might instead treat her like a broken thing, and that would be far worse.

"That's not it at all. I only—" The remainder of her words slipped her mind as they crested a hill and a valley opened up before them.

The green and yellow grasses appeared brown for a brief moment. Then she felt the energy of living creatures and realized it wasn't that the grass had turned brown, the valley was covered in bison. They stretched from hill to hill, filling the valley to brimming. Several of the creatures' massive heads lifted, turning to regard them. There had to be thousands. Rick slowed his horse to a walk and she quickly did the same. Rushing toward such creatures was the last thing she wanted to do.

Excitement so pure it hurt her inner eye shone from Lincoln. Ears perked, he sat up in his pack saddle hammock, tail thumping. Fergusson shared a long, pointed look with the pup. "You stay," he commanded in a whisper that was no less imposing because it was quiet. A pulse of compelling energy came from Rick. It reminded her of the way an alpha could back up another pack member with just a look. Tail and ears drooping, Lincoln laid back down.

For good measure, Catriona sent a thought to his mind. *They are dangerous. They must not notice us.*

His head cocked at her in question. *Hurt pack?*

Not on purpose, on accident. They are too big and scare easily.

With a huff, he lay his head back down.

Bringing her horse alongside Ayegi, Catriona leaned over and whispered, "Do we go around them?"

He shook his head. "We don't dare. If we crest the hill, there's a chance we could be seen. We should be safe enough if we stay to the outer edge," he whispered back.

She straightened in the saddle, eyes going wide as they grew closer to the bison. Some of the monstrous things stood as high at the shoulders as Rick was tall. But that wasn't the main thing that made her heart race. The two-foot-long horns on all but the juveniles looked like gleaming white blades waiting to tear into her. Even the females had horns. She supposed there was a kind of natural justice to that, but that didn't mean she liked it. They didn't exude the same nervous energy most prey animals did. While their thoughts were similar, they had an edge to them, a confidence drawn from capability.

The newspapers and Penny Dreadfuls were full of stories about the creatures. Still, she'd never imagined they'd be so big and proud. Her horse raised his head, ears perking forward.

Big creatures, aggressive, danger.

While every part of her agreed with him and wanted to urge Galiha into a canter and skirt up along the hillside to go around these things, she had a feeling it would be disastrous. And she knew Rick was right to go this direction. They couldn't afford to lose the advantage this morning's hard ride had given them.

We are safe if we stay quiet, go slow, she thought to Galiha as she stroked his neck. Though his hide twitched and jumped with nerves, his muscles relaxed beneath her a little.

Tearing her eyes from the creatures, she looked to Rick, her mouth opening. Head shaking, he held a finger to his lips. She closed her mouth and swallowed hard. Much to her relief, Rick guided them along the edge of the herd, though with them numbering in the thousands, they still had to go between some. A strong, musky scent drifted over her like a thick fog, seeping in until she feared she would never rid herself of it. Almost pig-like grunts came from a few of the bison as they passed by. Though it wasn't an aggressive sound, it still made her jump inside her skin. Thankfully, she had enough control over the instinct to keep it from showing. But Galiha noticed and each time she did it he pranced a little and pulled against the bit. With practiced breathing, she calmed herself and sent him soothing thoughts and energy.

For the most part, the herd ignored them, save for a few curious glances their way. Regardless, she began to shake as they passed a huge male with horns long enough to pierce clean through her body. Her concern was for naught, though, as the thing only rolled one lazy eye their way while he chewed on a clump of grass. Two-thirds of the way through the valley, with thousands of bison behind them, she began to relax. A pair of reddish-brown ones that couldn't have been more than a few months old began to push one another and romp about. Seeing them like that made them seem less frightening. It didn't hurt that they were nearly through the herd.

Out of the corner of her eye flashed a gray and white blur. Too late she felt Lincoln's excitement. She turned in time to see the pup leaping to the ground and bounding off toward the young buffalo. Excited barks echoed above the snorts and chuffs of the herd. The smallest buffalo bleated as though it were being eaten alive, turned tail, and ran from the pup. Fear filled it's mind, overriding all else. It didn't know exactly what Lincoln was, but it sensed he was more than a mere hound. For a brief moment Lincoln ran after it, tail high, floppy ears bouncing. One of the big males roared, the ululating sound seeming to resonate off Catriona's very bones and stopping Lincoln in his tracks.

Threat to herd! Stomp it! came the thoughts of the lead buffalo.

Bumps rose all along Catriona's skin. *No. Only playful. It's safe, we're safe,* she tried to press into its mind.

Head down, pointed horns leading, the big male ignored her and charged toward the pup, who seemed so tiny in comparison.

"Lincoln, come!" Rick bellowed, fear and concern giving his voice a hard edge.

Knowing what was coming, Catriona pushed her heels down to give herself the deepest seat possible. Rick's big buckskin horse launched into a canter. The packhorse followed. Her own horse danced beneath her, not wanting to displease her, but clearly terrified.

Danger, danger, must flee! Galiha screamed in her mind.

Go, she thought to him as she squeezed her heals to his sides. Galiha plunged into a gallop. She gave him full reins and let him know with a thought that she trusted him on which way to go. The painted mustang's instincts might just be what got her out of this alive.

Eyes glowing red as the danger began to kick in his true nature, Lincoln dodged left, leaving the male buffalo nearly stumbling over itself. If the pup thought they needed to fight things would turn very, very bloody. There would be no hiding his supernatural nature from Rick if it came to that. And if Rick witnessed Lincoln go down that path, at best he would get distracted at a crucial moment, at worst he would shoot the pup out of fear of the unknown. She couldn't let that happen.

Lincoln, this is not a battle, not a fight! They are only scared. We need to get away, not fight! she all but screamed into his mind.

He calmed a little. She whispered a prayer to the Tuatha that it would be enough for him to maintain control.

Run! came the thoughts of several bison. Chaos erupted as the herd fled for their lives. Catriona pushed her power out, using it to encourage the bison to steer away from them. Galiha's fear eased a bit at the feel of it. But the power only worked on those who hadn't completely lost their minds to fear—which were fewer and fewer of them with each stride they took.

Gray and white ears pinned, tail high, Lincoln shot straight for Rick, his long legs barely visible they moved so fast. He nipped at the heels of one of the huge creatures that was headed in Fergusson's direction. The thing squealed in terror and changed course abruptly. Bison hooves dug into the ground and threw clods of dirt and grass up as they took off. Suddenly grateful for the encompassing seat of the vaquero-style saddle, Catriona clung to her horse with every muscle in her lower body.

A young bison tried to dart around the front of Fergusson's horse. If it made it, it would run right over the top of Lincoln. But Catriona knew the pup could hold his own. Fergusson, on the other hand, had no idea. Rather than veer away from it, Rick went right for it, as if he were going to ram it in the side. He bumped into it, sending it stumbling off in the other direction, but not before Catriona saw its small horn tear a hole in the leg of his breeches. Still at a full out gallop, he called to Lincoln again, though at this point his voice was barely audible over the pounding of hooves. But he heard. The pup leapt. Clinging to the saddle horn with one hand, Rick leaned out so far she feared he may fall, his free hand reaching out. He caught Lincoln in midair and pulled him in against his chest, all without so much as slowing Ayegi.

Rick's head whipped back in her direction, his wild eyes catching hers like a net. "Stay closer!" he roared over the thunder of a thousand hooves.

That was precisely what she was trying to do. Getting closer would help her power encompass him in a globe of protection as well. But Galiha simply wasn't as fast as Ayegi. Her teeth ground against a pointless protest. Knowing her voice would never carry over such a cacophony, she steered Galiha to the packhorse's side.

Just a little faster and we'll be able to keep them safe as well, she urged. Galiha put his head down and found a second wind.

Though a few bison ran ahead of them and along both sides, most thundered behind them like a deadly storm waiting to swallow them whole should they miss a step. She prayed her horse's footing would be as sound as Rick had promised. Giving him all the rein he needed, she leaned forward in the saddle. Even with the packhorse in tow, they stayed ahead of the herd. Lincoln's excited energy sang to her like a battle bugle. Ears flapping in the wind, he craned his neck left and right, keeping an eye on any threats that might be too close.

Threat to pack. Stay away or else!

She sent soothing but firm thoughts to him. *No. They are not enemies to be killed. They are only frightened and want to get away from us. It is all right. You must stay. I can keep them away.* And she could, easily. Her power pulsed out around their little group in a sphere that urged the bison to move away from them.

Rick guided them along the outermost left edge of the valley where fewer of the charging mountains of muscle waited to plow them under. Almost instantly, Lincoln's energy calmed.

While part of her threatened to die from fright, another part of her—one that had been asleep for a long time—reveled in the excitement. She didn't know whether to scream or let out a whoop. From her open mouth came a sound that was halfway between both, one that was swallowed by the bisons' thunder. The hills parted moments later and they broke out of the valley onto open plains of grass that flowed to the horizon. Rick followed a small group of bison that veered left and she quickly mirrored him. They slowed to a comfortable lope, staying amidst the group as they headed straight for a large creek that cut through the valley. The majority of the herd rumbled past them, continuing across the plains.

Slowing to a trot, then a walk, they followed the small group right into the creek. Galiha's mind eased the moment they slowed. They moved farther downstream to get out of the way of the rushing creatures. Nearly up to her stirrups in water, she turned to watch the huge beasts charge onto the opposite bank and start up the hill. The thunder of the rest of the herd retreating far away echoed off the small hillside in an eerie way that made them sound closer than they were. Heart still pounding out a rhythm that matched their hoof beats, she had to remind herself to breathe. They had made it.

"Bad dog," Rick said in a tone that was filled with more concern than reprimand.

Fearing he would discipline the pup, she started her horse his way. What she saw made her sit up straight, leaving Galiha to prance and paw at the water. Rick petted the pup all over with gentle strokes that also seemed to be checking for injuries. The sight would have made her smile if her face wasn't still frozen in a rictus of fright.

When she could finally find her voice, she asked, "Is he all right?"

The roar of the retreating herd had died down enough that her soft voice carried easily to Rick. He turned to look at her. He nodded as he urged Ayegi over to her. Pup still clutched in one arm, he leaned over and placed a hesitant hand on hers. "Are you?" he asked, voice filled with something akin to guilt.

Unable to hold his gaze due to the raw concern in his eyes, she looked down. "I am."

Something bright red dripped into the water beneath his stirrup and flowed away. Her gaze flew up to his leg. The torn breeches revealed a long, deep cut that appeared quite painful.

"You're injured."

He looked down and shrugged. "'Tis only a scratch, no worries. Come along, we'll ride on through the stream for as long as we can to cover our tracks."

Still clutching Lincoln in his arms, he turned Ayegi downstream and started walking.

"That is hardly a scratch. We need to get it cleaned up." If only she had Ashlinn's power of healing. But to heal him would expose her. As it was, she was lucky her power was something subtle and easy to hide, and had served them well today.

Galiha followed at a brisk pace, passing up the packhorse to walk beside Ayegi. Galiha was a bundle of energy beneath her, muscles bunched as if preparing to launch into action again. *Calm. We're safe,* she assured him. He blew out a loud snort and shook his head, not in disagreement, but in disbelief that they'd made it.

Good herd leader. Grateful, he thought at her. Smiling, she gave his sweaty neck a good scratch.

Gaze fixed on the horizon, Rick shook his head.

"I'm not going to lose an hour or more of travel because of a scratch. I'll take care of it tonight when we camp."

She decided to try another tactic. "But what of the horses? Do they not need to rest after such a gallop?" It wasn't just for his sake, they really did. She felt their desire to stop.

Again he shook his head. "Nope. Standing still will only make them nervous, best to walk it off."

A frustrated grunt squeezed between her teeth. "Fine,

then. But if you are still bleeding by the time we leave the water, I am cleaning that wound. We cannot have you leaving a blood trail that points straight to us."

Brows raised, he finally looked at her. "Fair enough."

Pressing her lips together, she gestured with a hand for him to lead on. Frustrated beyond words, she allowed him to get a bit ahead of her. She had to, both so he wouldn't see his effect on her, and so his stoic expression wouldn't drive her to scream all manner of inappropriate things at him. The man confounded her in so many ways. Soon she found herself watching not only his wound, but the way his back flexed beneath his almost-too-tight shirt with each step his horse took.

She realized she wasn't just angry at him for taking the risk of going through that valley, she was angry he had put himself between her and danger. No one had ever done that for her and it left her feeling indebted. She detested that. Especially since she had never wanted to get herself in a position where she felt she owed a man anything ever again. Watching him pet Lincoln and hearing him chat with the pup made it hard to stay mad. The man had risked his life for a puppy, after all. How could she remain mad at someone like that? The thought only frustrated her more.

The stream soon sped to the point where Galiha had trouble with his footing. Its sandy bottom began to give way to rocks that the water tumbled over at an increasing pace as it traveled down a steeper slope. Rick's horse moved toward the left bank, drawing her gaze to his leg. Dried blood clung to the wound in a crusty mess.

"Are you sure we shouldn't clean that before we leave the water?" she asked.

Looking down at the wound, he shook his head. "That'll only make it bleed again, and like you said, we don't want to be leaving a trail."

With that, he started up the bank onto dry land. His packhorse was already stepping in the grass by the time she caught up. They said little the remainder of the day as she stewed in her frustration, and he seemed content to let her do so. At last, after an agonizingly long thirty or so miles, she decided she would simply have to return the favor of saving his life so she wouldn't feel as though she owed him anything. Using her power to push the bison away hadn't counted, not in her book.

The sun set while he led them into a copse of trees. Hot, hungry, and sore from being in the saddle all day, she eagerly reined her horse to a stop.

Once she had removed Galiha's tack and brushed out his white, red, and black coat, she set to gathering dry sticks and branches.

"What're you doing?" Rick asked.

She piled her load in a bare spot of dirt. "Gathering wood for a fire."

"We can't have a fire. It could be seen."

Drawing in a deep breath, she buried the part of her that wanted to cower and simply do as he said. "We have to boil water to clean your wound, otherwise it could get infected."

His eyebrows rose and his shortly trimmed beard moved as he chewed his bottom lip. One hand held Lincoln at bay as the pup tried to reach his exposed wound. "All right," he finally said.

Wide-eyed, she could only watch as he walked over to

retrieve his gear.

Finally, as he began to dig in his pack, she found her voice. "You're not going to tell me no, or at least argue?" The words were quiet, almost timid instead of filled with the bite she had intended. *Dammit, why can't I just be the old Cat?*

"O' course not. You sound like you know what you're doing," he said as he began to unbuckle his belt.

She straightened. "What're *you* doing?"

Not even slowing, he set his gun aside and reached for the fly of his breeches. "You've got to be able to get to the wound. Can't do that with me breeches on."

She whipped around so fast the packhorse jumped. Thankfully, he didn't try to bolt, just dug in and regarded her with wide eyes filled with concern. She struggled to push out words between her burning cheeks. She couldn't stop imagining him without his breeches on. "'Tis one thing to be under the cover of water with our backs turned, but this is pushing the boundaries of propriety a bit far!"

At the slip of her Irish accent her eyes squeezed shut tight and she bit her lower lip. For the four years she had been married she had worked so hard to root out that accent so she could sound like a proper high society lady. To have it rear its head because of this rogue, of all reasons, made her want to curse in Gaelic. Yet another thing completely inappropriate for a lady of high society. For more reasons than one. The effect this man had on her seemed to be terrible in every way.

Deep laughter rumbled behind her. "So there is an Irish lass in that tightly laced high society woman."

Wildfire scorched up her neck. A tart reply burned her tongue, but she couldn't unclench her teeth to release it. The long sigh that slid from Rick sent tingles along the back of her neck in the most delicious and irritating way.

"I have left me drawers on, and covered up everything but the wounded part of me leg. You may turn around with most of your sense of propriety intact, Princess," he said.

Eyes narrowing, she spun toward him on her heeled boots. Somehow, her gaze shot straight to his face, bypassing his leg that was bare from the knee down, and even his lap, which was covered by his leather coat. From his spot where he lay on the ground beside him, Lincoln shot to his feet, head cocked, ears perked up.

"How dare you speak to me as if I am some pampered rich woman after I just galloped through a herd of stampeding bison. You, sir, know nothing about me!"

Instead of glare or scoff at her as she expected, he grinned. Damn if he didn't look handsome doing it, too, with that scruff of a beard and those bright green eyes. Though her cheeks burned, she refused to give him the satisfaction of looking away.

"True enough," he admitted.

Having no idea how to respond to that, she set about gathering the items she would need from her pack. Lincoln trotted to her side, thrusting his nose in her way, investigating the contents of her pack. Next to them, Rick piled the tinder and wood, pulled out a box of lucifers, and started the fire, all while keeping his coat over him for the most part. She knew because she watched out of the corner of her eyes. Occasionally, a flash of skin drew her eye. To her surprise, he rigged branches to hold her pot of water over the burgeoning flames.

Mostly to distract both herself and him, she couldn't

resist pushing him a bit as she hung the pot of water over the fire. "Are you not going to tell me how foolish it is to bother boiling the water?"

Attention turning to his blood-encrusted wound, she knelt on the ground beside him. Her stomach churned at the discomfort of being in a position where he had power over her. She had to remind herself that he was not her husband. Despite being a bit of an arse, he seemed unlike Michael in every other way.

"No. Your sister-in-law was me doctor after all. Her practices kept many of the men in me regiment alive," he said in a tone that was so hollow it nearly echoed out into the twilight.

Pain of such a depth that it threatened to suck her in and swallow her whole flashed within his eyes. But he blinked and it was gone, replaced by the reflection of firelight. She turned to drop a small cloth in the warming water because she simply had to look away.

"You were wounded in the war?" she asked.

Leaning back against a rock, he let out a long sigh. "Weren't we all?" The words were barely a whisper.

Such vulnerability, especially from him, made her uncomfortable. He was supposed to be a pompous ass. She preferred him that way. He was easier to deal with than this glimpse of a man who struck something tender deep inside her. With a Herculean amount of effort, she focused on his wound rather than allowing her gaze to travel to his face. Hearing the vulnerability in his voice was one thing, but she couldn't bear to see it in his features. If she did, she feared he may creep like a mist through the mortar lines of the wall that protected her from all things masculine.

Stitches wouldn't do much for the ragged cut, and it wasn't quite deep enough for them anyway. They'd have to make sure it stayed clean so infection didn't set in was all. Using a fork from her pack, she retrieved the rag from the boiling water and returned to Rick's side. The moment it cooled enough, she began wiping the blood away. Even when she went over the deepest part of the cut, Rick didn't wince. Her gaze lifted to find him watching her with something akin to longing. The moment their eyes met it disappeared. Hardening her own expression, she lifted the small bottle Ashlinn had insisted she bring.

"This part is going to hurt," she warned.

Upon seeing the bottle, his eyes widened into a deeply furrowed brow.

"Damn," he muttered.

She looked back to the wound, hiding a grin behind the loose strands of her hair. So he knew what it was. To save the precious iodine, she dabbed a bit of it onto a clean portion of the cloth rather than pour it straight onto his wound. Squeezing the cloth to push the liquid out, she pressed it to the worst parts of the wound. Though he didn't flinch, Rick muttered a soft curse word in Gaelic that made her smile all the wider. So he could feel after all.

"We cannot have this getting infected," she said.

He didn't respond until she retreated to her pack to put her things away. "No, we can't. Thank you."

The sincerity in his words surprised her. "You're welcome."

As she dug in her pack, she heard fabric rustling behind

her. Part of her wanted desperately to turn around and catch a glimpse of him in his drawers, but she resisted. A lady didn't do such things, and she was trying very hard to be a lady, despite her past. Or rather, because of it. That was the old Cat, the one who had gotten herself into a heap of trouble and pain she had yet to dig out of. Much as she liked and missed the old Cat, she couldn't allow her to resurface. Alone in the wild with a handsome man made her want to oh so badly. But she didn't dare. Once the rustling stopped, she turned back around with bandages in hand.

Rick lay mostly hidden within his bedroll, wounded leg out and propped up on a rock. Curled into the crook of one arm lay Lincoln, sound asleep. The lack of anger he showed toward the pup spoke volumes about his character. Such things could be deceiving, though. She refused to drop her guard.

"Best save that for something worse than a scratch," he said, nodding toward the bandage in her hands.

The words sent a chill deep into her bones, but she nodded and put it away. She gathered a few things from her pack and started for the encroaching darkness—and privacy— the woods offered.

"Go, watch over her," Rick said so softly she almost didn't catch it.

Paws padded against grass and leaves. A moment later Lincoln stood at her side, arched tail wagging, big eyes watching her dutifully. Sentinel at her side, she went only far enough into the trees to be concealed to conduct her evening routine and change into something easier to sleep in. Unlike most pups, Lincoln did not leave her side, not even when a squirrel chattered at him from a tree. His kind were protectors first and foremost and not even the playfulness of youth could override that. Having him close comforted her and made her miss her friends. That Ashlinn had thought to send a fae creature with them to watch over her touched her deeply.

The snorts and sounds of the horses settling helped her find her way back to camp in the near dark. The scent of smoke drew her gaze to the cold fire pit where not so much as a coal smoldered. Her heart sank. So much for the idea of a warm meal. But the threat of someone following them held her protests. Today's wild flight shouldn't be for naught. If it could help them disappear, it was worth losing out on a warm meal. Lincoln trotted back to the mound of shadows that were Rick.

"You did good today," Rick said.

Knowing he couldn't see her expression in the spreading darkness, she allowed herself a smile. "Thank you, but all I did was cling to the back of my horse." It was part truth.

An alluring sort of grunt sounded from Rick. "Well, you did that quite well. Where others would have panicked, you kept your head."

It aggravated her to no end that she found his little noises and the tone of his voice attractive, but his words worked like a balm on that aggravation. Her attraction to men couldn't be trusted. Not after how her late husband had turned out. Besides, she had to stay focused, especially with someone pursuing them. Still…

"Thank you. But, you were the one who saved the day. Quite literally for young Lincoln there," she said.

He laughed, yet another of his sounds that made muscles low in her abdomen tighten, which hadn't gotten exercise in a few years.

"Couldn't leave me hound in peril. Best get some sleep now. We've got a long few days ahead of us," he said.

Dangerous as it had been, it had felt amazing to run with those wild beasts. Something of her old, reckless self had awakened. Past mistakes made her want to suppress that part of her, but it wasn't as though she would make them again. The naïve child in her was gone forever. What stirred today was more like her spirit reawakening. As much as her head spun with all the possibilities and problems that presented, slumber still managed to wrap her in an all-consuming embrace the moment her head rested on her makeshift pillow.

9

Rick

Day Four

Catriona had been gone for too long. With someone on their
tail, he shouldn't have let her go off on her own. Dropping an
armload of firewood beside the pit he had dug, his eyes strayed
to the opening in the trees through which she had disappeared.
It had gone against every instinct he had to allow her to go off
into the woods alone. But her insistence on needing a moment
for privy business had been difficult to argue with. Besides, she
was fae and they tended to fare better in nature than
civilization. He had barely let her out of his sight since the
bison herd incident two days ago. Though uneventful, today
had been a long, hard day in the saddle and he hadn't been
about   to begrudge her the chance to stretch her legs.

     That had been at least a quarter of an hour ago. Pink
tinged the edge of the horizon. Now he was willing to begrudge

her all manner of things. Eyes flicking to where the horses hung their heads in slumber beneath an oak tree, he hesitated. Grass and underbrush rustled at the tree line a moment before Lincoln shot out, fluffy tail wagging. Catriona followed not far behind. She had untucked her tunic and was using it as a makeshift basket. Greens and carrots poked up from within the bundle. All that bright red hair sat in a loose bun atop her head, held together by what looked like twigs thrust through it. Either exertion or the day's sun added a nice shade of pink to her sculpted cheekbones.

Realizing he was staring, he shifted his attention to the food she carried. "Where did you pilfer that from?"

Her brows drew together and her eyes widened as if to counter the movement. "I did no such thing. I found them in an overgrown garden that clearly had been left to go wild. The rundown shack nearby was half collapsed and clearly not inhabited. I only had to bargain with a few jack rabbits."

The tension that had been building in him eased and he moved his hand away from his gun. "Probably an old dwelling of those who kept the Pony Express horses."

Her green eyes lit up like sparks had gone off in them. It tugged at him in a way he was completely unprepared for. "Do you really think so? It appeared so rundown."

Nodding, he began stacking wood for the fire. "Aye. The elements and natives are slowly destroying them."

Lincoln bounded around him in a circle, leaping up to lick the back of his hand. He gave the pup a quick scratch behind the ears before returning to work on the fire.

"Is it not dangerous to follow too closely to such a known trail? And you're building a fire? What about Ainsworth's man?"

The concern in her voice made him look up from his task. Fear had replaced the excited spark in her eyes. Something compelled him to rekindle that excitement. "There've been no signs of anyone following for two days now, and so long as we keep the fire only big enough to create cooking coals, the smoke will be hard to see. Besides, we're far enough off the trail to be safe, no worries, lass." He regretted his easy tone and familiarity the moment the words left his lips, but it was too late now.

Her cheeks darkened, sending a delicious line of heat straight to his groin that he was powerless to stop. After a long, hard blink, he turned his focus to the flint and steel in his hands. It was not lost on him that starting one fire wasn't likely to extinguish another. Out of the corner of his eye he watched her dump the vegetables onto her blanket. He removed the knife from the sheath at his waist and handed it to her. Those lovely green eyes widened as they traveled the length of the blade, but she accepted it.

Once a spark ignited the tinder, he left the growing flame to dig around in his saddlebags. He dug out the small cooking pot from within. The sound of Catriona humming an old Irish tune stopped him in his tracks. The chop, chop, chop of the knife cutting through the thick orange carrots punctuated the beats of the tune. How she could make humming sound so lovely, he had no idea. But then, watching her red head bob to the rhythm and her slender shoulders sway ever so slightly, it became clear.

Never in all his life had he imagined he would see a high society lady kneeling in the grass chopping vegetables she'd just pulled from the ground with a knife and looking so...content. She handled the knife like she knew what she was doing. One of her means surely had cooks to do the work for her. So what if she was the hands-on type? That didn't disprove his first impression of her—or so he told himself. After four days on the trail, he had imagined she would be a sniveling wreck, ready to turn back and wait for the wagons. Especially after the incident with the bison herd, and knowing they were being followed by Ainsworth's man, who no doubt intended them harm. Neither had so much as riled her. It grew harder and harder to hang onto that first impression.

He sat the pot beside her and turned quickly away.

"My thanks, Rick," she said, casting him a quick smile.

Tuatha save him, but he liked the sound of his name rolling off her tongue, especially when she sounded so happy. "You're welcome," he managed without sounding too strangled.

This was the first time he had seen her so carefree, so open. With her hair all up in a messy bun and a smudge of dirt on her face, she looked wild and beautiful. But he knew better. Despite being a fae, she was still a lady of high society.

Albeit, one who wore breeches and rode a horse like a man.

"If I didn't know better, I'd say you were enjoying this," he said.

Her smile grew. "I am. It has been a long time since I've felt this free."

The statement frayed at the rough edges of the proper tapestry he had formed in his mind of her life. It made him wonder what her life had been like growing up. This was quickly going south of his intentions in starting the conversation.

"You don't miss your fine dresses and tea parties?" he asked.

She looked up, fixing eyes filled with wonder and anticipation on him. "I actually don't." She sounded surprised, but pleased at the realization. Her humming resumed.

"You are an enigma, woman," he muttered to himself.

"What was that?"

"I said, something must drive you to do this. What do you plan to do with the land?"

The chopping ceased and she glanced up at him from beneath her long lashes and hunkered down, almost as if she were cringing. "I'd rather not say."

"Afraid I will steal your idea?" he teased.

This time she didn't look up. Several carrots plunked into the pot before she answered. "No. I would just rather not be ridiculed."

Compelled by the mixture of sadness and pain in her voice, he placed a hand upon hers. "I would never ridicule you. If I've given you that impression, I offer me most sincere apologies."

She flinched almost imperceptibly at his touch but covered it with a shrug. "'Twas not an impression you gave me, but rather a response I have come to expect of those I tell my dreams to."

Though he enjoyed the warmth of her skin beneath his palm, he drew his hand away to make her more comfortable. "No one should scoff at the dreams of another, no matter what they may be," he said.

Members of high society could be quite vicious, something he knew all too well.

From behind a strand of brilliant red hair that had come free of her bun, he thought he saw the hint of a smile. She resumed chopping vegetables.

He decided he would have to go first. "I myself dreamt of starting a farm that could supply the local markets. Many scoffed at such a dream."

One red eyebrow lifted into her hairline. "That's a good dream, a practical one that helps others." The tiniest hint of an Irish accent slipped through her tone, a victory in itself.

A short laugh escaped him. "You sound surprised. So tell me then, 'tis only fair since I shared mine."

It was testing the depth of waters he knew he shouldn't step in, but the journey ahead of them would only feel longer if he didn't at least get to know her a bit.

Holding the knife as if readying to use it as a weapon instead of a tool, she finally met his gaze. "I want to raise horses, and my friends and I want to start a winery. A place like the wineries of Italy Deirdre's father used to talk of visiting. It will be a place that employs those who would have difficulty finding work in this war-torn country. 'Tis not an entirely selfless dream, but 'tis ours nonetheless."

"You would employ Freemen?" he asked, not hiding the surprise in his voice.

Her eyes held his and her chin lifted a bit in defiance. "I would."

Hiring those who had once been slaves was no small thing. Many would look down on her for it. Though they'd won the war and freed the slaves, people were slow to get used to the new ways and many were bitter about its effect on their livelihood. That she was willing to endure such cynicism impressed him. The resolve in both her voice and gaze stirred something in him. Slowly, a soft smile pulled the corners of his lips up. "Sounds like a selfless dream if ever I heard one," he said.

"Thank you," she said softly as she put knife to vegetables once again.

Hands going behind his head, he kicked back against his pack, stretching his legs out before him. "'Tis just that I had no idea me client had such a taste for the spirits," he teased.

Eyes going wide, Catriona sat up straighter. "While I do enjoy a glass of particularly nice wine, that's not the reason at all. Before leaving Ireland, my family was renowned for our horses and Deirdre's were renowned for the grapes they grew. Deirdre's family's grapes were so prized that the common folk couldn't afford their wine, the English and French courts bought it all up. And our horses were champions sought after by even the crown." Her voice quavered a bit on the last words.

"You're good with animals," he observed.

Her lips turned up into a secret little smile that she tried to hide behind the locks of her hair that had come loose. "'Tis what I'm best at, truly. I am better with them than with people. My whole family was."

Seeing her light up like that warmed his insides, but the fact that she had tried to hide her happiness ate at him. Had he really been so uncouth that he'd elicited such a reaction in her?

He indicated the pot of vegetables with a thrust of his head. "Well, you're certainly good at finding and picking the best of the lot."

Sore muscles protested as he rose to his feet. "I'll fetch some water for the soup and refill our canteens."

As he gathered the canteens, Cat's back became rigid as an English rider's. The knuckles of the hand that gripped the knife grew as white as the rings around her wide eyes. She looked to the shadows stretching out from the trees, then back to him. "'Tis almost dark. Is it safe?"

Taking his time, he bent over her to pick up the pot, reveling in the way her hair still smelled of lilac soap even after four days on the trail. Her shoulders relaxed, as if his nearness comforted her. Surely that couldn't be the case, though.

"The stream we passed on the way isn't far. I'll be back in two shakes of a badger's tail," he said as he tucked the pot under an arm and rose.

Lincoln leapt to his feet and trotted after him. He gave the pup a stern look and pointed to the ground. "Sit. Stay with Cat."

Dust puffed up as the pup sat down with a dissatisfied grunt. A moment later his tail started to beat at the stalks of yellow grass, and he turned his head toward her. Mouth half-opened with a quirky comment sitting on his tongue, Rick froze at the sight of Catriona. Pink tinged her cheeks, darkening until it seemed they might turn the very hue of her hair. His blood stirred. That decided it. He needed to call her Cat more often.

Though he took only minutes, by the time he returned darkness had settled over the land. The half moon and its cloak of stars lit his way well enough that the underbrush didn't trip him up overly much. The acrid scent of smoke led him back to camp as surely as a well-lit trail would have. He'd have to extinguish the fire as soon as the coals were hot enough to cook their meal. Couldn't have the smoke leading anyone else to them. Common sense had tried to convince him not to start it in the first place. But Cat had become increasingly nervous over the last few days and he knew both the false security of the fire and, more importantly, a warm meal, would make her feel better. One could only take so much hardtack and dried meat.

Truth be told—though he would only admit it to himself—his common sense was becoming less common when it came to this woman. Such an effect puzzled him. Not even his prior bride-to-be had possessed this power over him. It had been a proposal based on a good match socially and with both their families in mind. Still, he had been quite fond of the woman and suitably attracted to her. How was this so different? Perhaps because she was fae. That had to be it. Grumbling beneath his breath, he shook his head and forced his mind back to what was important.

A few more steps and yellow firelight revealed the outline of Cat and Lincoln huddled together near the fire. The light danced across waves of her long red hair that fell like a waterfall of fire down her shoulders to tease her cleavage. He hadn't seen her let it down in days. Shorter curls framed a lovely face fixed in an anxious look. While one arm was wrapped tight around the pup, the other hung at her side near her firearm, hand sitting on the hilt. The scents of fear and anxiety wafted from her. Seeing her look so vulnerable was highly unusual. An almost overpowering urge to protect her swept over him. So much for concentrating on what was important.

"Are you all right? Did something happen?" he asked.

Head popping up from where it had been resting on Catriona's knee, Lincoln emitted a soft puppy bark. Rick nodded to the pup, who then wriggled out of Cat's grasp to trot to his side.

"We're fine. It just took you longer than I expected and I began to grow concerned," Cat said.

Careful not to spill any more of the water than he already had, he carried the pot to the fire, eyes widening at the sight that awaited him. Large rocks surrounded two sides of the fire, a flat rock balanced over the two at the corner. Red coals glowed beneath it. The wet bottom of the cast iron pot sizzled when he sat it on the rock.

"Where on earth did you learn to do this?" he whispered.

She made a harrumphing sound. "Not all high society ladies are as useless as you assume."

Much as he hated to admit it, she had him there. "Fair enough. Truly, I'm impressed."

She rewarded him with a smug smile that told him he had accomplished his goal of distracting her from whatever had frightened her. He tried to tell himself that he only cared because clients were easier to deal with when calm. But the fire that roared to life in his blood when her green gaze fell on him begged to differ. He did his best to squelch the sensation—he refused to call it a feeling because that touched too close to things he didn't want to consider. While waiting for the soup to cook, he teased her about her choice and placement of rocks. In good humor, she dished out as much as she took, teasing him endlessly in turn.

After enjoying a meal in which her etiquette was refreshingly relaxed, he stretched out onto his bedroll and tried not to watch her from across the fire.

A bit of snorting pulled his attention back to the fire

where Lincoln stared hard at a stick in the pile.

"No, leave it," Rick commanded.

Something caught between a groan and a whine issued from the pup as he scooted back a step. Though his head remained pointed in Rick's direction, his big eyes strayed back to the branches slowly being consumed by the orange flames. A warm breeze carried the sound of a distant yip. Lincoln's head snapped in the direction of the sound and his ears stood up as straight as they could. His body tensed in preparation.

"Lincoln, stay," Rick commanded.

The pup whined and glanced his way. "Stay," he reiterated with more force. He didn't dare put a touch of his power in it. Cat would feel it for certain. The poor woman was jumpy as a doe already. If she felt his power she'd know what he was and would no doubt run all the way back to New York—or more likely, straight into a danger worse than him.

More yips echoed on the breeze, at least a half dozen.

"What is that?" Cat whispered, her tone tight.

She sat up from where she'd been lounging across the fire from him, looking almost as ready to run as Lincoln did. Those lovely lips of hers had drawn tight and the whites of her moist, wide eyes caught the firelight.

"'Tis only coyotes," he said.

"Are you sure 'tis not wolves?" she asked, voice so low he could scarcely hear it over the crackling of the fire.

The urge to lead her on and tease her surged within, but the way she trembled ever so slightly took the playfulness right out of him. "Aye, no worries," he said instead, surprising himself.

Her eyes flicked to him. "Coyotes are harmless then?"

"Aye," he lied with a shrug. They were harmless compared to him, but he couldn't say that.

Some of the shine left her eyes and her shoulders slowly dropped.

Another small yip carried on the cool wind as if in protest. Almost in unison, Cat and Lincoln's eyes widened and shot in the direction of the sound. To her credit, Cat looked completely at ease as she patted the pup on the head and murmured words of comfort to him. Rick let out a long breath, relaxed back against his bedroll, and kicked his feet up on a branch.

The night suddenly exploded with dozens upon dozens of yips that drew into ululating howls. A whimper escaped Cat as she sat bolt upright, arms clutching Lincoln so tight Rick wasn't sure if the pup's eyes were bulging or just wide with fright. The horses stomped and one of them snorted. Lincoln squirmed like a fish ashore until he had loosed himself from her grasp. His eyes locked onto a spot in the darkness and his muscles bunched in preparation to launch himself.

"Lincoln, no!" Rick commanded.

The pup's head snapped in his direction, then he froze.

"Come," Rick said as he patted his leg.

Like a shot of gray and brown fur, Lincoln was suddenly at his side, pressing against him, big eyes beseeching. "'Tis all right, boy, but you'd best not leave camp," he told him in soothing tones as he pulled a rope out of his pack.

Moving quick before Lincoln could spook again, he fastened one end of the rope about the pup's neck, and the other to his saddle horn. He wasn't sure if it would truly hold one of Lincoln's kind, but he hoped it would at least serve as a reminder of the command to stay.

"I thought you said they were harmless! They sound hungry and not at all harmless." Cat's voice rose several octaves on the last word.

Well over a dozen different canine voices serenaded the moon. From the sound of it, they were on the hunt. He wasn't about to tell Cat that. One of the horses snorted again, a tail swished, but otherwise they seemed unconcerned.

"For the most part, they are. But they love to draw out dogs and either steal them or…" He let his voice trail off.

Lincoln whined and lay down at Rick's side as if he understood the words. He probably did. Stretching out on his blanket, he stroked the pup's head until he began to relax.

Cat's wide eyes flicked from Lincoln to the horses. "What about the horses?"

"They wouldn't risk it. For one, the horses are too big. Two, Galiha and Ayegi aren't afraid of canines and will fight, making them very undesirable prey."

With a nod, Cat leaned back against her own saddle, one arm draped up over the horn in a bad attempt to look casual. "And are we undesirable prey?"

"You're safe enough between the horses and the fire," he said.

The fear that shone in her wide eyes told him he had gone just far enough to keep her safely within the camp for the night. Then he noticed her shaking ever so slightly. At first he had thought it was a trick of the firelight. But when she tried three times to brush back a lock of hair, missing due to her shaking, he realized he had gone too far.

"No worries, they're miles away," he assured her.

Pink lips pulling into a tight smile, she gave him the most unconvincing nod he had seen. Clearly empty words of comfort and a disarming smile would not do the trick here. He dug into his pack until his hand closed around a small, cool metal object. *It couldn't hurt.* By his calculations they had to be at least two days ahead of Ainsworth's man and he hadn't seen any signs of other travelers nearby. The risk was worth it if he could smooth that look of fear from her lovely features. For the sake of a calmer traveling companion that wouldn't keep him awake with worry, of course.

The cool touch of metal against his lips relaxed him and took him back to things he wanted to both desperately remember and desperately forget. With a gentle puff of breath he sent a few notes vibrating through the harmonica. Lincoln's head lifted and his ears popped up. Even Catriona perked up, her shocked expression looking more comical than the pup's. He paused to give her time to react, hiding his smile behind his harmonica.

She cleared her throat and blinked a few times before speaking. "So that's what those things sound like." The uncertainty in her voice left him wondering, but she went on before he could respond. "Quite…American."

He laughed and shook his head. "Aye, 'tis at that. I don't have to play, but it may help distract the pup." Falling purposefully silent, he waited.

Another series of sharp yips caused her eyes to shoot off into the dark. "Well, if it helps Lincoln, I suppose it will be tolerable," she said.

The badly faked bravado in her voice made him smile so large he couldn't have hidden it if he tried. After another yip made her jump, he brought the harmonica back to his lips and began to play. The mournful sound of a slow tune he had learned from a freed man in the war filled the night. Sad as it was, it was a song he had always liked. The way Catriona's lovely brow smoothed out and she relaxed back against her saddle told him it soothed her as much as it did him. That he had teased her into such a state stirred a bit of guilt. But he couldn't help it. The woman rankled him in a way no woman had for some time, and he hated it. Still, it wasn't her fault he mistrusted those of her station so much.

By the end of the song, Lincoln yawned and lay down with his head on Rick's leg. He started another song, one she might recognize. Her delicate red brows lifted.

"Scarborough Fair," she said between notes.

He lowered the harmonica. "Or the Elfin Knight, as me da called it," he said.

When she nodded with an approving look, he played on. Soon she hummed along. By the chorus she was singing softly. The sound of her voice both moved and soothed him in a way nothing had been able to do since the war. He closed his eyes as he played and listened to her sing. At the end of the song he paused.

"You have a lovely voice," he said.

In the firelight it was hard to tell, but he thought her cheeks might have reddened. Her head dropped and crimson locks of hair hid her expression. The peak of a high cheekbone through the hair stirred his blood. *Damn, but she is beautiful.*

"I think you've been out here in the wild too long," she teased.

"Not nearly long enough. But 'tis true. I've heard many a

good singer and you outshine the lot," he said.

When she didn't respond, he lifted the harmonica again and continued to play. Catriona's eyes watched him from across the fire for quite some time. They had softened considerably, the caution and fear draining from them with each note he played. An exhausted sleep soon stole over her. The peacefulness that smoothed out her features transformed her into a vision. Inspired, he played on long into the night.

10

Catriona

Day Six

After two days of near-silence from Rick, Catriona had endured as much of his surliness as she could. When he had played his harmonica she had thought maybe, in some small way, he might have done so for her. But now it had become painfully clear that his mistrust and dislike of her had not lessened in the slightest. The sight of a wagon and two men on horseback preparing to cross at the bank of the South Platte River came as a huge relief. Not only was she sick of the silence, but she had begun to think they were the only two people left on this planet. And that truly would have been disheartening.

Another wagon pulled by oxen and flanked by two more horsemen was already halfway across the river. The water splashing up from the horse's hooves made her acutely aware of how hot the late afternoon sun had already grown. Thanks to the heat she'd been looking forward to this crossing for the last several miles. To her dismay, Rick reined his horse to a stop at the tree line. The pup stopped and sat near Ayegi's front feet. Shielding his eyes from the sun with a hand, Rick scanned up and down the riverbank. While the shade of the trees offered a bit of relief, the water would be so much better. He held up a hand as if sensing she was about to urge Galiha forward.

"They look harmless enough," she whispered.

He turned one narrowed eye on her. "Looks can be deceiving, especially out here on the trail. We'll wait," he whispered back.

As if in a protest of his own, Galiha stretched his neck out and lifted his nose to sniff the humid air. She held his reins tight when he tried to walk forward. It had been a long hot day and clearly he was just as eager for the cool water as she was. They waited in the shade, sweating and thirsty, while the second wagon and horsemen began to cross. A little over halfway across, the wagon stopped. After much urging on the driver's part, it became clear they were stuck. The horsemen dismounted and began to push. Despite having the look of strong-backed farmers, they couldn't budge it. Two women climbed from the wagon, one taking the horses and leading them out of the way, the other joining in the efforts. Their grunts and shouts of encouragement to the oxen hitched to the wagon filled the quiet morning. The wheels rolled half a turn and stopped again.

"Damn it all," Rick muttered to himself as he urged Ayegi from the trees. He tugged his shirt free from his breeches to cover the butt of his pistol as he did so.

Surprised at his concern for the others, and more than a little pleased, Catriona followed.

"Hello there," Rick called out in a friendly tone.

As the settlers looked their way he waved and smiled. She had been about to call out her own greeting but the complete transformation of his face from surly and pinched to helpful shocked her into silence. She wasn't entirely sure if he was putting on a good front, or was truly concerned about the people.

"Looks like you could use a hand," Rick went on.

Two of the men at the back of the wagon exchanged a look and took several steps in his direction. It was no accident that they placed themselves between him and the women. Sensing their tension, Catriona finally found her tongue.

"A few more hands might make the difference," she offered in a tone that she hoped sounded as cheery as Rick's had been.

One of the men returned Rick's smile and nodded. The other eyed them with suspicion as he held up a hand. Rick reined his horse to a stop at the water's edge. Oblivious to the tension among the humans, Lincoln plunged into the water with abandon. The pup's long legs kept his head above the water even when he approached the women who stood knee deep behind the wagon. One of them—a girl who couldn't have been more than thirteen—giggled as he splashed about and tried to lick her hands.

"Well, I suppose we could use the help," the man who hadn't smiled admitted through his scruffy beard.

Rick rode right into the muddy water. The moment Ayegi stopped to drink, he swung from his back and plunged in, boots and all. Not to be outdone by her guide, Catriona followed suit. When Galiha blew out a relieved breath and stopped beside Ayegi to dip his nose in the water, she slid from his back the same as Rick had done. Cool water reaching almost mid-thigh shocked the breath right out of her and shot her eyes open wide. The day was hot, to be sure, but this water felt downright glacial. Skin began to tighten that she didn't want Rick—let alone these strangers—noticing. The thin material of her light green blouse did little to hide the roundness of her breasts where they poked above her corset.

She patted Galiha on the neck and sent him the thought, *Do not roll in the water. I will wash you soon.* He shook his head at her, sending droplets of water flying from the ends of his white and black mane that had skimmed the surface. Though she knew that could mean both yes and no where horses were concerned, the feeling he sent told her he wouldn't roll, for now.

"That's a good boy," she said aloud. At that he bobbed his head, his mind beaming with the praise.

Wading over to the others, she found a spot to place her hands against the wagon beside the youngest woman. No one would be looking at her breasts, least of all Rick, who was laying his shoulder against the wagon and preparing to push. All five of them found a spot as the bearded man began to count. As he did, she reached out and touched the mind of the oxen hitched to the wagon. Stubbornness born from heat and exhaustion filled them. They wanted nothing more than to stay in the water, no matter the consequences. She sent thoughts of the green grass waiting for them on the banks, how sweet it would taste, how it would fill their bellies and renew their tired muscles. Their minds perked up.

When Rick reached the count of three they heaved and the wagon began to move. It rolled forward, but only so long as they continued to push. Several arduous steps later, the cool water began to feel refreshing. It soon reached her waist, but the pushing became easier at that point so she wasn't about to complain.

The weight of Rick's eyes drew her attention from the worn wood of the wagon to him. Respect blossomed within his startling greens, that and perhaps a touch of desire. To his credit, the man's gaze had fixed on her face. Pink tinged his cheeks before he looked swiftly down and away, eyes catching on her breasts at last as he did so. She had expected many things of Corporal Rick Fergusson. Shyness had not been among them. She found it surprisingly appealing. He wore pink quite well. The remainder of the way across the river she tried to catch his gaze again in the hopes of rubbing it in a bit that she had caught him. But he didn't look back at her.

Soon the water grew shallow. Due to the muddy river bottom that squished beneath their boots, they would have to push until the wagon reached dry ground. The wagon began to roll back toward them. Rick suddenly shoved the young man beside him—who stood directly behind the left wheel—away and out of the path of the wagon. Renewing his efforts, he grunted and heaved with all his might. For a moment she felt his life energy pulse like the sun. The wagon rolled forward with a lurch and suddenly pulled away from them, having overcome whatever obstacle had pushed it back.

Rick dashed to the young man sprawled on his back in the shallow water and offered him his hand. "Sorry, lad. I saw you slip and you were about to get your foot crushed."

The young man nodded his head of unruly brown hair and took Rick's hand. "I was at that. Thank you so much, sir. But your foot."

With a shrug, he lifted it out of the water and moved it about. "I stepped elsewhere. Luck o' the Irish I guess."

Catriona swallowed hard. A crushed foot out here could be a death sentence. It would be so much easier to dislike this man if he'd stop being so damn chivalrous. She distracted herself by fetching Galiha, who was coming out of the water behind her. The gelding lingered at the water's edge and didn't shy away at her approach. In no hurry to leave the cool river, he waited, mind filled with patience and contentment. Lincoln danced alongside the horse, wagging his tail and bouncing on his hind legs as if to splash the horse on purpose.

Play, play, play, his excited thoughts drifted to her.

Still, the horse didn't move. Catriona shook her head at the big painted gelding as she took hold of his reins.

"You are quite unlike my thoroughbreds, creature," she told him.

He snorted and shook water from his mane, splashing it all over her and Lincoln. With a bark, Lincoln took off in Rick's direction. Laughing, she held an arm up to ward off the worst of it as the horse continued to shake.

Got you both! Galiha thought with glee.

"He is, at that. But 'tis not the only reason he lingers. He likes you," came Rick's slight baritone voice from directly behind her.

The sound stirred her blood and tightened parts of her that were already too tight considering current company. But then, if they weren't in their current company, that would mean they'd be alone together which would make it far more inappropriate. With more effort than she was comfortable with, she reined in her desire. It angered her that a man could stir her in this way. After her husband, she never wanted to be attracted to a man again. She took hold of that anger, focused on it, let it strengthen her resolve.

"Unlike his owner," she quipped as she cast him a reproachful look over her shoulder.

That one glimpse nearly undid her resolve. Breeches wet up to the waist clung to Rick's fit legs and outlined the bulge at his groin. Her backward glance became a stare as the sight captivated her. For a moment, she couldn't remember what she'd been mad about. It came rushing back when her eyes made it up to his face and she found him grinning like a cat on milking day. In a huff that ended in a frustrated grunt, she turned back to Galiha and began to swing up into the saddle. Once mounted, she found Rick's gaze still locked on her. The large grin on his face made her realize she had given him an eyeful, considering how her wet breeches clung to her behind.

"Never said I didn't like you," Rick said with a shrug of one shoulder.

Focusing a little too hard on wringing the water from her clothing, she urged Galiha forward. He jumped into an uncharacteristic trot all too quickly. The surprised grunt that issued from her along with the scramble for her saddle horn had Rick laughing with abandon. She mumbled a few curse words in Gaelic under her breath—something she hadn't done in years.

Rick's eyes shot open wide. He glanced in the direction

of the two wagons working their way onto the trail just ahead. "Gaelic sounds even more lovely coming from your lips," he said in a soft tone.

She grinned. "In my family we must learn it, but never speak it outside of the privacy of our home. But I did, every chance I could get. I kept up on the study of writing and reading it to further aggravate my husband." The memory of defying her parents' wishes to suppress their culture so she'd fit into high society better delighted her to no end. On the other hand, the one of defying her husband brought all manner of painful things back. Reacting to her, Galiha snorted. Her pain bothered him. It didn't make him fear some sort of danger. It made him feel protective. She scratched his neck and murmured words to him to ensure him she was all right. That danger had passed. Only the scars remained. Unfortunately, they could be just as painful.

"But your husband was Irish as well. I would think he'd want you to embrace your heritage, even if your parents didn't," Rick said.

Though she kept her head held high, she suddenly found herself wishing she'd held her tongue instead. "He believed it made us seem low class." More than that, it made him fearful of persecution and discovery. That seemed silly to her. The witch trials had been over one-hundred-and-seventy years ago. The world was much more modern and forward thinking now. It both surprised and pleased her to find that she remembered how to speak the ancient tongue of their ancestors. More so, defying him, even after death, felt good.

Blowing air out between his pursed lips, Rick shook his head as he swung up onto his horse. "That's a load of shite. No disrespect to the deceased intended. Forgetting our heritage is forgetting all our ancestors did to get us this far," he said.

The words sent a swelling of pride through her that made it impossible to respond. It was best she didn't anyway. To agree would be to sound low born, and to disagree would be a lie. She wasn't willing to do either just yet. Rick's ability to speak his mind so freely, to openly believe what he wanted, and to not care what others thought was enviable beyond measure. Enviable, and admirable. But she was no rogue free to do and say as she pleased. She was the widow O'Brian, head of the organization of the Widows of the 69th, and a fae. A woman of station such as herself had to watch her every move and her every word. She couldn't allow herself to forget that, not even out here in the wilds of America.

The bearded man from the nearest wagon waved and called out to them. "You're welcome to break bread with us if you wish. We'd be happy to have you as thanks for your help."

Rick waved back. "Thank you, kindly, but we'll have to pass. The missus and I plan to get atop the hill by nightfall. You folks take care, now, and safe travels to you," he called back.

Rather than ride up to and past them, Rick steered Ayegi off the rutted trail and onto the tall green grass of the hill beside it instead. After a good shake that sent puppy-scented droplets flying everywhere, Lincoln trotted next to him. The urge to protest had Catriona chewing her bottom lip. As much as she would enjoy a leisurely stroll alongside the wagons, they couldn't afford to take the time. They'd cross double the ground or more on their own. A squeeze of her legs and shift of the reins steered Galiha after Ayegi's buckskin-hued backside.

The people from the wagon called out farewells and

Catriona and Rick returned them in kind. Before them loomed the green, flower-spotted expanse of California Hill. Truly, it didn't look as intimidating as she had imagined it. People described it as an arduous climb that left wagons broken and horses exhausted. To her it merely looked like a good day's hack across the countryside. She knew she may not feel that way after the mile and half or so of traversing its two-hundred-plus-foot incline.

Once they were well away from the wagons, she looked to Rick. A slight smile pulled at his lips as his gaze cast out across the expanse of perfect blue sky.

"Missus, huh?" Catriona teased.

"Can't have them thinking ill of you," Rick answered in an honest tone.

"Thank you for that." She shook her head. "You're a puzzle, Mr. Fergusson. Not quite the rogue I initially thought you were."

Rick's dark brows rose into his long bangs. "You think me a rogue?"

The way all that dark hair framed his eyes made them stand out brilliantly. The scruff of beard he sported certainly lent to the roguish look, one that was quite handsome if she was being honest with herself. She found honesty overrated in this instance. Frustrated at how easily he distracted her, she forced her eyes back to the hill before them.

"Well, you certainly look the part, and your lack of interest in all things proper supported the belief," she said in as detached a tone as she could fake.

"But you don't think me a rogue now?" he pressed.

She could hear the smile in his voice, but she refused to

look at him to see if it actually pulled up his full lips. Just thinking about it was enough to make her jaw—and other muscles—clench. "I didn't say that. But I am starting to realize there's more to you," she admitted.

"Sound like maybe you don't entirely dislike me, either."

That drew her gaze, and a smile. "Not entirely," she said.

Something flashed in his eyes—concern, fear, maybe? But what on Earth could this man have to fear from her? Galiha suddenly lurched beneath her, pitching her forward in the saddle. Grabbing hold of the horn, she just barely managed to stop herself from going over his head. After a few limping steps, she reined him to a stop. A pinch of pain came from his left hoof.

She called up to Rick, who had traveled a few paces ahead. "Hold up, something is wrong with Galiha."

Not waiting for him, she dismounted. A touch at the back of Galiha's left foreleg made him lift it for her. She took a pick from her pocket and began to clean the dirt and grass from his hoof. The horseshoe moved when she knocked the pick against it.

"Oh no, he's about to throw a shoe," she said.

Leather creaked, and suddenly Rick's shadow fell over her. She looked up to find him hovering over her with a small hammer in one hand and horseshoe nails poking through the fingers of the other.

"No worries, I'll get him right as rain."

Her brows rose into her hair. "You can shoe a horse?" She blew out a sharp breath. "Of course you can." *Is there anything this man couldn't do? Damn.* A capable man was oh-so-attractive. As if he needed anything to make him more attractive.

She let go of Galiha's hoof and stepped back to give Rick room to work. He cleaned the hoof out a bit more, inspected it, and set to work putting new nails in. Galiha stood patiently for all of it. A flick of his tail on the last tap of the hammer caught Rick in the face. Laughter burst from Catriona before she could stop it. Inside, she cringed at the mistake. Outside, she tensed for a slap. But Rick only laughed along with her. It was a stark reminder that not all men were like her late husband.

Rick shook his head and patted Galiha on the shoulder. "That ought to hold you 'til we get to the next outpost, lad," he said.

Relief flowed through Galiha and he mentally sighed.

Rick turned to her and offered her his hand. After only a moment's hesitation, she accepted it. Solid as a rock, he steadied her as she began to climb into the saddle. Galiha took a step back and into her, sending her sprawling backward. Mischievousness oozed from him. A solid body slowed her fall. Arms caught her and pulled her against a hard chest. They fell to the ground in an undignified heap, but Rick absorbed all the impact and provided a soft landing for her. She ended up on his lap, wrapped in his arms. The warmth of his groin against her buttocks was scorching in a wonderful way that sent heat all through her. Only inches away, his emerald eyes drew her in. This close, she realized they had lovely swirls of a darker green running through them. But that wasn't all. A desire to match her own filled them.

Heart thudding faster with each breath, she forced her gaze from his. Her good intentions backfired as her gaze snagged on his lips. Though stubble surrounded them, it couldn't hide how soft and full they looked. She forced herself to look farther down still. His tunic gaped open, revealing muscles defined by hard work. He began to lean toward her. Caught like a rabbit in a trap she didn't want to get out of, she looked back up at him. Those luscious lips came for her, and damn if she didn't lift her chin to meet him halfway.

Before their lips could meet, his body tensed, and they were suddenly moving. He lifted her in his arms as if she weighed no more than a sack of flour. As he carried her to Galiha, his head remained bowed low, his face only inches from hers. The grin tugging at his lips, and the playfulness dancing in his eyes just about drove her out of her mind. Her mouth fell open, preparing to deliver a scathing remark, but words failed her.

This time Galiha stood motionless as he lifted her onto his back. Rick tucked her foot into the stirrup, his hand lingering on her calf, sending tingles straight up to her middle. Slowly, he drew his hand away and patted the horse on the flank. He gave her a crooked smile that was lazy and content with the look of a man who knew the effect he had on a woman. She wanted to curse him for the look, but instead, her lips turned up into a smile that she had to work hard to stifle.

"Sorry about that. He never pulls stunts like that," Rick said.

His gaze held hers, and he licked his lips as if savoring an imaginary taste. Forcing herself to look to up the hill, she made a "harrumphing" sound. "If I didn't know better, I'd think you both planned it," she said. While she'd meant for it to come out with a tone of indignity, instead it sounded breathy with anticipation.

Rick wiggled his eyebrows. "If I could have trained him to do such a feat, I certainly would have had him do it sooner," he said through a grin as he climbed into the saddle.

Shaking her head, Catriona laughed. Propriety dictated that she should be angry, or at least irritated that he had taken such liberties. But her body said something altogether different. This time, as they continued their trek up the hill, they shared a long look that she didn't feel compelled to break. Rick was different from Michael in every way. Perhaps opening herself up to him, at least a little, wouldn't be such a bad thing. In fact, it was beginning to seem like it could be a very good thing.

11

Rick

California Hill, Nebraska Territory

Twilight streaked the perfect blue sky with pink and red by the time they reached the top of California Hill. Considering they hadn't crossed the river until early that evening, they'd made good time. The wide-open plateau of grasslands offered them no shelter. They wouldn't be able to stop here for the night. But he had a place in mind. If only he could actually keep his mind on it.

He couldn't stop staring at Catriona, and worse, wishing he had kissed her. She would have let him. He could tell by the way she had lifted her chin toward him and started to close her eyes. It wasn't her fae power that drew him. Some fae had the ability to beguile, it was true, but she wasn't one of them. The power that flowed through her resonated with the land and its creatures. She was an earth fae, he was sure of it. The beguiling kind were a type of mind fae, something he had encountered in

Ireland once and gave a very wide berth to.

Pink and orange light outlined her curvy silhouette and played across her hair, making it look like it was on fire. Looking at her made him ache in the most wonderful way. But he couldn't look away. He wouldn't. When looking at her, he could see a future, something he hadn't been able to do since the war. He decided, propriety be damned, he was going to kiss her, and soon.

"Where will we camp?" Catriona asked, sounding a bit worried as her gaze scanned the grasslands.

He loved that she was quick to realize the danger of camping out in the open. Such astuteness made her an easier traveling companion. But it also meant she was afraid, and that was something he had hoped to spare her.

With a lift of his chin, he indicated where the opposite side of the hill began to slope down. "Ash Hollow is just down the way. We can shelter in the trees by the water at the bottom."

Relief softened her features and smoothed the lines between her red brows. For the last hour he had desperately wanted to do that with his fingers, but his words would have to do. For now. She was MacBranain's sister-in-law, for the Tuatha's sake. And a lady of high society on top of that. And fae didn't mix with his kind. But then, fae didn't normally mix with humans either, and yet Ashlinn had married Sean.

He squeezed his horse forward, needing to get Catriona out of his direct line of sight so he could focus. Ayegi lifted his buckskin head from grazing and set off at a brisk pace. Emitting a small bark, Lincoln took off like a shot ahead of them. In only a few paces, they began the descent through a smattering of tart-scented ash trees and sweet fir. The scents put Rick at ease, reminding him of home. And after nothing but open grasslands for a while, their cover was more than welcome. The heat of the day had already dried out his boots and breeches. The spring waiting in the bottom of the hollow sounded better by the moment. Ayegi seemed to agree, keeping up a good pace despite the decline that kept him back on his haunches.

Feathery boughs and lush green leaves provided much needed shade. The relief of having the hot sunshine off his skin drew a deep sigh from Rick. As he leaned back in the saddle to balance his descending horse better, his eyes shifted to the valley below. All the favorable campsites he could see were blessedly free of other travelers. To come across people was usually rare, but it did happen, especially in the summer months. The wagons back at the river were proof enough of that. One day later and they'd be sharing the valley below with that lot for the evening. Not a bad thing if they were good people, but Rick preferred solitude. The way his body reacted to the voice of Catriona talking to her horse contradicted that thought.

She was a talker, that one, always chatting with some animal or another. More often than with him. Not for the first time, it made him wonder about the nature of her fae power—wonder, and worry. Consumed by thoughts of her, he didn't see the swish of a horse's tail poke out from behind one of the trees below until it was too late. No sooner had he seen the black tail flick than a gunshot cracked through the stillness of the valley. A great pressure collided with his chest. Air left his lungs in a forced rush and he couldn't pull it back in. The pressure registered as blinding pain a moment later. He slumped forward. His abdominal muscles refused to work through the pain to pull him back up. Head-first, he tumbled over his horse's neck and began to roll down the hill.

Had he been able to catch his breath, he would have grunted at the pain his continued tumble caused, but he couldn't even do that. Finally, his grasping hands locked around a bush with roots strong enough to stop him. The jerking halt made fresh pain shoot through his chest. He pulled in a few burning breaths, but held his tongue. With a monumental effort and pain to match, he rolled over so he could check his chest. That alarming feeling of immense pressure was one he knew all too well. He'd been shot. Dirt, grass, and a few sticks soiled his beige shirt, along with a hole, but not a speck of blood. Of course there wouldn't be. Normal bullets couldn't pierce his skin. It still hurt like a dullahan's kick to get hit by one though. That thought made him rub the bullet hole scar below his left collarbone. They weren't as bad as silver bullets, that was for certain.

He rolled back over and forced himself up onto his hands and knees. A few blinks cleared away the blackness caused by the pain in his chest. It would be gone soon enough anyway. Fingers touching the cool metal of the flask he kept in his shirt pocket, a moment of panic came over him. Swallowing hard, he drew it out and inspected it. A small dent marred its surface, but the bullet hadn't penetrated it. Relief caused the air to rush from him lungs. His gaze scanned the hill. He had tumbled so far he could no longer see Ayegi or Catriona. How he had missed the trees dotting the hill, he had no idea. The rustling pad of inhuman feet through the grass and underbrush came from his left. He looked over just in time to see the pink canine tongue reaching for the side of his face. Relief over the pup being alive dulled his fading pain.

After a quick scratch to Lincoln's brown and grey head, he held a finger to his lips. The pup cocked his head. Rick's brow furrowed into what he hoped was a stern look. Lincoln plopped down. This earned him another pat to the head. For good measure Rick held his finger to his lips again just in case and pushed the urgency of quiet to Lincoln's mind. Knowing the dangers of the trail often called for a need for silence, Rick had taught him this trick while on the train. The pup had taken to it as if it were a game.

Underbrush rustled up the hill from him. Lincoln perked to attention, nose shooting in that direction, but he didn't move. The cream coat and black mane of Ayegi flashed in and out of the trees and bushes as he made his way down the hill. Shadows and yellow grass might have hidden the horse if not for the noise he made. But seeing as he was clearly not on the creature's back, that might work to his advantage by drawing attention away from where he lay. His gaze kept scanning the hill.

He had only heard one shot, but that didn't mean much. Hearing in the heat of the moment couldn't be relied on. Even for his kind. The mind played tricks on a man in danger of his life, made him forget what he heard. The war had taught him that lesson time and again. He was fairly certain there had only been one shot. That could merely be wishful thinking, though. The last thing he wanted to consider was that Catriona may have been shot as well. The thought was unbearable. Therefore, even if there had been another shot, his mind might have blocked it out. But he couldn't smell any blood. He took comfort in that small mercy.

An angry, feminine scream tore across the hillside, proving at least that Catriona still lived. Curses followed, as did grunts and the sound of flesh hitting flesh. Several paces up the hill and to the left he saw two figures struggling. A tree blocked most of his view. Long, red hair flashed in the dying sunlight. He shoved himself to his feet and started to climb. Getting to her was all that mattered.

The shadows hid his progress up the hill well enough and the sounds of the struggle covered any sound he made. Much to his surprise, Catriona could curse like a sailor, and in Irish to boot. He would have been impressed if he wasn't so scared for her. Some ten feet away and to his left, Ayegi stood. Motioning for him to stay, Rick passed him and kept climbing. To his relief, Lincoln veered off toward the horse. Another few feet and only one tree stood between him and where he had last seen Catriona. But all was quiet.

No, not completely quiet, he realized. A masculine voice whimpered. The smell of blood made his eyes pop open wide and sent a surge of frantic energy through him.

Through the feathery boughs he spied two figures on the ground. But all was not as he had feared. Catriona straddled a man who lay on his back. In one delicate hand she clutched a massive hunting knife that she held firmly against the man's throat. The torn edges of her blouse revealed far more cleavage than the garment was designed to show. Blood dripped from a cut on her right arm. Fury clouded Rick's vision as he stepped out from behind the tree, but the man's whimpers turned to words that stopped him cold.

"Please don't kill me, please."

Catriona made a sound between a scream and a growl

before finding her words. "Why shouldn't I?"

Her words got Rick moving again. He stopped where she could clearly see him, but hopefully wouldn't perceive him to be a threat.

"Easy, there, love. No need to do anything rash," he said in as gentle a tone as he could manage with his nerves screaming at him like a banshee.

Catriona's red head lifted a little, but she didn't turn his way or remove the knife from the man's throat. The man's gaze rolled Rick's way.

"That's right. Listen to your man, there. I only attacked you because Ainsworth made me. I wanted nothing to do with traveling out into the damn uncivilized territories," the man whined.

A small trickle of blood oozed out from beneath the knife blade as Catriona leaned forward. "And did Ainsworth make you try to rape me?" she asked in a tone so calm it chilled Rick to the bone.

The man's eyes opened wide and flashed back to Rick. "Make her see reason, man, please," he begged. Those eyes opened wider when they found no mercy in him.

"I'm finding myself disinclined to do so," Rick said. In fact, he found it difficult to keep his anger under control. The only thing that stilled his hand was Catriona being in the way.

The muscle in Catriona's arm tensed and Rick realized she might really do it.

"That settles it then," she hissed through clenched teeth.

"Cat, no!" Rick took a step toward her, hands held up. "Don't. I'm all for scaring the man half to death, but you don't want to kill him, trust me."

Though she tensed at his approach, she didn't look up. "Oh, trust me, I do," she said.

"Everything changes when you a kill a man, you change. You don't want that. This blaggard isn't worth that," Rick said.

Her arm started to shake.

"Please, Cat, don't let him do this to you," Rick pressed.

Twilight glinted off a tear as it slid down her cheek. She sprung up off the man and took several steps back, knife still in hand. One of the man's hands flew up to his neck where blood flowed from a shallow cut. His wide eyes shot from Catriona to Rick, and back again. Rick moved to stand between him and Catriona.

Over his shoulder, he asked her, "Are you injured?"

"No," she said. Her voice sounded strong, defiant. It allowed him to breathe a little easier. If the man had raped her, she would sound all too different. And if that had been the case, Rick feared he would have torn his throat out without a second thought.

"What's your name?" Rick demanded of the man.

A finely tailored suit of black pulled taut over an overfed frame with a paunch that made the man look pregnant. Black hair swept back from a clean-shaven face of severe angles. To be so clean out on the trail spoke of a meticulousness that bordered on narcissistic. Grass stains and several drops of blood now marred the perfection of his black suit.

"What's it matter?" the man snapped.

Is that a touch of an English lilt to his voice? It made Rick's hand tighten splay wide, aching to grab his throat.

"It would make it harder for the lady to kill a man with a name. But if you want to continue being a mule's arse, I might be inclined to let her back at you," Rick said.

Catriona moved in close enough to Rick's back that he felt her presence even though she didn't quite touch him. Her eagerness made him regret his words. The man's eyes shot over Rick's shoulder and he licked his lips.

"Cofield," he said in a rush.

Rick sighed. "Did Ainsworth send you for me or her?" He knew the answer, but he had to ask to see if he would be honest.

The man laughed, but it was a nervous sound void of humor. "I lied. No one sent me. You have supplies and a woman. I saw an opportunity and took it, is all."

While it was a plausible story—and a crime committed by all too many all too readily in these parts—the way his eyes kept flitting off to the left told Rick it was a lie. He had expected as much. But he didn't need to hear the truth. He already knew it. He could smell it.

"You're lying all right. Take your boots and suit off," Rick commanded.

The man's eyes shot open wide as he pushed himself up to a seated position. Rick drew his pistol and pointed it at his head and he froze, hand up before him. "Easy there, big mick, I ain't reaching for nothing," Cofield said.

"Watch your mouth, there's a lady present. Now do as I said and take your boots and suit off," Rick said, letting the cold fury searing through him fill his eyes. Though he didn't need the pistol to take the man out, he knew he'd respond better to it than verbal threats. And if it could prevent further violence, it would be worth it.

Adam's apple bobbing, the man nodded and removed his

boots.

"Where is his rifle?" Rick asked Catriona.

"In the bushes over there somewhere," Catriona said.

"Be a good lass and fetch it for me, would you please? Don't want him getting any ideas and trying to go for it," Rick said.

Footsteps moved away from him and started down the hill.

"What do you plan to do to me?" Cofield hissed.

"Better than you deserve. Now hurry it up before I change my mind."

Buttons popped free in Cofield's haste to remove the jacket he wore. He all but flung his boots off and tore his fine linen button-up shirt from his breeches. When it came to his breeches, he stopped.

"Those too," Rick instructed.

"Come on, man, have a spot of decency," Cofield complained.

Rick's eyes narrowed. "Says the wanker who shot me and attacked a woman because he thought her defenseless. Now shut up and strip. Everything off but your underclothes."

The man began to protest. Rick growled and lashed out, jabbing him in the nose with the fist of his non-dominant hand. Bones cracked and blood spurted as Cofield's head snapped back.

Oops. Too hard.

With no more than a whimper, the man did as instructed. Cowering in his long, white, cotton undershirt and pants, he tried to cover himself as best he could.

"Now, I suggest you start walking before the lady finds

your rifle and decides to shoot you with it," Rick said.

The man's eyes darted about. "You mean to send me off without a horse or clothes? I'll die of exposure!"

"'Tis a better death than you deserve."

Soft padded feet sounded behind Rick and to his left. A canine growl rumbled from that direction, the barest hint of a juvenile sound to it. Lincoln stepped up alongside Rick. Pup though he may be, he still stood taller than most dogs and outweighed any coyote Rick had ever seen. His light brown eyes, usually so filled with mirth, had turned crimson and glowed ever so slightly. Otherworldly power flowed from him. The white around Cofield's eyes grew as he beheld the pup.

"Run, and don't stop or he will catch up with you," Rick warned.

Lincoln's growl grew deeper, more menacing. He knew what Rick had said and understood the part he needed to play. Lips pulled up from his long canine teeth and pink gums. A squeak escaped Cofield. He turned and scrambled up the hill, legs pumping. A few barks from Lincoln made him scramble all the faster. When Lincoln went to give chase, a look and a motion from Rick stopped him in his tracks. The pup's head cocked and he eyed the fleeing man eagerly.

With a point of his finger, Rick commanded Lincoln to stay. The pup's ears drooped. If he caught him, which Rick had no doubt he would, the man would be doomed. As much as he despised the man, such an end would be difficult to ignore the supernatural nature of. Admitting to Catriona that he knew what Lincoln was right now wasn't something he was ready for.

Cofield had just disappeared into the trees when Rick heard Catriona approaching.

"You should have let me kill him. Now we have to worry about him at our backs for the rest of the trip," she said in a breathless voice that held a cold edge.

He turned to look at her, expecting fear-filled eyes but instead finding only her lovely brow furrowed with anger. Without a thought toward propriety, he holstered his gun and reached for the one in her hand. For a moment she held onto it, staring down at it, then finally handed it to him.

"If not him, it would have been another. This man he works for, Ainsworth, if he didn't get a telegram from Cofield when he reached the next outpost, he would merely send another man. And the bastard has men in nearly every territory between California and New York working for him," Rick said.

Those angry eyes shot to his. "But you don't really think Cofield will just give up, do you?" she asked.

"Perhaps. Maybe we scared him off. In which case he'll leave us be and let Ainsworth think he's still on our trail. If that happens, we're better off."

"If," she huffed.

"Better Cofield than a more capable man." The flicker of fury across her features stirred his back to life. "Don't misunderstand. I am not belittling the fact that you bested him. That was nothing less than brilliant. And if you hadn't, I would have torn him apart for daring to lay a hand on you."

"Well," she huffed. "I did have the matter in hand."

Laughter rolled from his lips, surprising him. "That you certainly did."

He flipped the cylinder release, popped it open with a flick of his wrist, and emptied the bullets from it. The army-issued Remington was a bit of a beast with a seven-inch barrel.

But it was a capable revolver to be sure, with its percussion caps and .44 caliber stopping power. He sent up a silent prayer to the Tuatha that Cofield had no idea what he was and had therefore loaded normal rounds.

"You've been shot! Rick, you've been shot!" Catriona exclaimed as she lunged toward him.

Her hands traveled all over him, groping him in a manner that wasn't at all unpleasant, despite the pain it caused. In all good conscience he knew he should speak up right away. He tried to tell himself that her actions merely stunned him for a moment. But deep down he knew better. He liked her hands on him, a lot.

"I...uh...I'm fine," he finally stuttered. "It was low powder, poorly loaded. It didn't even penetrate the skin, bounced off me flask." It was a half-truth, at least.

Face scrunching up in a look of confusion, her fingers found his flask and removed it from his pocket. She turned it over, feeling the divot left by the bullet.

"An Irishman saved by his whiskey, who'd have guessed," she said. The slight note of cheer in her tone lifted the darkness that had settled over them just a touch.

He decided to correct only half of what she said. "This flask hasn't held whiskey since me da died. 'Twas his."

She placed it back in his pocket with care. "Well, we're going to have to fix that hole in your shirt so you don't lose your good luck charm," she all but whispered.

This new softness in her voice scared him, made him think she might be close to breaking down. But not a touch of moisture shone in her green eyes. The fading light could have had a little to do with concealing such a thing, but he didn't think that was the case. From the way she squared her shoulders and stood tall and straight, he had a feeling she had shed the only tear she would over this incident. The blood trickling down her arm drew his attention.

A small but deep cut marred her left biceps. Grabbing his canteen from his waist and tearing a sleeve off his shirt, he set to cleaning the wound. She took the ministrations without a single complaint or so much as a flinch. In fact, she relaxed beneath his gentle hands and almost seemed to be soothed by his touch.

"A stitch or two wouldn't hurt, but I think if you keep this clean and covered you'll be all right. You aren't hurt anywhere else, are you?" Rick asked, trying to be as subtle as possible.

From the state of her clothes it was clear Cofield hadn't succeeded in raping her. The very thought threatened to send him into a rage that would reveal his true nature to her in a startling way. He tamped it down with fervor.

She stiffened and withdrew from him. "A few bruises is all. I'll be fine. Don't you think it best to fetch the horses and get moving? Seems like it would be a good idea to put some distance between us and this place before nightfall," she said.

It hadn't been the plan, of course, but they had little choice now. To stay here would be to invite trouble. While Rick didn't think Cofield would chance another attack now that they were on the defensive, he wasn't going to risk it.

"Aye. We should find Cofield's horse, too, take it with us so it doesn't wander back to him," he said.

With a thrust of her head, Catriona indicated three horses just down the hill from them. "Seems your gelding has already found her."

Fetching the horses proved easy. They came right up to Catriona. As they were tying Cofield's white mare to Rick's packhorse, Catriona's big paint came wandering up to see what all the fuss was about. More pain than he cared to admit throbbed throughout his chest as he climbed into the saddle. But it wasn't from the impact of the bullet. The distant, almost hollow look in Catriona's eyes made him curious about her past, and made him ache for her.

Over the last week he had learned she wasn't a woman who was easily rankled. She had bested Cofield, yet the incident had shaken her to her core. Something from her past must have been dredged up by the confrontation. Though curiosity ate at him, Rick knew by her cold eyes that now wasn't the time to ask.

12

Catriona

Day Nine
Chimney Rock, Nebraska Territory

For days they pushed on hard across the plains of knee-high green grass that bordered the Platte River. Well, she pushed and Rick tolerated her desire to keep moving. They didn't talk much after the incident. She didn't know what to say or how to say it. So they just rode. They covered a lot of ground even with the little white mare in tow. She turned out to be a halfway decent packhorse despite her small stature.

After an entire day of staring at the approaching spire of Chimney Rock, Catriona could hold her silence no more. For one, the damn thing was starting to unnerve her. The closer they traveled to it the farther away it seemed to get. But mostly, she began to feel guilty about giving Rick the cold shoulder. He had been so kind and understanding. But that wasn't what she wanted. She wanted the man who attacked her dead so he couldn't try to hurt her again. It was horrible of her, she knew, but she couldn't help it. He'd noticed her communicate silently with Lincoln in a way normal people couldn't. Men like him considered her kind witches, burned them at the stake, hanged them, drowned them, sometimes raping them before and after.

Two days of thinking on the matter finally made her realize Rick had been right. If she had killed the man another would have followed. And part of her wouldn't have been able to forgive herself for taking a life. As they finally rode into the shadow of the massive hill topped with a spire much like a needle, she found the words she needed to say.

"Thank you for stopping me from doing something I would have regretted deeply."

Rick started and sat up straighter, as if he'd been half asleep in the saddle. The brim of his hat lifted enough that she could see the green of his eyes. "You stopped yourself. I only provided the clarity you needed to make your decision," he said.

She squirmed. The next words did not want to come out, but she forced them. "I'm not a violent person by nature, I assure you." They weren't the words she had meant to say, exactly, but she found she had to work up to it. "In fact, I abhor violence."

"I never doubted your gentle nature," Rick said softly.

Catriona took a deep breath in an attempt to bolster her confidence. "I do, every day. You see…" She had to swallow to get the lump in her throat to go down before she could go on. "My husband was a heavy-handed man. It was more than just a man putting his wife in her place. I had to learn to be invisible, and when that failed, to defend myself." The rest wouldn't come out. It was too much, too hard. And parts of it she couldn't say. Like the time they'd gone for a ride in the countryside and she'd laughed at what she thought was a joke he'd made. How he had yanked her off her horse and beat her so badly he would have killed her if she hadn't asked her horse to kick him. Or the time she'd stood up for the cook who burned dinner and he had slapped her, and slapped her, and wouldn't stop until she called birds in through the open window to swarm him. And how he had locked her inside, forbidding any animals in the house, not even his own hound Scáth because he favored her over him.

A low sound like a growl rumbled from Rick. It caused Lincoln to perk up from where he had wandered off into the grass. "The bastard. Putting a wife in her place is a poor excuse for a weak man trying to make himself feel stronger," Rick said.

He wasn't wrong. Michael had been weak, both as a man, and as a fae. For some reason the women in his family had been born with the lion's share of the power.

The brim of Rick's hat dipped a bit and his eyes disappeared from sight. "Me apologies, I mean no disrespect to the dead. Me da taught me to never raise a hand to a woman who wasn't trying to kill me. I believe all men should teach their sons such things," he went on.

His words soothed her soul in a way she never imagined possible. And yet… "That's an interesting take on the lesson," she murmured without thinking about it.

For a moment his eyes went wide with something like fear. "Well, um, me da was an interesting person. Not bad mind you, just…different. Our family was…different." He cleared his throat. "Regardless, me point is, 'tis wrong what your late husband did."

To keep him from seeing her tears, she cast her gaze up to the magnificent spire thrusting from the hill like a lone tower. Never had she heard a man speak so openly about such things. And never had she imagined that one would hold such beliefs.

"Michael led me to believe all men disciplined their wives," she said. It made her feel profoundly ashamed to admit such a thing. But it was too late to take the words back.

Rick shook his head. "He deceived you. None of the good men I've ever known in me life have held such beliefs. Women are the bearers and nurturers of the seeds of life. They are sacred and should be treated as such. Surely your kind agree." At the last, his eyes widened again and he looked down and away swiftly.

Prickles of alarm danced across her. "My kind?"

One corner of his mouth quirking up, he shot her a dazzling smile. "High society, o' course."

A sigh of relief eased from her. Of course that had been what he meant. For a few moments the only sound was the soft steps of the horses' hooves moving through the grass. "That's a beautiful way to think of women. And yes, many of my…kind, believe that," Catriona finally said.

The scruff of Rick's beard moved into a semblance of a smile. "Me da's words, but I believe them through and through."

"I think I would have liked your da."

The smile he gave her lit up his face. "He would have liked you, for sure," he said. The joy faded slowly and his eyes shifted to the rock. "Me deepest apologies," he said.

"Whatever for?"

"For misunderstanding you. You don't like to be called Mrs. O'Brian because you don't like *being* Mrs. O'Brian, I'm guessing."

Unable to speak, she just nodded. Part of her wanted to tell him the whole story. She tried, but fear paralyzed her lips. Only two other people knew the entire story and not because she'd chosen to tell them, but because they'd been there. Not that she'd have it any other way. They were the two people closest to her in the world.

"True enough. I'm not ashamed of the name. 'Tis a good name, to be sure. Ashlinn is proof of that. I'm ashamed that I was Michael's wife." That much was easy enough to say. The rest she had to steel herself for. "All the ladies envy me, hate me, for marrying the finest catch in all of New York. Their opinion of him, not mine, though I certainly believed it at first."

As she spoke, her gaze traveled the massive rock formation to their right, seeking strength in its crags and crevices. Her words stilled when she saw something move up on a distant outcropping. A mountain goat, perhaps? No. Mountain goats weren't that big. Hidden half in the shadows of the rocky hill, a painted horse of white and brown stared down at her. But it wasn't just painted by nature. This horse had a black circle drawn around its left eye and stripes down its neck. On its bare back sat a man with long, black braids of hair draped over a naked chest. Halfway up the hill as he was, she couldn't make out much more, but she was relatively certain the things thrusting up from his head were massive feathers. They were too far away for her to pick up any feel of the horse's energy or thoughts.

"Indian," she croaked in a hoarse whisper.

"I know. Don't look at him, just keep riding as if you didn't notice," Rick said in a low voice.

Her heart pounded as though leaping from a starting gate. She tilted her head so the brim of her hat hid the man from her sight. Placid as ever, Rick's big buckskin meandered closer as if on his own volition. But she knew better. The tension in Rick's legs and back gave it away. Ayegi crossed behind Galiha and moved up between her and the hill. Rick's eyes traveled over her in a calculating manner that wasn't at all pleasant.

"Stay sharp, be ready with that pistol just in case," he said.

"Why?" she asked, hating the high pitch her voice took on.

"Just in case he attacks, we're in his territory, after all. But with that in mind, don't be trigger happy either," Rick said.

She did as he said, her hand straying to the pistol she wasn't at all sure she'd use. The fact he'd warned her not to be too quick to shoot eased her mind some. Responding to the tension in her body, Galiha perked his head up, ears going forward, and increased his pace to a brisk walk.

Danger? he questioned with both his mind and actions.

In return she sent him thoughts of uncertainty along with confidence and assurance she would protect him. He snorted, amused by this, but calmed nonetheless.

She didn't slow him. If anything, she wanted to urge him faster, but she resisted. Beside her, Ayegi matched the pace.

"Do you think that's why he's here? To keep an eye on

us?" she asked.

Rick's chest rose and fell with a massive sigh. "Aye. This was his land before we came." The sadness in his tone made her curious about his past beyond the war.

She needed the distraction to keep her from losing it and urging Galiha into an all-out gallop. "You sound like a man who knows," she said softly.

"We're driving them out just the same as the English have been trying to drive our kind out of our land for centuries," he said.

A sudden pang of sympathy for the Native Americans tore through her, leaving guilt in its wake. Tears stung her eyes. "Oh Tuatha, that's awful. I never thought of it that way."

"Aye, 'tis. But don't go getting too sympathetic. Can't have you hesitating if we have to fight them," he warned.

"Them?" she croaked.

"I've seen three. They only want us to think there is one."

On instinct, her gaze shot to the hill before she could stop it. The one she had seen was gone. Using the small brim of her hat to hide her face, she did her best to scour the hillside. Her hand strayed to the pistol at her waist. Could she really use it? Cofield's attack flashed in her memory. Delicate fingers wrapped around the walnut handgrip.

"Bet the lasses wouldn't scoff at me now for wearing breeches. This is a tale I will most certainly have to tell them. In fact, I think I should write to them and warn them to do the same, else—"

"Shhh," Rick interrupted.

Her hand strayed away from the pistol. She straightened a bit, eyes narrowing as they turned on him. "Why? I was whispering."

Rick's eyes narrowed right back at her. "Even the softest sound carries out here. And ready that pistol."

Making a sound between a groan and a growl, she put her hand back on her weapon. She literally had to bite her lower lip to keep from arguing. All manner of terrible outcomes began to play through her mind. Her heart beat faster and faster until her breath sped and sweat began to trickle between her shoulder blades. In response, Galiha's hide twitched beneath her. They rode in silence until they reached the edge of the shadow cast by Chimney Rock. The tension in Rick's body eased and his shoulders dropped. His eyes looked out over the fields beyond the rock where dozens of dark shapes moved. They were not horses. She could hold her tongue no longer.

Steering Galiha as close to Ayegi as she could get without running into him, she leaned over and whispered as quiet as she could, "What is it?"

"Bison," he said through a grin.

Her skin prickled as she recalled their last encounter with a herd of bison. "And this is good how?" She really hoped he didn't have a similar plan in mind. It would take every ounce of courage she had to ride into another herd of those things. And a good dollop of stupidity. Her power could only do so much.

The expression of relief on Rick's face as he turned to look at her made her worry. "Because, the Cheyenne are here to hunt them, not us," he said.

The tails of six horses whipping in the wind as they galloped out after the bison herd confirmed his words. Seeing the distant grasslands swallow them brought a relief so powerful that she shuddered.

"We're in the clear. Best not to tempt fate, though. Feel like racing a bit?" Rick asked.

She grinned back. Heels down to get deeper in the saddle, Cat took up her reins and squeezed Galiha with both legs. At the same time, she sent him and the white pack horse feelings of playfulness along with a thought; *let's run.* The lazy gelding transformed. His hind legs launched them into a gallop that had her grabbing for her hat. From somewhere behind her, Lincoln let out an excited bark. A moment later, Ayegi galloped up alongside her, his black mane flipping up in the wind he created. Rick let out joyous laughter. Green eyes flashing with excitement, he wiggled his dark brows at her. She rose to the bait and raced alongside him. The wind felt amazing after a long, hot day in the sun, and the rhythm of the paint galloping beneath her brought a soothing familiarity. The stress of the last few days slid away with the wind.

A chance look in Rick's direction at the wrong time brought it all scorching back. Tension pinched deep lines into the corners of his eyes and between his brows. From beneath the brim of his hat, he watched the retreating Native Americans. One hand clutched the reins, the other lay on the butt of his pistol. Contrary to his words, he clearly didn't believe they were safe just yet.

13

Rick

Day Twelve

After a sleepless night of listening to the ululating songs of the braves' hunting party, Rick woke Catriona at the first hint of light and pushed them on. He couldn't help it. The sounds had instilled in him an almost desperate fear of attack. Visions of old battlefields danced behind his eyelids each time he so much as blinked, making each sigh of the wind and groan of the trees prickle across his nerves. Worse than that, was the fact he didn't want to raise arms against these people. This was their land and he was an uninvited, unwelcome guest.

Though no native songs filled the next night, he couldn't bring himself to build a fire or sleep then, either. The risk still felt too great. Between the natives and Ainsworth possibly sending another man if Cofield didn't check in via telegram, they didn't dare slow down. On the third day they rode late into the evening until the only thing he could see of Catriona was the shine of the fading light on her dark red hair and the white patches on her paint horse.

Finally, when she looked ready to fall from the saddle, he chose a suitable enough site between a few large boulders that would give them a defensible position. The horses dropped their heads to graze on the tall grass the moment he and Catriona dismounted.

He patted his horse on the neck as he removed his saddle. "Apologies for asking so much of you, Ayegi," he said to him.

One hand in the middle of her back, Catriona stretched until things popped. "Ayegi, I do love the exotic sound of that name. Will you tell me about the natives you got him from?"

His eyes locked onto the curve of Catriona's backside as she bent to set her saddle on the ground. The way the breeches clung to her made him like them on her more and more. He knew the ploy well. She was trying to get him to talk, as she had been for the last several days. All manner of topics had poured from her as they rode across what remained of the Nebraska territory: the weather in California, what type of grass grew best in what soil, which animals were native to the area, how to best fertilize, and on and on. He hadn't minded. She had a pleasant voice that was high enough to be feminine, yet deep enough to be pleasing to the ears in a way that was almost sensual.

She loved to talk, for sure, but he knew it was more than that. Silence made her nervous. He could tell by how tense she became when things were at their stillest. Always, her eyes scanned the horizon, and always she pushed on to the limits of her endurance. It pained him to see her afraid. He wished he hadn't told her about Ainsworth's men using telegrams to give him updates. But it was better to have her afraid than careless. Intelligent as she was, she would have figured it out eventually anyway.

As they worked together to string up a line between two trees, he gladly focused on his knot tying. He took his time removing Ayegi's gear. Once they tied all the horses to the line, though, he had no excuse not to look at her.

She took her cap off and shook out her long, red waves. Golden rays of receding sunlight made her hair look like coals about to burst into flames. "Please, do tell me about them."

It took him a moment to remember what she had asked. Those eyes, that smile, they would not be denied. She deserved the chance for a distraction. He told her of the natives' love for horses, how they often even brought them into their tents when the weather was bad. Eyes widening, she grinned like a lass before diving into a slew of questions. To keep that look on her face, he indulged her, telling her about everything from the women's clothing, to the men's headdresses. She squeezed every detail he could recall out of him with question after question. Once he could recall no more, she began chatting about everything she'd ever read on natives.

While she talked, they set up camp together. The routine had become second nature, hardly requiring words between them. Which was good considering he couldn't get a word in. But that was all right. Her lovely voice soothed him, and right now he'd take all the soothing his raw nerves could get. Anxiety over the possibility of being followed plagued him as much as it did her, maybe more. Darkness fell as he coaxed the flames of a fire to life. He hadn't wanted to start one, but the braves were days away and they needed to cook the rabbit he'd caught on the trail today. He wouldn't have done it, but their stores were running dangerously low due to how often they left the trail to shake any possible followers.

After they finished their meal, Catriona sat staring at him from across the fire. He stared right back. With a view like that, how could he not? The way she cocked her head to the side and stroked her chin made him smile. She held his stare with a boldness that stirred his blood. Yellow flames crackled against the wood between them, softening her face with a lovely glow. Were it not for the slobbering and occasional crunch of Lincoln gnawing on a bone at his feet, the mood would have been quite romantic. Of course that made him extra grateful for the pup.

Normally he could hold out indefinitely, but something about this woman made him intensely curious. "Out with it. What are you thinking?" he said.

She looked down and away, hiding her expression behind a curtain of red hair. "I shouldn't pry."

The prickling sensation traveling up his back told him he should have let it drop. But it was too late now. The sad tone of her voice pulled him in. "If you don't ask, I'll be subjected to that look for the next four weeks," he said through a sigh.

Her eyes narrowed and brows pinched together, but the curiosity didn't leave her face.

"Aye, that's the one. Ask away," he said.

A smile flitted across her lips and the beginnings of a blush colored her cheeks. Both faded all too quickly as she met his gaze full on. "Did you meet my husband, before he deserted, I mean?"

Pain raked across her face at the last words, but she held his gaze. Such strength floored him. Shaking his head, he broke eye contact for her, using the excuse of throwing another stick on the fire. "No. There were many battalions within the 69th regiment, and he wasn't in mine."

Silence heavy as a wool blanket fell between them. Even Lincoln paused in his chewing, cocked head pointed in Catriona's direction. She looked down and didn't look back up. The pup dropped his bone, trotted over, and plopped down across her feet. The barest sniffle sounded as she scratched between Lincoln's ears.

"You shouldn't feel ashamed. The man was responsible for his own actions. His shame shouldn't be yours. Society has it all wrong in that aspect, in many aspects, truly," he said.

She swiped at her eyes before looking at him. It had grown too dark to read her expression.

"Thank you," she said. After a moment, she went on. "Most of the time I'm angry at him for deserting his fellow soldiers, his country. Other times I imagine how it must have been and a part of me understands. Countryman fighting countryman, brothers fighting brothers in some cases, or so I heard. It had to be terribly hard."

He could only nod in answer. Her eyes weighed heavy on him but he stared at the flames, unable to look at her. The words stirred up the images of bloody battlefield after bloody battlefield. A long moment of silence stretched between them before he could get words out of his constricting throat. "It was so much worse than anyone can imagine."

Catriona scooted close enough to reach over and touch his arm. The almost otherworldly warmth of her fingers served as an anchor that drew him back to the present. Her gentle eyes regarded him with so much concern that it sent a pang of longing through his heart.

"My deepest apologies. I didn't mean to bring up painful memories," she said.

Trapped by the allure of her eyes, he couldn't look away or hide the raw emotion broiling in his own. For a moment, he couldn't tell if his pain reflected in her eyes or if it was her own. It didn't matter either way. He had caused it either by bringing up something that hurt her to remember, or by causing her to sympathize with him.

"No worries, 'tisn't your fault. The memories are always there, waiting for me every time I close my eyes," he said.

She took his hand. The small, delicate feel of her made an almost overwhelming protectiveness sweep him. His fingers closed around hers.

The contact gave him the strength to go on. "Sometimes they consume me. A shout, the crack of a gun, or the sight of blood can bring the memories back so strongly that it feels as if I'm living them again."

Her free hand stroked his arm, and she nodded. "I've been through a trauma of my own. Nothing compared to yours, o' course. I found when I'm trapped in the memories reciting the different types of birds or horses helps bring me out of it."

His brows rose at the possibilities. When the flashes came he had always been at their mercy. He'd never thought about anything being able to pull him back out of them.

Catriona shook her head and looked down. "I'm sorry, 'twas foolish to mention."

She tried to pull her hand away but he held fast to it.

"Not at all. I think that's a brilliant idea."

A small smile pulled at the corners of her lips. "In that case, was there anything during the war that brought you comfort?" she asked.

His free hand touched the harmonica in his pocket. "Aye, music."

"Next time it happens try to think of a song, or the sound of an instrument playing. Maybe it will help," she said.

"I will, thank you," he said, giving the last two words the weight they deserved.

He couldn't tell her the episodes made it so hard to think that such a thing seemed nearly impossible. He couldn't explain that they plunged him so deep into the memory that he was literally reliving it. But most of all, he couldn't admit that they sometimes happened while he was awake. If he did, she would most certainly think him insane. Besides, maybe her advice would help. Maybe he'd be able to think through the next episode. It certainly couldn't hurt to try.

Hand still in his, she lay her head on his chest and relaxed beside him, her body deliciously close to his. "You're welcome," she said through a yawn.

Though his eyes flew open wide and his breath caught, he did everything in his power to stay relaxed. Good sense and memories of what had happened the last time he'd let himself get this close to someone told him to pull away. His heart told him not to. The more he grew to know her and not just her social standing and secret race, the more he wanted to draw her closer. The turmoil ate him alive from the inside out. Her soft, rhythmic breaths soothed him and soon had him nodding off for the first time in two days.

14

Day Thirteen

Rick's soft groaning from the depths of heavy sleep stirred Catriona awake. Stretching the stiffness out of her limbs, she sat up. The hours she had spent in that position made her entire body ache. But she didn't mind at all. Above them, the stars faded against the coming light of predawn. Rick groaned again and rolled over. Before he even settled into position, he rolled onto his back. His chest rose and fell at a rapid pace. Behind closed lids covered in sweat, his eyes rolled left, right, and back again. A few words were audible between his groans.

"No…Sean…watch out…"

Chills climbed across her skin, banishing the comfortable warmth where his body had lain against hers. This had to be one of the nightmares he'd spoken of. She couldn't even imagine the horrors he had endured and might be seeing again in his dreams. The moment she thought it, she discovered how very wrong she was. Her imagination turned out to be far more powerful than she had given it credit for. It was no wonder he hadn't slept in so long. She couldn't let him relive such a horrible experience. Whispering his name, she reached for his shoulder.

Her fingers worked like the spark to a powder keg. At the barest touch, Rick exploded toward her. He flew to his feet, arms swinging. A cry burst from her as one of his hands connected with the left side of her face. Rather than knock her aside, he grabbed her by the neck and shoulder. Closed lids still hid his rapidly moving eyes. His hand gripped her throat tighter. His eye teeth and the set directly behind him had extended into fangs. Power rolled off him the likes of which she had never felt before. It was overwhelming, animalistic. Oddly, impossibly, she had a sudden flash of his thoughts. But it was more than that. It was as if she was inside his mind, seeing what he saw.

Standing waist deep in a river, he fought with a man in a confederate uniform. Behind them a town burned. Rick swiped at the man, but with claws, not a fist—long, curved claws that grew out from where his fingernails should have been. The man swiped back with claws of his own, baring fangs at him. Rick ducked easily. As he did, he slashed at the man's stomach. Blood sprayed. With a hiss, the man stumbled back. One more strike and Rick would have him. But the man drew a pistol. The crack of gunfire filled the air. Pain exploded into Rick's shoulder.

"Rick! Wake up…Rick…" The last word came out as no more than a croak.

His eyes didn't open.

Using a technique Ashlinn had taught her, she spun away

from him and thrust her arm out against his, breaking his hold on her neck. Nails scratched her flesh as she broke free. No, not nails, claws. Suddenly, Lincoln bounded to her side. Head bobbing from one of them to the other, he seemed confused as to whom to bark at. He knew, Linc knew Rick was something other than human, and he didn't care. It made her feel minutely better, but still. Ash puffed up around her as Catriona stepped back into the cold campfire.

This time, she tried screaming into his mind like she would an animal out of control. *Rick, wake up!*

Arms going to his sides, he swayed. Slowly, his eyes opened, blinking as though trying to clear something away. Several more moments passed before the fog of sleep began to lift from them. His fangs and claws disappeared. The logical side of her tried to make her wonder if she had even seen them in the first place. But she knew better. Logic didn't always apply to her world. *What are you?* she wondered. Unexpectedly, the thought didn't bring fear. When he'd been in the grip of his dream, with some sort of animalistic side at the surface, she had felt a kinship with him, an understanding she only felt with animals and fae beings.

"Cat…what…where?"

Lincoln stopped barking. Hair stood up along his back as he cocked his head at Rick. The motion drew Rick's gaze slowly, as if it took a lot of effort. The nightmare must have had him completely in its grip to leave him this disoriented. That knowledge quenched a little more of the fear that threatened to finish the job of choking her. Rick's eyes widened as they worked their way back to her.

"Oh no," he whispered.

She tried to will herself to stop shaking, to force her fists open, but she couldn't. He took a step toward her, hand reaching out, and she flinched. It wasn't that he was something more than human. She'd met a lot of supernatural beings in her life. It was more basic than that, a trauma of her own leftover from a bad marriage. The pain and shame that flashed over his face made her feel terrible on more than one level. The shame was something new. All the times Michael had hit her, he'd never once been ashamed. And the bastard had been wide awake and usually sober. She didn't know how to take Rick's shame.

"What did I do?" Rick asked in a voice thick with mounting tears.

The sound of his pain chipped at the wall that had erupted around her heart. But her fear—the fear of being struck, however unreasonable she knew it was in his case—kept her from going to him. Hell, it made her want to turn and run.

"I...um..." She couldn't finish because no words would come to her.

He moved a step closer, and it took every ounce of control she had not to bolt. Her entire body shook with the effort. Tears stung her wide eyes. She blinked rapidly to try to dry them so they wouldn't fall. Showing weakness had always gotten her beaten worse in the past. But it was more than that, this time, with this man. She was fairly certain he hadn't done this on purpose, and she didn't want him to feel bad if he hadn't. If. Even from what she knew of Rick, that doubt remained. Because there seemed to be plenty she didn't know about him.

His hand reached toward her neck, stopping short. "Oh

no, you're bleeding. You're bleeding," the last words were no more than a garbled sob.

Letting out a pain-filled cry, he sank to his knees and dropped his head into his hands. His shoulders shook with silent sobs. For several moments, she stood watching him weep in the predawn light. Soon, Lincoln trotted over to him and licked at his hands. He leaned his head toward the pup a little. The weeping broke a hole through Catriona's wall. Seeing him like this was too much. He had been through too much.

She went to him and smoothed his hair. After a few strokes, her hand stopped shaking. He rose up on his knees and she moved into him, cradling his head against her stomach. His arms wrapped around her waist. Their gentle, hesitant pressure eased the anxiety that tried to stir to life within her.

"I didn't mean to. I swear it, I would never raise a hand to a woman or anyone who wasn't trying to hurt me," he said against her stomach.

She made shushing noises. "I know. You aren't that kind of man. 'Tis just the war trying to keep you in its grasp. But you're here now, you're with me. Everything is going to be all right."

Not a single sound issued from him as his body shook with sobs. Were it not for the movement, she would have thought he'd stopped. The way he hid his pain reminded her of how she had hidden her own. From the muscles rippling in his arms to the width of his broad shoulders, he seemed a pillar of strength that nothing should be able to shake. Yet here he was, as shaken as she'd ever been on her worst day. And she had undergone some truly bad days. Letting out one soft whine, Lincoln licked at both of their arms.

She swallowed her fear and forced her body to stop shaking. Deep breaths helped. It was a skill she had become adept at over the years with Michael. But this wasn't Michael. Rick hadn't hurt her knowingly or willingly. His mournful, horrified sobs made that clear. The sound of them filled her with the instinct to protect him, odd as that was. When her hand grew steady enough, she began to stroke his hair back from his forehead. Her other hand snaked around his shoulders and cradled him gently to her. Rick relaxed against her more with each stroke of her hand. She held him close until the sobs that racked his body finally stopped.

15

Rick

Day Fourteen
Wyoming Territory

The Wyoming territory stretched out before them in seemingly endless plains. The slate gray sky hung so heavy above that it almost felt like he could reach up and touch it. Moisture made the air thick, heavy, and almost difficult to breathe. In the distance a darker layer topped the clouds and sheets of rain fell across the plains. A strong wind blew the sweet scent of wet grass to him.

"How bad do you think the storm is?" Catriona asked.

Concern wrinkled her brow beneath her little bowler hat, which wasn't going to keep her dry. He should have insisted she purchase a brimmed leather hat like his before they left. But, at the time he'd wanted to teach her a lesson. Now…

"Bad," he admitted, eyes on the darker clouds.

Was that a flash of light he saw in the distance, or just the sun trying to break through the clouds? Tuatha, he hoped it wasn't a flash. It might be a boon, though. Yesterday, he had thought he'd seen a rider on the horizon behind them. While it could have been just another traveler, it wasn't likely. Travelers were few and far between lately, especially lone riders. He couldn't help but wonder if it had been Cofield. Or even another man. Ainsworth would get impatient if he didn't hear from the man. The bastard had men all across the territories and states protecting the goods he shipped across America. It was only a matter of time before he sent another who was close to the area he'd last heard from Cofield.

If only that were their only problem at the moment.

Cat turned and began to dig in her saddlebags. Clinging with only her legs, she did so as the horse continued to walk. And damn if she didn't do it with ease. Only a few of the clients out of New York whom he'd escorted could ride as well as she did. But then, she was fae, one who's power seemed to be tied to animals. He felt it this morning when she'd awoken him, a connection, almost as if she had been there in the last moments of the nightmare with him. But that was impossible. Wasn't it?

And he could have sworn his claws and fangs had been out when he'd awoken. But she didn't act as though she'd seen them. Or if she had, she wasn't mentioning it. She continued to surprise him at every turn. After her tenderness this morning, he found he didn't hate that about her after all. He'd only hated it because each new surprise endeared her more to him. Now, he thought maybe that wasn't such a terrible thing.

From her bags she removed a bundle of sturdy, dark blue

cloth, tucked it under one arm, and stuffed her hat into her bags. She closed and tied the flaps with a double slipknot. Turning back around, she shook out the bundle of cloth—which turned out to be a hooded cloak, of all things—and fastened it around herself. She pulled the hood on and did up the buttons about her neck and shoulders to keep it in place. A slight blush painted her cheeks when she found him watching her.

"What?" she asked.

"Nothing, 'tis just that you look a bit like you walked out of Tír na nÓg." He couldn't hide the smile that tried to break through.

Her eyes widened and she swallowed hard, but she covered the reaction with a shrug and flip of her red hair. "Smirk all you want. It might be out of fashion, but 'tis of good canvas that will keep me dry." The playfulness in her voice was somewhat forced.

At least she sounded a bit like her spunky old self again. Since the incident this morning she'd been quiet and withdrawn. A veiled hesitance akin to fear hid in her eyes now and that crushed him. Had she seen his fangs and claws after all? If so, she might think him a dullahan—dark fae creature— of some sort. It wouldn't be too far from the truth. Or was it the fact he had choked her in his sleep addled state? Either would be reason enough.

Smiling, he did his best to feign a light-heartedness he didn't feel. "Aye, it looks as though it will at that. Does that mean you want to keep going?"

She lifted her chin. "O' course. We can't lose half a day's travel because of a little rain. Besides, 'tis nothing but open fields to the horizon. No sense stopping where we don't have cover. Time is of the essence, after all. I will not be denied that land."

"True enough," he agreed, trying not to sound too relieved.

The one eye he could see behind her hood glared at him. She placed a hand on her hip. "Then what is that smirk for?"

The light tone made him smirk all the more. "You amaze me is all," he said. He held up his hands in mock surrender. "And I mean that in a good way."

Giving him a slight nod, she picked up the reins and squeezed Galiha into a trot. "Good," she called back. Fanlike tail of gray and white wagging in the air, Lincoln trotted after her.

If his heart wasn't still so heavy, he would have laughed out loud. All he could manage was a smile, but it was a happy one. Lincoln came running back, hopped a circle around him, barked, and bounded after Cat once again.

"All right, all right."

He squeezed Ayegi into a trot and caught up. As he looked over his shoulder a distant shape caught his attention. Toward the horizon, barely visible, he could make out the outline of three figures on horseback. At this distance it was hard to tell who, even what, they were. The lack of a wagon didn't bode well. Those who didn't travel with a wagon were in a hurry for one reason or another, or weren't settlers. Either way it could mean trouble. He kept them half a day's travel east of the main trail, so there shouldn't have been anyone out here. Not wanting to worry Catriona, he kept it to himself. With nothing but open plains as far as the eye could see, it did them no good to worry just yet. That didn't stop him from turning now and then to subtly check on the figures.

They remained there, no closer, no farther away.

Rain doused him as they entered a literal sheet of it that turned everything dark as twilight. One step they had been dry, the next they rode in a torrential downpour. The horses hung their heads, tucked their noses in, and trudged on. Thankfully, enough grass covered the land here that it wouldn't easily turn to mud. Over the next hill, though, it was hard to say. No canyons or hollows lay ahead so flash flooding wouldn't be an issue. But if they had to veer off course, they'd have to be careful. As they trotted on, Rick went over what he knew of the area, plotting out alternative routes just in case.

The grin Cat cast his way as she guided Galiha closer was tight and tense as the horse that pranced beneath her. His own gelding was also a bundle of coiled energy. Nervous horses made for a very bad sign. As if to solidify his concerns, the darkening skies above swallowed their shadows, leaving them in a hazy near-dark.

Cat cupped a hand over her mouth and leaned in his direction. "Wyoming weather isn't exactly welcoming," she said in a voice that shook with nerves.

"Not always," he said, raising his voice so she'd hear over the roaring patter of rain.

His gaze flicked back in the direction he had seen the riders. They now rode close enough he could make out feathers thrusting from their hair and could tell they rode bareback. It looked like Wyoming might hold more than bad weather for them.

"Shite," he murmured to himself. To Cat, he said, "Wouldn't hurt to canter them a bit, get closer to the trees faster."

A rumble of thunder shook the ground and cut off his last words. Ayegi's black mane arched, and he stomped as if in agreement. Forgoing any words of comfort the gelding wouldn't hear over the pounding rain anyway, he patted his neck instead. With the barest squeeze of his legs Ayegi leapt into a canter, head thrust straight out into the building wind. Cat kept pace easily enough. The big paint could really move when he was properly motivated. And now that his pack horse's burden was lightened by the addition of Cofield's horse, both of them easily kept up.

After only a half mile or so they had to slow for the little mare they had taken from Cofield. Being tethered to Cat's gelding, which was much slower, helped her, but not enough. The poor thing's sides heaved with each breath. The rain had plastered her dark brown coat to her, revealing how underweight and out of shape she was. At the next trading post he'd have to sell her. Unfortunately, she was nowhere near the shape for a trek like this as his own packhorse was. It was no wonder they'd been able to keep ahead of the man for so long. Cat kept looking back at the mare, calling out an encouraging word now and then, but the horse wouldn't speed up.

The size of raindrops grew so big a single one covered nearly half of the back of his hand. Their collision with everything earthbound became a cacophony of pattering. Another boom of thunder added a little speed to the mare's pace. The world brightened for a brief moment just as Rick looked back over his shoulder. Through the curtains of rain the three figures rode not more than a hundred yards away now. Thunder rumbled again, shaking not only the ground, but the very air around them. As he looked back at Cat, a streak of lightning zagged down through the sky not far behind her. Her eyes went wide.

Grass flew as the horses dug in and barreled forth into a canter. Rick chanced another look behind them. Their followers had gained enough ground that he could make them out despite the heavy gloom cast by the clouds. Three braves in hunting gear rode astride sure-footed appaloosas speckled with black spots. And they were gaining fast. A sinking sensation gripped him along with a certainty that the natives weren't just running from the storm in the same direction. Whether it was the horses they were after or just a chance to kill two people they saw as threats to their land and families, it didn't matter. Nor did his sympathy for them when it came to surviving. He needed to distract them to keep Cat safe. If he could do so without harming them, he would. Even if it meant showing them what he was.

Thunder boomed overhead again. Lightning crackled across the clouds, not quite breaking through, but skirting their underbelly. The storm would hopefully help in what he had planned. He veered Ayegi as close to Cat as he could without risking clipping Galiha's heels.

"Head northeast, find the trail. Meet me at the fort!" he yelled over the building noise of the storm.

Her eyes shot open so wide he saw more white than green. The near panic on her face pinched at his heart. She shook her head so violently the hood of her cloak fell back. He motioned with his head behind them. She turned to look and went white as a banshee. While she wasn't looking he willed one of his fingernails into a claw and sliced clean through the rope that tethered the white mare to Galiha.

"I'm going to lead them away. Take Lincoln. Don't look back and don't stop for anything," he yelled.

The way her brows pinched together made him fear she would argue. She sat up a little straighter, letting Galiha slow his pace. Just when he began to fear he'd have to slap the paint on the rump and hope she could stay on his back, she nodded. She leaned back in the saddle, slapped the horn, and called to Lincoln. The fleeing pup looked to him.

"Lincoln, up!" Rick commanded as he pointed at Cat.

Barely missing a step, Lincoln veered toward Cat and leapt in midstride. Heavy as he was, he knocked Cat back. For a breathless moment, Rick feared she might topple from the saddle. Somehow the woman maintained her balance and managed to grab hold of the massive pup. She gave him such a long, pointed look as they loped along that he started to reach out to smack Galiha on the rump. Right before he could, she leaned forward and squeezed the horse into an all-out gallop. They took off like a shot. Only heartbeats later they faded into the gray haze of pouring rain.

With a thought, he let his fangs extend and willed his fingernails into wickedly curved claws. He slowed Ayegi to a lope and steeled his heart for what he'd have to do. No matter the cost, he wouldn't allow them to get Cat.

16

Cat

Day Fifteen

With the thunder pounding overhead and lightning crackling all around—even touching the nearby hills—Cat couldn't have slowed Galiha down if she had wanted to. And she didn't want to, at least not a first. She knew the natives might kill her if they caught her, or worse. Ever since noticing them following she'd tried to reach out to their horses and encourage them to stay away. It worked, but only as far as her mind could reach, which wasn't far enough.

It tormented her to leave Rick to confront the danger alone, but clearly there was more to him than met the eye. She hoped, prayed to the Tuatha, that whatever it was would be enough to keep him alive. As much as she wanted to turn back and help, Galiha ran like the whole Cherokee nation was on his heels. Trying to stop him would be like trying to stop a train.

How long they fled into the gray miasma of rain, she had

no idea. She only knew the rhythm of the horse beneath her and the warmth of the massive pup she clutched to her chest. He was bloody heavy. Thankfully, her saddle was a bit big, allowing him to squeeze mostly between her and the horn, which helped hold him in place. It made her very grateful for the odd Spanish style. Every now and then she glanced back, hoping to catch sight of Rick on their heels. But he wasn't there.

Running calmed Galiha, quieting his mind until scarcely any fear remained. It had to be his normally mellow demeanor. Most of her horses would hang onto their panic like a shield for as long as they could. Being bred and raised as hunters and jumpers, they tended to be temperamental.

Lincoln didn't share Galiha's calm. He raged inside. But it was his nature to protect. More than that, his kind were bred for battle—not the Irish Wolfhound he so resembled, but the true fae creature he was. It took all her willpower and a fair amount of mindspeak coaxing to get him to stay on the saddle.

On the other hand, the white mare who did her best to keep up remained terrified no matter how much she tried to sooth her. But considering how slow she was, that wasn't entirely a bad thing. It kept her moving. Severed lead rope hanging, she plodded along at a lope that made Galiha's look fast. Rick must have cut the rope when she wasn't looking.

Three successive bangs in the distance made Cat flinch. They sounded like gunfire, but with the crackle of lightning, boom of thunder, and roar of the rain, she couldn't be sure. Galiha slowed to a trot after what felt like forever.

New herd member can't keep running, he thought.

A glance back showed her several paces back. Head hung

in exhaustion but eyes still wide with fear, she plodded along at a trot. *Don't worry. We won't leave you,* Cat told her with mindspeak. She felt more than heard her let out a loud snorting breath of relief. In a few strides, she nearly caught up. Hoping to see Rick, Cat peered behind the mare, but the rain swallowed anything more than thirty feet away.

She couldn't leave him to fight and possibly die for her. She just couldn't. Besides, the mare needed to rest. Shifting her weight back, she sent a thought to Galiha. *Slow down. We need to rejoin our other herd members.* He dropped to a fast trot. Her stomach sank as she realized she didn't know which way to turn to go back to Rick. The endless gray may as well have been the black of night. As if in answer to her prayers, the haze began to lift and the rain grew lighter. The noise of the storm swallowed the sob of relief that tore from her. Muscles tensed in preparation to give Galiha the cue to turn, she froze.

The clouds above her swirled in a vortex. She stared at them transfixed, horrified.

The stories of such storms were the things of nightmares. What had the papers called the phenomenon? Oh yes, a funnel cloud. Terror resonated through her. Staring at the base of a forming tornado, she could only hang onto her Galiha. The wind shifted and the big paint squealed and reared. His front legs kicked out as if trying to attack the storm itself. When he came back down and his feet hit the ground, he launched like a cannonball. In only two strides he left the little mare behind.

Run, little mare, run. Do your best. We will find you later, Cat told her. Though it tore at her to leave the mare behind, it was that or quite possibly die. Apart they both had a chance of surviving. She had to let that comfort her for now.

Free of his burden, Galiha shot forward at a reckless pace. Part of Cat feared she should slow him down. One misstep and they'd all tumble to do the ground. At this pace such a fall would likely be fatal to them all. But they were still beneath the forming funnel and the wind already tugged at her so hard she had to cling to Galiha with all her strength. She wanted to look back and check on the mare, but she couldn't. The wind had become so strong she couldn't even turn her head. Each breath she pulled in, the wind tried to steal back.

Lincoln wiggled in her arms. His mind screamed, raging against a foe he could not fight. *Easy, boy. Be still. We have to outrun it. Trust me and Galiha*, she soothed. Nuzzling his head into her armpit, he did as he was told.

They ran and ran and ran. Soon the wind eased along with the rain. Tree-covered hills stretched in the near distance. She chanced a look behind them. The mare was nowhere to be seen in the gray soup of rain and clouds. Overhead, the base of the massive funnel cloud extended out toward the horizon for easily a hundred feet or more. A darker gray core lay in its center, drawn upward like a cone. Rain flowed backward up into the cone, along with grass, leaves, and even small bushes. The sight held Cat in thrall until the wooded hills engulfed her.

Even the thickest of trunks swayed and bent in the wind, providing moving targets as they fled past them. Sides heaving, Galiha soon slowed to a fast trot through the near-dark of the forest. Cat kept him at that pace for some time. Not only did she want to continue to put distance between her and the storm, letting him slow too quickly would be bad for him. Once the forest grew too thick for easy passage, she slowed him to a fast walk. The teardrop leaves of aspens torn from their branches blew about almost as thick as the rain. Small twigs and forest debris smacked her now and then, but the size and frequency decreased with each step.

After what felt like a lifetime, the frantic swaying of the branches eased. Rain pattered down steady but gentle in comparison to only moments ago. The distant drum of thunder and the metallic taste in the air kept her from relaxing. She sucked in a deep breath, grateful to be able to do so again. Clutching the shivering pup tighter, she guided Galiha deeper into the forest. Rick's words played over and over in her mind. She kept moving as he had instructed her. It would do no good to make it out of the storm only to have the natives catch up to her. She rode until the storm faded and the sky darkened with nothing more menacing than the coming of night. Not knowing where Rick or the natives were, night itself was menacing enough.

Once she could no longer see through the trees, she let Lincoln down and dismounted. Her shaking legs barely kept her upright. With the pup literally underfoot—as much as a three-foot-tall canine could fit underfoot—she walked Galiha. Hand out before her, she felt her way through the trees. Hours later it seemed, a slip down a blessedly short hill into a small hollow finally forced her to stop. The danger of going on was too great in the thick darkness. She hunkered down in the hollow with Lincoln, covering the two of them with her cloak. Galiha stood over them, mind quiet as he succumbed to exhaustion and slept. Wide eyes staring out at the dark, she went through each and every member of the Seely court she could recall the names of, begging them to watch over Rick.

The rustle of light steps in the forest duff nearby snapped Cat's eyes open. The forest all but glowed with the soft, pastels colors of early dawn. Yellow aspen leaves appeared translucent in the illumination of small beams that broke through the branches here and there. Birds filled the still morning with their sweet tunes. But the calm didn't fool her. Something had awoken her.

Breath held, she listened hard as she looked around. Her gelding's white, brown, and black coat made him blend into the aspen and fir trees so well she had to look twice to find him. Head still drooped in slumber, Galiha stood not ten feet away like a massive equine sentinel. The rustling came again, closer, and a little louder this time. But only a little, as if whatever—or whoever—made the sound was attempting to be stealthy. Hands over her heart to try to stifle its pounding, she held her breath. Lincoln popped up from her side, eyes wide, slightly flopped over ears as perked as they could get. *Protect*, his thoughts insisted. Before she could think to grab hold of him, he shot away from her.

She stifled the impulse to call after him. If someone was out there, she couldn't risk them hearing her. One or more of the natives might have escaped the storm. And there was always the threat of Cofield being out there somewhere. That thought lingered in the back of her mind every waking moment. She understood and respected Rick's insistence that she not kill the man, but if she had she wouldn't have felt the need to constantly look over her shoulder.

Just when she thought about drawing her pistol, she felt a

simple, harmless mind touch hers. At the top of their little hollow a small, gray form scurried at Lincoln's approach.

A long, deep breath eased from Cat. "A rabbit," she murmured with a shake of her head. It had been just far enough away she hadn't felt it's mind before Lincoln herded it her way. Stretching out stiff muscles, she rose slowly. Yesterday's wind had blown rain into every crack and crevice it could find in her cloak, soaking her quite effectively. A night spent on the ground hadn't helped matters. Already the morning air was warm enough that she wouldn't consider herself cold, exactly. Miserable, most certainly, but not cold. The blue sky peeking through the branches overhead promised it would get warmer. Perhaps she'd dry out if she got moving. After a long moment of listening, she rose and went to her still saddled horse. One of Galiha's eyes opened and rolled her way as she dug around in the saddlebags. She pulled out her canteen and a bit of hard tack for a makeshift breakfast. It was tasteless, but that hardly mattered. She wouldn't have tasted even a full breakfast of bacon, eggs, and potatoes. Her mind was far too distracted.

She wondered if Rick had escaped the natives, or the storm, for that matter. Where was he now? He could be lost, hurt, or worse. The thought of anything bad happening to him squeezed her heart until she swore it would stop beating. She had left things on such a bad note with him that she felt awful. If she had any idea which way to go, she would have tried to find him. But that would only get her lost. He could be anywhere.

Unable to finish her meager breakfast, she leaned her head on the saddlebag. The movement awoke Galiha enough that he started munching on the grass at his feet. At least the horse had the good sense to eat when he could. Her shaking hands stroked his neck and mane. She felt bad leaving him saddled all night, but she had wanted to be able to ride away quickly if needed. And she'd already lost too much to risk having to leave behind her saddle and saddlebags. The thought made her throat constrict.

Lincoln bounded over the hill and down into their hollow, tail wagging with abandon, tongue hanging out the side of his mouth. The pup made her think of Rick all the more. Cat sniffed and blinked back the tears that threatened to spill. She scratched the tall pup behind the ears.

"No rabbit for breakfast, then? Well, here."

She offered him the hardtack she had left and shook her head as he ate it. Lips pulled back, eyes squinting, he chewed and chewed. *Tasteless, not good. But it pleases Alpha if I eat it,* he thought. A short laugh bubbled from her, surprising them both.

"Well I didn't say 'twas good." The very thought of being an alpha to a creature such as him seemed absurd to her. But then, he was only a pup. It would be some time yet before he reached his full capabilities.

Rising, she pulled the small compass Rick had given her out of her pocket. After a bit of turning this way and that, she nodded and climbed into the saddle. Galiha's head lifted. Her hand came to rest on the butt of her pistol. From this height she could see out of the little hollow to the quiet forest beyond. Green and yellow leaves along with small branches littering the forest floor were the only signs of yesterday's chaos. The peaceful morning seemed somehow wrong after last night's storm. But no sign of anyone else existed. A long breath eased from her.

Ears perked, Lincoln looked up at her. *Ride with Alpha?*

"Oh no, I've had enough of that for a bit. You'll be walking today," she told him.

A slight tug on the reins lifted Galiha's head. Looking out over his long, black mane, she twisted the compass this way and that until she found north. From there she gave the direction of northeast her best guess and guided Galiha from the hollow. She once again held her breath as they crested the top of the hill. Nothing more menacing than sun-drenched downed branches and tall, half-naked trees awaited in all directions. Breathing a little easier, she started into the forest. Lincoln bounded out a few feet ahead. The pup tried to look every which way at once, nearly landing on his rear a few times. After several moments of this his ears and tail drooped.

Male alpha isn't here. His inner voice sounded so disappointed it tugged at her heart.

"I know, boy. But he's going to meet up with us," Cat said in a soft voice. Her eyes scanned the trees for natives. Yes, that was why she kept quiet. It wasn't because the doubt and fear she felt might be detectable in a louder voice. She wouldn't allow herself to believe that was why. To do so would be admitting she thought Rick might not meet them at the fort. Admitting that wouldn't allow her to keep going.

Each time Galiha's hooves came down on a branch and sent a resounding "crack" through the forest, she flinched. Keeping a close eye on the compass, she did her best to travel in the direction she knew the next station lay. She soon gave up putting the thing back in her pocket. She strung it on a leather tie strip from her saddle and hung it around her neck. Hours ticked by. Or at least, she thought they did according to the movement of the sun. Things of that nature had never really been her strong suit. But she knew for certain when high noon arrived. The sun on top of her head was hard to mistake for any other time. It beat down on her, roasting her within her cloak. She didn't want to stop to take it off, or even to rest or eat. Rick was out there on his way to the next station. He could already be there, waiting, worrying about her. Getting there, to him, was all that mattered.

A mournful whining from several paces back gave her no choice but to stop. No more than a slight shift back of her weight stopped Galiha. Pressure from one foot turned him the direction they had come. As she often did, she marveled at his training—and the man who had trained him. Urgency shot through her at the thought, but she fought it down. Lincoln lay ten paces or so back, prone on the ground, head resting on his paws. Despondency filled his mind.

"Not the only thing that matters, I suppose," she muttered as she dismounted. She would rest, for his sake, and Galiha's.

As Galiha lowered his head to graze on the spots of green grass growing here and there, she dug in the saddlebags. Pulling out hardtack and her canteen, she sat down on a fallen log next to the horse. Warm water that tasted of creek loam and rocks slid down her throat, not quenching her thirst so much as satisfying it. She held the cracker in her hand as if considering it. Lincoln rose slowly to his feet and trotted over to her. He plopped down on his haunches in front of her as if the small trip had taken every bit of energy he had left. Both his mind and eyes screamed of his sadness and worry for Rick.

She handed him the cracker. "I know how you feel," she

said, petting his head as he worked at eating the chewy thing. More than that, she knew the pup had the ability to slip between realms, allowing him to travel to other locations in this realm in a blink. If the desire struck him powerfully enough, he could go searching for Rick in that manner.

"Thank you for staying with me," she told him aloud as she continued to stroke his head.

When finished with the cracker, he licked his lips—and half the side of his muzzle—and perked his ears up.

"Sorry, boy. That's all we can spare for now. I don't know how far the fort is—or when we'll find it," she told him.

She might have to hunt. It wasn't something she enjoyed, but she could do it if she had to. Sighing deep as only a pup can, Lincoln curled around her feet as much as his body would allow and promptly fell asleep. His thick, wavy hair fluffed up through her fingers as she petted him. The motion soothed her almost as much as him, lulling her into a weary state. Heat radiated off him. The poor thing. She had been pushing them far too hard for as hot as it was.

The thought reminded her of her cloak. She undid the buttons and removed it. The cool breeze wafting through the forest swept away the heat that had begun to stifle her without her knowing it. It lifted like a weight. Long locks of red that had come free from her braid blew back. She took another long drink of water and offered some to Lincoln. He raised his head enough to lap at it. If they were going to make it, she would have to take better care of all of them. Careful not to disturb the pup, she rose, strapped her cloak to her saddle, and poured water into a cup for Galiha. The horse managed to get his lips in the cup and suck the water from it. At any other time such a sight would have made her laugh.

Her gaze scanned the woods as she contemplated how long to let them rest. Every sigh of the wind, creak of a branch, rustle of a leaf, or strange call of a bird drew her attention. The streets of New York and even the small farm she'd grown up on were so very different from this place. Without Rick here she felt vulnerable, exposed, and she hated it. She hated that she needed him here to make her feel comfortable. But mostly, she hated that she *wanted* him here with her. After Michael died, she had vowed never to need a man again. Yet here she was...

The loud crack of a large branch breaking yanked her from her thoughts. Birds cried out and took to the skies in a flurry of dark wings. Cat spun toward the noise, fumbling for her pistol. For a terrifying moment that thrust her heart up into her throat, she couldn't figure out how to free the weapon. By accident really, she pushed back the leather guard that lay over the hammer and drew it. Twice her shaking thumb tried to pull the hammer back and failed. Giving up on that method, she used the entire palm of her left hand to pull it back. The resounding click made her acutely aware that she may actually have to fire at someone.

It would have been simpler to ask the forest animals to help her, but she refused to endanger them.

Another cracking branch pulled her wide eyes to the right. A huge, dark shape moved in the trees. Lincoln popped up. The gray and black hair along his back stood on end and a low growl that made him sound much older than his few months rumbled from him. The pistol barrel shook before Cat as her left index finger moved toward the trigger. Around the edges of her vision things began to go dark. Oddly, it helped bring the shape into focus.

So tired. So scared. Must find herd. The mournful thoughts echoed in her mind and squeezed her heart. The thing pushed through the underbrush, revealing an equine head. Cat's finger began to twitch against the trigger as she looked to the horse's back. The fear she detected from the horse could mean many things. The trigger flexed slightly beneath her finger pad. Two more steps and a little white mare emerged, without a rider—the very one she'd been using as a packhorse. The makeshift packs hung half off her left side, the leather scuffed and torn in places, but intact. Breath releasing from her in a loud rush, Cat moved her finger away from the trigger and lowered the pistol. The mare jumped a bit at the sound of the exhale, but held her ground.

It took a few tries, but Cat finally eased the hammer down and holstered the pistol. Murmuring soothing words, she approached the mare. The horse shied away at first, but let Cat get a hold of her rope without too much fuss.

Inside, the poor creature's mind filled with relief.

"'Tis all right now, girl," she soothed.

Aside from a few scrapes and scratches on her legs and rump, she appeared well enough. Cat adjusted the skewed pack. Only a few items of clothing and maybe a cooking pot seemed to be missing.

A wave of hope big enough to sweep her away surged through her.

Since the mare had survived, maybe Rick had as well. She held tight to that hope and refused to think further on it. Too much thought would introduce doubt and she wasn't going down that road. The man was more than he seemed, of that she had no doubt. Odds were that 'more' had helped him survive. Refreshed to the point of near-bursting with energy, she tied the mare to Galiha and mounted up. With Lincoln bounding along a few steps ahead, they set out once again.

The compass soon led her out of the forest. She hesitated at the tree line, scanning the open fields of green before her. Yellow and purple wildflowers dotted the gently rolling hills. Nowhere among them could she see any people. Breathing easier, she started out into the open. While no people meant no natives, it also meant no Rick. At the top of the first rise she beheld a sight that brought tears to her eyes. Wagon wheel ruts cut a path through the low part of the valley. The short grass between them indicated they were well used.

She let out a little whoop of triumph. Lincoln barked and hopped through the tall grass to her and the horses' sides. She grinned down at the pup. "We found it, lad, we found the trail!" More tears of relief came with the words.

An overzealous squeeze of her legs moved Galiha into a trot. She wanted to urge him into a canter but she didn't dare, not with the little mare tagging along. Besides, they could maintain a trot much longer than they could a canter. It encouraged her to remember those were Rick's words. Settling in for the bouncy ride, she did her best to contain her excitement. Rick could be down this trail. Rick *would* be down this trail.

Hill after hill passed as the sun made its way to the horizon. She eventually slowed the horses to a walk. The lack of any people soon became discouraging. How far down this trail could the fort be?

By early evening, her tidal wave of hope withdrew and

doubt began to creep into its place. Off to her left and slightly behind her, the horizon began to take on a pink hue as the sun grew closer to it. If she were lucky, she had an hour before it set completely. Being stuck out in the open would be far too dangerous. She urged the horses back into a trot. The mare slowed them down more than she was comfortable with, but she didn't want to leave her behind, especially after touching her mind and feeling her fear of that very thing.

No worries, we will not leave you behind, she spoke in her mind, assuring her. The relief that surged through the poor thing relaxed her enough that she actually increased her speed some.

In the distance Cat began to see a shape that resembled a rock formation. Something like Chimney Rock, only flatter, perhaps? She didn't recall reading or hearing about any such thing on the eastern side of Wyoming. But she was discovering that a lot of what she'd read about the California Trail wasn't true. The closer she grew, the more the shape revealed itself. It wasn't a rock formation at all, but a building. A very large one. Suspicion almost caused her to slow the horses. Then she realized what the place was.

"Fort Laramie. By all the Tuatha, Lincoln, that's Fort Laramie!" she cried.

Lincoln gave a little "woof" as if in agreement and kept trotting along a few paces ahead of them.

They reached the gates of the fort just before the sun dipped below the horizon. Ten-foot-high walls of great pine logs ending in sharp spikes rose up before her. Pungent scents of people and animals cramped together mingled with aromas of roasting meat and bread. In this case, she would happily take the bad with the good if it meant hot food. The two uniformed men standing before the open gates nodded to her as she approached. When she grew close enough to see their faces, they removed their caps in a hurried manner. The one with salt and pepper hair approached her.

"Ma'am, are you in distress?" he asked.

Lincoln sauntered up and sniffed him. The man drew back, eyes widening. She could hardly blame him. Despite being only a pup, he came easily to the man's hip. Even a seasoned soldier would be wise to be wary of such a large dog. If he knew what Lincoln truly was, he would have run for the hills.

She saw the chevrons on the man's shoulder marking him as a corporal. "No, Corporal, thank you. I'm quite all right now that I've made it here. I was separated from my escort during the storm. The fort is open to travelers I do hope," she said.

He nodded. "O' course, ma'am. All are welcome. There's trading and lodging to be had within."

She smiled at him, doing her best to hide her relief. "Thank you. If you can direct me toward the lodging, I would be most grateful. And has a man left word about a woman coming to meet him, I wonder?"

The soldier shook his head, and her heart plunged. She did her best not to let it crush her into a thousand pieces. Just because Rick wasn't here yet didn't mean he wouldn't be soon. The soldier went on to tell her all about the boarding place while trying to casually step away from Lincoln. The pup followed him step for evasive step, clearly enjoying the game.

"Lincoln, come," she commanded. She gave the corporal a smile and nodded. "Thank you once again. And if a man by the name of Rick Fergusson asks after me, would you please let him know where I'm lodged?"

The man nodded deep enough for it to be considered a bow, then put his hat back on. "Will do, ma'am."

Knowing Rick wasn't here, each step Galiha took inside the gates dragged her deeper into a well of misery. She wanted to turn the horses around and gallop out to find him. Being under the guard of the army while he was still out there felt terribly wrong. The safety of the walled fort embraced her into its shadow. And she didn't want it. She had thought maybe she wanted Rick back by her side because of the sense of safety he represented. Now she realized, she couldn't have been more wrong.

17

Rick

Day Fifteen

Rick dropped the reins—guiding Ayegi with only his legs—and let his claws extend as he charged toward the natives. As he had left Cat, he'd released his packhorse, but the faithful fellow still followed along behind. Rick's resistance to violence melted away in the rush of survival. Letting these men get to Cat wasn't an option. While he felt for their plight, he couldn't risk them catching Cat and harming or enslaving her.

But fighting natives wasn't anything like fighting the confederates. There was a good chance he could show them what he was and appeal to their superstitious side. It had worked in the past.

Letting his power build, knowing it made his eyes glow in the darkness of the storm, he let out a ferocious growl. The spotted horse to his right squealed as it skidded to a halt. It reared up, front legs pawing at the air, eyes wide and filled with terror. The half-naked native tumbled from his horse, which promptly shot off to the left. Gaping, the man crab crawled backwards as fast as he could.

The man to Rick's left hollered out a war cry and raised a tomahawk with a blade as black as night. Obsidian. It wouldn't even break his skin. Still, he couldn't risk his horse getting hurt. A press of Rick's legs and Ayegi veered away from the man. This put them in the path of a third man. Moments too late, Rick realized the third man had a bow aimed at him. He threw himself as far to the left as he could while remaining in the saddle. Something punched him in the left arm, right between the muscles. His fingers jerked and he dropped the reins. An arrow fletched with the two-toned feathers of a golden eagle stuck out of his arm. The arrowhead had to be silver. Ignoring it, he swiped at the man with his right hand as they rode past, raking fingernails that had transformed into claws across his abdomen.

Only feet away, the man with the tomahawk launched himself at Rick. That he could do so not only from the back of a galloping horse, but also collide so accurately with Rick was a marvel. But Rick had little time to appreciate his enemy's battle tactics. He blocked the tomahawk swing and tumbled from Ayegi's back. Pain seared into his left arm again as the arrow broke off. He and the native crashed to the ground and rolled, ending up in a heap of tangled limbs. He wrestled the tomahawk from the man's grip.

The man ended up on top of him by sheer luck of the tumble. As he went for Rick's throat, Rick slammed the flat side of the tomahawk against the man's face. A lift and thrust of his hips sent the native flying. Half conscious, he groaned as he rolled to a stop a few feet away. Blood seeped from a small cut amidst the white face paint streaked across the left side of his face. The wound wasn't fatal by a long shot. Rick breathed a bit easier.

For good measure, he snarled at the man, making sure he got a good look at his fangs and claws. After a gasp, the man said something rapidly in his native language and began scampering backwards.

Rick rolled to his knees and tried to stand. The vibrating ground proved too difficult to find footing on.

"What the..." The raging storm swallowed his words and his breath right along with them.

Only two things he had ever encountered made the ground vibrate. Seeing how there were no trains this far west, that only left one thing. He scrambled to his feet and stumbled past the groaning native. Almost as an afterthought, he picked up the native's tomahawk, shoving it into his belt. Better there than ending up thrown at his back. Heavy rain painted the world gray, obscuring anything over twenty feet away. Neither Cat nor the natives' horses were anywhere to be seen. The clouds above him swirled in a massive circle that was picking up not only speed, but grass and dirt as well. He started running in the opposite direction of the storm-born monster.

From out of the gloom to his left emerged Ayegi, running in his direction. Rick turned and ran in the same direction as the horse. At the last moment, he veered to the side. When Ayegi came alongside him, the horse slowed. Rick grabbed the saddle horn and vaulted up onto Ayegi without missing a step. The horse ran for all he was worth, legs pumping, straight into the gloom. He couldn't see more than a few paces in front of them.

Reckless as it was to run blind, not running from the building tornado could be a death sentence—even for one such as him. He trusted his horse's instincts and let him do the steering.

Shapes soon emerged from the gloom—trees. They swayed and gyrated like fifty-foot-tall men in the throes of a wild dance. Going into a place with so much possible debris flying around would be a risk, but they had no choice. At least, he didn't, because there was no stopping Ayegi at this point. One wrong decision and they'd be dead. Rick decided he'd leave the big decisions up to the horse.

They cantered all out into the forest. The amount of leaves and branches flying about forced him to hunker down and squint. He did his best to simply be a responsive rider so he wouldn't pull Ayegi off balance. The horse leapt, dodged, and skidded about, avoiding trees and flying debris. They ran so hard and so long that he started to worry about Ayegi overexerting himself. The wind eventually started to die down. The amount of leaves and branches whisking through the air decreased. Rick reached for the reins.

Too late, he caught sight of a large white barked branch as it flew at him. It collided hard with the side of his head. The last thing he saw before being plunged into darkness was the ground approaching at high speed.

Head throbbing with a powerful vengeance, Rick groaned as he clawed his way back to consciousness. The pain made him want to stay in that darkness, but he couldn't. Cat was out there somewhere. He had to get to her. Ayegi, Lincoln, Galiha… Any one of them might need him. He had to wake up. Never in his life had he had such a headache, not even after an entire bottle of good Irish whiskey. He lifted his head from the blanket of yellow and green leaves. A blow of pain so sudden and forceful struck him that for a moment he thought he was being attacked. But further movement revealed that it was the movement itself causing the pain.

Bright sunlight bathed the battered forest around him. It assaulted his eyes with each agonizing blink. He forced himself to a sitting position. The sharp ache in his left arm was dull in comparison to the continuous throbbing in his head, but it served to remind him of the arrow. Two inches or so of an oak shaft stuck out of the side of his arm. In the mass of dried blood he couldn't see the arrowhead, but he most certainly felt it. Gritting his teeth, he wiggled it to get a sense of the shape. The resulting jabs of pain told him it lacked barbs on its backside.

"Thank the Tuatha for small favors," he mumbled, the last word developing into a muffled yell as he yanked the arrow out.

The wound started to bleed, but that was a good thing, for now. It needed to be flushed and bleeding was a good start. Gently, he probed at his head with his fingers. A large bump had risen on the right side, but his hair seemed free of blood.

"I take it back. Thank the Tuatha for large favors."

Satisfied he would live, he patted himself to get a feel for what sort of resources he had left. His pistol nestled in his slightly askew holster, eight bullets remained in the slots along his belt, and the native's tomahawk was still tucked through the left side of the belt. Weapons but no food wasn't necessarily a bad thing. Water was another matter, especially since his mouth felt as parched as Nevada. He would need to find water soon.

But, to do that, he would need to get on his feet. A tree standing not two feet away would help in that matter.

The crunching of branches to his right had him reaching for his pistol instead of the tree. He turned in that direction, pistol thrusting out, thumb pulling the hammer back. Ayegi's long, dun-colored face lay not two feet away from the barrel of his pistol. The horse chewed a mouthful of grass as he watched him with mild interest in his big brown eyes.

He lowered the pistol. "For the love of Goddess Áine, horse, you scared me half to death. But 'tis good to see you."

Ayegi took a few steps closer and sniffed at his head. Rick reached up and scratched the horse's chin, gently moving him away at the same time. "It hurts bad enough. I don't need you bumping it. It'll heal in no time."

He holstered the pistol and grabbed hold of Ayegi's bridle. "Up," he told him.

Ayegi lifted his head, easily pulling Rick to his feet. The world swayed beneath him, threatening to drop away, and his head throbbed like it might explode. For it not to have healed completely, he must have been hit extremely hard. Rapid healing was one of the perks of his kind, but even he couldn't immediately heal bad wounds, especially those created by silver. With that thought, his arm ached. He leaned on Ayegi until the wave of pain passed as much as it was going to. Hanging onto the bridle with one hand, he took a few tentative steps. The world swam far more than he was comfortable with. Murmuring words of praise to his horse, he leaned heavily on him as he worked his way back to his saddlebags. Much to his relief, nothing more than a few scrapes marred Ayegi's hide.

From his battered saddlebags, he removed his extra

canteen of water and a large green bottle. He took a longer drink than he should have from the canteen. The powerful thirst made him wonder how long he'd been out. Legs apart, knees bent, he tore the sleeve from his shirt. He braced himself with a few deep breaths that only served to make his headache worse. Focusing on his head, he opened the canteen and poured it over his arm. Pain seared into the wound, but not nearly as bad as he'd expected. To the best of his ability, he cleaned the blood and forest debris away and probed the wound to get it clean as possible. That part hurt a bit more. He put the cap on the canteen and put it back in the saddlebag.

The green bottle shook in his unsteady hand as he uncorked it. He stuck the cork in his pocket because he knew he'd drop it. The acrid odor of the tincture within wafted up and attacked his nostrils. Nose wrinkling in disgust, he turned his head away. Only two other times had he been subjected to this awful stuff, but the nurse who administered it the first time had sworn by it. If that nurse hadn't been Ashlinn—his best friend's wife and Cat's sister-in-law—he wouldn't be doing this right now.

What had she called the stuff? Oh, yes, iodine.

Having stalled all he could, he poured the tincture over his wound sparingly. Fire erupted in the wound as though he had dumped molten metal in it. A cry of pain pushed against his clenched teeth and pursed lips. The damnable stuff foamed in a most unnatural seeming way. It must have gotten shaken up in the commotion. Ashlinn had sworn it was purely science, but the stuff felt more like dark magic. Considering both that the stuff had been reserved for officers in the war, and that Ashlinn's patients had the highest rate of survival, it was worth the pain. He poured a bit more on for good measure before he could lose his nerve. For all he knew, it was magic. Ashlinn's fae ability was healing after all. Which was why he subjected himself to it even though his healing was nothing short of supernatural.

Finished torturing himself, he put the bottle back in his saddlebags and withdrew a clean bit of cloth that he kept for just such an emergency. Normally healing wasn't something he had to worry about much, considering silver was one of the few things that could really hurt him. But he had made this trip often enough to know that some of the natives in the area used silver in their arrowheads. They had things in their own culture that required silver to defeat, and they had figured out he was similar enough to them. Each trip he made became more and more dangerous. It was definitely time to stop.

As best he could with one hand, he wrapped the cloth around his wounded arm and tied it off. Taking hold of Ayegi's reins, he began looking for something to help him mount. Just swinging up into the saddle wasn't an option. Thanks to the insistent head wound he'd most assuredly end up on his backside. A half-downed tree nearby looked like it would do the trick.

With one hand on Ayegi's shoulder for support, he led him over to the tree. Ever so slowly, he stepped up onto the downed tree and climbed in the saddle. It took a while for the world to stop spinning and the urge to vomit to pass. The saddle horn served as his anchor. Once the world settled and his vision cleared, he spotted his packhorse grazing nearby in the trees. He whistled short and quick. Stars exploded behind his eyelids, making his vision go white. The clop of a horse's hooves approaching made it worth it.

"Good boy," he soothed as he leaned down and grabbed the horse's dangling lead rope.

For a moment, he had to cling tight to the saddle horn while the pain the movement caused passed. With sincere promises of treats to come, he tied the lead to Ayegi's saddle horn. He hung tight to both the saddle and consciousness as he set out to find the trail that would lead him to Cat.

18

Cat

Day Seventeen
Fort Laramie, Wyoming Territory

Chipped nails of her left hand drumming on the watchtower windowsill, Cat peered through the sailor's glass the soldier had provided. After a sleepless night, she had made her way to the gates at the first light of dawn. Each hour that had ticked by challenged her resolve to wait. Finally, she had convinced the latest guard on duty to let her into the tower that overlooked the surrounding valleys. Nothing but fields turning golden in the later afternoon sun lay out there.

"I'm sorry, ma'am, my shift is almost over. I've got to ask you to leave so I don't get into trouble," came the soldier's voice.

Doing her best to repress the protest that sprang to mind, she started to lower the glass. A sound from the soldier stopped her.

"Look at that, there comes a rider now," he said.

She whipped the glass back up to her eye. Her pulse pounded in her ears for a terribly long moment as she scanned the horizon. The soldier said more, but she couldn't hear it over the rush. Then she saw two horses and one rider approaching. They were still too far away to make out any details, but she didn't need them. The power that sang through her blood told her it was him. It shouldn't have since it didn't work with people, but there was no denying it. She thrust the glass back at the soldier so fast the impact caused his breath to expel in a grunt.

"Apologies. My deepest thanks!" she said as she spun and took off for the stairs.

Wood ground against wood as the soldier shoved his chair back in a rush and stood. "Wait, ma'am. It's dangerous to go down the ladder on your own!"

Already flinging the hatch open, she started down the ladder with no intention of waiting. Thanks to the breeches she wore, she didn't need the man's assistance. Even in a dress with a full bustle she could have made it, though it would, of course, have been considered quite the scandal. Not that anyone at this fort would care much beyond the entertainment factor. By the time the soldier put a foot on the ladder, her booted heels were touching the dirt.

Tail wagging with enthusiasm, Lincoln greeted her with a bark.

Here, he is here! the pup thought as he hopped around her.

Yes, he is! she thought to him as she scratched his head.

"That's a good boy," she said aloud while freeing him from the pillar he was tied to with one easy pull. Her shaking hands took two tries to remove the rope from his collar.

At over a hundred feet down the wall, the gate seemed a world away. Each step was an agonizing test of her restraint. Being a grown woman, she couldn't run through the fort without raising all kinds of alarm. She walked as fast as she could, weaving in and out of people and carts selling wares. The frantic pace could barely be called a walk. Lincoln jogged alongside her, darting away only to go around an obstacle or a person, then darting straight back.

After several agonizingly long moments in which she began to fear her heart may burst from anticipation, she reached the open gate. She slowed her pace and returned the guards' cordial greeting as she strolled out, pretending she hadn't a care in the world aside from a refreshing walk. She managed to maintain that walk for almost twenty feet. Then she saw him. Rick's big buckskin gelding trotted toward her, his packhorse in tow. She could just make out Rick well enough to see his beard lift up into a grin. With a whoop, he urged the horses into a gallop. The breeze caught his chin-length brown hair and threw it back.

Abandoning all concerns over how it may look, she ran to him, Lincoln fast on her heels. The distance between them couldn't close fast enough. Just before reaching her, Ayegi slowed. Rick vaulted from the cantering gelding's back and hit the ground running. The feat took her breath away as surely as the run. In another few steps he swept her up into his arms. The relief that engulfed her literally made her knees give out. He held her up easily. To feel him solid and alive against her seemed too good to be true. She didn't want to move too much in case it was a dream and she might startle herself awake.

Until that moment, she hadn't realized just how much she had feared he was dead, and how much it would have devastated her if he had been. He smelled so good, like horses, pine trees, rainwater, and musk. After several long moments of holding her tight, he drew back only enough to take her face in his hands. The rough, callused palms clashed with how gently he cradled her.

His gaze drank her in, long and deep. She lost herself in the raw emotion there and never wanted to be found again. Their lips collided with a ferocity that rivaled that of the storm they had escaped. His soft lips gave and invited her in. A completely unexpected passion swept her up. This was one natural disaster she was finished running from. If it destroyed her, so be it. She sank against his hard chest, sighing into his mouth as it opened to her. His tongue invited her to dance and she accepted eagerly. The strong scent of blood wrapped around her.

Wait, blood?

Eyes going wide, she pushed Rick back slightly. "Are you injured?"

Bemusement filled his heavy-lidded eyes. "I can honestly say I'm not feeling a drop of pain."

As she pulled back farther, she saw his bandaged left arm. "O' course you're not, you daft man." She sighed and rolled her eyes as she tugged at his makeshift bandage. To his credit, it was quite well done.

He winced and she nodded. "Not a drop, hum?"

Still grinning, he shrugged. "'Tis only a scratch."

She put one hand on her hip. "Enough of that manly act, now. What happened, and how bad is it? Out with it."

He opened his mouth to speak and then grinned and closed it. Something bumped her gently from behind. She turned to see Ayegi right behind her, his lips tugging at a lock of her long, red hair. Sighing, she extricated her hair from the horse's mouth and scratched his nose. Rick's warmth drew away as he bent to greet and pet Lincoln. Watching the two of them made her smile so large it ached. The pup licked Rick's face and he endured it with laughter. She left them to their moment and stroked Ayegi.

An arm soon draped over her shoulders. She leaned into him and held tight to his waist, her eyes closing for a moment. Never had she felt so content, not even in Michael's arms. Especially not in Michael's arms. She forced the thought aside. This was not a moment she would allow him to ruin.

Rick took hold of Ayegi's reins with his free hand. "Let's get back to the fort and I'll tell you all about it," he said.

"All right, but I'm holding you to that."

They walked together, neither willing to let go long enough to climb on Ayegi's back. The distance between them and the gate closed all too soon. No doubt the soldiers had seen them embracing. But, from a distance they wouldn't have noticed the tenderness or passion she and Rick showed one another—nor their reluctance to let go. Up close would be another matter. If she was to be completely honest with herself, she didn't really care about appearances for the first time in a long time. During the short time she'd spent in the fort, she had come to realize people here knew Rick. She didn't know what impression he cared to give them, and she wasn't about to force him into something he wasn't ready for. She let go and took a few steps away.

The soldiers at the gate perked up when they saw him. "Corporal Fergusson! How goes it, lad?" the elder of the two asked.

Rick grinned and shook the man's hand. "I dodged a tornado and ended up with naught but a scratch, so I can't much complain. How about you and the lads here?"

They chatted companionably for a short time, exchanging information about traders, trappers, and the activity of the local native tribes. Though Rick smiled and kept up a casual air, Cat could see the tension in the lines around his eyes and in the tightness of his lips. At first she thought it was pain until she realized the tension grew worse at the mention of the natives.

Finally, the men took a breath and she jumped into the conversation. "I should be getting the corporal here to the doctor. You gentlemen have a good evening." With that, she hooked an arm through his and started walking. She gave them a charming smile to soften the interruption, and quiet their protests.

"Good evening to you too, ma'am, and you, Corporal," the elder of them said.

"Aye, a good evening to you both. And do come meet us for a drink at the tavern tonight, Fergusson," the other called.

Rick waved back at them. "Will do, lads." He leaned close to Cat. "Thank you for that," he whispered.

Cat inclined her head. "I've discovered those two can talk all day."

Rick's brows pulled together. "How long has it been since the storm?"

She returned his pinched look. "Two nights. Why?" Her heart pounded as the fear of what he might have undergone out there struck her.

Rick's eyes went wide. "A branch knocked me out. I just woke this morning."

She held tighter to his arm, suddenly fearful he may topple at any time. Though truth be told, he looked well enough considering. She couldn't imagine—didn't dare imagine—how fast a branch caught up in tornado winds would have been moving. "Rick, you really do need to see a doctor."

"Nah," he disagreed in a distracted tone that worried her.

"Please, for me."

A long breath blew from him. "All right. I can deny you nothing. But truly, the arm was only a scratch, and me head feels fine now."

They stopped off at the stables on the way and paid a man to care for the horses. A few buildings down they came to the makeshift hospital, a log building with a dirt floor and gaps in the walls. The lone nurse within got Rick to a cot straight away and began removing the bandage from his arm.

Her nose wrinkled. "What on Earth did you put on this? It stinks to high heaven," she said as she discarded it.

"Iodine. Me nurse in the war swore by it," Rick said.

"Poppycock! Anything that smells that foul can't be good for you."

Cat shared a look with Rick. She smiled wide, knowing full well the nurse he spoke of was her sister-in-law, Ashlinn. Fae healing ability aside, the woman was ahead of her time when it came to medical practice and brilliant to boot. If she swore by this iodine, Cat would do her best to find more of it for Rick's wound.

When the nurse had the bandages cleared away, she rested a hand on her hip and looked at Rick from beneath her brows. "Trying to gain sympathy from your lady friend?" she asked.

Grinning, he gave her a mock-shy look before glancing down. "Nah. I just heal fast. I tried to tell her 'twas only a scratch," he said.

Leaning over to get a look at the new pink skin, Cat was struck mute for a moment. It looked like a puncture wound of some sort. But it was healed as if it were weeks old. "He was struck in the head with a branch during the tornado. It knocked him out for some time," she said.

The nurse made an unconvinced humming noise. "I'll have the doctor come in and look him over just to be sure," she said.

With a shake of her head, she left the room. Shortly after, the doctor came in and gave Rick a perfunctory once over, checked his pupils, then handed him a flask.

"Fancy a wee nip?" he asked.

Accepting it, Rick knocked back quite a bit more than a wee nip. "Thank you kindly."

The doctor met and held his gaze as he accepted the flask back. "What kind of Indians were they?" he asked, voice hard.

Cat scoffed inwardly at how fast news traveled.

"I thought Cherokee at first, but they were almost certainly Paiute."

The man's face pinched into all kinds of angry lines. "We've been having trouble with them. Just you or a wagon train?"

"Just the lady and me."

A prickly flush of fear worked its way through Cat, speeding her heart into a frantic rhythm. Her damnable red hair was likely what had attracted their attention. The anxiety eating at her must have shown on her face, because Rick took hold of her hand. She gripped tight and leaned heavy on the side of the bed.

"How many?" the doctor asked.

"Three," Rick answered.

"Any get away?"

Rick's eyes closed for a long moment and Cat had a feeling he was considering how much to reveal. "Possibly. The storm made it hard to tell."

"You kill a few?" the doctor pressed, sounding all business.

Rick's teeth ground together. When he answered, he looked away from her.

"Hard to say in the chaos of the storm." Guilt weighed heavy in the words.

Pieces of Cat's heart felt as though they broke off at the words. The man was already haunted. Now he'd possibly had to kill men because of her. His hand tried to slip from hers, but she held it tight.

The doctor rose from his chair. "Right then. I'd best report to the lieutenant that we may be expecting trouble. He may want a word with you later."

At a nod from Rick the man tipped his cap to Cat and strode from the room. Cat harrumphed.

"That seemed more like an interrogation than a medical exam," she said.

A shrug from Rick led her to believe he had expected it. "The doc is the first one to hear of any trouble with the natives, which means he's the one responsible for getting that information to the fort's lieutenant. They're just doing their best to keep the fort safe." Though his words seemed heartfelt, a layer of pain lay beneath them.

"I understand that, but he didn't have to be so cold about it."

"He's a doctor, and a military one at that," Rick said as if that explained everything.

This time when he tried to pull away, she let him. If he couldn't stand to touch her after what he'd had to do for her, she had to respect that. Tears threatened her eyes and tightened her throat. "I'm so sorry you had to kill men because of me," she whispered.

His own misty eyes locked onto hers and he grabbed her hands. "What, Cat? No, no. I'm not sure if I actually killed any of them. And if I did, I wouldn't blame you. I was afraid you'd be ashamed of me for what I did."

She lifted his hands and kissed the backs of his knuckles. "I would never be ashamed of something you had to do for me, or for protecting your own life."

He pulled one hand free and stroked her face. "You're amazing, woman," he whispered.

Eyes on his lips, she began to lean in to him when shuffling steps outside the open door stopped her. The rail-thin nurse whisked back into the room, barely hiding a smile by keeping her head down. "I didn't mean to interrupt," she said.

She handed Rick a wrapped bundle and set to checking the dressing on his arm. "That's a skullcap and ginger tea for your headache. Drink it as often as necessary. It'll do a fair spot better than the whiskey the lads will no doubt try to talk you into medicating with," she instructed.

"Yes, ma'am," Rick agreed obediently.

Still smiling, she sneaked a sly look at Cat.

"So how long have you been courting our corporal here?" she asked.

Mouth gaping, searching for words, Cat just stared at her. Not even an inkling of an idea of what to say would come to her. Her smile froze as she looked down at their clasped hands. Did she dare respond? Her heart wanted this. Her head didn't. But what did Rick want? More than anything, she wanted to look at him, to see how he felt, but she couldn't. What if he didn't feel the same? Or what if he did?

His index finger slid beneath her chin, lifting it. Slowly, she gained the courage to raise her eyes to meet his. They stared at one another for a long time. In the depths of his green eyes she saw her own turmoil and raw emotion reflecting back at her. But she saw something else as well, something fiercely loyal and daring. A part of her that she'd never even realized had been slumbering stirred and began to waken.

His answer felt as though it were more for her than for the nurse.

"We've only just begun."

19

Rick

Day Eighteen

The first light of dawn revealed an empty horizon touched only by golden rays. It should have soothed him to know his night terrors had been no more than shadows of his fears. But it didn't. An urgency had settled deep in his gut that wouldn't be denied. In the war he had learned to trust his gut. Listening to it had saved his life more than once. It wasn't just Cofield or another of Ainsworth's men he feared now, but a threat that could be even bigger. Not just to him and Cat, but possibly to the entire fort. His sailor's glass clicked softly as he compacted it. The guard leaning up against the wall beside the open gate stirred and blinked rapidly. His bloodshot eyes spoke more of overindulgence than being overworked.

"Still nothing out there, eh, Corporal?" he asked.

"Nothing yet, Private. But I'd keep a close eye out if I

were you," Rick warned.

"Oh, aye, for sure. Savages have been active this month." Rick hated that he used the word savages to describe the natives. It wasn't fair to them considering they were just trying to protect their home. Oblivious to his ire, the man went on. "Picked off three of our cattle just last week. They like to stand out there on the horizon as if they're trying to goad us out into the open. And the last wagon train to come in had a spot of trouble with them, too," the soldier said. "I don't rightly think they'll bother us here at the fort, though. You're safe as can be behind these walls."

Chills danced across Rick's skin. He snorted. "The people of Fredericksburg thought the same thing," he grumbled half under his breath.

"What's that?"

Tucking the sailor's glass into his belt, Rick ran a hand down his newly shaven cheeks and cupped his chin. "Nothing, just war memories." He clapped the young man on the shoulder. "Your captain know of these issues?"

"Aye. He's not worried about a few savages, not with an entire division of the U.S. Army behind these walls," the soldier said.

Rick cursed in Irish beneath his breath. He fixed the soldier with a hard stare. "Well, he should be. Best stay alert. 'Tis only a matter of time."

The man nodded. "Oh, of course, of course. I was just catching a wink while you were here."

As Rick strode away, the man stood taller and faced the open gate like a sentinel. But Rick knew better. He'd likely be asleep in another few minutes. The unease in his gut intensified as if in agreement. His pace increased, his stride lengthening to eat up the hard-packed dirt. The winding path through the stands and random wooden buildings felt twice as long as it had coming here. The makeshift maze of streets still lacked more than a half dozen people at this early hour. But it was the layout of the place that slowed him down more than the people.

Why did the damn lodge have to be so deep into the fort? He hadn't wanted to leave Cat to come out this far, but he'd had to check. Now he questioned the wisdom of doing so. It was a completely irrational fear, he knew. She couldn't be safer, for the moment, at least. The feeling in his stomach wasn't anything rational, but it wouldn't be denied. He started to jog. A spot of mud sent him sliding into a cart and nearly crashing into a gray-haired woman carrying baskets of apples.

"I'm so sorry, ma'am. Here, let me carry those for you," he offered, ashamed his distraction had caused the collision.

With a gap-toothed grin, she eagerly accepted his offer. Several minutes later and several streets out of his way, they finally reached her stand. She made him take a pair of apples for payment then he all but dashed away. As he jogged past the dusty entrance to the stables, Cat's voice drifted out. From the timbre and words it was clear she was speaking to the horses. The sound made him smile and eased some of the tension that had crawled up around him. Turning into the stables, he found her in Galiha's stall, standing on a stool so she could brush the big paint's back.

Her red hair hung loose in long waves that reached nearly to the belt of her breeches. The rounded shape of her rear those breeches outlined banished the last of the chill brought on by the soldier's words. As her arm moved in a rhythm, he caught glimpses of the pleasant manner in which her linen blouse outlined her breasts. He could tell by the way they moved so freely that they sat above her corset, unlike some of the more modern designs that covered them. He rather liked this design, a lot.

"You going to stand there ogling me, or are you going to pick up a brush and help?" she called sweetly over her shoulder.

Grinning, he rested his arms on the stall door. "I think I'll just ogle a bit longer."

A short laugh was the only warning he got before she tossed a brush that he just barely managed to dodge. He picked it up, dashed into the stall and chased her around Galiha, who did no more than twitch an ear at them as he continued to eat. When he caught her, he tickled her until she laughed so hard tears sprang to her eyes. His arms settled naturally around her as their laughter trickled off. Her slender arms wrapped around him as well.

Smiling, she ran a hand along his right cheek. He winced as her soft skin caught on the stubble he'd missed. "You shaved," she said in a tone that managed to sound both pleased and disappointed at the same time.

Her teeth tugged at her bottom lip. That one little motion drove him wild. Blood rushed straight to his groin, making his breath catch. He wanted nothing more in the world at that moment than to bend and kiss her full, pink lips, but he didn't dare. Already he had taken liberties with her that he had no right to do. Sean would pummel him good if he found out about how he had conducted himself with Cat. The man was his closest friend, a person he respected more than anyone.

Looking into Cat's eyes, he had to reconsider that last thought.

Then there was the not so slight problem of what he was and what she was. Before he could allow things to progress, he would have to tell her. Though it would likely drive an immovable wedge between them, she deserved to know.

Her pink tongue shot out and wetted her lips. He had to shift his hips back slightly so she wouldn't feel how his body responded to her. As if she knew exactly how she affected him, she leaned a touch closer, eyes sparkling with mischief. If the kiss wasn't unwanted, he couldn't help but wonder if it would really be considering taking liberties…

"I see heavy thoughts behind those handsome eyes," Cat said in a playful tone.

He hoped his smile didn't look as forced as it felt. Mustering his will, he drew back as far as her arms would allow him. "I've disrespected you and the MacBranains by taking liberties with your affections."

Cat laughed, hard and abrupt, as if the fit surprised even her. The sound sent fantastic thrills down through his core. Damn but she had a way of undoing him that made him want to beg for more. Light as feathers, her hands trailed down his arms, sending wonderful chills throughout his body. Her eyes narrowed into a sly look that made his blood pump faster.

"Why, Patrick Fergusson, what on Earth makes you think *you're* the one taking liberties?" she asked.

He muttered a prayer to the god Cernunnos in Gaelic. The look of desire his words stirred in her eyes made him ache and swell all at the same time. "You are a marvel, woman, unlike any high society lady I've ever met," he said.

She gave him a coy look. "Maybe I'll tell you why when

we get back on the trail."

Heat rushed to his cheeks, but it wasn't embarrassment or even attraction. If she was willing to tell him her 'secret' then he should be ready to share his. But the thought terrified him. He forced a grin. "I'd like that. I want very much to get to know you better."

Her long lashes batted as she pulled away and turned back to Galiha. "Do you now?"

The bait was too delicious not to take. He walked up behind her, put his hands on her hips and leaned down to whisper in her ear. "I think perhaps I do."

She shivered but recovered quickly with a flip of her hair. "You *think*?" she asked.

He leaned down and kissed her neck. "I know," he said in a husky voice right against her skin.

The sigh that slid from her just about melted the rest of his resistance. Just about. When she leaned back into him he moved away. He stepped around to her side, waiting until she faced him. If he didn't do something to slow things down, they would burn out of control before he could tell her. "But I think that nurse might have been onto something."

Her eyebrows rose. "How so?"

"About us courting. I think that's a fine idea."

"Do you now?"

"You say that a lot."

One corner of her lips rose. "Do I?"

"You do."

With a flourish, he took hold of one of her hands. Doing so without gloves on would have been quite improper in the circles she was used to running in, something he was acutely aware of in that moment. But she didn't pull away. Of course she didn't. Not only had they been far more intimate than merely hand holding, but she truly wasn't like other high society ladies. Certainly not like the one who kept him running in fear from every emotional connection that tried to form. Until now. Cat had broken that cycle.

"I have sent off a telegram to Sean, telling him that I intend to court you officially, should you accept me offer," he said.

Her eyes flew open wide. "You have?"

Suddenly fearful that he had misread her feelings, he swallowed hard. Old insecurities tried to edge their way back in. She gripped his hand tighter, banishing them.

"What I mean to say is, I'm honored. But, Rick, I'm a broken woman. There are things you don't know about me." Her eyes dropped from his halfway through her words.

Rather than forcing her to look back up, he just leaned his head against hers. "And I'm a broken man. There's no harm in us getting to know each other better. That's what courting's all about, after all," he said.

She was quiet for so long that anxiety began to worm its way around his heart. What if she had only been flirting with him and didn't desire anything more? If that were the case, he didn't dare tell he the truth about himself. All manner of other doubts started to work at him.

"You, o' course, have my utmost respect, and I won't ever take liberties with your affections that might compromise you," he promised. And he meant every word of it. Propriety was a thing he liked to toy with, but honor was another altogether. "And we will get to know each other, share our secrets without judgment or fear of reprisal. And then you can decide if you'll have me."

Cat whisked away from him, thrusting her head up into the air. "Your terms are acceptable, Mr. Fergusson. I agree to the courtship," she said.

Using the excuse of brushing Galiha, she ducked around the other side of the horse. "But I make no such promises about not compromising you," she said in the same formal tone she had used to accept his offer.

Mouth dropping open, he stared at her over Galiha's back. The twinkle in her eyes made his knees want to give out. Exclaiming in Irish, he set to chasing her around the horse again. Outside of the stall, Lincoln barked and put his front feet up on the door. Already, the pup was big enough to see over the nearly five-foot-tall door. Laughing, Rick drew away from Cat.

"Looks like we'll have a proper escort to look after your honor," he said as he scratched Lincoln on the head.

It was as good an excuse as any to stop short of embracing her. Since they had made it official—or as official as it could be without Sean's consent—he was determined to do this properly. Mistakes of the past would not be repeated, not with Cat. She was too important to him. He moved Lincoln off the door and forced himself to leave the stall. All manner of improper things might occur if he didn't. Appealing as continuing to push the boundaries of propriety was, he couldn't allow it, not until she knew all his secrets.

"We need to get on the trail as soon as possible," he said.

A forlorn sigh eased from Cat. "It was so nice to sleep in what serves for a real bed out here. I'll miss it," she said.

Rick halted in midstride and leaned back to look at her.

"What, no protests?"

She sat the brush aside and picked up Galiha's saddle blanket from where it hung over the stall wall. "O' course not. We've got to make up lost time." For a moment, she disappeared as she bent down on the other side of the horse. "I sold the white mare and replenished our provisions. I hope that's all right," she said.

He loved that she had thought to do that. "Brilliant. Precisely what I would have done."

She stepped out of the stall and grabbed the saddle off the rack, struggling a bit with its weight. Intent on helping, he dashed back and opened the door for her. "Let me help with that."

Before he could take it from her, she strode back into the stall and slung it up on Galiha's back. Her enduring independent streak struck him. Even after everything, she still insisted on taking care of herself. Never in his life had he met a high society lady who would put her own saddle on when the opportunity existed for someone else to do it for her. He simply couldn't figure this woman out, and he loved that.

"I've got it, no worries," she said through a grunt as she adjusted the cinch.

"You are a marvel, woman, an absolute marvel."

Shaking his head, he left her to it and went to saddle up Ayegi and prepare the packhorse. Less than an hour later, they were mounted and riding through the gates of the fort. He took them straight to the trail and headed due west at a good trot. It would be the quickest way to make time, but he planned to cut away from it as soon as possible. Only after nearly half an hour did he finally slow the pace to a walk. The huge fort still loomed in the distance behind them, but at least it was behind them.

"Good to know I'm not the only one eager to leave that place," Cat said.

"Truly? Why? I would have thought lingering somewhere with food that wasn't dried and a bed that wasn't dirt would appeal to you," he said. He kept his tone playful, but his real intention was to keep her from asking him why he'd wanted to leave so badly. No need to worry her.

Eyes going distant and back straightening into a rigid line, she paused before answering. "They were a little too comfortable behind their wooden walls for my liking. I don't believe the natives would have been so bold as to attack us that close to the fort if they felt the soldiers were a real threat. And the animals in the fort were unsettled, which is never a good sign."

It took him several long moments to recover from the shock. When words finally came, they spilled out before he could realize they were likely the wrong thing to say. "You think an awful lot like a man."

Jaw tightening and eyes going wide, she looked long and hard at him. "Not at all. You'd do well—as would all men—to know that women think just as strategically. We just don't often speak our minds or get heard when we do."

"You are right, o' course. Me apologies. I didn't mean it that way," he attempted to recover.

Her brows smoothed out. She shrugged as if it were of no consequence. But it was to him, very much so. "I know you didn't. Most men would mean it precisely that way, but not you."

His saddle creaked as he leaned over to touch her arm. "I respect you and your thoughts. Please, always speak your mind with me."

Moisture sprung to her eyes and her face went smooth as glass, without expression, as if it could counteract the emotion in her emerald eyes. Thrusting her head high and flashing him a wicked smile, she said, "I will."

Though her voice was teasing, he could read in her posture how serious she was, and how much his words touched her.

Ayegi perked up when he picked up the reins. "What do you say we put this fort far behind us and get across this state?"

Hiding a smile, she picked up her reins as well. "I say that sounds like a fine idea."

A shift of his weight and squeeze of his legs and both Ayegi and their packhorse took off. Cat swung out wide to give the packhorse room to run alongside Ayegi, a formation they had found allowed them to move faster for longer periods of time. Better than that, he found it put her right in his line of sight. Long, red waves of the most beautiful hair he'd ever seen trailed out behind her like a silken banner. He thanked the saints for Ayegi's sure footing, because with Cat beside him, there was no way he would be able to keep his eyes on the trail. Barking for the sheer joy of it, Lincoln took off running ahead.

For the first time in weeks, Rick let himself relax. It would only be for a moment, but what a beautiful moment it would be.

20

Cat

Day Twenty-Eight
Wyoming Territory

Long days spent in the saddle mostly at a trot helped them cut days off their trek across the plains of the Wyoming territory. Unfortunately, it left Cat so exhausted by the end of the day that she scarcely had the energy to stand, let alone court Rick. The tender looks and shared conversation contented her for the time being. No matter how she prodded, Rick kept most things about himself and his family under lock and key. She did learn that he loved this country, sympathized with its natives, and had a knack for horses. Despite all the knowledge about horses he displayed in their conversations, he just didn't strike her as a horseman. So much about him remained a mystery.

Until she learned more about him, she couldn't tell him her secret. That required a level of trust they weren't at yet. They were close, and getting closer every day, but the threat of being stoned to death or burned at the stake held her tongue. True, it had been a decade since her kind had been burned as witches in this country. But the risk wasn't worth taking. That, and she wasn't ready to see the disbelief, and then fear, and then condemnation in his eyes.

And telling him when he was so clearly under stress seemed a bad idea anyway. Part of the reason for his stress was all too apparent. Though he tried to hide it, she saw him looking over their shoulders all too often. Whether it was Cofield, another of Ainsworth's men, or natives he worried over, she couldn't tell. To ask would only make his anxiety worse, so she pretended not to notice. Twice she saw figures in the distance behind them. Rather than point them out, she made excuses to ride harder, faster, and farther. It made for long days and sleepless nights. Some courtship.

At the western edge of Wyoming territory, as the sun set on their twenty-eighth day, she set her mind to finding out more about Rick. From the high branches of a cherry tree, his voice drifted down to her. "Too bad we can't make a pie. Me mum used to bake the most amazing cherry pie when I was a lad."

She held a blanket out for him to drop the cherries in, moving this way and that as he crawled throughout the tree. Any she missed Lincoln snatched up, then just as promptly spit out, tail wagging wildly all the while.

"What part of Ireland were your parents from?" she asked.

"Me mum is from county Cork, but me da is from Edinburgh," Rick said.

Surprise froze her in place for a moment, causing her to miss a handful of cherries he dropped. Lincoln pounced on them before she could retrieve them.

"Truly? You're half Scot? I thought you were jesting when you said it earlier," she said.

"Truly. Does that change your opinion of me, Princess?" he asked, tone playful but hiding a hint of concern.

"O' course not. But it does explain a few things," she teased.

Several cherries pelted the top of her head.

"Hey! Get down here where I can properly retaliate!" she hollered.

Laughing, she threw one back up at him, and missed the mark terribly. A squeak of surprise burst from her as he dropped from the tree and landed right in front of her. "How's this?"

Another squeak came from her as she dropped the blanket and took off running. Rick chased her around the tree, Lincoln right on his heels. Their laughter and the pup's barking filled the tiny valley. Soon the laughter got the better of her and she couldn't run anymore. She collapsed into the tall grass beneath the cool shade of the tree and breathed deep of the sweet yellow buttercup flowers all around her.

It had been years since she'd felt this relaxed. Considering the constant fear of being chased down and murdered in her sleep, that said something horrible about her life so far. But she wasn't about to dwell on that right now. A moment later Rick lay beside her, propping his head up with his hand so he could look at her. Lincoln gave one last bark before trotting off to investigate something in the tall grass. If she weren't able to read his mind, she would almost have thought the pup was giving them privacy on purpose.

Cat's gaze shifted from the scattering of fluffy white clouds above her to the man at her side. Nearly two weeks of beard growth covered his strong jawline and chin in a brown scruff that she very much wanted to run her hands over. Mirth filled his green eyes as if he knew exactly what she was thinking. He had been every bit the gentleman he had promised over the last several days. Too much for her liking, really. But it was refreshing in a way that made her feel relaxed and safe like she'd never thought she'd feel around a man again. In the beginning of her courtship—if it could be called that—with Michael, he had always secreted her away and pressured her to lie with him. He had only ever been a gentleman when others were looking. But her family had been desperate for her to marry a man of fae lineage and he was one of few such eligible bachelors within a hundred miles.

"You have the most beautiful laugh," Rick said, pulling her back to the present.

"Thank you. It's been a long time since I've laughed this much," she said through a shy smile. Compliments that had nothing to do with how she looked were another thing she wasn't used to.

"Meself as well," Rick said.

Curiosity seized her as she took in his lazy, contented expression. "You didn't really like me at first. What brought you around?"

He lay back down on the ground beside her, folding his hands beneath his head. At first she thought she had pushed too far, too fast. But then she realized if they were going to court seriously, she needed to know him better. Pressing into uncomfortable territory and truths was the only way to do that.

She would not make the mistake of getting involved with a man she didn't know well enough again.

"You're different from other high society ladies. At first, I didn't see that. You seemed just like them in the beginning. But you've relaxed, shown me the real you," he finally said.

She looked back to the sky. "You make me feel like Cat again, not Catriona O'Brian."

His hand found hers and his fingers wove through hers.

"Well, I'm sorry you ever lost the old Cat. I rather like her," Rick said.

The tender tone of his voice touched her so deeply it actually hurt a bit. The few years she had known and been married to Michael, he changed her so much that she could scarcely remember her old self, let alone ever hope to be her again. According to Michael, she had needed to rise up to the standards of his family and social circles. Here this man was saying he liked the old Cat better. It amazed her beyond words.

They lay together in silence for a long time. It was a comfortable silence that she hated to break, but after a while, she had to know something. "You have a jaded opinion of high society women," she said.

"Aye, I do."

When he didn't say more, she realized she was going to have to push a lot harder. "Why? Was it something I did?"

He lifted her hand and kissed the back of it, long and tender. Had she not already been lying on the ground, she may have swooned. "No, not at all." After a long sigh that sounded like it started in his toes, he went on. "Me parents found a good match for me, a woman of exceptional breeding with a desirable dowry. We got on well enough during courtship that I thought we might be in love." His voice grew hard at the last sentence.

Cat waited, giving him the time he needed, watching the drifting clouds rather than him to take the pressure off.

"We set a date. Then I heard about the 69th regiment. Sean told me he was joining up, to try and make a difference, to make this *his* country. It seemed like a good cause, and I couldn't let him go alone."

"O' course not," Cat agreed when he paused again. Such feeling toward his fellow man, and honor toward his friend was admirable—and very attractive.

The corner of Rick's lips that she could see lifted into a smile. She opened her mouth to say more but he spoke before she could.

"I was left standing alone at the altar. She didn't show up."

Red-hot fury blazed through her. "That's terrible, Rick. To do that to a soldier bound for war…what a horrible thing." The last word broke as tears overwhelmed her. In a moment she recovered and squeezed his hand tight. "But her folly is my gain."

Rick rolled over and propped himself up. He moved a lock of her hair from her face and bent down to her, eyes closing. She rose up to meet him. For well over a week she had been hoping he would kiss her again, and she wasn't about to let him back out of it now. Their lips molded together. The pressure was gentle, with a restrained eagerness behind it. That eagerness both excited and scared her.

Pushing her fear down, she parted her lips and invited his tongue to chase hers back into her mouth. It did, and the soft sensation of it between her teeth set her on fire. She rose up on an elbow and pressed against him. The feel of his hard chest against her made her nipples rise to attention. Wonderful tingles traveled down through them straight to her core. Rick's hand slid behind her head and into her hair. She wanted more, needed more. Her free hand moved to his lower back and she pulled him up against her. The hard erection that pressed into her groin made her moan. One of Rick's hands moved to her left breast, turning her moan into a gasp.

Large paws beat down the grass not far from their heads. Cat's eyes flew open to find Lincoln standing over them, a large hare dangling from his mouth. The hare's black eyes rolled in her direction and its ears twitched. Fear and resignment radiated from it.

I have brought meat! Lincoln exclaimed, his voice proud and excited in her mind.

With a screech, Cat flew back and to her knees. Lincoln's tail wagged, slapping flowers and the heads of grass with each swipe. He dropped the big hare before Rick and let out a proud bark. The second the hare's feet touched the ground, it launched out of the pup's reach and took off.

"Pup, your timing is impeccably bad," Rick said with a laugh.

Lincoln cocked his head, barked once more, then took off after the hare. *Don't worry. I'll get it back!* he said in mindspeak.

They laughed at him bounding through the grass at a lazy pace, as if he cared nothing for actually catching it. Rick rose and offered her his hand. She accepted, letting go to brush grass from her clothing.

"Looks like he makes a good chaperone after all," she said.

She couldn't possibly be angry at the pup, he was far too precious. Besides, with the moment passed, her anxiety set back in full force. It was best to wait. Rick needed to know the full truth about her before they passed the point of no return. Some men would be repulsed at the very thought of touching one of her kind, falsely thinking them to be a witch, to be beguiling, or to be evil. Not that witches were evil either, but narrow-minded people ruled by fear refused to believe that.

Seeming to sense her conclusion, Rick offered her his arm. "He does indeed, and just when I've gone back on me word to protect your honor and not be too forward. I cannot apologize enough," he said.

"You don't need to apologize at all. I wanted to kiss you, and more. And what I want is important, is it not?" she asked with a sly grin.

"Absolutely. What you want is of the utmost importance," he agreed as they walked back to their campsite. "You shall be the ruin of me, woman, and I shall enjoy every moment of it."

The kiss had awakened something so powerful in Cat that she couldn't sleep. Over the dying embers of the fire she watched Rick doze off. His hard chest rose and fell with a rhythm that seemed almost delicate, fragile in comparison to his strong body. She desperately wanted to go to him, crawl into his sleeping roll, and finish what they had started. The ache was stronger than anything she'd ever felt for Michael. She had never wanted her late husband as much as she had really just wanted him to stop pressuring her. Not that he wasn't attractive. He had certainly been that. The pressure had just always ruined it. What she felt for Rick was completely different, and strange, but in a scintillating way.

The soft sounds of his deepening breaths made her long to hear them beside her ear, feel them along her skin. On her right, Lincoln snored away, his gangly puppy legs kicking in the throes of a dream. She grabbed the edge of her blanket, preparing to move it aside, when Rick stirred.

His breathing quickened, became almost distressed sounding. Firelight glistened off sweat forming on his brow. Blankets flew from him as he tossed and turned. His head thrashed. Between groans she could make out a few words that chilled her: *all the bodies.* She was up before she realized she had moved. This time she didn't run to his side. Stopping well out of reach, she sat down on his side of the fire. She had to do something to ease his suffering. The only thing she could think of was to sing. The first thing that came to her mind was that song they had played together weeks ago. Something told her it would just the thing to soothe him and help pull him out of the nightmare. The words of "Scarborough Fair" were thankfully ingrained in her memory so she didn't have to think about them. It came out breathy, her voice shaking.

Damn it to hell, he needed her. She had to pull it together.

Her eyes closed and she recalled their wonderful kiss from earlier. Slowly, her voice smoothed out, became more confident. Soon she sang with depth and emotion. The sound filled the night, rising over the crackling fire, and eventually over Rick's groans. Halfway through the song Rick's thrashing slowed. With a long exhale, his body relaxed. Something in him tugged at her.

Impossibly, she slipped into his mind.

A bloody cornfield turned to a beautiful green meadow dotted with bright red poppies tall enough to brush against his hands as he walked. Golden rays of the sun bathed him in their warmth. Tiny sprites flitted from flower to flower ahead of him, their iridescent wings reflecting the light. Peace and calm filled him.

Not wanting to intrude, she pulled back out of his mind. That should not have been possible. She couldn't enter the minds of people. What was this man? Oddly, the thought didn't frighten her. How could it when his energy felt so familiar, so safe?

After a hard swallow, she picked back up where she had left off in the song. By the last chorus, he rolled toward her and his eyes fluttered open. She sang the chorus once more just to make sure he was fully awake. He sat up and she tensed in preparation to bolt, just in case. At the end of the round of chorus, she paused.

"That was so beautiful," Rick said in a sleepy voice.

"Are you awake?" she asked.

"Aye, thank you. Your voice pulled me from the depths of hell." The gravity of his tone brought tears to her eyes. He sat up and looked down at his hands. "I didn't scare you, or…hurt you, did I?" The shame and fear in his voice pinched at her heart.

She went and sat on the edge of his blanket. Slowly, so he didn't startle or pull away, she reached for his hand. This time she held no fear of him. He wasn't like Michael. He wouldn't hurt her. "No, not at all."

Her first instinct was to say how it had been her fault last time. But she didn't let those words out. Both Deirdre and Sadie had been trying to teach her not to take the blame for the actions of others. And, more importantly, not to excuse the violent actions of a man toward her. While she knew Rick hadn't been in his right mind—or even awake—and she didn't blame him in the least, she couldn't let herself accept the violent behavior, either. Not after what Michael had done to her. To do so would be to step backward in her own healing and lose the progress of confidence her friends had worked so hard to build back up in her.

Rick squeezed her hand gently. "Thank the Tuatha. That was quite clever of you to sing. Thank you for remembering our song together. It was exactly what I needed."

A shy smile crept to her lips. The way he always invoked and spoke of the Tuatha warmed her, gave her hope that he might accept what she was without judgment or fear. "I had to do something. I couldn't just let you suffer like that." She left out the part about how much his words had unnerved her, and how she needed to cover the sound of them. Knowing the war was horrible was one thing, hearing a person relive it was another altogether. One day she'd be ready for that, but today wasn't that day. She had her own hell she was still recovering from.

"You're amazing," he said as he lay back down. He opened his arms, inviting her to lay beside him.

Forcing her reservations aside, she lay down and snuggled into the crook of his right arm. From his warmth seeping into her to the scents of river water and soap emanating from him, everything about him soothed her. He made her feel more wanted than she ever had in her life.

"'Tis me turn to watch over you as you sleep. I'll be awake for a while now, you rest. I'll wake you if I get sleepy," he said.

The idea of falling asleep in his arms both thrilled and scared her on several levels. What if he fell asleep again and had another nightmare episode? But what if he didn't? To be held and cherished while she slept would be a dream come true. Michael had never wanted to do that with her. But how could she sleep with such a fear looming over her? She wanted to trust him, more than anything, but she also wanted to survive the night. In the end, she took a leap of faith and allowed his beating heart to lull her to sleep.

21

Cat

Day Thirty
Utah Territory

Miles and miles of hills and fragrant pines soon lulled Cat into a sleepy haze. The exhaustion of constantly having to look over her shoulder for a threat that may or may not be there was exacting a high toll of her piece of mind. Every shape on the horizon, every shadow, seemed to hold a potential threat. They hadn't seen another soul for days. Still, a part of her feared that it wasn't a matter of *if* one of Ainsworth's men would catch up to them, but *when*. Learning he had men scattered all along the outposts of the California Trail to protect the shipping of his goods stole a good amount of her sleep.

The mountains of Utah with their pockets of hidden snow and lush plant life were breathtaking, but days of such travel left her exhausted. She constantly had to shift her weight forward or back depending on the hill they descended or climbed. They had been descending since yesterday. Leaning back in the saddle began to feel close enough to lying down to rest. The heat of the day only compounded matters, nearly putting both her and her horse to sleep.

It felt as though she had been in the saddle so long her buttocks were in danger of taking on its shape. She decided that once they reached California, she never wanted to sit in a saddle again. When she voiced this, Galiha snorted. "Well, maybe not for a few months, at least," she told the horse as she patted his neck, dropping the last words to a whisper.

A familiar scent that she couldn't quite place tickled her nostrils. In her half-awake state, she began to think about New York. Oh how she missed Deirdre's spunkiness and Sadie's down-to-Earth manner. She even missed Ashlinn's immeasurable good will that made her so hard to live up to. It felt as though she hadn't seen her friends in an eternity, her people, her kind. She hadn't realized being away from other fae would make her feel so isolated, so hollow. It felt as though an enormous piece of her were missing. Then she realized what spurred the thoughts. The familiar smell was the ocean, or salt water, rather. She sat up straight and looked to Rick, who was grinning like a fool.

"I was wondering when you'd notice," he said.

"We're close to the Salt Lake?"

He nodded. "We should reach it in the next hour or so."

"And the town?" She tried not to sound too eager and failed miserably.

"We'll have to pass right through it. I figured we could stop there for the night, replenish our provisions, and get a good night's rest before crossing the salt flats. We'll need the rest if you want to push across them fast," he said.

"I do. But do you really think 'tis a good idea to stop and rest?" As desirable as a real bed and meal sounded, she didn't want to lose time. With another man out there who wanted her land, she had to push all the harder. No one was going to steal her dream away from her and her friends if she could help it. The sooner they arrived, the sooner she could start building and readying the land for horses. And she had to plant the fields by fall or she'd lose the window this year.

"We don't have much of a choice. The horses need the rest after these mountains, even if we don't," Rick said.

She scratched beneath Galiha's mane. "Hear that, lad? Perk up. There's a comfortable stall full of hay waiting for you down there."

His contented thoughts floated to her. *Open is good. Travel with herd is good.*

The gelding continued down the tree-choked slope at his leisurely pace. Undeterred, Cat began asking Rick all manner of questions about Salt Lake. From his descriptions, it sounded like a significant town. Not a city like New York, or nearly as advanced, but large enough to be considered civilization. Her curiosity about the people of Utah was eclipsed only by her excitement over visiting a real city again. She had never thought she'd miss the bustling streets of New York, and more importantly, the vendors and restaurants. This prompted her to ask all about the eating establishments.

Rick entertained her every question with a seemingly endless patience that surprised and delighted her. Because of it, she kept talking and asking. She wasn't used to a man being so open and tolerant of her chatting. It refreshed a part of her she hadn't even realize had been parched.

Excitement mounted in her as the trees parted and the valley cradling the town unfolded before them. Log buildings and dirt streets stretched across the open space in a gridwork of civilization. It was so much more than she had expected. After Fort Laramie, she had thought she may never see a proper town again. At the time it hadn't bothered her. Fort Laramie had been enough to stave off the wilds. But now, with the promise of diverse trade and the security of law and order that not even Ainsworth would dare to challenge, she breathed easier. More than that, she looked forward to it.

And she wasn't the only one. Galiha's stomach grumbled. *Hungry. Food?* his thoughts floated to her.

Yes. Down there, she thought back to him.

Ears perking forward, he picked up his pace nearly to a trot. Ayegi and the packhorse did as well. Soon they rode on the dusty streets amidst wagons and other riders who called out greetings. She was so busy looking at the shops they passed, that it surprised her when Rick stopped them at a hitching post a few streets in. He dismounted and was at her side before she could even get a foot out of a stirrup.

The assistance down was nearly as welcome as the feel of his hand in hers. The other lingered on the small of her back as her feet touched down. The muscles of her buttocks screamed at the change in position and she swayed. Rick steadied her with gentle pressure. She tested out taking a few steps, nodding to him once her legs held.

The building they had hitched in front of was two stories of finely hewn logs with several large, clear windows on each level. A covered porch wrapped around it. Over the large wooden door hung a beautifully painted sign declaring it the Traveler's Inn. Inside the windows, Cat saw several tables with chairs atop them.

"Oh, to eat at an actual table," she said through a heavy sigh.

Tucking her arm through his elbow, Rick escorted her to the door. "We're not eating here," he said.

Her excitement began to wane. "We're not?"

"No, this is only our lodging. They have the finest rooms and baths, but I have somewhere special in mind for dinner. I hope you don't mind shopping for a dress."

Her heart lurched into a fast rhythm that forced her to concentrate on maintaining a collected composure. "I don't mind at all."

Even if she had to haul herself back into the saddle and ride to a tailor, she wouldn't pass up the opportunity to dress up for him.

Rick stopped and looked at Lincoln, then pointed to the ground. The pup plopped down with a tired grunt. "Stay. I'll come sneak you in later. This isn't the type of place that allows dogs."

Rick opened the door for her. Lincoln's head cocked and he all but vibrated with the desire to move, to follow.

We are safe. Stay outside and watch over the horses. We will be right back, she assured him.

Tail thumping in the dirt, Lincoln lay down not far from Ayegi's hooves as if too tired to move anyway.

She paused to look long and hard at the animals. "Are they safe here?" she asked Rick. What she really wanted to ask was if they were *all* safe here, but she didn't dare say it. Voicing the fear felt like making the threat more real.

The gentle smile Rick gave her told her he understood exactly what she meant. "We're safe here. Ainsworth doesn't transport goods through Utah."

She breathed considerably easier as he opened the door for her.

The scents of lavender oil and soap wrapped around her as they stepped inside. The wooden table and chairs shone with the evidence of the oil as did the wooden floor to a far lesser degree. The clicking of her boot heels on the floor was music to her ears. Floors meant fewer spiders and snakes, two creatures she would be very happy to have a break from. Each puff of dust coming off her clothes and tracked in by the soles of her boots made her feel a tad guilty. More than a tad, really. It brought up old memories she didn't want to recall.

Hinges on a swinging door near the back of the room creaked. A woman emerged, wiping her hands on her flour-dusted apron. Though she smiled, it was tight with disapproval as her eyes flicked down to the tracks they were leaving on the floor. Those unwanted memories of Cat's multiplied until she looked down in shame.

"Good afternoon, ma'am. We require two rooms, beside one another if at all possible," Rick said.

The woman looked them both up and down before turning and waving for them to follow her. "Come along then. I'll get the hot water for you both on straight away."

The words "hot water" made Cat instantly forgive the woman's haughty manner.

An hour later, Cat was bathed, refreshed, and back in the

inn's main hall. She had put her simple traveling dress on, but even it felt dusty from the trail. Without a hoop, it didn't quite sit right so she kept tugging at it. Bringing a hoop hadn't been an option when every available space had to be used for things that could keep her alive. Until now, she hadn't wanted one. The moment Rick came down the stairs she forgot all about the fit of her dress. In dark breeches and a blue shirt, he managed to look casual and stunning at the same time. He still wore a pistol on his hip. Despite it, he managed to look quite civilized.

He offered her his arm. "Stop tugging, you look lovely."

She hadn't even realized she'd started again. A nervous, tittering laugh escaped her. Her cheeks burned at the sound. "Thank you. It just feels improper."

"No worries. I won't judge you for being out of fashion. Besides, all I see is you, not the dress," he said with a charming smile that melted her anxiety.

They left the inn behind for the bustling streets. Wooden sidewalks lined the buildings, offering them a clean, safe place to walk away from the wagons and horses. Shops selling all manner of goods and luxuries unfolded before them: candle makers, glass blowers, bakers, potters, butchers, and more. She had forgotten the amazing feeling of having every need literally within reach. What had seemed so common before now felt like a precious luxury she had always taken for granted. How many times on the trail had they eaten dried meat and crackers to get by because there had been no game, fruit trees, or berries readily available? She would never look at a shop window or cart filled with food the same again. Rick had to peel her away from the windows of several shops due to the lure of something as simple as preserves or meat on display.

She felt like a lass seeing a town for the first time. It was once again wondrous, but also opulent in a way she had never realized before. Most of the people walking the streets wore functional clothing, much of which was quite conservative. By the time they reached the tailor she began to feel guilty about buying a dress for a night out.

"It seems silly to buy a dress for one dinner," she said, hesitating on the sidewalk.

Rick smiled. "You are a rare gem."

A very girlish giggle came from her. He lifted her hand and kissed the back of it. "If it makes you feel better, we'll sell it back tomorrow."

She cocked her head thoughtfully. "Or trade it for a nice pair of riding breeches and a new blouse."

Rick let out a short laugh. "I love how practical you are, dear lady."

Again, heat rushed to her cheeks. She dropped her head, unable to meet his gaze with her cheeks burning so hot. But her embarrassment was only part of the reason. Truly, she needed to look down at the stairs as she ascended so she didn't step on her dress. It amazed her that after only a few weeks of not wearing the things, she had forgotten how to move in them.

The moment they walked inside the shop, Rick took a step away until all that touched was their interlocked arms. While she missed the feel of his body pressed alongside hers, the sights in the room were adequate to distract her. Rows of shelves filled with bolts of fabric in several different colors and patterns stood on the left side of the room. On the right sat a desk with a man behind it cutting fabric. When the bell over the door chimed he popped up and greeted them with a crooked-toothed smile.

"Hello, hello, what can I do for you folks today?"

"Good day, sir. The lady and I are visiting a fine dining establishment this evening and hope you might have time to tailor something you have on hand for us," Rick said.

Smiling wide and nodding, he looked to Cat. Before he could speak, she jumped in. "And I'd like to trade it tomorrow for some sturdy traveling clothes, if that's possible."

The man began to walk around her, digging in his apron. "Of course, not a problem in the slightest. Such beautiful red hair, perhaps something in green satin..." He spoke mostly to himself.

"I would love gold if you have something in that color," she interrupted his murmurings.

His wide eyes sparkled with inspiration and his murmurings took on a whole new enthusiasm. "Yes, oh yes, I have just the thing..." His words trailed off into whispers about measurements, lace, and other things too quiet for her to follow.

A woman emerged from the back and escorted Cat into the depths of the shop. For a few hurried moments she took her measurements in the privacy of a back room with a curtain for a door. When finished, she took her out to the main room to give her options for accessories and shoes. While they waited, she and Rick were served afternoon tea by a finely dressed young man who couldn't be much over eight. From the similar eyes and chin, she guessed it was the tailor's son. The boy kept them company and they swapped news with him while sipping tea. Cat was so relieved at the chance to sit on soft, comfortable furniture that she was disappointed when the tailor brought out bundled packages for them.

Before Rick could try to offer, she stepped up to the counter and paid for her own items. The woman taking her money raised her eyebrows but didn't say anything. Rick's tight lips tried to hide a smile, a protest, or both. Once finished, she moved away to allow him to pay for his own items. Courting or not, she wasn't about to allow herself to become indebted to a man ever again if she could help it. And in this case, she could.

The late afternoon sun cast a golden hue over the town as they stepped back out onto the street. The number of wagons and the foot traffic had decreased by half, leaving the air clearer of dust and refreshing. Or maybe that was just her building excitement making the entire world feel like a more hospitable place. Stolen glances through her hair at Rick's handsome profile only heightened the feeling. She felt giddy as a schoolgirl with an infatuation but without the pressure and anxiety that came with it. The only other infatuation she'd ever had was Michael. That had come with all sorts of pressure.

She floated all the way back to the inn on a cloud of excitement that kept her chatting randomly about the array of shops and the warmth of the community surrounding them. With smiles and nods, and not a single complaint, Rick escorted her to the door of her room.

"Will half an hour be adequate, or would you prefer longer to get ready?" he asked.

The question took her completely by surprise, leaving her mouth hanging. She'd never been given a choice in such matters. It took her a moment to think it over and seize the rare opportunity. "An hour would be nice, thank you." The deviation was due in part to test his response and in part because she would need extra time to get into the complicated layers that went with such a dress. Doing it on her own wasn't impossible, but it wouldn't be an easy task.

Stepping back, Rick kissed her hand. "O' course. I shall see you in an hour."

The kiss lingered, his soft lips and warm breath thrilling her as much as the control he had just given her. He spun away and strode to his door across the hall. After unlocking and opening it, he turned around and bowed deeply to her. That handsome grin left her breathless and swooning as he closed the door. She leaned back against the wall and tried to capture her runaway heart.

Busy as she was primping her deliciously clean hair and getting into her layers of clothing, the hour couldn't go fast enough. While at the tailor's, she had heard Rick and the man talking through the thin walls. It had sounded as though the man had a fine suit he was tailoring to Rick's size. She had never imagined a man like Rick would wear a suit. Now she couldn't stop imagining it. Her mind conjured up the image as she struggled with her corset. The darn thing proved impossible to get properly tight on her own, but she managed to make it at least serviceable to hold up her breasts.

Looking at them pale and pouring over the tan corset reminded her of Rick's hand on them. Her nipples popped to attention at the memory. Tingles spread through them, then down her abdomen and between her legs from there. She grabbed her right breast and gently pinched the nipple, imagining the touch was Rick's. Moisture made the sensitive folds of skin at her apex slick. She moaned aloud before remembering how thin the walls of such an establishment could be. That served to snap her out of her daydream with jarring speed.

She stared at her reflection in surprise. Even though she was the only witness, her cheeks flushed scarlet. The sight made her smile. It had been so long since she'd desired intimacy with a man that she had nearly forgotten how powerful the urge could be. Shaking her head to clear the desire away, she let go of her breast with reluctant slowness and reached for her dress. Focus didn't come easily after that. For one, even the brush of fabric kept her nipples hard, and each step made her acutely aware of how her slick folds rubbed together. Once she had her dress on, she splashed a bit of water from the basin on her face. Hands on the vanity, she leaned close to the foggy mirror and stared herself in the eye.

"Get hold of yourself, woman. Can't have him thinking you're a tart who opens her legs for any man," she chastised herself.

With a deep breath, she straightened and smoothed her golden-hued dress. Lovely as it was with a square neckline bordered by lace and gathered at the waist, the thing felt confining after wearing breeches for so long. It didn't help that the corset forced her to take such short breaths. While she had always worn it with her blouse, the loose fit had allowed her to keep the corset loose as well. This fine dress made no such allowances. If she hadn't cinched it up so tight she risked splitting a seam. Turning this way and that in the mirror, she admired how the hoop held the gold fabric out and helped it move. Comfort aside, it was lovely, and it was nice to wear something lovely again.

That done, she turned to the special items she had purchased—three long, white, silk ribbons and a handful of tiny rosebuds. Closing her eyes, she cleared her mind, and took three deep breaths. As she breathed, she felt her connection to the earth and its creatures, to the moon and the stars above.

Her fingers began to weave the ribbon into a plait, working in the rosebuds as she went. She chanted softly as she did so, the words the barest of whispers.

"Danu, mother Goddess, I invoke thee and ask you to lend me your wisdom." As she chanted, she envisioned the power of the one she invoked going into the crown, infusing it.

"Brigid, Goddess of fire and hearth, I invoke thee and ask you to lend me your protection." Flowers and silk came together in her hands, her energy pouring into them.

"Aengus, God of love, I invoke thee and ask you to help me make good decisions in matters of the heart."

The plait of flowers and silk buzzed with energy, warming her hands. She placed the crown atop her wavy, red tresses, working it in and through them until it was secure. Energy poured over her and soaked into her being. As it did, she felt protected and clear-headed.

A knock on the door got her blood pumping to sensitive regions all over again. Well, at least there was no need for rouge. She ran her hands over her hair in a few spots, bit her lips for color, and walked to the door as slowly as she could make herself. It turned out just short of a mad dash she was grateful Rick couldn't see.

"Hello, Miss Catriona. 'Tis Patrick Fergusson come to fetch you for dinner," Rick's semi-formal voice drifted through the door.

The fact that he had called her Miss Catriona instead of Mrs. O'Brian made her smile so big it hurt her cheeks. She was of a mind to tell him how much this touched her when she opened the door, caught sight of him, and lost all ability to speak. A charcoal suit tailored just right accented his broad shoulders and muscular arms, as well as all the right lines of his legs and groin. Fine black shoes had replaced his dusty, brown boots. Her breath caught when she tried to speak. Despite the absolutely dashing figure he cut, it was his face she couldn't stop staring at. The beard and mustache were gone. A strong jaw offset fine cheekbones, balancing out to give him a mature, handsome visage. He had pulled his chin-length brown hair back with a charcoal-hued ribbon and tucked it into a bun in the style she had seen in paintings of ancient Japanese warriors. Without all the scruff on his face, his green eyes stood out in a manner that captured her without mercy. Lessons drilled into her by an insistent mother were all that helped her scramble together an ounce of etiquette.

"Mr. Fergusson, thank you for coming to fetch me. You look…" She struggled for words that wouldn't sound like she wanted to tear all his fine clothes off. "You look quite dashing."

But the words proved unnecessary. Rick's wide-eyed look of shock made it clear he hadn't heard a thing she said. He murmured something in Irish as his gaze slowly traveled up her body. By the time he reached her face, desire burned in his eyes like sparks around an emerald.

"You look absolutely stunning, like a fae queen. I feel remiss in calling you princess before," he finally said in English.

She looked down before the heat could fully enflame her

face. His elbow extended toward her.

"Shall we?" he asked.

She nodded and straightened, doing her best to be the portrait of poise and collection that she felt so far from. Curiosity soon distracted her from her nerves and allowed her to notice some odd things about Rick. The confident, easy way in which he carried himself made her think he wasn't a stranger to fine clothing. Most lower class men fussed when they had to dress in such a manner. She realized she didn't know much about his life before being a guide.

Her curiosity grew into something she could barely contain. Not that his class mattered. She had enough money, and he clearly wasn't the type to seek such a thing. But then, he never seemed to want for or complain about money. The way he had paid for their lodging that first night in Omaha, how he replenished their supplies at each outpost even if they didn't need it, how he replaced his traveling clothes so readily, it all spoke of someone unconcerned with money. It didn't make sense. It was as if he wasn't the penniless rogue she had thought him to be.

If he didn't want for money, why on Earth did he risk his life escorting people across America? The trip was a grand adventure, to be sure. But she couldn't imagine anyone enduring it more than once if they didn't have to.

The crowded dining room downstairs with its clanging plates and chatting patrons didn't allow her the chance to make inquiries. With many murmured pardons, they made their way through the inn's dining room and out into the streets. Golden lamplight lit the mostly empty streets in scattered pools. Only a few wagons and horses traversed the streets, working folk on their way home from the looks of it.

The normalcy of it all struck her as unusual after weeks on the trail. Nostalgia wrapped around her and made her miss her friends terribly. The heavy scent of salt in the air didn't help either, as it conjured up memories of the bays back in New York. At the same time, she was quite excited to be on Rick's arm walking through a civilized city. It smelled a bit worse than she remembered. The slight sweetness of manure mixed with the tang of lamp oil, while the sweat of hard-working people mingled with the perfume of the upper class. Neither mixture was pleasant in any way. It made her realize how much she was going to love living in the country again.

Things were simpler in the country, purer as she got to live closer to the animals and land. And of course it was safer away from people who didn't whisper behind fans and hands about her and her friends' oddities. They hid what they were as well as they could, but prying eyes eventually noticed.

"I don't believe I've ever seen you this quiet. You're all right, I hope?" Rick asked.

She smiled up at him, stricken once again by how handsome he was beneath all the scruff he had shaved off. Another part of her missed it. The ruggedness held a certain excitement and danger that had been very appealing.

"Quite, thank you. I think I may just be in a bit of shock at discovering the civilized man who was hiding beneath that beard," she said.

Rick groaned, an enticing sound that did wonderful things to her. "I've gone and done it now. My roguish façade has been ruined," he said.

With a laugh, she looked to the darkening sky in a gesture

equally as dramatic. He joined her with easy laughter that sounded like it came from deep in his soul. It was a lovely sound to hear coming from a man so haunted. That thought made her look to the people who walked the streets and sidewalks. While she knew Rick wouldn't lie to her about Ainsworth not moving his goods through Utah, she couldn't help but fear he might have men here anyway. Silly and irrational though the fear was, it refused to go away. No one looked twice at them save to smile or ogle one or the other of them. All in all, the strangers seemed innocent of wishing them any ill. She did her best to believe that and breathe easier.

Less than half a block later, Rick opened the door to a dining establishment where they were met by a gentleman in a fine gray suit. At hearing Rick's name, he nodded and escorted them inside. The view within made her forget all about Ainsworth and his men.

Fine tablecloths lined with delicate lace draped round tables meant to seat a couple. A high ceiling made the smallish room feel spacious. Several feet lay between the two dozen or so tables, making it clear the owners cared more about their guests' comfort than the amount of them they could fit into the room. Large, yellow candles sat amidst centerpieces of fresh daisies and buttercup flowers on each table. Aromas of roasting meat and vegetables filled the air. Cat's mouth began to water. Maybe it was a good thing she hadn't been able to get her corset very tight. A warm, finely cooked meal wasn't something she'd had often of late.

Their host led them through the room and out a large oak door that looked like it could withstand an entire regiment of Rebels. It opened onto a lush garden of raised beds sitting in rows that spread out in a maze framed by tall fruit trees. Shadows draped it all, broken up by pockets of light shining down from windows of surrounding buildings—windows that were above head height. No one would be able to see this secluded garden. Cat's curiosity piqued as their host led them down a path of flagstones set in low-growing mint that released its lovely fragrance with each step they took. The man paused at a planting bench to light a candle and take it with them.

A hesitant smile tugged at her lips as she looked over at Rick. He hid a smile of his own as he gave her a sideways glance. What was he up to? She trusted him more than she thought she'd ever be able to trust a man after Michael, but this was all quite unusual. They ducked beneath the fruit trees and skirted around what looked like a blueberry bush. The dark made it hard to tell, but she smelled blueberries, so it seemed likely. On the other side, starlight spilled down on rows of grapevines growing up trellises. Dark or not, she would know their silhouettes and scents anywhere. Rows of more grapes spread out like the spokes of a wheel from a little gazebo aglow with candlelight. They reminded her so much of Deirdre's grapevines that it made her heart both hurt and swell.

They walked between the rows to the gazebo. A small round table set in the same manner as those inside the establishment waited in the center of the gazebo. Grapevines grew up the support beams of the structure, their leaves and fruit hanging down to add a screen of extra privacy. Rick had to duck to get beneath them. A large orange and white cat slumbering next to the support beams on one side stirred. Its eyes shot open wide and locked on Rick.

Predator. Danger! its mind screamed.

No, no danger. It's all right little one. We mean you no harm, Catriona told it.

But it was gone in a flash.

A rustling in the fruit tree above the grape arbor gave her a glimpse of feathers. The sleepy thoughts of an owl drifted down to her. *Not time to hunt or torment cat yet. Sleep more.* She couldn't help but smile at that. Together with the cat's, his presence must be what kept the smaller birds away from all the fruit.

Three big yellow candles cast a lovely glow on fine porcelain plates. The place looked nothing short of magical to her. Somehow she managed to mumble her gratitude when Rick pulled out her chair for her.

Their host rattled off the menu, but she couldn't concentrate long enough to listen to him. Too much beauty lay around her, drawing her attention away. Grapes hung everywhere in big clumps, and they smelled divine.

"Catriona, what would you like to eat?" Rick asked after a moment of silence she didn't realize had fallen until it was too late.

Cheeks warming, she struggled to recall anything their host had said. "I'll have whatever you recommend," she finally told Rick.

Normally, she would have seized the opportunity to choose for herself. But she had already ignored the poor host, she wasn't about to ask him to repeat himself. Besides, she had a feeling more opportunities for such independence would arise with Rick.

A short distance away, a frog croaked. *Hello?* The sound was soon echoed by another, and another.

Cat gone?

Sing!

They struck up a lovely chorus of frog song that delighted and entertained her.

Their host made a motion with his chin and a man with a violin stepped out of the shadows between two rows. With promises to return shortly, their host took his leave. The violinist remained back at the edge of the rows. He was close enough to the gazebo to be considered a proper chaperone, but far enough away to give them adequate privacy for conversation. At a nod from Rick, the man set bow to strings and began to play. Beautiful music that tugged at her soul filled the warm evening air. It mingled with the sound of crickets and a few frogs quite nicely. She enjoyed it for several moments before her excitement got the better of her and loosened her tongue.

"However did you find such a place? 'Tis downright magical," she said, keeping her voice quiet so it didn't compete with the music.

Eyes alight, he delved into a story about a need to find a watering hole here that served more than water. He told her how he had endured the company of a horribly tiresome fop all the way from Omaha and either had to unwind or end up leaving the man here. He had a way of telling the story that made her laugh with the unrestrained joy of a young lass and beg for more details. His animated manner and quick wit made him quite the storyteller. But what truly impressed her was the way he listened to her responses and engaged her as though what she had to say was more important than his own words.

All too soon, their host returned. Once she saw the bottle

he cradled in one arm and the two delicate wineglasses he carried, she instantly forgave his interruption. He set the glasses down with softly spoken apologies for interrupting. A loud pop sounded as he uncorked the bottle.

"Per the gentleman's request, our finest white wine for the lady." He went on about the age of the vines that had produced the grapes and even touched a bit on the town in Italy the vines had originated from.

While she wanted nothing more than to get back to her privacy with Rick, she knew the man's conversation for what it was; time to allow the wine to breathe. That he knew to do so would have impressed Dierdre. Finally, he filled their glasses.

"I do hope you enjoy it. I shall be along shortly with your meal," he said before turning to disappear into the dark.

Cat thanked him and picked up the glass with something close to reverence. It wasn't the alcohol that made her feel that way, but the gesture by Rick. That he had thought to bring her to such a place touched her deeply. She looked over the glasses turned golden by the candlelight and stared at him in awe for a moment.

"A single table amidst the most beautiful setting I've ever seen. How did you arrange all this on such little notice?" she finally asked.

Rick's crooked smile was evident even behind his raised glass. "I have me ways. And I knew how much you'd love it. That motivation was enough. Do you mind if I make a toast?"

Blushing hotly, but doing her best to ignore it, she raised her glass. "Please do."

"To new beginnings," he said.

She echoed the toast through a smile that pushed her

burning cheeks up high. They clinked glasses and she raised the wine to her nose. The lovely, slightly heady aroma told her it would be delicious before it even touched her tongue. It didn't disappoint. In fact, the taste was fine and smooth without the acidic bite of many lesser-made wines.

"How did you find an establishment that serves wine here? I thought this was a city that frowns upon spirits," she asked.

"Oh aye, 'tis, but like I said, I have me ways." After a long sip of wine, he set his glass down, folded his hands together, and rested his chin on them. "Enough about me for now. I want to know more about you."

Heat scorched along her skin. The world swayed a little and sadly, not from the wine. Picking at the edge of a fingernail, she looked down at it as if it required her full attention. There were many things she didn't want to tell him. Things that might change his opinion of her. But, if she were to take this courtship seriously, she knew she had to.

Rick's hand settled atop one of hers. Though the touch was gentle, she jumped. "Me deepest apologies. I didn't mean to make you uncomfortable."

His gentle tone gave her the courage to meet his gaze. "There's no need for you to apologize. If we're to give this courtship a fair chance, I don't want secrets between us. There are things you need to know about me. If you change your mind, so be it."

Breathing deep, she drew her hand from his and sat back in her chair. She forced herself to hold his gaze and bear the shame she had coming. "I'm not like other high society ladies because I wasn't always one. I was born a farmer's daughter. I became pregnant with Michael's child and his family forced him to marry me. I lost the baby." There was more to say, but already her voice began to fail her.

Rick moved his chair closer to her side of the table and took hold of her hand once again. He raised it up and held it against his cheek for a long moment. "It brings me great sorrow to know you have suffered such a loss. But, Cat, what social circle you were born into, and what misfortune has befallen you, doesn't change how I feel. You could still be a farmer's daughter and it wouldn't change me mind."

Tears sprung to her eyes, preventing her from holding his gaze any longer. She widened her eyes and looked up, trying to dry the moisture. Every day this man astounded her with how wonderful he was. Stubborn, sarcastic, a touch ornery, yes, but wonderful beyond measure. Eyes going distant, he lay her hand back on the table and leaned back in his own chair. Many would say such things because they were a penniless rogue looking to raise their station, but that didn't feel like the case with Rick.

"Now, 'tis me turn, I suppose. Me family is wealthy and I've inherited that wealth. Me da bought a large plot of land in California. He wasn't a prospector. He just wanted a safe place in the country for our...family. But he found gold in the creek that ran through our property, a lot of it. So sadly, I'm not the romantic portrait of a penniless rogue many imagine me to be."

She could only stare. It explained many things, so many, that she was surprised she hadn't guessed at it before. Perhaps it had been because she liked the dangerous idea of him being a penniless rogue. The irony of their situation struck her as humorous. A fit of laughter soon stole over her. It grew until she couldn't stop. Moments into it, Rick joined her. They laughed until tears squeezed from their eyes. The violinist gave them a wide-eyed look, but kept playing as if they weren't laughing their fool heads off. Only when their host returned with their food were they able to stop. The man hid a smile as he bowed his head and took his leave.

The aromas of juicy meat, rosemary, and lemon made Cat suddenly quite serious. After trying a bite of the deliciously flavored chicken, she raised her brows at Rick. "Romantic rogue, hum?"

He squared his shoulder. "Aye, I rather liked the idea of you envisioning me as a rogue. It held a certain romantic danger. Alas, I'm nothing more exciting than new money."

"That makes two of us, Mr. Fergusson," she said.

The warmth in his eyes spread over her in ways she longed for his hands to do. Things deep inside her awoke and tightened in a most exciting way. To calm herself, she turned her attention to her food for a while. Divinely seasoned in comparison to their meals on the trail, it was almost adequate to distract her. The way Rick kept licking his lips with slow, obvious pleasure undid all of her carefully planned distraction.

She looked quickly down. "You are much more than new money. You're honorable, kind, and have a rare respect for a woman's mind."

Listing those qualities didn't take her mind off his delicious lips or bulging arms like she had hoped it would. But it did serve to remind her that there was much more to him that she liked than his fine physique.

"Thank you for such kind words. Me mum would be proud to hear them," he said. The reverent tone he used when he spoke of his mother made her look up. Love for the woman shined in his eyes.

"I'd love to hear all about her," Cat prompted.

All but glowing with pride, Rick delved into stories about his mum. The way he spoke of her made it clear he revered the woman almost as a saint. Throughout the meal they exchanged stories, laughed, and enjoyed the violinist, who turned out to be quite talented. Rick even accompanied the man on the harmonica for a few songs. To Cat's surprise, the two very different instruments blended well together. Even the frogs seemed to agree as they joined in. The two men shook hands and slapped backs as they exchanged compliments afterward.

When their meal was finished and their host came to clear away their plates and refill their glasses, Rick complimented the man on his kindness and asked him to extend his gratitude to the chef.

Smiling at Cat, he asked, "Will you excuse me for one moment?"

"Of course."

Rick stepped away from the gazebo with the man. Their heads leaned together and they spoke in hushed voices she couldn't quite hear. Rick tucked coins in the man's hand and clapped him on the shoulder. He left with a smile and a nod.

Those small interactions impressed Cat. She was used to high society men ignoring the help and entertainers to the point of being rude. The actions of the man spoke of an exceptional upbringing and made her want to meet his parents. Or, his mother, rather, since he said she was the only one he had remaining.

As Rick rejoined her, she set her second empty glass of

wine on the table. "I don't mean to be a lush, but this wine is divine," she said. But it was more than that. She hadn't felt safe enough in a man's company since Michael to indulge in wine.

Dimples formed in Rick's cheeks, a sign she had come to realize meant he was holding back a smile. His hands found hers, as they so often had tonight. The thrill of his touch danced through her. Somehow it managed to remain just as strong and wonderful each time.

"So you've said, repeatedly," he said, allowing his grin to break through. The expression—so full of joy—made him look absolutely dashing.

She giggled, beginning to feel the effects of the wine. "So I have."

"But I'm glad you feel that way," he said, gaze lifting to look beyond her.

Her head turned at the sound of footsteps brushing on the flagstone just as their host sat a small wooden box in front of Rick. The men nodded to each other and the host took his leave with a huge grin. Soft violin notes drifted to them as the violinist began anew. The tune thrilled her and made her blush at the same time—*Scarborough Fair*. Rick moved the box in front of her.

"I know we've only begun our courtship, but I've known you now for a little over a month, so I hope you'll accept this small token of me affection," he said.

"Rick... I..." She didn't know what to say, so she let her voice trail off.

Her eyes fell to the box. At no more than three inches or so tall and wide and maybe twelve inches long, she had no idea what it could hold. It was too long for the traditional courtship gifts of jewelry and too short and small for flowers. She undid the little latch that held it closed and opened the lid. The oiled hinges didn't make a sound. On a bed of black satin sat a long, healthy-looking root. She knew it instantly by both scent and appearance. It was a dormant grapevine.

Her watery eyes shot up to him. The vulnerable look of doubt on his face almost held her tongue. "Patrick, this is…this is…" Her throat closed and she found she couldn't finish.

He jumped in quick as if he feared she didn't like it. "You mentioned you and your friends wanted to start your own vineyard and raise horses."

"I did," she forced out in a whisper, turning her shining eyes up to him.

The doubt melted away, turning into a pleased smile. "You like it then?"

She opened her mouth to speak, but her body threatened to reduce her words to a sob, so she closed it without making a sound. Her moisture-filled eyes returned to the bare root. "It's perfect," she murmured.

His fingers wove through hers. "Then you must accept it. I'll be heartbroken if you don't." It wasn't a command, but more of a plea.

After that she couldn't possibly refuse. Keeping her head down to hide the depth of emotion she knew burned across her face, she drew the box to her and clutched it tight. "In that case, I accept," she said in a quiet tone.

"Excellent! I hear sprites like this particular grape, so perhaps when the vines take root and produce, they might attract a few," he said with a sparkle in his eyes. But was it teasing, mischief, or something else? Cat couldn't quite tell.

Either way, her cheeks heated and she looked down.

The man spoke of the Tuatha at times, and dropped little comments like that on the rare occasion, but such was the way of the Irish. They longed for the old days and old ways, even if they didn't truly believe they were real. The question was, did he?

"Sounds perfectly magical," she said as she stroked the box.

Humming low in his throat, he covered her hand with his. "Just like you," he whispered.

The table moved slightly as Rick rose. "I'll be right back," he promised.

He dashed off into the darkening shadows and shared a few hushed words with the violinist. The lovely notes of a tune with just the right cadence for a waltz filled the air. Rick returned to her side and offered his hand.

"Miss Catriona, may I have this dance?" he asked.

She lifted her hand with a flourish, giving him a coy look from beneath her lashes. "My dance card has nothing but your name on it this evening, Mr. Fergusson," she said.

As she rose, she took great care to set the box back away from the candles. The risk was miniscule, but it was one she wasn't willing to take. The contents of that box were far too precious to her. Never had a man given her such a thoughtful gift. Not only did it mean he listened to her and cared about what she wanted, but he embraced her friends being part of her life as well. That in itself was a treasure.

Carrying her hand as if it were something equally as precious, Rick guided her out onto the short-trimmed grass before the violinist. There in the candlelight, they danced a slow waltz that had her heart beating a conflicting rhythm.

The bare skin of Rick's hand against her own sent little thrills of excitement based partially on the impropriety of it. Societal rules said she should wear gloves, but she hadn't. Partly it had been because she'd spent so long on the trail that it seemed terribly impractical. But mostly she had forgone wearing them because she simply hadn't wanted to. At the time of the decision she had felt a rebellious thrill. Now she felt an altogether different thrill. Then there was the hand on her waist. Though satin and cotton layers separated their skin, the heat that radiated from his hand scorched her in a most welcome manner.

Sharing gazes that further tested the boundaries of societal acceptances, they danced long into the night. Rick's feet and hands were as quick and talented as his wit. He guided her effortlessly around the garden with a grace that ensured her heart pounded whether it was a polka or a slow waltz. Dancing alone with a man rather than in a group felt rebellious in itself. But dancing with Rick, here alone save for the violinist, felt downright scandalous. And Danu help her, but she loved it. The man kept his hands where he was supposed to and made not one untoward comment. The look of desire in his eyes told her of his restraint and thrilled her to no end. Every bit of it delighted her—from his obvious desire to his honorable ways.

The evening ended all too soon. After tucking more coins into the hands of their host and the violinist, Rick escorted her back to the inn. They chatted along the way about the journey left ahead of them. Cat began to grow excited in an entirely different way. Only eighteen days or so lay between them and their destination. That was less than three weeks. At the door to her room, she stalled with all manner of questions about the trek across Nevada.

Was it truly that hot? What did a rattlesnake sound like? Were there natives there?

The questions flowed almost in an endless stream. She was curious, sure, but she really just wasn't ready for the night to end. Finally, Rick's eyes scanned left and right. He put a hand on the wall she was propped against. He leaned close enough she could smell the lemon soap scent lingering on his skin. That, along with his lovely eyes so close to her own, made her breath catch and her knees weaken.

"We have a hard week ahead of us. 'Tis best if you get a good night's sleep," he said.

She couldn't stop watching his lips as he talked. How she wanted to touch them, lick them... They descended on hers with an urgency that matched her own. Her arms wrapped around his waist and pulled him to her. The brush of his chest against her breasts drew a moan from her that poured down his throat. He groaned in response and cradled the back of her head. The way he touched her made her feel like something precious and delicate, two things she had never felt like.

After a long, wonderful moment, he drew away and took a step back. She grabbed hold of his hand. A plea for him to come inside waited on her tongue, but she didn't let it loose. The last thing in the world she wanted was for him to think her a tart who wasn't taking this courtship seriously. If she invited him in like she so desperately wanted to, he might think just that. Her history with Michael made that fear a distinct possibility. Besides, she couldn't lie with him until she told him the truth about what she was. And if she did that, there was a strong possibility he'd turn away from her.

"What if you have nightmares? Perhaps you should sleep on the floor in my room," she suggested instead.

He lifted her hand. Eyes closing as if in deep indulgence, he kissed it long and slow. A shiver ran through her that she couldn't have stopped if she had wanted to.

"There is no fear of nightmares this night, I assure you," he said when he relinquished her hand.

The words might have made her blush if her blood wasn't already rushing down to her breasts and groin. Part of her felt foolish. Of course the man had been having nightmares since the war and had endured them without her help until now. But it was nice to know their evening might bring him a good night's rest.

She managed to scrounge together a modicum of propriety. "Well then, Mr. Fergusson, I bid you a good evening and look forward to seeing you on the morrow."

Rick bowed as he took another step back. "A good evening to you as well, me dear Cat."

That would have undone the last thread she had on her control if he hadn't promptly spun and stepped into his own room. Resisting the urge to sigh, she clutched the box containing the grapevine root to her chest, wishing it were him. It was going to be a very long eighteen days if she couldn't get her desire under control.

22

Rick

Day Forty
Nevada

The desolate landscape of sagebrush and sandy soil coupled with the scorching heat to force them into traveling by night across Nevada. A week into it and Rick found himself missing the salt flats. But they couldn't slow down or stop. Though he'd never tell Cat, he had noticed a man trailing them in the town of Salt Lake the morning they'd left. He refused to steal her peace from her by worrying her needlessly. He had ditched the man easily enough. It was part of why he'd booked them rooms in a place separate from where they had dined. While he had wanted to be right about Ainsworth not having men in Utah, he hadn't been willing to risk Cat's safety on hope alone. And he was glad he hadn't.

A few days of sticking to the hills and skirting around the

salt flats of the Utah territory helped keep them hidden from prying eyes. Nights crossing Nevada convinced him they had lost any tail. Unfortunately, traveling at night like this exhausted both him and Cat and put the horses on edge. But Cat helped with that. She murmured to them, stroked them, and brought them a sense of calm even he couldn't. Much to her credit, the woman kept pushing on, never wanting to slow or take a break. He'd never met a woman like her, and not just because she was fae. He'd met plenty of them back in Ireland. That wasn't what made her special. *She* was what made her special.

She talked a lot less when they traveled in the dark, and he missed the sound of her voice.

Worse yet, they were forced to stay on the trail, stopping at the old Pony Express stations for water. Most were no more than deserted sites with a wellhead, but that was all they needed. The horses survived on scrub grass and the grain he had bought in Salt Lake. Though they were making great time, they needed a break. Toward the beginning of the seventh night, when he smelled the fresh, clean scent of river water, he made a decision. At first Cat didn't notice as they veered away from the trail. Lincoln, on the other hand, moved with a new spring in his step. He led the way with his fanlike tail of gray and white swaying above him like a teetering sail.

The cooler night air wasn't quite enough to stop Rick from sweating. He was so, so tired of sweating. As they slept each day away beneath the shade of a tent or rare tree, he sweated. Even at night, he sweated until the hours waned toward dawn. Usually the nights in Nevada were cooler, cold even. But not this year. With temperatures in the day tipping over into dangerous levels, the sandy soil held and radiated heat even at night. Hot nights were a rare and unwelcome occurrence in this state. Even Cat tugged at her collar and fanned herself.

He smiled as he anticipated her reaction to their destination.

One hand on a nicely shaped hip, Cat guided her horse closer. "You haven't strayed from the trail in days and now you have a mischievous look on your face. What are you up to, Rick?"

Dark as it was with only a half moon out, he had been hoping she wouldn't notice. But he should have known better. After all, her astuteness was part of what he admired about her.

"'Tis a surprise."

"A hint, then?"

Squeezing with his legs, he urged Ayegi to go faster. With an unladylike curse that almost made him laugh aloud, she urged Galiha into a trot and caught up.

"It wouldn't be a surprise if I told you," he said.

"Come now, just a hint is all. That's not telling me."

She went on to ask every manner of question conceivable about where they were going and why. Her renewed energy was reward in itself. He played along, giving her vague answers that kept her asking more questions. It did him good to see her so animated again. The chatting kept her distracted enough that she didn't even notice the slight incline they started up.

Galiha nearly gave it away when one hoof slipped on the smooth rock. "Is this path safe?" she asked.

"Aye, just let him choose his steps. He'll get you there safely," he assured her.

Not wanting her to get ahead, he urged Ayegi into a brisk walk that soon had him moving out ahead of her. A cool, clean scent that he could taste on the back of his tongue touched the air just as the ground leveled out. Soft moonlight illuminated boulders framing two sides of the plateau they had ascended. It would hide them quit effectively from anyone who might be in the valley below looking up. Nearly as important as that was the spring-fed pool of water nestled between the hollow of the boulders. At barely more than the depth of a water trough and only twice as wide and long they wouldn't be able to submerge in it easily, but it would be more than adequate to water the horses, refill their canteens, and even wash their clothes and bathe.

As Galiha stopped at the edge to drink, Cat swung down from the saddle.

Much to his surprise—and delight—she began peeling her boots off.

"A dip in the river would have been welcome, but this gives us cover from prying eyes. 'Tis perfect," she said.

Rick dismounted beside her as Ayegi joined Galiha in trying to suck down the entire contents of the pool. A moment later Lincoln stuck his head between them both and lapped at the water.

"I'm glad you're not disappointed." He removed his boots and gun belt. "You may want to turn away, for the sake of propriety. I've endured the heat for far too long, and 'tis long past time for me to wash up," he said.

She surprised him by reaching for the waist of her breeches. "Aye, that makes two of us!" she said with a delighted laugh as she turned away.

That laugh did sinful things to his body that made him roll his eyes closed and beg the Powers That Be for restraint. She had pulled her tunic free of her breeches and had the hem up several inches before he finally forced himself to turn away. Apparently, the Powers That Be weren't listening. In a desperate attempt to stop himself from growing any harder, he set to removing Ayegi's saddle, then moved on to do the same for Galiha and their packhorse. He removed the bridles and halters as well. They wouldn't wander far, not with the grain they could surely smell tucked away in the saddlebags. The monotonous routine helped him gain a bit of control over his rebellious body.

Bellies full of water, the horses moved off to graze on the grass that grew around the plateau. Droplets of water splattered him as Lincoln bounded around him then dashed off to circle the horses. Laughing at the pup, he stripped down to his undergarments. Cool air rippled across the thin, cotton underpants, hitting his scrotum, and helping tame his erection a little.

"You can clean up first, I'll step around the boulder to give you some privacy," he said over his shoulder.

"Will you help me with my corset?" she asked. The sultry sound of her voice undid all the good the cool air had done him.

"Of course," he said before good sense could stop his words.

He started to turn but hesitated.

"Don't worry. The darkness will preserve your modesty," Cat teased.

Her voice had a lovely, lazy sound to it that pulled at things deep inside him, things that he feared would never reawaken completely. It wasn't just desire she stirred in him. That scared him, but it also thrilled him to know that part of him wasn't dead.

"Me modesty? 'Tis hardly me modesty I'm concerned with," he said as he turned.

All her long, wavy, red hair hung loose and draped over a shoulder, exposing her back to him. Moonlight shimmered across the silky laces of her corset, crisscrossing in a mesmerizing pattern. The pattern led his eyes down to the curve of buttocks, covered only in cotton drawers. A strangled sound escaped him before he could mask it. Cat let out a wonderful giggle that sent tingles straight down to his erection. It took all of his restraint not to moan. If her voice could do that...

His eyes rolled back so he closed them and took several deep breaths. It had been a very long time since he'd lain with a woman, but that wasn't it. None had elicited this response from him since his bride-to-be. Even then, his desire for her had been different, more basic. Cat pulled at something deeper inside, something more than just the need to copulate. And though he wanted to deny it, he couldn't lie to himself. It had nothing to do with her being fae and everything to do with her being Cat.

"Are you implying you're not modest, Mr. Fergusson?" she asked in a teasing tone.

"Not as modest as I should be in this situation," he admitted.

She took a step forward. At first, he thought maybe she was reconsidering disrobing. He let a long breath out. It would be for the best. But then she bent over and he thought he might lose his mind. Water splashed. A few cool droplets flew past her and landed on him. Drawn in by a force he could no longer fight, he walked up behind her. His fingers made short work of her corset ribbons. It was all he could do not to use his claws. But then she'd have no laces. As alluring as that might be, it would prove troublesome for her later on the trail. She took a deep breath, and the confining device loosened. Her head turned toward him just enough for him to see the mischievous smile lifting one corner of her lips.

"Will you help me slide it off?" she asked.

Her hips wiggled in a wonderfully enticing way as he slid the loose corset up over her head. He tried to fight the urge to touch her any further, he really did. But his hands had a mind of their own. They trailed back up her half-bare legs, over her hips, and to the curve of her waist.

"You have an effect on me," he admitted.

Her hands reached back and touched his legs. The gasp that pulled from him was beyond his power to stop. Only inches lay between them. He froze.

She leaned her head back close to his shoulder. "As do you on me," she whispered in a husky voice that told him she fought the same battle of restraint as he did. Knowing that only made his battle harder—among other things.

One move and he could be pressed up against her. His muscles shook with the effort of holding back. The part of him he kept hidden from her paced in its cage. Her hand moved up his leg and to his arm, almost scattering his restraint. Almost. If he made love to her without telling her what he was, even if she could accept it, she may never forgive him. His soldier training kicked in.

He took a step back and squeezed his eyes shut tight. "Cat, I want you, so much. But more than that, I want to show you the honor and respect you deserve." The sound of cloth moving over flesh made his knees weak, and his will weaker still. By the Goddess Brigid, what had she taken off?

"And I want you to know that I am a respectable woman, one who takes this courtship quite seriously. But I am still a woman, one with desires and wants. One who wants you," she said in a soft voice that tingled across him.

Eyes still closed, he reached out and found her bare waist. Not a stitch. "Nothing could question your respectability in my eyes," he said in a tone that was scarcely more than a moan of desire.

Both of her hands now worked their way up beneath his shirt. He lifted his arms and allowed her to pull it over his head. Her wet hands trailed down his bare chest. The sensation made his erection jump. Despite his best efforts to keep them shut, his eyes shot open. Shadows and long hair hid enough of her curves to leave him wanting so much more.

"Rick, do you intend to abandon all attempts to court me if we lay together?" Her voice was low and sultry, sliding over him as easily as her wet hands.

"No."

"Will you do so if our joining is less than perfect?" she all but purred near his ear. Her fingers worked at the laces of his breeches.

His voice came out strangled. "No. Such things can be worked on. It isn't the copulating that I desire most, but you."

"And I you," she purred as her hands locked behind his neck. "Which is why I want to reveal my final secret to you now, here, in my most vulnerable state."

Tension sang through his muscles and he froze. "Cat, you

don't have to—" A delicate finger against his lips stopped his words.

"I do have to."

"And there's something I must tell you as well, something that may make you run for the hills, but please don't. It might put you in danger, and I promise, you are in no danger from me, not ever," he said.

She grinned. "Now I am intrigued. But me first. And if after I tell you, you think me daft and wish to call off our courtship, I will understand. But I must tell you."

"All right then," he encouraged.

"I am a fae."

"I know."

"Now don't be so quick to prote—wait, what?" Face scrunched up, brows nearly touching, she gaped for a moment before finding her words. "I'm not jesting."

"I know. Neither am I. I smelled it the moment I met you on the steps of the wine shop," he admitted.

The lines on her face smoothed out until her skin resembled porcelain. "Smelled me?" It wasn't fear, exactly, in her voice, but it wasn't mirth either.

Sighing, he took a big step back. When his thigh touched a boulder, he stopped and contemplated getting out of the pool. But her words stopped him.

"The way Lincoln accepts you, obeys you, you're not human, are you?" she whispered. One hand touched her breastbone as if she were having trouble breathing. She wasn't, he could hear her breath strong and sure. Her heart was racing, though.

There it was, that caution bordering on fear that he'd been

dreading so much. But there was no turning back now. She'd shared her truth, it was time for him to share his.

"First I must say again, you are safe with me. I would never harm you. Despite what I am, it is not in my nature. Protection is more of a part of who and what I am than violence, though many believe the contrary," he began.

"And what are you?" she asked.

"I am a *faoladh*."

Much to his utter and complete surprise, she gasped and took a step toward him. She reached up to touch the side of his face. "A werewolf. I thought your kind were extinct." Of all the things he expected to hear in her voice, joy had not been one of them.

Her bare breasts rubbed across his chest, her hard nipples causing pinpricks of desire to shoot straight through him. The tip of his cock brushed her stomach. She pressed closer until it was trapped between them, the length of it rubbing against her soft skin.

"I would never fear you," she said on an exhale. "But you may fear *me* after I reveal my last secret, though." She let her hand drop away from his face. "My fae power is mindspeak with animals. I can hear their thoughts and converse with them in their minds."

The way the bison parted for them, how Galiha took to her so quickly, it all made sense now. "Why would that make me fear you? Wait, can you read me mind?"

Laughter erupted from her. "No! Especially considering the outstanding job done of hiding your power and nature from me." She recovered the step he'd taken away from her. "But I do feel drawn to you, comfortable with you like I'm not with most other people."

"Whew." He swiped a hand across his forehead before getting serious again. "I sense Lincoln is a fae creature as well, but what I'm not certain," he prompted.

"He is a *failinis*," she said.

Eyes opening wide, he uttered a colorful Irish word before asking, "A fae war hound?"

"Aye," she said with a smile.

"And Ashlinn and Sean gave him to me? Wait, do they know what I am?" he asked, the last dropping to a whisper.

"Certainly not. Ashlinn would have told me."

"I plan to tell them. The timing just hasn't been right," he said. He thought back to the way Sean had been in the stables. "But I do think Sean suspects I'm…more than human." And he had still trusted him to bring her all the way across the country.

"'Tis no easy secret to share, just as mine, Deirdre's, and Ashlinn's isn't," she said without an ounce of judgement in her tone.

These revelations, her quick acceptance of him, they made her all the more precious to him. More than ever, he did not want to foul this up. "Revealed secrets aside, maybe it is best if we wait, as is proper. You are so precious to me that I don't want to dishonor you, or make you feel like you aren't worth waiting for, because you are." At the last he couldn't stop his gaze from traveling down her naked torso.

She huffed. "You listen to me, Rick Fergusson. All my life I've done what others wanted me to do, living my life to please them. I'm finished with that. It would please me to have you right here, right now, and that's what I aim to do," she said in an authoritative voice that sent delicious thrills through him.

"Even knowing what I am?"

"Especially knowing what you are."

"In that case, I am yours for the taking." He had awakened this amazing woman and he wasn't about to do anything that would put her back to sleep. Still... "Sean will have me bullocks for this," he muttered.

Cat giggled. "Not before I do."

At those words, he finally dropped the walls he'd been so carefully hiding his power behind. The smile that graced her lips and lit up her eyes remade his long-broken heart. Mouth open in awe, she cupped his face in her hands staring at him like he was one of the great wonders of the world. Slowly, she trailed her hands down his body, finally reaching and grasping his erection, shattering any lingering restraint he had.

23

Cat

Both silky smooth and iron hard, Rick's erection was a wonderful contradiction that felt oh so right in her hand. He was big enough to thrill her, but not frighten. Her hand moved up and down the length of it. The resulting moans that tore from his throat as he threw his head back made her giddy with excitement.

One of his arms went around her back, the other found her left breast and began to massage it. Pleasure pulsed through it and down between her legs. He rolled her nipple between his fingers, causing her hand to convulse around his erection. They cried out almost in unison. This caused her to fall into a fit of delighted giggles. Rick's responding laughter vibrated against her skin as he began to kiss her neck. He lifted her onto one of the boulders. After a long look at her, he bent to suck and nibble at her neck in a way that made her long for him to do it to other parts of her.

Back arching, she pressed against him, thrilling at the feel of his hard chest rubbing against her nipples. His kisses trailed down. She shook with anticipation as his mouth hovered over her breast.

"Are you certain?" he asked in a wonderfully husky voice.

In answer, she arched her back and pushed her breast into his mouth. He sucked and nibbled until she thought she might climax before he entered her. Was such a thing even possible? Such pleasure wasn't something she'd experienced with Michael. Then Rick's hand moved down between her legs and she knew all things were possible. First one finger, then two entered her, exploring gently. She wanted more, and pressed against him to let him know. It only took him a heartbeat to find a rhythm that had her throwing her head back and moving her hips in time with his thrusts. Then with the fingers of his second hand, he began to make circles against the nub at her entrance, building the most exquisite pressure in her that she'd ever felt. As she shuddered and convulsed around his fingers moments later, he whispered sweet things in her ear about how amazing she was.

When she could finally utter something besides cries of pleasure, she told him, "Me? Hardly. You're the amazing one. I didn't even know such pleasure was possible."

With a laugh, he resumed kissing her neck. "It pleases me more than I can tell you to know *I've* pleased you," he murmured.

This shocked her to silence for a moment. The idea of a man finding joy in her own pleasure was foreign to her, but very much a welcome idea. Since he was open to such forward thinking, maybe he'd be open to more experimental ideas. She had seen something in one of Deirdre's books that put a woman in a position of power. Such a position would ease the anxiety snaking around her heart—an anxiety born of an abusive husband.

At her urging, he sat down on the boulder next to her.

"Then perhaps you'll indulge me a little more," she said.

She put her knees to either side of his legs and hovered just over his erection. Moonlight lit his face, revealing wide green eyes filled with excitement. It was all the permission she needed. Slowly, she lowered herself onto his erection until he was buried deep inside her. The supporting hand around her back helped her rise and fall onto him, but allowed her to find her own rhythm. Even in this he allowed her independence. That was almost as breathtaking as the feel of him moving in and out of her.

The unique position and freedom of movement stimulated parts of her in a way she'd never imagined possible. Before long she climaxed again, this time so powerful that her vision went white. She collapsed against him.

"You are so amazing, beautiful," he whispered to her as he stroked her back.

Once her heart started beating something close to a normal beat again, he began to move. "I want you to try and touch me mind when I come, to feel how precious you are to me. Can you do that?" he asked, placing a kiss on her neck.

She pushed herself up enough to look at him. "Are you sure? It wouldn't be an intrusion?"

Laughter bubbled from him. "No more than me cock is intruding in you."

Heat flushed her cheeks before spreading out from there. A tentative smile worked its way onto her lips. Easier than she thought possible, she reached into his mind, finding it wild and free, much like fae creatures. She felt both his human and wolf side, not as if they were two separate beings, but two halves of a whole. They were both warm, inviting, beautiful. Such pleasure and joy filled him that he all but glowed from within with it. She meant the world to him. He would fight for her, die for her, live for her. Most importantly, she could feel that he would never harm her in any way.

Tears traced hot tracks down her cheeks. She hadn't realized she'd closed her eyes until Rick's callused hand brushed her cheek. "That bad, hum?" he asked. "I knew me mind would be dark, but—"

Shaking her head, she grabbed his hand and kissed the palm. "No, not at all. It's beautiful, you're beautiful. And the way you see me is…" The lump in her throat wouldn't allow her to finish.

"As a treasure. That's what you are, a treasure," he said.

Heart swelling, she bent down and kissed him long and slow. He grasped her hips and began to move. Together they found a perfect rhythm. Not long after, he shuddered inside her and cried out her name.

He held her close and tight as if he never wanted to let go. More soft, wonderful words poured from him, as did lazy kisses that trailed across her shoulder and neck. It made her feel precious and cherished. She had thought such experiences were only stories told in Deirdre's forbidden books and those written by their fae ancestors. But then, before this trip, she would have never believed men like Patrick Fergusson existed outside of fae tales. She had never been so glad to be wrong.

24

Cat

Day Forty-One
Nevada

For the last quarter mile or so, Rick's attention had shifted from her. It was subtle, and he was trying to hide it, but it was impossible not to notice. Up until now he hadn't been able to take his eyes off her. She steered Galiha closer to him, stepping up out of the wagon wheel rut on her side of the road. "You've been looking over your shoulder for the last quarter mile. What is it?" she asked.

The last light of day flashed across his half smile. The smile faded as he glanced over his shoulder once again as if his body were trying to give him away. Her own gaze flicked in that direction. Dusk obscured much of the horizon behind them, but not so much that she couldn't make out the shapes moving in the distance. They were too far away for her to feel their horse's minds. Instead, she touched Rick's mind and found caution and an almost overwhelming protective instinct.

"Natives or Ainsworth's men?" she pressed when he didn't answer. She wasn't certain, but she thought he might be able to smell them.

"Too clumsy and obvious, and they smell of cotton, starch, and gun oil. It has to be Ainsworth's men. Do you feel up to a run?"

She straightened in the saddle and took up her reins. "No."

Rick looked at her with open-mouthed shock. It was early in their evening's travels, barely an hour in. Clearly, he realized she wasn't worried about Galiha's constitution yet.

"Um, ah…" His voice trailed off.

She lifted her chin. "I'm finished running. We put ourselves at risk when we run. 'Tis best to make a stand in the place of our choosing. I know you don't want to kill, and I respect that. But these men want to kill us, and I'm tired of giving them chances to do it," she said.

Her head turned his way, but the pale light of the half moon wasn't enough to reveal her expression. But he shouldn't need to see it. Her tone should be enough to tell him all he needed to know. She would not be swayed by anything short of him throwing her over his saddle. Appealing as that sounded at any other time, she wouldn't allow it now.

"Can we buy him off?" she asked.

Rick shook his head. "No. Ainsworth is not only wealthy, but he's powerful and ruthless. He inspires a certain amount of fear in his employees."

"Then we need to be scarier. I'm not suggesting we kill

them, but I'm prepared to do what it takes to stop them from trying to kill us," she said.

"Well, maybe if it's Cofield…"

"You don't really think that man would have the bullocks to come after us again after what happened last time, do you?"

Rick shook his head. "Not the bullocks, no. But I think he'd be afraid of Ainsworth enough to try again. Ainsworth likely has something over the man. He always has something over his men."

They couldn't just strip him and leave him again. At over a hundred degrees during the day, a man would almost surely perish before anyone else came along to help him. It would be a death sentence. She wasn't entirely sure she could do that any more than pull a trigger. But, if the man was threatening them directly, that would be a different situation altogether. Not only did she have the land and her friends to think about, but possibly even a future with Rick. Every moment, she feared ambush or one of them being shot in the back. She was tired of being afraid. More than that, she was tired of risking her future because of that fear.

"You said you showed him your fangs. Do you think he'll figure out what you are and come armed with something that can hurt you?" she asked. It was difficult for her not to sound a little jealous. She would love to see his fangs. The thought rather excited her.

A smile teased at his lips as Rick shrugged, letting her know he'd heard the note of jealousy. "Hard to say. Most people don't believe people like us exist, even when faced with the evidence they will try to use logic to dismiss it. Trick of the light, overactive imagination, heat of the moment, they'll make up any excuse to try and convince themselves what they saw wasn't real."

"But there's a chance," she said. "We have to be extra careful. Are the legends true about silver?"

"Yes. That and the claws of another shifter will do the job well enough," he admitted.

This shot a flare of nervousness through her. She shifted in the saddle, wanting desperately to look behind them. Penny Dreadful novels sometimes featured stories of werewolves, and they always noted that silver would kill them.

"Wait…where's Lincoln?" Rick asked as he scanned the moonlit landscape.

While he wandered off a bit now and then, the pup never got out of sight. Until now. The low scrub and sagebrush couldn't hide Lincoln's tall, gangly form. And yet he was nowhere to be seen. Cat reached out for his mind and found nothing.

"I can't feel him anywhere near," she said.

"Bullocks," he cursed in a harsh whisper.

With the mounted forms she'd seen in the near distance, they couldn't risk raising their voices to call out. Rick whispered the pup's name quietly in several directions. Not so much as a rustle sounded in response. It wasn't like Lincoln not to at least respond with a bark.

"Something's wrong," Rick whispered to Cat.

"Bastard. If he has tried to hurt a hair on that pup's head, I'll shoot him myself," Cat hissed beneath her breath. "His powers haven't fully awoken yet, and without us there to kick in his protective instinct, I don't know how much he'll be able to do against armed men."

A growl tore from Rick that rose the hair along her arms. "I will wrip them apart if they try to hurt him."

Gaze flicking back to the figures in the distance moving ever closer, Rick moved his big buckskin over until he walked so close he almost brushed Galiha. Without looking, he touched her arm. "Go to the trees to our left, hide," he said.

"No."

His wide-eyed gaze locked onto hers. "Don't be stubborn about this. If they hurt you…" He swallowed hard and closed his eyes.

She put her hand on top of his. "You saw how that ended for Cofield last time, and he ambushed us. This time I'll be ready. Don't look at me like that. I can handle myself. And I won't kill him unless I have to," she said.

Part of her loved that he wanted to protect her. Another part of her needed to do this, not just for Lincoln, but for herself. She was finished letting others control her life. The pinched look on Rick's face made it clear he wasn't happy.

"Rick, I can't let anything happen to you because this Ainsworth wants my land," she said.

If anything, his look became more pained. He took hold of her hand as they rode toward the trees. "He wants my land, too. Part of the reason Sean asked me was because you and I will be neighbors. My land lies on one side of the creek while yours lies on the other," he said.

She gaped at him for a moment, unable to speak. While that changed many things, it didn't change the most important thing. "We'll discuss that later. But it doesn't change the fact that I want to help. That I *can* help."

He let go of her hand and took up the reins. Before he

could protest, she cut in. "And I would be just as devastated if anything happens to you as you would if anything happens to me."

Even after what they had shared last night, if he insisted she just hide, she wasn't sure what kind of a future they would have together. After how horrible her late husband had been, she hadn't ever expected to let herself take the risk of loving again. Now that she had, she was determined to make sure it was the right man, one who would respect her independence.

"All right," he said through another heavy sigh. "But we separate and flank them. And, you wait for the right opportunity before showing yourself."

In a few more steps, they reached a small copse of trees. Hanging on to the horn of his saddle, Rick leaned as close to her as he could. "You go that way, quiet as you can. Stay in the cover of the trees. There are two men out in the open and likely a third, possibly more hidden. Don't drop your guard, always assume there are more. And please, be careful," he whispered.

She nodded in answer and squeezed Galiha into motion, steering him in the direction Rick had pointed. At Rick's urging, Ayegi went trotting off in the other direction. The shadows of the trees wrapped around her, burying her in the overwhelming scent of juniper. Most of them were short and full but several reached high into the dark blue sky. Their gnarly, often twisting trunks lay in every direction, looking almost silver in the moonlight. The scent was so strong it almost made her sneeze. She fought back the impulse, but just barely.

The big paint stopped. She touched his mind.

Hard to see.

It's all right. Take your time, she told him.

While these trees weren't as thick or tall as pines or firs, they were numerous enough to present a challenge. Galiha started moving again before she could see even a foot in front of her face. All this time on the trail, the sure-footed horse hadn't steered her wrong yet, so she let him have his head. She contemplated drawing her pistol. Her eyes were slowly adjusting to the dark, but her hands shook so badly she could barely hold the reins. The weapon wouldn't do her much good in her state. Better options were available to her anyway.

The darkness gave her a small sense of security. But if she could hide in it, so could others. Her heart thudded faster. Sweat made the reins slide a little too easily in her hands. Not that she had to worry about Galiha. He wasn't prone to spooking at things, not even in the dark. She was another matter. Every little sound made her heart speed faster and her breath catch. Thankfully, the fallen needles and berries from the junipers were so numerous they covered the ground in a thick carpet that absorbed nearly the sounds of Galiha's hooves. But if it concealed his, it concealed that of the men's horses as well.

She couldn't allow herself to relax. Too much was at stake here.

Rick began to shout. "You better not have hurt my dog, or so help me I'll stake you out for the rattlesnakes."

Damn him! He hadn't said he was going to draw them to him. She stopped Galiha and listened hard. Between Rick's continued threats, she heard the slight creaking of a saddle off to her right. Along with it came the thoughts of an exhausted horse.

So tired. Must sleep soon.

305

From the sound of the creaky saddle, the man was maybe fifteen feet away. She held her breath until she heard the soft grunt of his horse as sharp spurs met his sides, then the sound of him trotting off in Rick's direction. Tears stung her eyes. Another few strides and she would have all but walked right into the man. But she hadn't. Gritting her teeth, she banished the tears with a few blinks. The man hadn't noticed her and she had to take that as a point in her favor.

Still holding her breath, she listened hard for any other sounds. No thoughts of animals came to her. Acutely aware of every sound her own tack made, she squeezed Galiha into motion, following the man who rode toward Rick.

Careful. We must be very quiet now, she told Galiha.

Unable to see all the limbs, let alone trees, she allowed him to choose their path. In a few steps her eyes adjusted enough that she was able to make out the outline of most things. She ducked beneath branches or leaned out of their way when she could, worried about even the small sound they might make brushing against her. Her heart felt like it rose higher into her throat with each step they took. Soon she could scarcely breathe. She hardly *wanted* to breathe, for fear of the sound it would make. Even that might get her discovered.

Not far away up ahead, she felt the exhausted mind of another horse. A few moments later she made out the shape of a mounted man moving through the trees not fifteen feet away. Whoever it was, they were growing too close to Rick for her comfort. From what she could tell, they never looked back, so she was confident they didn't know she trailed them. Still, she'd have to be extremely careful. These men were clever. Again she thought about drawing her pistol, and again she resisted the urge. Better options were available.

She felt Lincoln's mind not far away. Such a powerful relief flooded through her that it brought tears to her eyes. Something too short to be a packhorse trailed along behind the mounted person ahead of her.

Pack? Lincoln asked.

Yes, but be quiet for now, she told him.

Stayed calm like alphas taught. No fight. Want to fight.

Soon, she promised him. *We will surprise them. Wait until I say.*

The mirth that filled him at that would have made her smile at any other time. These fools were about to see what served as entertainment for a *failinis.* They had no idea what was coming.

As they moved through a spot of moonlight Cat saw the unmistakable flash of Lincoln's gray head and wide eyes looking back at her. He whined and tugged backward, but something held him fast, probably a line tying him to the man's horse.

Protect pack.

No, not yet. Wait, she insisted.

He whined in protest.

"Shut it, yah little bastard, or I'll smash your brains in," the mounted man whispered so low she barely heard it.

The words made a wave of fury surge through her. *Linc, quiet. Wait,* she made it a command.

His head perked up. His ears stood taller.

"I knew it was you, Cofield, you cowardly bastard. Who are these three you've got here with you?" Rick demanded.

He sounded so close. The man she followed had to be

nearly on top of him. Cofield and three men, Rick had said. Though he couldn't see him, he must smell the hidden man. Good, that meant he knew right where he was.

She stopped Galiha for a moment to listen. It wouldn't hurt to get a bit more space between her and the fourth man. At this distance, if Galiha stepped on a stick the man might look back and see her. Taking a chance, she urged the horse just a little farther to a big juniper tree with branches high enough that they could slip under them. It wouldn't conceal them completely in the rising moonlight, but it would break up their shape enough to fool a first glance.

Yes, she felt the mind of three other horses. Caution and fear clouded their minds—fear of Rick. They sensed what he was. *Good.* That might work in their favor.

"Let us have the woman, Fergusson, and we'll let you go," Cofield said.

"You'll have a hard time getting to her even over me corpse, if you could manage such a thing. Which you can't," Rick snapped back.

Leaning forward in the saddle, she peered around the twisting tree trunk. The scrubby desert opened up and in the open space stood four men. The broad, tall one was without a doubt Rick. Few men could hold themselves with that kind of confidence. Besides, she felt his energy as surely as she could feel Linc's or the horses'. Since they'd lain together he hadn't put back up the walls that blocked his true nature from her. While she couldn't read his thoughts, she could feel his power—so calm and ready. Moonlight outlined his silhouette, revealing a pistol in each hand pointed at two different men. Cofield stood ten feet or so away. Between her and them were not only a few trees, but Cofield's fourth man. He had dismounted and was hiding behind a tree. He leveled what had to be a rifle by the shape in Rick's direction, bracing atop a tree limb.

"That can be arranged. Tell us where she's at, or you both die," Cofield said.

Linc, come. But be quiet, she thought to him.

The pup ears perked. *Time to protect pack?*

No. Time to play a game. Be sneaky. Come to me.

Game! She could see his tail wagging in her mind's eye.

White teeth flashed. Fae power flared. He bit the rope clean in half with one chomp. Hunkered low to the ground, he started to slink toward her.

Rick's head rose a touch higher. "I'm not a daft fool. Ainsworth wants me land as much as he wants hers. I have no illusions about how this is going to play out. I told her to run. You'll never catch her. That paint she's on is faster than a rattlesnake."

That brought a smile to her lips. While Galiha could move when properly motivated—by say a tornado—to call it fast was being generous.

"Oh but you are. You showed me your true nature. We came prepared. There's silver bullets in these here guns of ours. You get shot, you ain't getting up," Cofield said, satisfaction thick in his tone.

Chills danced along her spine with icy pinpricks. Alarm shot through Rick's energy.

Lincoln reached her side. He stood on his hind legs, front paws coming to rest against her stirrup. Holding her finger to her lips again, she petted him with her free hand. After allowing him a few licks, she motioned for him to get down.

Good boy, the best boy. Now stay here, by this tree.

I win game?

Almost. Stay quiet, sneaky, and you will win.

He walked the few feet to the base of the tree and sat down.

Her attention shifted back to Cofield as he made a grunting sound. "I know she won't go far without you. A woman unescorted in these parts won't last long. She's a smart lass, she'll come back for you within the hour I imagine. Now, put those pistols down or my man in the trees will air you out a bit."

Desperate, she concentrated with all her might, trying to send a thought to Rick's mind. *The fourth man is a sharpshooter with a rifle pointed at you. Make him think you are surrendering, then Linc and I will take him by surprise. Trust us to do this, please.*

After a long moment of hesitation in which he looked around him, Rick started to lower the pistols.

Galiha, run the sharpshooter down. The horse dug in and launched himself forward. They barreled down on the unsuspecting man with a burst of deadly speed. Galiha's steps never faltered, not even when they treaded right over the would-be shooter. The rifle went off. More gunshots followed. She hauled on the reins and brought Galiha to a skidding stop before he could run out into the melee.

The rifleman started to push himself up. Curses and grunts of pain issued from him. She leapt from Galiha's back. The drop unbalanced her and she went down to a knee. The rifleman started to scramble over the ground, his hands searching. A huge, dark shape appeared between her and the man. Light glinted off white canine teeth as they clamped onto the man's hand. The man screamed in pain. The energy and mind of the creature told her it was Lincoln, but it didn't look like him anymore. His need to protect her had made him change into his true form. Red eyes glowed from within a canine face filled with far more sharp teeth than any dog of this realm possessed. Muscle filled out his formerly lanky body and claws that gleamed like knives tipped each of his paws.

With the man's hand still in his jaws, Lincoln swiped out with one of those paws and raked his chest. Muscle and bone glimmered in the moonlight. A ragged intake of breath was the only semblance of a scream he could utter because those claws opened him up all the way to his lungs.

Good boy, Linc. Good boy. You can let go now. We need to go help Rick, she thought to him, not wanting him to dip too deep into his nature and not be able to transform back.

As he let go of the man's hand, the sharpshooter flopped to the ground and commenced his death throws. Not giving him another thought, Lincoln trotted to her side, his glowing eyes leaving fading trails in the dark.

Together they dashed toward the clearing where Rick had been. Screams, snarls, and growls told them which direction to go. On instinct, Cat reached out to Rick's mind. It felt wilder than ever, filled with rage and an intense need to protect. But most importantly, she couldn't detect any signs of pain. She prayed to the mother Goddess Danu that meant he hadn't been shot. She burst through the tree line.

The moonlight revealed a massive wolf launching into the air, its jaws open. It collided with the only other figure left standing. A scream filled the night. Despite the clear danger, Cat lurched into a run. She tripped over a body and went to a knee. Before her the tangle of wolf and man fighting stilled. The wolf rose, leaving the man cowering on the ground in fear. Cat realized two bodies lay on the ground around her, neither of them moving. It didn't matter, they didn't matter. Only Rick did. The wolf started toward her, but stopped well out of reach.

He was a beautiful creature to behold. Tall and proud, he had to be near two hundred pounds, and all of it muscle. Blood darkened his muzzle and chest. A coat of gray and brown accented with white helped him blend into the beige and gray colors of the Nevada landscape. But those glowing green eyes would stand out anywhere. People without magic wouldn't see the glow, but their unique color would still make him stand out.

Hesitation, shame, and worry emanated from him.

"You're breathtaking," Cat said.

Surprise filled his mind.

"'Tis true," she said, wincing as she stood. A rock had connected with her left knee when she'd fallen. It would develop quite the bruise come morning.

A concerned whine issued from Rick, and he took a step toward her.

"I'm all right, just hit my knee when I fell," she told him.

Lincoln trotted past her, right up to him. Rick went still as Lincoln rubbed his neck along his. The transformed pup trotted a circle around the wolf, hopping and barking, then dipped down low onto his front legs, tail wagging. Rick stared at him, eyes wide, surprise radiating from him.

Cat couldn't help but laugh. "I take it this is the first time you've both seen the other's true form."

Lincoln made excited puppy growls that indicated he wanted to play. The wolf licked the side of his face. Cat took another step toward them and winced again as pain shot through her knee. Rick's head whipped in her direction. He took a hesitant step closer.

"Please don't feel shame. You protected yourself and us. It matters not whether you used pistols or claws to do it," she told him.

The wolf's tail and head rose higher. He walked up to her. Avoiding the wet spots that were likely blood, she stroked the side of his face. Such soft fur.

His body warmed and began to vibrate slightly. A moment later his wolf form flowed into that of a man. The beauty and natural flow of it made Cat gasp. It was like water pouring from one vessel to another, smooth and effortless. One moment he was a wolf, the next, a man. The sight of all that bare, beautiful skin of his sent a flush through her. Shoulder length brown hair hung loose and shaggy about him.

Concern in his eyes, he reached a hand toward her. "Are you all right? Did they harm you?" he asked.

Scoffing, she shook her head. "Asks the man who just took out three armed opponents intent on killing him." She took his face in her hands. "I am fine. How are you?"

Hands running over him, she checked for any wounds that the dark might be obscuring from her. None existed. The rifle had missed its mark. A long sigh of relief eased from her.

She tried not to think about the two still bodies, barely outlined by the moonlight as if the ground were slowly devouring them. A groan sounded and the third body, off to the right away from the others, stirred. Cat drew the pistol from her waist and spun in the direction of the sound. Cofield struggled to his feet. She leveled the weapon at him. Her finger slid inside the trigger guard. After all the trouble and anxiety he had caused them, she wanted him dead. But she couldn't make her finger pull the trigger back.

"Don't, Cat. 'Tis bad enough to kill a man in the heat of battle, but don't do it like this. This would destroy you," Rick all but begged.

The concern he showed for her conscience, again, stilled her finger. That he cared so much for not only her physical well-being, but her emotional one as well, was a rare and beautiful gift. She let the barrel sink toward the ground. It wouldn't have done any good even if she had pulled the trigger. She hadn't cocked the damnable thing. Rick's hand came to rest on her shoulder. His lips touched her forehead with something close to reverence. Lincoln let out a little whine as he rubbed against Rick's legs. The warmth of Rick's body pressing against hers disappeared as he reached to pet the pup.

"A monster and a witch, a fitting couple," Cofield said through a snarl. Head lifting with a snap, he suddenly scrambled for her.

Without even thinking about it, she whipped the pistol around and slammed the butt of it into the side of his head. He went down hard and fast and didn't stir. The urge to keep beating the man with it flooded through her. She resisted, but it wasn't easy. It would have been easier if she dropped the weapon, but she wasn't about to do that.

"Good on you, Cat," Rick. "I can hear a heartbeat. He's alive." The disappointment in his voice reflected her own.

At the same time she felt relief. It was quite disorienting.

A querulous canine noise came from Linc and he rubbed up against her. "What's the matter, lad? Are you hurt?" she asked him as one hand brushed over his fur and her mind reached out to his.

Predators come. They don't like Rick and me here.

He pushed into her so hard it almost forced her back a step. A long howl broke through the night not far away. Another joined it. She wasn't sure, but she didn't think they were coyotes. The sound was deeper, richer. Chills danced up her arms.

"Rick, is that…"

"Wolves," he finished for her.

Talking to prey animals and reasoning with them was one thing, predators was another altogether. She might be able to convince them they were no threat, but considering what Rick and Lincoln were, that would be no easy task. Add to that the scent of blood filling the air and they were in some serious trouble. Could Rick and Lincoln dispatch the wolves? Almost certainly. But Cat abhorred violence toward animals, particularly when it wasn't necessary and was no fault of the animals. They were in the wolves' territory. It wouldn't be right to kill them.

Rick checked Cofield over, removing a small pistol from his boot and a knife from his belt. As he stood back up, he whistled. Their horses came trotting out of the dark. After a quick pat to Ayegi's neck, he dug around in the saddlebags and pulled out a pair of breeches and a shirt.

While he dressed, he said, "We need to leave before the wolves get here."

A wave of nausea swept her. It felt wrong not to bury the

bodies, even though the men had been about to kill them. But it didn't feel wrong enough to risk those she cared about. Rick grabbed Galiha's reins and led him over to her.

"Wait. We should leave him the knife at least. We aren't the monsters he is," she said.

Rick touched her cheek, then nodded. She took the knife from him and went to Cofield. Shaking from the irrational fear that he might awaken and lunge at her again, she bent down. She tucked the big knife into his hand so if he awoke he would know the kindness they had done him. He deserved the guilt that would bring. Pistol pointed at him, just in case, she backed up until she bumped into Galiha's shoulder. Rick helped her into the saddle. For once, she didn't protest. As bad as she was shaking, she didn't think she could have made it on her own.

He gave her hand a reassuring squeeze. The dark hid his expression. "You're sure you're not injured?" she asked. She couldn't ask if he was all right, because she knew he wasn't. He had just killed two men. His shoulders slumped with the weight of it. But she hoped that was all they slumped from. Cofield had mentioned silver bullets and she'd heard more than one gun shot.

"No. I was too fast for them. What about you?"

Howls echoed over the last word. "No. They didn't touch me, let's go," she said.

"Change back now. You've done good," Rick told Lincoln.

In a blink the pup's form shrank to its normal size, his mouth full of fangs reduced to the far fewer and duller ones of a normal canine, and his eyes changed back from glowing red to gold.

"That's a good lad."

Scooping Lincoln up, Rick placed him in the nest between the packhorse's packs and told him to stay. The command was unnecessary for the pup laid down immediately. The moment Rick settled into the saddle they took off at a brisk trot. Cat spared one last glance back at Cofield, who had just begun to stir. That, or it was death convulsions from the head injury. She couldn't bring herself to care either way. Soon it wouldn't matter, because the howls of the wolves grew closer by the heartbeat. Guilt over those feelings might come later, but right now she was content with her indifference.

25

Cat

California

The rising sun behind them streaked the rolling hills with gold and painted the horizon orange. Sweet fragrances of a multitude of wildflowers that grew amidst the tall green grass drifted to her on a warm breeze. That warmth meant they had made it. There was still time to build and plant before fall took hold of the land. Both this and the beauty of the land brought tears to her eyes. Though she shook from head to toe, she dismounted, leaning heavily on Galiha until she knew her legs would hold her. Her feet tingled at the touch of the ground beneath them. Tail swinging, Lincoln licked at her hand as he dashed past to find some wildlife to harass.

"This is my land?" she asked in a choked voice.

Rick walked up to her. Pride and affection radiated from his beautiful energy. "Aye, much of it." He pointed to the west.

"Mine lies just over there. See that creek?"

A silvery line wound down between the hills before them, so far away it looked like little more than a string. She nodded.

"That's the border between our lands." He went on to further explain the boundaries, pointing to trees to the north and a group of boulders to the south. But she heard little of it.

"Mine," she whispered.

Tears slid down her cheeks in hot streaks. They obscured her view, but didn't make it any less beautiful. It was one thing to live in a fine house in New York that she'd never lifted a finger to create. But this, this was a chance to build something of her own.

"You could plant the first vine right here. I'll build you a gazebo on this very spot if you want. And you can put the first pasture right there in that meadow. Can you imagine it, horses and grapevines stretching as far as the eye can see in all directions?" Rick said.

She could, oh how she could. The mention of him building something for her, here, in this amazing place, enabled her to tear her eyes from the hills to look at him. He fidgeted as if nervous. It wasn't the same kind of nerves he'd battled over the last week.

It had taken days for the nightmares to leave him be after the encounter with those men. Each night she had sung to him, kept him rooted in the present, helping him battle his demons. He had grown better with each passing day until she thought he had put it behind him enough to stave off the worst of the nightmares. This seemed different, but it still worried her. She hated that he may still be battling his conscience over something he'd been forced to do in part because of her.

"That will be lovely," she said, imaging the rows of vines stretching out from this point, surrounded by pasture filled with horses.

Part of her couldn't help but wonder if Rick would be in that future, or if he even still wanted to be. Over the last week he had been kind, and even affectionate to the point of a gentle touch here, or the occasionally grasping of hands there. But they hadn't made love again. That worried her more than she cared to admit. Over the last few days she had begun to fear something, or someone, waited in California that would alter his plans and end their courtship. She wouldn't blame him if he chose another—or even no one—over her after the things he'd had to do because of her. His kind were endangered, after all. If there were a female *faoladh* in the area it only made sense that he would choose her.

It was important to her that he knew she wouldn't blame him or hold him back from doing what was right for his kind. And yet, she couldn't speak past the swelling lump in her throat to express it. The thought of living next to him and not being with him was too much. Eyes closing, she held her head high. The sun caressed her face with a warmth unlike any she'd felt in New York. Painful as it would be to be without him, this place felt right, it felt like home. With or without him, she could do this. She would do this.

A rustling of grass directly before her made her open her eyes. Rick knelt in the green grass and yellow wildflowers, looking up at her with such tenderness that it made her heart clench. He ran a shaking hand through his nearly chin-length hair and swallowed hard.

"I know you've been through a terrible marriage in which

you were treated horribly by a man who changed after you took your vows. But I promise, that with me, what you see is what you get. I will not change, nor will I ever raise a hand to your or speak an ill word against you."

As he paused she swallowed hard in an attempt to dislodge the lump that had grown in her throat. He went on before she could even think about finding words.

"And I know you haven't had a chance to confirm me family and social status, and I promise to give you ample time to do so. But I am compelled to ask, once you do and should you find them to your satisfaction, Catriona O'Brian, may I have your hand in marriage?"

After a gasp that nearly turned to a sob, she put a hand on her hip. "Patrick Fergusson, your family and your social status mean nothing to me," she teased, the effect ruined by a sniffle.

His head cocked to the side and she nearly laughed aloud at his resemblance to Lincoln. The confident man she had traveled with had morphed into this timid, unsure lad before her. She found it oddly charming.

"And that means…?"

Now she did laugh as she grabbed his hand. "It means that I wouldn't care if you were the penniless rogue I thought you to be. 'Tisn't your wealth or your family I want, but you."

A smile pushed up his scruffy cheeks. "You wouldn't mind marrying a *faoladh?*" he whispered.

Yet again she had to swallow so she could speak. "Of course not, you daft fool, I'd be honored. I'll marry you and none other," she said in barely more than a whisper.

Rick let out a huge whoop that sent a handful of birds in a nearby tree into frantic flight. He launched to his feet, swept her up in his arms, and spun her around as he clutched her close. Laughing, she kicked her feet up and clung to him with all her strength. Lincoln appeared and began running circles around them, barking with enthusiasm. Finally, Rick set her down on her feet. She swayed, but he held her steady. He cupped her face in both hands. After a long look, he leaned down and brushed his lips against hers. Arms around his neck, she pulled herself up and deepened the kiss into something that would burn away his lingering propriety. He groaned into her open mouth. Clothes soon began to fall on the grasslands of their new home.

EPILOGUE

Deirdre

Nevada

The plants sang their exuberant song of late summer to Deirdre, drawing her deeper into the juniper forest. All around her rich, deep reds, oranges, and gold hues decorated the land. Bone tired not from traveling, but from the tedious company of their escorts, she walked deeper into the trees. The moments she could steal for herself were precious few. Thinking her off answering nature's call, the men hired to escort and protect her and Sadie wouldn't come looking for her for at least another few moments. Most of the aloof brutes were likely catching a nap anyway. In this bloody heat it was almost impossible not to given the slightest opportunity.

The very thought made her tug at her cotton dress where it clung to her sweaty thighs. What she wouldn't do for a hoop to keep the blasted material away from her. Or better yet, a brisk ride on her horse to get the wind moving through her hair. But, due to the dangers of the trail, her escorts were adamant about not letting her stray far from sight. As if she were a dog that needed to be kept at heel. Her jaw clenched. If only they knew what she truly was they would understand how little she needed their help. But their knowing would put her in far more danger.

Another week and they'd reach California. That kept her going when she wanted to strangle their escorts. She knew it was wrong to think ill of these men. They were friends of Sean MacBranain's, her good friend's husband, men he had fought alongside in the war, men he trusted not only with his own life, but hers and Sadie's as well. And they had proved true and good in every aspect. Maybe if any of them were interesting enough to be attracted to, she would warm to them more. But the lot of them were too stoic, boring, or repressive for her tastes. Despite the fact they weren't her kind, she had tried to get to know them and weigh their characters for something more than a passing acquaintance. After all, she was ready for a romance that would sweep her off her feet. Clearly, it would not be with one of them.

The day's heat lost some of its bite as she stepped into the shade of a large juniper tree. Letting out a long breath, she leaned against the twisted trunk. The rough bark scraped at her back, snagging her dress, but she didn't care. The life energy thrumming through the tree soothed her, causing a sigh to slip from her lips. It surrounded her, touching her energy, recognizing what she was through it.

What she wouldn't give for a river. Even a stream would do. Water wasn't exactly plentiful in Nevada. Regret pulsed from the tree.

No water nearby, Steward. My roots are deep and still barely touch what lies ten times my height into the ground. The communication from the tree didn't exactly come to her as thoughts, but her mind translated it that way. It came more like feelings, impressions, but she understood. The plants tended to think of her as a steward, a protector, which she endeavored to be.

The snap of a branch yanked her from her musings with a

start. She slid around the tree trunk away from the noise. As much as she wanted this trip over with, she wasn't ready to crawl back into a stifling wagon just yet. Bluish juniper needles brushed against her hair, catching in the long, dark locks. She grabbed the branch before it could snap back and make any noise.

Oddly, no one called out to her. If it were one of the men, or even Sadie, surely they would have called out. A grunt filled with pain sounded close by, too close by. Deirdre froze. She broke through the paralysis to reach for the knife she kept nestled in her deep cleavage.

"Is someone there?" came a man's raspy voice.

Her fingers closed around the small handle of the knife.

"Please, I mean you no harm. I need help."

She remained silent and hidden. Something about the man's voice made the skin on the back of her neck tighten. But did she dare judge a man on an undertone? It could merely be pain. Leaning around the trunk, she peered through the branches. A lone man in torn and bloodied clothes stood amidst the sage brush. He leaned heavily on a makeshift cane. Bandages that looked like they might have once been the sleeves of his shirt were wrapped poorly around his right calf. In a holster resting on a belt nestled a large pistol. Both the remains of his tattered shirt and his breeches hung on him as if he'd recently lost weight, or the clothes weren't his. The pockmarked skin of his face ran a shade just north of death. Dark circles surrounded his squinty eyes.

The sight of him only confirmed what she had heard in his voice; he wasn't to be trusted. Her little knife felt woefully inadequate. But if she needed them, the trees and sage brush would answer her call.

"I know you're there. I can see you through the tree. Please, help me," he said.

Her conscience wouldn't allow her to just leave the man. "Put the pistol on the ground, step away from it, and I'll come help you."

Using the branch he had fashioned into a cane, he limped a few steps closer. "Oh thank you so much. You're a Godsend. I—"

"Stop right there and put the pistol on the ground," she commanded.

Gaze skittering about, she considered calling to her escorts. The energy of the tree pulsed in response to her anxiety.

Help steward, it thought/felt. Its branches swayed as if in a breeze, though one did not exist.

No. I'm fine. But thank you. I will ask if I need help, she thought to it. A few deep breathes helped her calm herself. It would not do to upset the tree and make it think she was in danger. When plants thought she was in danger, things tended to happen that made it difficult to hide what she was. And when she couldn't hide what she was, bad things followed.

The man stopped, free hand going up to show he meant no harm. "Sorry, I got so excited. I haven't seen another soul for a week is all. Thought I was going to die out here alone," he practically whispered.

It occurred to her that each time he spoke he had whispered, even when he'd grown excited. The skin on the back of her neck grew even tighter. Suppressing her anxiety grew difficult. What she wouldn't have done for a bow at that moment. What good was being a champion archer if she didn't have a bow at a time like this? But like most of her belongings, it was packed away in a wagon.

The man finally did as she commanded and lay his pistol at his feet.

"Now take a step back," she said.

She could call for help. Maybe she should. But she knew if he did mean her ill, he could be on her before anyone from the wagon train could reach her. Or worse yet, Sadie would be the one to reach her, then she'd be in danger, too. Her friend was still weak from heat exhaustion. No. It was better to take care of him herself. He took two small steps back. Emboldened by his obedience, she stepped out from behind the tree.

The man's beady eyes opened wide. "You're even prettier than you sound," he said, voice too eager for her liking.

"That is hardly a proper thing to say to me considering the nature of our meeting," she said.

His eyes traveled over her, feeling like the cool, slick hide of a snake against her skin. As she feared they would, they caught on her cleavage. "Name's Cofield, in case you want to call it out later," he said through a sneer full of broken and crooked teeth.

He lunged for his pistol. Several small roots of the tree she'd been leaning against shot out of the ground and wrapped around his hand, pinning it against the dirt. Teeth bared, she strode to him and placed a boot on his hand. His bones ground beneath her heel. He cried out. The second he looked up, she asked the tree to send a root beneath his chin, applying just enough pressure to make sure he knew it was there. It did so in the fraction of a heartbeat. Gasping, his eyes shot open wide.

"Your first mistake was being a blaggard who would attack a woman. Your second was taking me for a daft fool. I'm not going to give you a chance to make a third," she warned him in a voice that was as steady as her iron control.

"What is this witchery? You're hurting me," he whined. "Please, I've been attacked by bandits and wolves. I was just afraid."

"Of a woman?"

"It was a woman who did this to me." He pointed to a scabbed-over gash on the side of his head.

"A woman bandit?" she asked, raising her voice loud enough that she hoped the men from the wagon train would hear.

"Yes," he insisted.

Shifting her foot, she ground her heel harder against the butt of the pistol. "Let go."

"You have my hand trapped."

"Then pull it out. That or I'll crush it, your choice."

As he pulled, she asked the tree to let him go. The roots retreated into the ground. His eyes grew wide as he watched them go. Despite his shock, she felt him try to take the pistol with him as he pulled, but he couldn't get it out from under her foot. Once his hand was free, she covered as much of the pistol with her foot as she could.

"Crawl away from me, slowly."

He shuffled backward on his hands and knees faster than she was comfortable with, but she let him go regardless.

"You're like her, a witch," he hissed.

Gaze locked on him, she bent and picked up the pistol. When her hand closed around the grips, he dove for her. She

328

brought it up, but he blocked the arm holding it and bore her to the ground. While his hand wrapped around her one wrist, she slammed the butt of the pistol into the side of his head. As he fell, she twisted so he went face-first down into the sage and dirt. She scrabbled away and to her feet.

A brand new wound on the opposite side of his head from the other one bled freely. The fluttering eyelid that she could see soon disappeared in a wash of red. Though it was a lot, to be sure, she didn't think it was a fatal amount of blood. Having grown up with a brother, she knew just because a head wound bled a lot didn't mean it was that bad. The fact that the man seemed only half-conscious was another matter.

Steward needs more help? the tree asked.

No. Others are coming. They would see. I am safe. Thank you, she told it.

Footsteps pounded through the scrubby forest toward her. Pistol held at the ready, she took a step back from Cofield—just in case—and turned in the direction of the steps. A tall Negro woman with skin that shone like brown porcelain plunged through the trees. She stumbled to a halt, barely remaining on her feet. Her gaze moved between the still Cofield and Deirdre. With a shake of her many braids, she shrugged off her shock and half-jogged, half-stumbled toward Deirdre.

Deirdre met her part way, grabbing hold of her arm to steady her. "I'm all right, Sadie."

"I had a dream you were in trouble and knew something was wrong. What happened? Who is that?" Sadie asked, only the barest hint of an accent in her voice.

Deirdre's eyes narrowed at the man. "A fool who did not know whom he was tangling with. He called himself Cofield."

Holding tight to Deirdre's arm, Sadie leaned in the man's direction. "Did you kill him?"

"Not sure."

Sadie covered her face with one hand. "A fool indeed." The exhaustion weighing each of her words struck a vein of concern in Deirdre.

"You shouldn't be out here. You haven't yet recovered from being in the heat too long yesterday," Deirdre said.

Two more sets of steps pounded their way. "That's precisely what I told her, but she insisted she were in danger—oh. Oh my, are you all right?" came a man's voice.

A man old enough to be her father flanked by a tall, skinny man came through the sparse trees. The older man, Jack, approached the two of them. The skinny one, Sam, went to Cofield.

"I'm a fair spot better off than he is," Deirdre said.

Jack held his hand out for the pistol and Deirdre gladly gave it to him. She hadn't the first clue how to use the damnable thing. But it did seem to work rather well as a blunt weapon.

"He's alive, though knocked well and good out," Sam called from where he crouched by Cofield. "What should we do with him?"

"Bollocks," Deirdre murmured under her breath.

Sadie slapped her arm. "Deirdre," she reprimanded.

Eyes opening wide, Deirdre asked, "What? He's dangerous."

"I only meant to mind your language."

The half-smile on Sadie's full lips helped sooth Deirdre's nerves.

Jack ran a hand through his thinning, dark hair. He looked to Deirdre as he so often had during their journey west. While he was officially in charge of their wagon train, he had quickly learned that no one was in charge of Deirdre Quinn.

She shrugged. "Leave him here for all I care. He clearly meant me ill."

Sam's brow pulled down into a scowl that nearly made his eyes disappear. "He attacked you. He's dangerous and should be handed over to a lawman for punishment."

Eyes going wide, Sadie's grip on Deirdre's arm tightened. "Won't it be dangerous to take him with us?"

Breathing out sharply through his nose, Jack flicked his wrist, popping open the cylinder of the pistol that held the bullets. He spun it, mouth moving in a silent count of each bullet within, flicked it back closed, and pointed it at Cofield. "We've less than seven days to go. We'll keep him bound. Go fetch some rope, Sam."

With a nod, Sam rose and took off at a jog. A groan issued from Cofield. Not wanting to leave Jack alone with the man, Deirdre waited for Sam to return. He did so in a few moments, rope in hand.

She nodded to Jack. "You seem to have this well in hand. I'm going to get Sadie back to the wagons."

Jack nodded to her in return. "Of course."

One arm going around Sadie's back, Deirdre turned her in the direction of the wagons. The way her friend sagged against her proved the outing had been too much. She hated that the woman's prescience had drawn her out of the comfort and shade of the wagon. On the other hand, the bit of excitement had gotten her own blood flowing, and that was a welcome change. Deplorable though Cofield clearly seemed, at least he brought intrigue to their day. Regardless, she wasn't about to let her guard down around him for one moment.

It was going to be a long week.

*Continue reading in **Desiring A Witch**, coming winter of 2023.*

AUTHOR'S GRATITUDE & HUMBLE PLEA

Thank you with every bit of my heart for reading. If you enjoyed the read, I would be eternally grateful for a review on retail sites and any mentions on social media.

Wait, please don't go!

I know the words "please review" tend to make people run for the hills because we all have extremely busy lives, and many just don't know what to say in a review. But trust me, they truly make all the difference to an author because they affect the way the retail sites handle the book exponentially, which in turns greatly affects the book's sales—or lack thereof.

So what do you write? Short and sweet is great as long as its from the heart. One to three things you loved about the book will do. A review can be as short as a sentence, or as long as you like.

ACKNOWLEDGEMENTS

Thank you to my ARC team, and my Booktok besties who have inspired me to keep going, and have given me more support and encouragement than I could have ever imagined. Lucky doesn't even begin to describe how I feel to have met and become friends with all of you.

Thank you to Lizzy Gayle, fantastic author and out of this world friend, who cheers me on every step of the way and keeps me believing I can do this crazy thing.

To readers old and new, I cannot thank you enough for reading. You are the blood that keeps my creative heart pumping. Entertaining you brings me so much joy.

ABOUT THE AUTHOR

When she's not writing, Heather can be found on the slopes, the hiking trails, or paddleboarding. She enjoys the outdoors nearly as much as the worlds she creates. No need to travel to the Great Northwest, though, you can find her on social media and her personal site.

www.heathermccorkle.com